Saving Kandinsky

A novel

Mary Basson

Saving Kandinsky is a work of historical fiction. Aside from the well-known actual people and events, the characters and events depicted are either products of the author's imagination or are used fictitiously.

.

Saving Kandinsky is a novel based closely on the lives of the historical figures who inhabit its pages. For enhanced enjoyment, visit the companion website for images of the art referred to in the novel.

savingkandinsky.com

ISBN 0-9911496-0-2

1.Münter, Gabriele, 1877-1962—Fiction. 2.Kandinsky, Wassily, 1866-1944—Fiction. 3.Women artists—Fiction. 4.History—Fiction. 5.Art—Fiction. I. Title.

.

To Alex, Duncan, Jacob, and, of course, Steve.

Contents

Old age hath yet his honor and his toil.
Death closes all; but something ere the end,
Some work of noble note, may yet be done,
Not unbecoming men that strove with Gods.

From "Ulysses" by Alfred, Lord Tennyson

Part One

Part One

Kochel
Early Summer, 1902

Inside the mountain Gasthof, the boys were singing Schubert. Grouped around the wide hearth with its fine summer fire, they huddled in pairs—tenors, baritones, basses—sharing the sheet music one of them had copied for all to read. Inside, the boys sang "*Wie schön bist du,*" melding their voices in poignant intervals, their low tones steeping the night with sweetness. "*Wie schön bist du,*" they sang, "You are so beautiful." But Ella was not with them, not inside, not singing. Ella was outside the Gasthof under the forest canopy, leaning against an old beech tree cushioned by thick ivy. Dark green leaves coiling in her curls, she was lifting her face to find his, again and again.

Chapter One

The Mountain's Palette

Kochel
Early Summer, 1902

SQUINTING in the rosy air, Ella stopped to listen. Had she been day-dreaming when he called? She set her bicycle against a tree and stood motionless, straining to catch his whistle. Wind rumpled the masses of phlox, their blue nearly orchid in the early light. Toward mid-day, they would turn azure; by nightfall, indigo. But no whistle came, nor footstep. He must be behind her, hiding, laughing, and she turned, half-expecting to find him out. But all she saw was the curve of the hill, patches of lavender on the sunny slopes, moss undulating among the rocks. All right, then. There was more to the day than a whistle. She set the legs of her easel among the woolly edel-weiss. As the sun rose higher and the air turned apricot, the day's colors pushed into her head and took up all the room for listening. And then at last she could work.

Beyond the stony outcropping, shafts of sunlight polished the Kochelsee white like a dinner plate. A lake breeze pushed up the shore slope, combing through heliotrope, lifting the brim of her yellow hat. She tied the ribbon firmly under her chin and secured her sketching paper with a clip. She wanted to capture the contrast of clouds caught between two hills rising black above the bright lake. She would not even try to draw their tops. The hills should be diagonal borders holding something airy and ephemeral between. But the clouds shouldn't be shapes, exactly. More like weightless hollows, easy to blow away. Cloud bubbles. No, not that either. More formless. She almost thought her eyes were failing, for she could not fix the clouds, so slowly they grew higher, denser, finer, thinner. And still she heard no whistle, her ears traveling down the hill and into the deep woods. No whistle at all.

When finally the light began to fade and the late afternoon sucked away the clouds entirely, she rolled up her paper, put her charcoals in their tin, and wiped her blackened hands on the grass. She pulled her smock over her head, turned it inside out, and folded the cloth neatly. Careful with its giraffe legs, she disassembled the easel into her canvas bag. She strapped on her rucksack and cycled slowly back to the Gasthof, looking keenly about her. Still no whistle.

The dark-beamed dining room was deserted when she arrived. She was taking her usual seat at the table just as the others burst in, bustling and noisy with glasses and water and silverware.

"Gabriele," one of the boys said. "We didn't see you all afternoon."

"That Fraulein Münter," another one grinned. "Elusive as always."

"I was near the lake." Ella turned to the boy near her. "Was Professor K with you?"

"You didn't know? He went to the station to pick up his wife from Munich."

Something twisted low inside her. *No*, she wanted to say. *Please, no*. The boy must have misspoken. She must have misheard.

"His wife?" She clutched her napkin.

"She's staying with us for the rest of the summer." Doncker grinned across the table.

"A looker." Palme winked.

"Leave it to Professor K." Muehlenkamp gave a little drum on the tabletop.

Ella excused herself, though Frau Puntel had not begun to serve the soup and flanken. She stumbled up the stairs and down the narrow corridor, one hand on her mouth, the other scraping the timbered walls until she got inside her door. Fighting the desire to whimper, she climbed into her bed. She tucked the cold, white cover over her head. She began to cry. On the strength of a single word, she had changed.

Wife. He had a wife, and she, Ella, was not who she had thought just minutes ago. Then, she was a girl listening for her suitor, a girl singled out by a very great man, a girl such a man might want to marry. Now, she was a fool. For the last several weeks—no, long before that—she had been kissing a man now said to have a wife. And not just kissing, either. She had been ready to give herself to him entirely. It had almost happened. She had wanted it to happen.

That she had made such a mistake with a man hardly surprised her. She had never known how to be around people. Her short life to date had been riddled with stupidities, with clumsy and indecorous gaffes, with failures in judgment. Even as a schoolgirl she had sensed her own ineptitude, rarely dawdling with the other girls or taking part in their games. She didn't know how to laugh or tease or whisper in a girl's ear. She didn't know she was lonely.

Her fears were confirmed one rainy afternoon as she lurked outside the parlor, eavesdropping.

"...is it because something's wrong with Ella, Mother?" The voice was Emmy's. "I know she *can* talk. But she's so gloomy. I think something's the matter. Pass me that blue thread, will you?"

"I don't know about *wrong*, exactly. Papa thought when she got to school, she'd come out of herself. But, well, that's why I'm taking her to Herr Doktor, though Papa thinks..." Mama's voice dropped then.

"Ella? Is that you, dear? Come here and sit with me and your sister."

She never told anyone what she'd overheard and she had no memory of any visit to Herr Doktor, but the words "*something's wrong*" rang in her ears for years.

On her eighth birthday, Papa gave her a case of charcoals and a thick pad of paper. The gift puzzled her. She'd expected the new dress from Mama and the books from Emmy and Carl. But she didn't know what to do with the charcoals. "These pencils are magic," Papa had said. "If you tell them to, they can speak." He had lifted her onto his large lap. "Look at the tree by the gate or the path to the house. Is it a brave tree? Or a smiling path? Or a stubborn house? Make your pencils show us what you see."

Ella couldn't tell at first what she'd shown on her paper. Still, the charcoal felt comfortable in her hand, as though the black stick were another finger willing to live alongside the others, able to work with thumb or pointer or pinkie. What she could tell was that with the charcoal in her hand, she was talking somehow.

For a time, drawing was as good as having friends. She entered her work as though she were opening the door to a room where she might circulate among the forms and shapes inside. Like a choreographer among dancers, she could direct the space. Stand this way, she might say to a line with her arm around its shoulders. Bend here, she might insist. But she never used words. For the time she was working, she was unreachable even by her own consciousness. Until, that is, she met Professor K. And then she'd made that other mistake.

She kicked her boots. "*Dummkopf.*" She flung back the coverlet. "*Dummkopf.*" He was over a decade older than she, a man well-respected, attractive beyond measure, a capital man. Why wouldn't such a man have a wife? People said that men took advantage, but she was at fault. She'd not known the proper way to respond to his attention. Anyway, what vanity made her think she deserved to be the object of his interest? She of all people. Her eyes swam, and she pressed them shut. She had thought that if she let him kiss her, he would want to marry her.

And how many kisses there had been! She could count three in Munich, though she had re-imagined those first nights so many times, she couldn't be sure. She thought it was three. The time after class when they were caught in the rain on the way to the tram. And two more the next night. Then just the day after the summer session began here on the mountain when she fell from her bicycle—that counted, too. It was not a real fall, to be sure, more a slow leaning toward the road when she turned her foot on a stone and sat clumsily on the ground. K had put his bicycle down and come to help her, his lips warm on her skin where she had scraped it. That night his kisses had been placed where she found them most meaningful, seven she recalled. Sometimes it was hard to establish where one kiss ended and the next began. Her fingers still remembered the planes of his back under his shirt.

The next afternoon they had cycled around the lake to paint *en plein air*. On the far side, shielded from the other students, they had kissed again. But then he had jumped up from the grass and begun pedaling quickly back to the camp. She had worried afterward that she had not pleased him. He might think her naive. Last night in fact, so foolish now that she considered it, she had let him lead her outdoors while the others were singing, and far behind the lodging house, under the heavy shadows of the beech grove, he had held her very close and kissed her—what was it?—eleven times. Or twelve? And she had felt his body hard against hers, his hips pressed on hers as she leaned against a tree, her own body warming and yielding. She had let him stroke her breasts through her shirtwaist, marveling not just at the pleasure of his touch but also at her audacity, following him up the dark stairs toward his room, wanting to take him into herself and hold him there. But when he lifted the latch and the door swung open, he had hesitated, and she had pulled away then. Giving oneself over to a man in that way was not to be done lightly. After all, he was her teacher. And besides, other than the talk of art, she hardly knew him. Her mother, had she lived, would have been horrified. Even Emmy would disapprove. And yet, she had wanted him.

She wiped her cheeks with the wide hem of the sheet. "Stop being a goose." Even aloud, her words seemed insufficient.

Twenty-five altogether. One kiss for each year of her life. She had fallen in love with a married man, an unfaithful man. Pearl light groped about the high dormitory room through its single window. She should not have been so stupid.

The floorboards in the hallway groaned. Ella tucked the cover over her head. It would not do for Olga to see she had been crying.

"Is it your tooth, again?" Olga sat on the edge of the bed. From the first day, she had trailed behind Ella on their painting excursions. "You have such the talent!" she had said once, requiring no flattery in return. Ella could not have given it.

" Only a little. I'll be all right."

"You should eat something, though. Frau Puntel's dumplings are quite soft."

"I can't go downstairs."

"No, of course. I, myself, have had the toothache. In Moscow, I had to have the—what do you say?—the *dental* to remove it." She opened her mouth and stuck a finger in. "So you to stay, and I will here bring some soup." She wiped her wet forefinger on her broad hip and left the room.

‡

Months before at the new Phalanx school, when Ella had finished her first still life in oils, Professor K had judged it lively and colorful, and she had taken the canvas back to her room in the pension, wishing her parents might have seen how accomplished she had become.

She pictured her mother stout and serious in a black dress, her father in his great white beard. What would they have said of the twenty-five kisses? That at her age, she should know better? She burrowed deeper under the duvet.

Before long, she heard Olga's steps on the stairs. She had soup on a tray. "And when you have finished to eat and feel better, you must come down and drink some beer." Olga patted the bed. "The beer will help you to sleep, and the sleep will cure the toothache. I will wait for you in the lodge."

Olga's mothering calmed Ella. In fact, of course, there was no toothache this evening, though there sometimes had been. Just last week Ella had had her dinner on a tray. But how could she listen to the idle talk of the students and wonder if Professor K would also come to the table and bring this wife? She groaned. He has a wife. All along he has had a wife.

A smarter girl would have been more cautious. How stupid of her. She was hardly a child, though perhaps in these matters she was less worldly than many girls. Even Emmy had spoken with her, a sisterly talk, warning her to be on her guard, that men might want—well, she would not say just what. Might want what a married man could expect? Yet what could Emmy know of such a man, she who had never even left home.

Ella wiped her eyes and sat up. In truth, she was flattered that such a brown bird as she had drawn his attention. Plain little Ella, people said. But he had seen something fine in her. He had said as much, that something in her soul marked her as different. And she could see that he was different, too—profound and spiritual—nothing like the pallid instructors at the Ladies Academies, nothing like the foolish, randy boys she'd known in school. He was mature, dignified, intelligent, even brilliant, the kind of man to see beyond her shy smile. Who wouldn't be flattered? Who could blame her? She had been the one he'd favored.

And after all, perhaps what the boys said wasn't true. They liked to brag and swagger and tease. They did it all the time. They could be wrong, couldn't they? They often were.

After a bit, she got up and finished the soup Olga had brought her. She moistened a cloth at the washbasin and cooled her face. She tidied her hair and shirtwaist and adjusted the broad belt at her slim waist. All right, then. Others might flinch from the truth, but she was not raised that way. "See what there is to see," her father always said. She would have to go downstairs and learn for herself. If there really was a wife, that would be it. At least she would know.

The narrow steps under her feet felt insubstantial, as though she were stepping on the clouds of the afternoon, and her legs softened under her long skirt. The tray in her hands was the firmest thing about her, and she clasped its side to her waist for ballast.

Though a dove-gray light lingered outdoors in the early summer until well after nine, the evenings were chilly. With their backs toward a blazing fire, Olga and the boys clustered in a half-moon around Professor K seated in the largest armchair, his legs extended toward the flames. A small fair-haired woman crouched on a low stool at his feet, her arms wrapped around her knees.

Professor K rose and made a little bow toward Ella. "Ah," he said. "Our final student. Miss Münter, please allow me to introduce Miss Anja Chimiakin from Moscow." The little woman rose and extended her hand.

Ella gestured toward her mouth. "Excuse me," she said. "I have had a toothache."

"Please join us." Professor K pointed to a bench. "We were discussing the Finns."

Puzzled, Ella took her seat next to Olga's ample figure.

Miss Chimiakin? This woman at his feet was a "*Miss*," like herself, a *Fraulein*, and not Frau K, not his wife at all. So then the boys *were* wrong. Ella clasped her hands in her lap.

"We were just speaking of the value of folk arts." Professor K sat back in his chair. "Since you ask," he addressed a student, "I have, indeed, read the *Kalevala*—the Finnish scholar Lönnrot's edition. The best way to encounter the *Kalevala*, though, is as music, chant passing back and forth like dueling angels."

He let his eyes rest on Ella, and she held her breath. He pulled in his outstretched legs and crossed his ankles in their short boots.

"But back to what we were saying. Yes, of course, folk art like the *Kalevala* expresses the spirit of a whole people. The fine arts, though, need not be national or political. Instead, art must express the innermost soul of the artist."

The boys nearest the fire, who had been feeding straws into the flames, grew quiet and turned toward him, their faces solemn and expectant.

"Let me tell you," he continued. He had been studying in Vologda when he read the *Kalevala*. There he was, high above even the Arctic Circle. One bitter night as he sat reading in his room, a truth began to form within him: the nature of art is expression, not imitation.

"We artists can—we really must—go beyond superficial realities. We must express essential thought, pure thought." His eyes glistened behind their round spectacles. "Think this way, my friends. The truest art should be like music, completely abstract."

"Wait, wait, Professor." Palme interrupted. "What about *Die schöne Müllerin*?"

"Of course, I am not speaking of the love songs and ballads we like to sing together. These have quite a different purpose."

Muehlenkamp chuckled, his eyes lowered away from the Professor.

"My friend, I, too, love our Schubert songs. But, students, think of a string quartet as a conversation among four intimate friends—Beethoven, if you like. The phrases, the rhythm, the dynamics of the sound—think how they work to express a spirituality." He raised his hands clasped softly and then released the captured bird of his thought. "But not narration. Not representation." His eyes flashed from left to right, taking in the group. "Am I not right? Yes? There may be harmony, of course. But not story. The future of art will not mean merely copying nature. No, my friends—art will be visual music—abstract and expressive."

Ella glanced at Olga by her side. Like her, Olga clutched her hands, a fold of skirt caught between her fingers. Just barely shifting her weight, Ella let her arm brush against Olga's. When they got back to their shared room, Ella would ask her what she thought about Professor K and his new ideas. Olga might not take to them.

"Professor K," Schneider said. "I don't understand. Are you suggesting that our paintings should not represent—well, bowls of fruit or sunsets, if you will?"

"Herr Schneider, I admire the leap of your reasoning. And some day—yes, some day, you will be right." He let a pause grow fat in the room, ballooning into the corners. "Art will be pure spirit. But no story—indeed no picture at all."

Schneider looked down at his hands. The boys near the fire cleared their throats. Ella heard Olga swallow hard. It *was* remarkable what Professor K was saying: "No picture at all." Even Olga would see that.

Professor K smiled at Anja Chimiakin gazing up at him, and then he once again scanned the group, Socrates among the Athenians. "My young companions, we must leave behind our flowers and fruit. The expression itself, and not its objects, is the art." He leaned back in his chair to let the force of his words settle about the room.

"But Professor," began Muehlenkamp, the oldest student. "Why are we here in Kochel learning to paint *en plein air*? If we are to forget painting apples and roses and hills, as you say, we could have stayed in Munich."

"In all that heat," Palme said, laughing. "For my part, Professor, I am just as glad to be here with you on the cool mountain. And I promise you, I will not paint a single apple the entire summer."

"Carlchen, you idiot," said Muehlenkamp. "I was talking of symbols." He turned back to the Professor. "What should be our subject, Professor K, if we are to forget the things we see? When we are painting together, you keep telling us to *look*. What are we looking for?"

"Gentlemen," Professor K began, "and Ladies, of course. You must look to see the essence of the thing, and then imbue that object, that landscape, that figure with the intensity of your spirit. You must give the object some quality of your own soul." He took a small pipe from the pocket of his short jacket and nestled it in the palm of his hand. "Like many of you, as a boy I painted the subjects of the folk stories my grandmother read to me—both German ones and Russian, too. I love them still—how could I not?" He cleared his throat and, leaning forward in his chair, gestured with the empty pipe in his hand. "But the question is not *what* are we painting." His statement was a provocation to suspend time, and he used the pause to fill his pipe from a small, leather pouch, tamping down its contents, teasing his students with his delay.

From her bench, Ella inhaled the earthy aroma of his tobacco. She remembered the scent of his cheek, his beard. She remembered the taste of his lips.

"No, the question is *why* do we paint? Not what. Why." He fumbled in his jacket. "Now, who has a light for my pipe?"

Muehlenkamp was first with a match. Cupping the flame with his hand, Professor K drew in long lungfulls, his chest expanding into his jacket with the effort.

"We paint because of who we are—emotional beings, spiritual beings." His was the voice of the prophet from on high. "Yesterday we were as children painting what we saw through our eyes. Tomorrow, we will paint what is true in our souls."

Ella's hands trembled. Alone in her little room in Munich, she had spent hour upon hour gazing at the ceiling from her iron bed, finding shapes and faces in the fine cracks and lines in the plaster, feeling her soul rising to them, giving them purpose and life. It wasn't just his physical self that drew her to Professor K. He spoke thoughts she had no words to express. Her mouth grew dry.

"Olga," she whispered, "has Frau Puntel brought out the beer?"

"Ah," the Professor said, "our young invalid needs to drink. Palme, find Frau Puntel in the kitchen, why don't you, and bring us her big blue jug of beer. And some of her salty pretzels as well."

So Ella knew he had been listening to even her slightest breath.

After refreshments, Professor K began again.

"I have a game before we sleep tonight. Everyone must participate." He glanced at Ella. "My game will help us in our search to see without our eyes."

The students looked at each other.

"So—you all remember the story of Hansel and Gretel, yes?"

The faces upturned toward him, gleaming.

"Well, while you were working this afternoon, I played Hansel for you all. I have dropped a path of stones—nice substantial ones, mind you, no breadcrumbs!"

Palme and Muehlenkamp laughed.

"I want you to go out in the moonlight tonight and follow the bright stones where they lead. You will find your way with *all* your senses, not only your eyes."

"Alone, Professor K? Will we be out in the dark night *alone*?" Olga's voice trembled.

"Miss Stanukovich, I would not distress you so. Each will have a companion." He set a small stack of paper on the table before him. "I have your names here. Just before you depart, you will receive your partners." He rubbed his hands together and then raised his index fingers. "There is just one rule—no talking while you walk. Instead, let your senses speak and listen. Hear the wind. Feel the mountain air. Open yourselves to the glories of the night and let your soul expand into its mysteries. Be one with the night. Right now, off you go!"

There was a flurry of excitement, the putting on of jackets and collecting of wraps. Ella, catching the energy of the others, ran to the dormitory room and grabbed her shawl from its drawer. Perhaps she would be alone with him, his partner. She would ask him to clarify what she meant to him and what to make of this woman who had joined the group. Surely she, Ella, held a special place in his heart. Yet if there were an uncomfortable truth to be known, she would know it.

Papa had not been a man to hold back. An adventurer, himself, he had often told his children, "Go on, take a chance. The world is large enough to hold you." Laughing together at some slight done to them at school, her brother and sister would chant his words until the wrong or error shriveled beneath their feet. They would romp about the sitting room stomping on its remains. "The woorrlld is biiiig enough," they would shout. Ella could not join in their merriment, but inwardly she felt bold. She would make the world big enough for herself. Wrapped in her shawl, she whispered Papa's words as she descended the stairs. "Go on," she told herself. "Go on."

The boys had already assembled and were taking names from Professor K's hands.

"Miss Stanukovich," said Doncker, "you and I will brave the night together."

Olga giggled, her plump shoulders rising toward her ears.

Wuest and Brumder became a pair. Then Palme and Kleuwer. Schneider and Muehlenkamp.

Ella stood alone. But Professor K was speaking to Miss Chimiakin, his face close to hers, frowning, his voice muted but sharp, a razor sheathed.

"But I am not the slightest bit tired, Wassily Wassilievich." Miss Chimiakin put her hands on her hips. "And I want to be with the group. This Fraulein will be my companion." She pointed at Ella. "You must wait here to greet us all when we return. *Au revoir.*" She turned from him and took Ella's arm.

Within minutes Ella walked out into the night with the woman said to be her lover's wife.

Just outside the doors of Puntel's hotel, a meadow swept toward piney woods beside a mountain lake, untrammeled and remote. For some minutes as Professor K stood in the open door of the lodge, feeble rays spilled some meters into the dark, but once he closed the door, the little light dissipated into the night. A moon full to bursting shone at intervals through thick clouds driving past its face in gusts like a woman sobbing intermittent tears into a folded cloth. The night was alternately bright enough to see shapes and so black a walker could not find his own feet with his eyes. Creeping forward, adjusting to the dark, Ella listened for a time to the scuff of boots and shoes ahead of them. Then the evening grew utterly still.

What a curious turn things were taking. Perhaps this Miss Chimiakin knew about the kisses and thought to punish Ella, to lead her into the dark and then leave her. Or something else. Well, she, Ella, might be small, but she was brave. On cold nights when the boys and girls from the Gymnasium gathered for Crack the Whip on the frozen pond, little Ella would skate alongside the whip, not holding on or joining in, but keeping up, her legs pumping, a little satellite orbiting alone. *Faster*, she would tell herself, *Move*. Why, at twenty she had sailed to America with just her sister for company, even joining a Texas cattle drive with her brother Carl and his American wife, Mary. They rode on horseback, laughing as the dust flew up from the dry roads and covered their hair and clothes. This tramp through the Kochel meadow near the lake was nothing in comparison.

As the path veered away from the comfort of the lodging house, Miss Chimiakin drew close to Ella.

"This walking in the night is difficult, do you not agree? I had not thought it would be so dark."

Ella put her finger to her lips.

"Fraulein Münter, I know we are not to talk, but supposing...?" She shuddered. "I never walk out like this at home."

Through the thin cotton of her shirtwaist, Ella felt little fingers pressing on her flesh. She cringed at the touch but she did not remove the woman's hand from her arm. "I can see the stones."

And for a time, Ella *could* see Professor K's stones. He had spaced them close together at first. But as the path circled the meadow and neared the woods, Ella found the way harder and harder to read. What seemed like a glowing stone might turn out to be a patch of bare earth or a section of bleached-out tree bark blown onto the grassy plain near the woods.

"Do you hear the others, Fraulein Münter?"

Ella shrugged, the earth mute through the thin soles of her boots. As they walked up a slight incline, mounds of root growth turning their feet, Miss Chimiakin lost her footing and fell, nearly pulling Ella down with her.

"I am so sorry. Oh, forgive me, Fraulein Münter. I can see nothing!" Sitting awkwardly, Miss Chimiakin clasped her ankle.

How irritating she was, this woman. It seemed Professor K's game required someone of stouter constitution than this Miss So-and-So. But what could she do? She could hardly abandon the help-less woman. And besides, she had no wish to walk through the dark alone. Ella helped her companion rise. "If we go slowly, we'll be all right." But the night had grown darker, the air denser. A canopy of leaves soon stood between them and the moon. In minutes, Ella could see no path at all.

"Fraulein Münter, I think I *have* injured my ankle. I must sit down." The woman rubbed at her boot. "This game is not a good idea. Wassily Wassilievich should have come with us."

The woody patch they had entered was unfamiliar, the dark im-penetrable. No shape presented itself, no sound directed her. The air felt moist, suggesting perhaps that they were near the rise overlook-ing the lake, perhaps near enough to stumble into the water, their heavy skirts and boots pulling them down. Nor could Ella see the ground beneath her feet to tell if they had stopped atop a jutting shelf, a wrong step sending them tumbling over. Yet they must walk on. Ella took careful step after step.

"The path is quite narrow. Put your hands on my waist and step where I do. Put your weight on me."

They walked some minutes in tandem then, Ella frowning into pitch. The game was ruined. She had wanted to do as Professor K had instructed, to see her way without her eyes, but how could she, tramping along with this helpless woman trailing behind her, hang-ing on her? Worse, until Ella could clarify the woman's identity, every activity was sure to sour. The uncertainty was unendurable. "Miss Chimiakin," Ella said at last, "have you known Professor K a very long time?"

"Professor!" Miss Chimiakin smirked, pulling on Ella's dress. "Yes, I have known Wassily Wassilievich since we were children. We are cousins and schoolmates as well." Miss Chimiakin's voice wrinkled.

"Oh, please, can we sit? My ankle is beginning to swell." She bent over and moaned as she loosened the laces of her boot.

Cousins. So that was it, then. And yet the information gave Ella little peace. The little woman sitting before the hearth had not looked up at Professor K like a cousin. And they had not argued like cousins. Ella frowned into the dark.

"Come, we are far from the lodging house." Ella helped Miss Chimiakin to her feet, and they continued on into a blackness Ella had only experienced in the depths of a winter's sleep. They appeared to be in a forest, now, and Ella walked with her hands outstretched lest a sharp twig pierce her eye or the brush of a long limb scratch her face. Fearful that she, too, might trip, she grasped at the slender branches on either side to steady herself as the ground shifted and rolled. Worse was her utter lack of direction in the dark. When they came to a part of the woods where the growth was thick, Ella passed an overhanging bough to her companion's hand, urging her to duck, not to catch her hair. Further on, the leafy mold beneath their feet hardened, creased, and folded. "There's a root just here." Ella tested the ground with the toe of her boot, her voice low and intense. "Don't trip." Long minutes passed, each step a treacherous gamble. At last the woods seemed to thin, and the girls found a grassy knoll on which to sit and slow the beating of their hearts.

"I cannot walk further, Miss Münter. The pain is too great." Miss Chimiakin removed her boot and rubbed her ankle.

"Shall I go on ahead and get help?"

"Yes, oh yes. I am sorry to ask it." Miss Chimiakin began to whimper. "Or rather, no. Don't leave me. I cannot stay here on my own. Oh, Fraulein! What should we do?"

Ella wrapped her shawl around the trembling woman, then scoured the blackness with her eyes. She might have to go on alone. But where? She peered into the dark just as a housekeeping wind picked up and rearranged the sky, and as the moon flickered overhead, she saw a grove she recognized, well beyond the lodging house. Under this stand of beech trees, she had kissed Professor K eleven times.

"I think I know where we are now. It's not far. You can make it." Ella took the woman's hand and pulled her up. "Let me bear some of your weight." She positioned Miss Chimiakin's arm around her shoulder, drawing her close, their hips and skirts brushing as they lurched along the grove.

The wind blew stronger now, dense clouds passing in brief intervals in front of the low moon. Light flared and darkened unnervingly. Each time the moon shone and their eyes grasped the contour of a tree or bush, the light dissolved into a deeper blackness, leaving them blinder than before. Ella put out tentative steps again and again, her ears straining for direction, her eyes sore with the futility of sight, sure of the general direction but uncertain of the terrain. Then just ahead, she saw a dim glow close to the ground.

A fragrance, moist and floral, seeped toward them from the dull light the way a beautiful woman enters a room, her scent announcing her loveliness. On the far side of a chalky space, small white forms caught snatches of moonlight. They had come to Frau Puntel's moon garden, the broad white beds designed to light a nighttime path to the kitchen door. Balled hydrangeas and saucer-wide peonies shone as bright as lamps each time the moonlight poured upon them. Pale roses and lilies and phlox bloomed knee high. Snowy clusters of geraniums, daisies, and impatiens glowed among a drift of white-leaved hosta.

Beyond the flowerbed, Professor K and the others sat silently.

"Wassily Wassilievich!" Miss Chimiakin called out.

But Professor K crossed toward Ella.

"Thank God," he said.

"Miss Chimiakin has hurt herself."

Professor K swiveled to Miss Chimiakin and put his arm around her shoulder, assisting, reassuring.

"It *was* a very black night for a ramble," Palme shoved his fists into his pockets. "The two girls should not have gone by themselves."

"I'm not sure why any of us went," Muehlenkamp grumbled.

"I thought the walk was splendid." Doncker edged close to Miss Stanukovich.

"Oh yes, Professor," said Olga. "I was frightened, but Herr Doncker was marvelous. We *did* see without our eyes!"

Doncker touched her hand.

"I think we've all learned something tonight, Professor." Wuest got up from the ground and brushed the seat of his pants.

Professor K turned back to look at the students following in his wake. "Then the game was a success."

That night, Ella slept fitfully. Her legs jerked spasmodically, and in her dreams, she reached out blindly in the dark, stepping again and again onto a surface that would not bear her.

In the morning, Ella set up her easel on a knoll on the far side of the lake so that yellow masses of wild mustard framed a lower border angled against brilliant water. Yesterday, the scene inflated her spirit. Today, though, her soul lay within her leaden as the load on her back.

The night walk had ended badly, and the question of the Chimiakin woman remained unresolved. Why had Professor K behaved so mysteriously, not at all like the man who had talked with Ella, walked out with her, kissed and touched her? Perhaps Miss Chimiakin was something more than a cousin. One could marry one's cousin. An uncle of her mother's had done so. As brave as Ella had felt at the start of last evening, by the end, her nerves were worn, her confidence abraded and bruised.

The turmoil in her heart was at odds with the brilliance of the scene before her. The sun shone strong enough to squeeze out the bluest blue from the water's depths, and today's patch of wild mustard was vigorous, holding onto its winter growth late in the season near this high mountain lake. Small clusters of yellow petals radiated on short petioles from stems so firm the brisk breeze barely rearranged them. It would not do to waste the day. Ella unpacked her rucksack and shook her curls. She could do this—set aside her discomfort and make herself think in pure color, the possibility of primaries and dyads—yellow with green, blue and red-violet. She could immerse herself in work. Painting was a tonic, a restorative.

The mustard and the lake would supply the stable base of her picture, the green of overhanging leaves and the red-violet of anemone just to the left forming a triangle to move the eye up and back. As the sun passed overhead, Ella lost herself in the work, sometimes mixing paint from two or three tubes, sometimes easing dabs on her cardboard palette to use straight from their container. She wanted to imbue her canvas with clean lines, the energy and purity of the scene, the colors strong enough to make her gasp. Concentrating, she muffled the clanging memory of the moonlit walk, the clinging woman she could neither befriend nor neglect, the cool and perplexing distance of Professor K. Gradually, her nerves quieted and the clench that dampened her spirit loosened its hold.

She ate her lunch in silence. Frau Puntel had wrapped wedges of two nice cheeses with a thick slice of dark bread spread with spicy mustard and folded in half. Ripe peaches and a square of dark chocolate. Ella had brought her own canteen of water from the well near the house. She settled herself under a stand of old larches on the edge of a wooded area banding the lake and ate the cheeses and fruit, the only sound the modest licks of water against the green banks where the mustard grew. The air grew heavy and fragrant with the humid forest growth just behind her, and she lay down on her side in the warm grass, her canvas bag under her head. She dropped into a nest of sleep. In her hazy dream the sun grew strong against her back and wrapped her in a thick coverlet. But when she tried to fling off the warmth, a man had nestled himself around her, his arm enfolding her, his hand very near her breast.

"Don't awaken, my friend," he whispered.

Ella felt the weight of his arm, the rise and fall of his chest as he breathed in time with her. Alarmed that he should be so close, she rose and stumbled away from him to where a growth of maidenhair ferns grew in feathers above barky humus. She knelt among them and brushed her skirt to calm herself.

As though he owned the very air, Professor K rolled onto his back and clasped his hands beneath his head. "This mountain summer shines with the beauty of an icon, all gold and lapis. Do you feel it, Fraulein Münter?" He inhaled deeply as if to suck in the whole of the afternoon's air. "Has your work gone well today?" Then supple as a feline, he raised himself in one motion and walked to her easel where she had placed it under a tree for protection from the full sun. "Wonderful colors you've mixed," he said. "What a fine yellow! This is the mustard, yes? The small scrapes of the knife are quite good." His voice was full and strong, the call of a mountain horn. "I can almost see the blossoms moving in the breeze. And the lake—quite a fine blue you have here! You have almost caught the thing, itself."

Crouched low under the green-black canopy, Ella trembled. His presence so suddenly here, so near as she slept, unnerved her. What should she make of it? There was still the mystery of this wife and the oddness of the evening before. And his words to her now, like compliments to a prized student. Surely she meant something more to him. She couldn't think what to reply, what to understand, what to expect.

"You are a true artist, you know. I esteem you most highly. Young as you are, I sometimes think I have nothing to offer you. The best I can do for you is guard your talent and let nothing false creep in. Your own spirit must lead you." He picked up her palette knife and stroked it clean of paint. Stooping to wipe the color onto her smock spread out now on the grass, he lay the knife in its folds. He rose, then, stepping toward the glade of ferns, facing her directly, his voice deep and insistent, his eyes intense. "This is not fair. This is not all. Fraulein Münter, you must hear me—there is in your soul a light that blinds me! Please believe me, our time together in the past, when we talked of the soul's freedom, it—it was most satisfying to me. As artists, you and I, we see that the ordinary, the conventional constraints of the world need have no authority. I'm sure you understand. You and I, we—"

"Is Miss Chimiakin your wife or your cousin?" Ella stepped away from the shadow of the forest verge. She raised her chin.

He strode back to her painting on its easel, his shoulders tight, a pulse in his neck throbbing. He picked up a tube of her paint, and then another. "What is this garish green you are using?" He swept his hand across the tubes on the easel's shelf and flung them on the grass. "You are never to use this color!"

Ella retreated to the shadow. His harsh words sprang up brush and bramble between them.

Through the tangled growth, as though to carve a path, he called out. "Miss Chimiakin is my cousin. I have known her from childhood. She was my schoolmate at University, and we became companions." His voice dropped and he paused. "But yes, she is also my wife."

Ella steadied herself. Reaching behind her, she clasped the lines and ridges of a tree's coarse bark.

He placed his hands upon his face, his long fingers pressing on his eyes. "Miss Chimiakin comes from a line of aristocrats on the same side as my great-grandmother. To take my name would degrade her. It is often done so in Russia. You could not have known." He crossed the grassy space between them. Several paces from where Ella stood, he stopped and held himself erect and still. "Fraulein Münter, I was wrong to take advantage of your youth. I was wrong, certainly, to betray my wife. And yet I am not sorry for our moments together. Your friendship has given me much joy, and I have developed a deep affection for you, though I have no right to claim it."

"Miss Chimiakin?"

"My wife knows nothing of our particular friendship. You were most kind to her last evening, and she is grateful, as am I." Again he took a step toward her. "My marriage—I believed—I believed we could all be here together." With a long exhalation of breath, he pressed the heels of his hands against his eyes. "It was an ideal, a fantasy. I was mistaken." For some moments, he said nothing.

Nor could Ella speak. So much had occurred, she could not take it in. Tears threatened in her throat, but she would not let them rise.

"Fraulein Münter, for the love of God, forgive me. Say at least that we can be artists together. We will say no more about the intimacy between us."

Her voice, when she found it, was thin as though a weight pressed upon her airways, her little breath wasted in her chest. "If you say." But what was she to do with the stone inside her? What pocket in her skirt could contain it?

They stood in silence, the mid-day insects muted in the sun. He raised his head toward the bright water. "This arrangement cannot be. I am—*uncomfortable*—with you here. I cannot leave the other students, nor can I send my wife back to Munich." He faced Ella once again, his back toward the canvas with the offending colors. His voice was low, little more than the lap of lake water against the grassy bank. "Fraulein Münter, I must beg you leave Kochel. There may be other teachers for you in Munich. Forgive me."

He picked up his bicycle from the grass and pedaled away. When the path curved around the lake, he was out of sight.

Ella walked to her things on the grass and bent to collect her palette knife and smock. She put them into her rucksack, fumbled with the flap, dropped the knife onto the grass. The twenty-five kisses were a folly. She had been naive to allow them, a goose to count them. She had lost her way when she let herself be kissed, when she fell into a fantasy of spiritual communion. And now he wished her to leave—the mountain, the class, his wife, himself. Her eyes filled with tears, and she had to sit down.

It was some time before she could bring herself to pick up the containers of paint lying on the grass. She threw the tube of emerald green into the lake.

The next morning was grey and rainy. Herr Puntel drove the horse and wagon to the lodging house door. Palme hoisted Ella's heavy trunk, her traveling valise, and her rucksack onto the wagon where Kluewer secured them, covering the bags with a tarpaulin. He lifted up her bicycle onto the wagon bed. Olga, holding Ella's arm, gave advice.

"You must not let the dental to pull your tooth right away. He must give you a poultice for your jaw and the herbs to soothe the swelling. And when you are better, I am hoping you will return to be with us here." She squeezed Ella's arm. "I will miss my friend."

"Olga, you forget—my father was a dentist. I won't let anyone pull the tooth."

"Here, take my handkerchief. Now you must come back."

"Yes, well...I cannot say."

"But you must. We will paint together. You can teach me to ride your bicycle."

Holding her umbrella over her head, Ella climbed into the seat beside Herr Puntel.

"Goodbye, Olga. Goodbye, boys. Perhaps I'll see you in Munich in the fall."

Palme waved. "Good luck with your tooth."

"Safe travels," Schneider said.

Ella waved back as Herr Puntel shook the reins and the horses started down the slick mountain road.

In the dim Kochel station room, Ella purchased her ticket and posted a note to her sister.

> Dear Emmy,
>
> I am coming to Bonn and will arrive on the late train Sunday. Can you make up a bed for me? Don't wait up. I'd like to stay with you for a while. Will my brother-in-law object?
>
> Love,
>
> Ella

With her finger in the grit of the train window, Ella drew a face, round glasses, a small beard. Bringing her finger to her lips, she kissed it. Then, with the side of her hand, she wiped the glass. She cleaned her hand with Olga's handkerchief and folded it neatly into the pocket of her skirt for safekeeping. From time to time as she dozed along the journey, she reached into her pocket and found it there.

Galerie

"Gabriele Münter Painting in Kallmünz," 1903
Wassily Kandinsky
Oil on canvas
23" × 23"
Städtische Galerie im Lenbachhaus, Munich
Gabriele Münter Bequest

In this expressive depiction of an artist at work, Kandinsky portrays the painter Gabriele Münter with her back to the viewer, a position both he and she were to replicate later in successive paintings. An early work of Kandinsky, this painting, while not realistic by virtue of its lack of significant detail, is nonetheless fully figurative.

The figure who represents Münter stands before an easel slightly to the left of the painting's center, absorbed in her work. She, in the foreground, stands on a lawn covered in burnished autumn leaves beneath bare trees, their warm colors in contrast to the deep blue of her painting smock. She glances toward the subject of the small painting she is working on, a group of houses separated from her by several stone steps and a fence. The hamlet, a collection of rustic structures in the painting's background, is depicted in golds, tans, and ochres.

The painting's surface is heavily textured with bold impasto diagonals on either side of the vertical figure of the painter at work. More care is given to light and atmosphere than to the details of buildings, trees, or the human figure.

The effect is energetic and passionate.

J. Eichner

Chapter Two

Tables and Chairs

Bonn
Mid-Summer, 1902

As MUCH AS she hated it, she would have to concoct a lie.

Gradually aware of herself under Emmy's starched sheets, Ella rolled onto her stomach. The ruse of the injured tooth that the students in Kochel had accepted would not deceive her sister. She might insist that Ella have her tooth looked at here in Bonn, an enterprise that would surely expose her. Emmy would frown at her haste in bolting and upbraid her for traveling so far with a disorder not severe enough to have weathered a single day's journey. So toothache would not do. Perhaps she could tell Emmy that the painting sessions were not satisfactory. She had quit lessons before when the teachers had patronized rather than challenged her. But what if she decided to return to Munich in the fall and resume study? She might, after all, want to go back.

She would have to find something to say to Emmy. But not the truth.

Foolish Ella! She had slid into a romantic fascination like a stupid schoolgirl. To be singled out by such a prominent figure, a man of significance—who wouldn't be flattered? But shame on her, too, for continuing to desire this forbidden man. In the space of a train ride, the insult of her hasty departure from Kochel had boiled into a sweet syrup thickened with desire. "I've met a man," she whispered to her pillow and rolled onto her side, pressing her knees inward, a warm ache in her groin pulsing and spreading. But before long the little figure of Miss Chimiakin supplanted his image, and Ella began to thrash about, her head abuzz with hornets. Oh, but he had wronged her. He was most to blame. A married man—he had deceived her! Her teacher—he had taken advantage of her!

Yes, but she had encouraged him. She had wanted it.

Thrust into a thrilling drama but ashamed of her tangled feelings, she fell victim to a confused knotting of self-recrimination, longing, pride, resentment, and lies.

She mustn't tell Emmy.

Since long before the end of her childhood—she marked it at the death of her mother—Ella understood that a young woman measured her success by the attention she could garner among eligible men—attention leading to marriage. She had assumed she would be like the other girls, like Emmy herself, but when the courting season came round, once again she had found something wanting. Before Mama got sick, a minister's son had called for Ella. He was studying theology, and they had strolled arm in arm beneath the leafing trees, their bodies cool as the night breeze between them. Ella feared telling the earnest young man that she had stopped attending church services, that what he knew as "faith" had no pull on her. What future was there for her with such a man, playing the role of pastor's wife, active among the ladies' groups, gracious at teas, attentive at the rituals of birth and death? Worst of all, he had no imagination—doctrinaire rather than inspired. How could she go forward? Yes, she wanted a comfortable home of her own, but the nest he offered pricked rather than warmed her and she could not see herself building a life with him. At any rate, he, too, lost interest, confessing that he was about to propose marriage to a girl in Cologne with whom he had been corresponding.

"Did you do something to offend him?" Emmy asked.

"I just didn't suit him. Besides, he was ordinary."

"What's wrong with that?"

"It's just not what I want."

"Oh, Ella. I wish you could get along better with people."

"Oh, *I* don't. I don't wish that at all."

Nearly a year later, Ella acquired a second gentleman, a spirited university student whose weekly singing lessons fell the hour before her own. Handsome and popular, he had walked her home a few times, cavorting as they went, but Ella felt all elbows and feet, briary in the midst of his windy expansiveness, dim-witted about his jokes. She could not eat in his presence and was absolutely tortured when she had to excuse herself to execute some necessary bodily function. While the other girls glided gracefully into the clear waters of easy sociability, she mucked about on the reedy shores. He, too, stopped calling after a bit.

She felt most at ease in the little workspace she made in the back bedroom. Emmy scolded Ella. "You've got to make an effort. You won't find a husband in a paint pot. Especially now that Mama's gone, you've got to be more sociable. You know that's what she'd want." Ella had nothing to say. She returned to her silent studio and her canvas.

Of course she wanted a husband. Knew she *should* want one. Emmy made it clear enough. According to her, Ella's talent should be nurtured in a public setting, a conduit for male approval. Every class she took was an opportunity to attract a suitor. But the men she met were nothing to Ella. She preferred to paint, happy for the solitude, happier still to be free, unhindered by conversations and expectations. When she got a new Kodak, she had an excuse for keeping herself apart from the group of girls and men who went to the dances.

"You're hiding behind that thing," Emmy said.

"I'm not," Ella retorted. "You've seen my photographs. I'm good at it. Leave me alone."

"You've got to get out more."

"I'm not you, Emmy!"

"Not to mention the expense of all these classes. Are you sure you want to spend your inheritance like this?"

She couldn't make Emmy understand. It wasn't just a question of classes. She felt something she couldn't name. She wanted to—but she couldn't say what it was. Something was stirring within her and it wanted out.

That fall she left home to study at the Ladies' Academy in Munich. Away from her sister's constant scrutiny and disapproval, Ella could do what she liked. She liked to draw, to sketch, to paint. She thought she'd really like to sculpt. But before long the Ladies' Academy became a disappointment. Little was expected of her. No one thought she could do anything important.

"Remember Fredericka Schloemer?" Emmy had written her then. "She's opened up a little hat shop just behind the Hauptbahnof. I think she'd take you on, if you'd like. Shall I speak to her?"

Ella shoved the letter under her portfolio. Hat shop!

She had heard of a new school called the Phalanx. It was said to have a serious purpose. She would enroll there.

The school was progressive, the students interesting. Almost at once, it seemed, Professor K understood her. He shared his own sketches and loaned her books. He regarded her as a person with thoughts and aspirations. He let her know that as a draftsman, she shone above the others, including the boys. Even better, he spoke of the spirit and the soul of art, ideas trickling within her. When he talked, her liquid thoughts took shape and form, and she felt herself enlarged. Within days of meeting him, she wanted to please him. Within weeks of meeting him, she set herself a goal: to astonish him.

The work of seeing well challenged her. She fattened her notebooks, drawing the same subject again and again to master its lines and find its central focus. She made both thumbnail sketches and large gestural studies, tried the popular flat *Jugendstil* style as well as rounded-out images with shading. She thought of herself differently, then, forgot she was Ella. She became the gesture, the image, the effect. She stayed until the studio lamps were exhausted, and she took her papers home to scratch and erase until she toppled into her bed smudging the sheets.

The Phalanx students worked day and night, weekdays and weekends, indoors and outdoors. When spring came, Professor K organized bicycle trips into the countryside, encouraging the students to develop their repertoire of images. When they reached a promising vista, they dismounted and set up easels near the road or off in the trees. Once when the group of students had passed a long day sketching and hiking, the others turned back toward the train, leaving Ella and Professor K to cycle down a country lane alone, their shadows long and purple on the new grass beneath them. Ella was pumping slowly now, and he rode a bit ahead. When she rounded a bend in the road, she could not see him before her.

"Fraulein Münter," she heard behind her. He had pulled off the lane and leaned his bicycle against a tree alongside a small stream. "Come here."

Ella needed no further invitation. She plopped down gratefully and lifted her face to the breeze while he unstrapped his canvas bag from its rack on the rear of his bicycle. He sat down next to her and propped his sketchbook on his outspread knees. With a few strokes, he drew in the outlines of the scene before him—the brook, the cluster of cottages on the right, the long meadow, the stand of evergreens in the distance.

"It will be sunset soon." He lay his sketchbook on the grass.

For answer, Ella picked up the page and drew shadows under his trees, deepening the slope of his meadow, putting his cottages in relief.

He smiled when he saw what she had done. Placing the paper onto his own lap, he feathered in the lines of the horizon, suggesting a darkening sky. "We should paint together, too," he said, not lifting his eyes.

"Should we?" Ella reached over him to darken the drawing further, fingering her charcoal on its side to blacken the trees. She took back the sketchbook and settled it on her skirt.

Supporting himself on one arm, he crossed the other over her to fill in the foreground with his pencil. Held between the arm behind and the one drawing on her lap, Ella held her breath. What would come next? But when he had finished, he merely leaned back. "Look at the red of that sky," he said. "I hear it like a tuba."

Ella squinted at the horizon, saw thick stripes of crimson and scarlet, vermillion and carmine pressing the contours of the land, the shades sinking into one another as though each color had weight and mass and the purpose to penetrate the surface of the earth itself.

"Listen to the reds, Fraulein." His voice was deep and low. "For me, the world is one—art, music, color, sound—all one." He placed his hand on the sketch on her lap, smearing the charcoal, ruining her trees. "You hear it, too."

Ella hesitated. "I'm not sure."

"Of course you do," he replied. "Your soul hears what mine hears."

With each outing, Ella saw that his physical energy and the rhythm of his casual conversation complemented hers, and as her admiration grew, her initial awe of him diminished. Chatting, packing up at the end of a session, she forgot that she was his student. And as she cycled alongside him, she felt what it was like to be a healthy young woman. With him she was at home in her body, connected head to toe, brain, shoulders, lungs, limbs splendidly strong, riding easily along the bumpy country roads, stopping to share a chocolate bar from his pack, admiring the shaft of light on a bed of moss. His fine back on the bicycle in front of her was all the scenery she needed. When they were together, she forgot that they were two people, separate. She wanted to be so near him that they were not two.

Lying now in Emmy's bed, Ella warmed again with desire. But soon Emmy would return from the long end of the garden where she was tending her rabbits and chickens at this hour and begin clanging about with pots and pans. Ella would have to get up, kiss her, and detail yesterday's precipitous departure. She burrowed deeper and kicked her bare feet against the bed. She hated to be false to Emmy, but what else could she do?

She would fabricate a different love affair—not with Professor K— but with the kind of man her sister would understand, an ordinary man. Ella would say she had kissed a man and then had fled. Carl Palme would serve. She would say she had kissed Carl Palme and, fearing his advances, had run. That was close enough to the truth. She need not say he was a Russian, her teacher, a married man.

Telling it, Ella found herself falling into the fiction of her own devising, weaving a tale of her time on the mountain made up of threads of truth but not its essence. Ella said she'd flirted in the beech grove with Carl Palme, a stupid boy, and nearly let him have his way with her.

Emmy sat at the table and listened. "Oh, Ella," she smiled. "Every girl has a few stupid men in her life. No harm was done. You shouldn't have run away. You're not a child, you know. You need to find a husband before very long, and a kiss or two is the price a girl pays from time to time. You won't find any husband at all if you stop a man from kissing you. You want that, don't you—a husband? Children?"

"I'm not sure."

"Ella, of course you want a family! But you'll have to find a nice fellow first." She leaned over and patted Ella's shoulder. "I'm going to ask Georg to introduce you to some of the men in his office. Lots of men will want you, especially now that you've grown up to be so pretty and talented."

"You know I'm not pretty. I've never been."

"Don't be silly. You have lovely eyes and such soft brown hair. Oh, Ella, you'll get over this! You will. Anyway, I'm glad you're here. And so is Georg. We want you to stay a long time."

After Mama's death, Emmy had opened her home to Ella, and the Schroeter home was welcoming, a model of conventional domesticity. If Emmy was right, Ella could have that, too. Perhaps she could resume private painting classes in Bonn, though the serious art schools wouldn't have a woman. Still, she could consider staying here with her sister, finding her way, finding a husband too.

For days, she tried on the part, tried to think like the other girls she knew. She cast a shadow of herself into the intimate audience of Emmy and Georg. But another Ella lurked in the dark backstage, listening for her cue to join the hero before the lights. When she sat at the table peeling potatoes or stitching a tear in a garment, *his* face or voice or scent lay just behind, beside, beyond her, and she measured her happiness by the intensity with which she could conjure up his presence. Emotion rumbled deep within her like a mountain stream wearing down the core of a cave with its rushing force, sometimes far below the surface, sometimes spraying its way upwards until the rattle of a rock shower on the tin roof of her mind drove away thought. She was unsettled by the power of her feelings but could not trust herself to speak them. Too much shame at her own poor judgment stood between the rush of emotion she associated with Professor K and the relief she might have felt in confessing.

"You're so silent, these days." Emmy lifted her stirring spoon from her broth. She brought up Carl Palme and his kisses, and Ella blushed over her needle. "Wouldn't you like to write to him?" Ella shook her head, glad she had not betrayed herself with the truth.

Gradually, Ella adapted to the rhythm of the Schroeter household, muddling through the days with Emmy, shopping and cooking, cleaning and mending. She tagged along with her sister to Emmy's rabbit hutch and watched her coo and fondle the larger animals, nuzzling against them while they wriggled in her hands. One morning, holding the pups, Emmy remarked on the coloration and variety that two adult rabbits produced, but Ella turned away, visibly uncomfortable. Later, when he came home from work, Georg did the slaughtering, and Emmy seemed quite pleased when a pair of skinned rabbits appeared on her wooden table, ready to be braised or fried. Ella kept her distance, looking askance at her sister then, astonished that she could separate the creature she kissed from the one she cooked. "I could never do that," she said.

"You will," Emmy replied, "when you have a home of your own."

Ella worried then. Was she a nuisance in the house? Ought she to leave her sister and brother-in-law to their own lives? Might her presence, in time, wear a hole in their well-knit intimacy? There were nights when her sister seemed withdrawn and a little sad. She'd leave her needlework in its bag and turn out the light early. It must be that Ella was a bother to the little family. Emmy and Georg were a couple she wasn't a part of. But being an outsider to their life wasn't so easy for Ella, either, and as the summer nights passed, both their enthusiasms and their concerns chafed at her. It was a chore to appear cheerful, to do her part, to contribute to a family that wasn't hers. Once, Georg and Emmy invited in a neighbor family. Emmy doted on their little boy, and she bought treats for him—plum küchen and a ginger cake. But Ella felt awkward with the child and could find no game to amuse him. The next Sunday, Emmy urged Ella to accompany her and Georg to the old Dopplekirchen for services. Georg sang in the choir. Afterwards, as they strolled home, he made a point to take both sisters by the arm.

"I'll just walk behind," Ella said. "The street is too narrow for the three of us." But it wasn't just the street she meant.

Yet there were cheery evenings, Georg dancing with his wife to a schuhplattler rhythm. And they all sang together the new volkssänger tunes. Then Georg took the floor with "Da unten im Tal," the old Swabian folk song his grandfather taught him, and he brought out his concertina. Emmy smiled at Ella. "Wouldn't mother have loved him? If only she'd lived—" Her voice broke off. "If only, I'd—" She turned away then and left Georg to put his instrument in its case.

Another night Georg offered to help Ella set up a small studio in the attic eaves.

"You'll want the nice light to do some of your art, won't you?" he said. But she didn't push him.

The next evening, though, she walked down the path through the shrubbery to the back garden. Georg was sawing wood, his tool a bass continuum underlying the higher-pitched song of mid-summer insects.

"What are you making?" Ella leaned against the back side of the rabbit hutch.

Georg squinted in the dim light and lined up his saw against the pencil line he had drawn. "Emmaline is talking about having a little business. You've heard her. Breeding and such." He finished his cut and lay the board on the grass.

"I guess."

"I thought I'd get another hutch ready before the next litter arrives."

"Do you mind? Working after supper, I mean."

"Not at all. I'm glad to put my hands to something."

"I can see you're good at it." Ella thumped the hutch behind her with her knuckle.

"There's no pleasure if you don't try to be good at what you're doing."

"I know."

Georg straightened. He blew at the teeth of his saw, scattering
dust. "I'm a music man, myself," he said. "I'd have music about me
all day long if I could. I'd sing and I'd play my instrument, too. But I
don't have the talent, you see. I might have had, when I was younger,
if I'd stuck to it. But I was foolish, like a lot of fellows, and I was lazy,
too. I thought the music would always be there when I was ready to
get to it." He tucked his saw under one arm and with the other carried
the sawhorse to the lean-to shed behind the rabbit hutch.

Ella waited until he returned, and she followed him up the path
to the house.

"Are you trying to tell me something?"

"I suppose I am," he said as the first star of evening popped like a
pinprick through the dark blue sky.

Later in her little room, Ella looked again at the night sky. How
far away she was from her old life, her old room in the colorful
Schwabing neighborhood, the noisy pranks of the art students at the
Phalanx, the camaraderie and cut-ups, the winey scents of solvents,
the squirt of paints pressed from tubes, the mess and the exhilaration
of trying to make something that had never been before, something
you alone saw and knew. But she couldn't go back. She was hopeless.
She didn't belong anywhere. She closed the lace curtain and crawled
into bed.

In the park that day, Ella had watched a mother call in panic
for her little boy, first frozen in place, then dashing along one path
and then another. The mother had searched and searched, a mad
woman, hollering and crying, racing this way and that until the child
was found. But Ella could not find that other Ella, the one a childhood teacher once called *independent*.

When Emmy brought up Georg's workmates, Ella turned away. "I'd rather not."

"Then, won't you go back to your drawing, at least?" Emmy said. "Shouldn't you have *something* to do?"

"You think I'm just playing. But I'm not. Drawing is important."

"Well, do it then, if it's so important."

But she did not take out her pencils or her canvas. Her rucksack stood in the corner of her little room, her colors and knives inert. The days brushed by her, a rock in a dry streambed.

When Ella had been with them almost a month, Georg took a vacation from work, and the three spent a week bicycling in the Idar-Oberstein area. Emboldened by splendid weather, vigorous exercise, and good spirits, Ella sent Professor K a picture card, telling Emmy as they walked to the post that she admired her teacher but barely knew him. "He has artistic theories, not like the usual teachers."

"Why don't you go back?"

"I—I can't say for sure."

She felt like a smudged image, layers of Ellas superimposed on one another, their outlines dirty and bleeding.

One late August morning broke pleasantly cool, a forecast of crisp days still months ahead, and Georg awakened with a hunger for *pickert*, a peasant potato dish his grandmother had made. After morning chores, the sisters set out to the market for raisins, a necessary component, but then dawdled at a milliner's and then a draper's where Emmy took one bolt after another to the shop window to see the wool in natural light. Ella sat on a wooden chair while the shop girl and Emmy traded agitated narratives of shrinkage and fading and moth control. "Haven't we spent enough time here?" Ella muttered. It was long past noon, hours since breakfast, and Ella was hoping they could stop for refreshment.

"Is it nearly time to go?" Ella joined her sister at the counter. Emmy lifted the watch she wore at her waist and gasped. She bid a hasty farewell to the shopkeeper, pulling Ella down the Hochstadenring and past the Endenicherstrasse. "I can't believe I nearly forgot. How could it have gotten so late?" She began to run. "You should have said something."

"What about? Where are we going? Can't we have tea?" Ella trotted after Emmy.

"Later."

Plumper than Ella, Emmy grew breathless, puffing as they crossed one busy street and then another, their boots clapping against the cobblestones, their net bags swinging against their skirts.

It was not like Emmy to forget an appointment. But now Ella might have to wait for ages while Emmy conferred with her doctor or priest. What a nuisance! She could have stayed at home and read her book. Where was Emmy dragging her?

Rounding a corner into a quiet neighborhood lined with chestnut trees, Emmy stopped before a black iron gate. 14 Poppelsdorfer Allee. A spiked fence separated the stone building from its neighbors and framed a set of wide steps before a polished black door. Emmy lifted the heavy knocker and let it fall back with a loud clap onto its brass lip. "Her name is Madame Szendrey," she panted. "We're going in."

Emmy led the way into the dim interior, a long hallway flanked with doors shut like tombstones. Inside one door, a rope of amber light lay at the foot of a heavy curtain. Emmy pulled the curtain aside, and the sisters entered a close, darkened parlor. Three people sat at a small table.

"Come in, dears." A clip in the woman's voice suggested Romany. "I've been waiting for you."

Ella could hardly see the room, its walls blotted in deep maroon paper above a dark figured carpet. Thick velvet draperies covered what must have been a window at the back. Atop a small pump organ, a gathering of porcelain frogs surrounded what looked to Ella like a human lung under a glass globe. A dark green cloth covered the center table, and the chairs around its perimeter sat low to the floor, forcing those seated there to crouch, backs curved, heads thrust forward, as though the chairs were meant for children. Over the table, the dim halo of a domed lamp seemed to pull into its orbit all who sat there.

Their hostess took command and gestured toward Emmy, then Ella. "Frau Schroeter, please take the seat next to Frau Holzinger. And this young lady will be seated next to me." The woman spread her fingers on the surface of the round table and lowered her heavy head.

The room grew still. "I call us away from the glare of the day." Madame Szendrey leaned over the table and extinguished the lamp.

From then on, Ella could see nothing. But she knew, at least, where she was.

It was not her first séance. Some weeks after their mother died, just sixty-one, Emmy, still engulfed in grief, convinced her younger sister to accompany her to the edge of the city where an old woman sat in a dingy room and attempted to contact their mother's spirit. The session had been a failure. Emmy had cried convulsively throughout the woman's clumsy attempt to reach the spirit world. Afterwards, Emmy admitted she had heard and felt only her own desolation.

"You can't have thought you'd actually speak with Mother." Ella had been exasperated, annoyed to have been so duped.

"It wasn't the session. It was *me*. I couldn't stay still enough to let her in. It was my fault."

Ella frowned. The medium's voice had been raspy, and in the lamplight Ella had been repulsed by sagging flesh and hairs on the woman's chin. "That's not it," she had said. But plagued, herself, by fits of grief, she had not wanted to object. In her own dreams she had stared into a watery vortex into which she might plunge.

Now in the blackness, Ella tightened her shoulders. For a time they sat in a capsule of near silence, the everyday noises of Bonn's busy neighborhoods far away. A clock ticked.

"Place your hands on the table, my friends," Madame Szendrey instructed, "and locate the seeker next to you." Five pairs of hands brushed the table. On Ella's left, plump fingers patted the soft cloth until they reached Ella's hand and took it. On her right, Madame Szendrey set her large hand atop Ella's and wove her fingers firmly in her own. The room settled into itself.

Gradually Madame Szendrey began to wail, *ahhnngahhn-ngahhnng, ahhnngahhnngahhnng.* Her voice came from the walls, the floor, the table, from nowhere. It became a bagpipe, a slashed throat. "We create an energy, yes, oh yes, we draw another energy to us." Up and down in cadence, rising and falling, swelling and diminishing, she moaned to an unseen. "Feel the light. Feel the light." Silence alternated with sound. Sound melded into words. Words dissolved into prayer, supplication, incantation. "Come to us. Come to us. Come to us...."

In the close air of the room, Ella thought she might scream. Though she could not see Madame Szendrey, Ella felt the woman jerk back and forth in the chant, pulling Ella's gripped hand toward herself and shoving it away again, scraping the fibers of the table cover with the heel of Ella's hand, abrading it. A hard metal ring on the medium's finger pressed into Ella's flesh like a chain. Ella wanted to free herself, to rise from the table, but the room was so dark, she dared not try to stand or raise an alarm. She did not know how to tell Emmy they must leave.

Madame Szendrey began to speak again. "The air is rising upon my cheek. We are joined. Come, spirits. Float upon that air above us, who so want your guidance and your counsel."

Ella did feel a draft of thick, warm air, but it seemed to dissipate almost instantly.

Then Madame Szendrey spoke in whisper, a breathy utterance like a gas escaping. "Ahhhhhhnnnnnnngh. Yes. Yes. Yes, yes, yes, yes. I feel you here among us." Her voice rose, an urgency. "One of us wants you. Frau Schroeter? Fraulein Holzinger?"

Ella held her breath. Was Emmy going to say something?

Fraulein Holzinger's chair squeaked under her weight. "Papa? Is it you, Papa?"

Ella thought she heard a low rumble.

Fraulein Holzinger grew agitated. "What did he say? Did Papa speak?"

Madame Szendrey cried out. "Give your daughter a word!"

The rumble beneath them resolved in a shushing sound, a kind of muted wind. Ella thought she heard a groan or grunt. There may have been a cry, silence and sound intermingled, indistinguishable and nightmarish.

"Fraulein Holzinger, your Papa says that you should hope. But he is fading, now. Let him go. Sleep, beloved spirit. Farewell, most beloved spirit."

Fraulein Holzinger began to weep. "Papa..." An older voice next to the crying woman joined in, lower and more subdued.

Madame Szendrey trembled. Again as if in a kind of spasm, she jolted Ella's hand in hers to and fro along the table. Her hand became unattached to herself, the object of another's whim, and though she tried to stiffen her elbows to her sides and claim her hand, in the murmuring incantation, she had no strength.

"Fraulein Holzinger, be comforted. Your Papa is at peace." The medium hummed throatily.

Then like a forest growth after rain, a pale and sudden shift. The room grew cool. A curtain flapped. "But now, Frau Schroeter. What is this? Something is moving, coming closer. Ah, it is for you, Frau Schroeter. A message is coming, coming here." Madame Szendrey sighed and softened. "Ah, little spirit. Your Mama is here."

From across the table, Ella heard a whisper, "Oh, my dearest!"

Above the scuffle of hands, the breath of tears. Was it Emmy? And then Madame Szendrey began again, a low murmur rising and falling, slow, insistent. "We feel you, angel infant, dearest beloved, and we know you for our own. Come to us." It *was* Emmy, crying hard. Madame Szendrey was droning now, a soft thrumming, more than reverberation, less than song. "Bless your Mama. Brush her cheek with your sweet breath. Come and say farewell. Say goodbye to your Mama at last." Madame Szendrey spoke firmly now. "Goodbye, angel infant. Go on into your angel life. Love will keep you with us always."

Madame Szendrey released Ella's hand. "Frau Schroeter," she said, "be at peace."

"But she didn't speak!" Emmy sucked syllables from a pool.

"Dear heart, think of how small she was, how unformed. No, she could not. But she came to you to say goodbye. Take comfort in that. She knew you as her mother, and she came to you."

Emmy gave herself over to sobs.

Once again Madame Szendrey's presence filled the room like a warm wind. She moved from her chair; a yellow gleam encircled the table again.

"The world of the departed is not our world. Happily, we sometimes glimpse their aura, but now we must rejoin our separate lives."

The group at the table shifted uncomfortably. The medium continued. "Let us cherish this moment within us and let the presence of spirits linger in our hearts as we go. Quietly, quietly we move again in light."

Ella followed Emmy down the hallway and out the door. On a bench beneath a chestnut tree, she pulled her sister to sit beside her.

"Was the baby well grown?"

"I'd felt her move. They said five months or six. They wouldn't let me see. It was awful then, just blood and more blood."

Ella stroked her sister's hand. "Why didn't you tell me?"

"There are things a married woman can't...I couldn't...."

Ella tucked her sister's arm under her own. "You should have, though. I should have known."

They sat for a while in the late afternoon sun. Passersby nodded. Men lifted their hats.

"Love hangs on, Ella, longer than you know. Even when the person has died. I hope you never have to learn that." Emmy dabbed at her eyes. She blew her nose. "I never told you another thing, but I've wanted to. Don't be angry. When Mama was in a coma at the end, you were—away. I wanted you to come home. I wrote you letters, but you never came. It mattered to me. You don't know what it was like, hearing her breathe, waiting for the next breath and then the next one. Dying wasn't just part of Mama's life. It was part of *my* life. You should have been there."

Ella grew still on the bench next to Emmy. She hadn't thought it mattered. Mama couldn't hear or speak. She hadn't thought about Emmy.

"You'll have another baby, you and Georg."

They watched a young couple walking together, she holding his arm at the elbow.

"That's right." Emmy stood. "Of course it is. I tell myself that." She took Ella's hand. "Come on, now. Let's have tea and sweets."

Ella put her arm around her sister's waist and the sisters walked toward the shopping street.

The night Papa died, or rather the afternoon of the night he died, Ella had come home from school feeling hot and confused. She was eleven and accustomed to being greeted when she came in the door, but everyone at home was busy. Something, it seemed, had happened. Emmy met Ella and shooed her into the parlor, a room no one ever entered without an event or ceremony. "Stay here and read your book. I'll bring you something to eat. Mama's busy." Emmy closed the heavy sliding doors behind her. But Ella couldn't read or eat. She stretched out on the stiff horsehair sofa and fell asleep. When she woke up, it was dark outside. She couldn't get up. She was very hot now.

Before long, Emmy came to her and sat on the edge of the seat cushion. "Ella, sweetie," she had said. She was crying. "You need to come to Mama."

Even through her own tears, Mama had seen that something was wrong.

"Tell Herr Doctor to come back," she had told Emmy.

Ella, it seemed, had the measles.

She was in bed for three weeks while all around her there was bustle. Papa had died suddenly, a heart attack she was to learn much later. A funeral had been held in the church, despite his announced atheism, and a burial. Ella missed it all, tossing and itching, a sick child in the house of mourning, only vaguely aware of visitors, of weeping. She was frightened, of her illness, of her absent father, of her grieving mother, of death itself. Her constant caretaker was Emmy, just eighteen. On one of the first mornings after her illness set in, Ella had turned in her bed to see Emmy hanging a heavy drape over the lightly curtained window. "There," she had said. "That's to protect your eyes until you're well again." And then she sat beside Ella and read to her.

Until that moment, Ella had barely noticed her siblings, so much older than she were they all. They were part of the furnishings of an orderly household, like the kerosene lamps and the chopping block, neither authorities like Mama and Papa nor playmates. In that gesture at the window, Emmy became one of the parent generation, an adult, giver of wisdom, protector. Ella turned to Emmy as she might have looked to her mother. Not until the séance today when Ella saw her grieving for her dead child did Emmy become her sister, some-one from her own generation, able to share experience as well as di-rect it. A responsibility she had been ducking perched on her shoul-ders, wrinkled and thick.

The next morning she woke up resigned to get on with things. She had spent enough time in fruitless fantasy. She dressed and went to the kitchen.

Bare to the elbows and dusted with flour, Emmy had regained her typical good cheer. She was making strudel, rolling the dough in a wide band, the floury wooden roller stretching the dough larger and thinner. Stopping her work, she brushed her hands together to shake off the flour. "Ella, Georg has a fellow he'd like you to meet. He's going to ask him home for dinner tonight. It's all right, isn't it, Ella? Isn't it a good idea?"

Miss Chimiakin flew into the room, and Ella lowered her head.

"Come on, Ella. Say you'll meet this man."

That other life was over for her. That business of kissing was over.

"I suppose. I won't promise you I'll take to him, you know." Ella looked up from her breakfast. "But if Georg likes him..."

"Yes. What harm? I think he works in the printing department. Georg couldn't tell me a single thing about his looks, though." Emmy grinned over her dough.

Ella shook her head from side to side. She could never marry a man who couldn't describe his own friend.

Emmy returned to her rolling. "So, when the strudel is done, we'll go to the butcher. I was thinking of veal shanks and spaetzle."

‡

The evening began well enough. Ella wore her dark blue skirt and a pretty shirtwaist embroidered on the sleeves. Her hair was soft and curled close to her face. Her waist was slim. She looked like many girls at twenty-five, she thought. Undistinguished. Herr Schuler was a tall, thin man with fair hair and light eyes, much taller than Professor K with his lithe, compact form. Ella felt little when she shook his big, moist hand. Seated stiffly in Emmy's parlor, Herr Schuler said he had never been to Munich but hoped to visit there one day. Ella said she was taking pleasure in being with her little Bonn family. She asked if he enjoyed his work. Herr Schuler said that he did. He'd met Georg there, in the office. The conversation was like riding a lame horse.

"You work with print?" Ella crossed her ankles. Apparently this is how one did it. A woman feigned interest in a man, and eventually in time the man might return the favor.

"Lithographs. It's pretty interesting. We did a fine map a few months ago—loaded with color." Herr Schuler rubbed his palms along his long thighs. "There's a scholar fellow named Haeckle who's got us making sea creatures, now. We have to load the presses five, six times for each plate. Like I say, it's interesting work. The images have to line up just right or they get blurred."

"My sister is a printmaker, you know." Emmy nodded toward Ella.

"*You* are a printmaker, Fraulein Münter?"

"Not like you. I do art." Ella looked at the cabbage roses on Emmy's carpet. "Mostly I paint."

"We have a whole chest of Ella's pictures in the attic." Emmy moved to the edge of her chair as though she might go right on up and bring paintings down to show him.

"It that so?" Herr Schuler said. "So you paint a bit?"

Ella sniffed. "I'm not sure what you mean. I suppose I paint quite a lot from time to time."

"I can't say I've ever met a woman who liked to paint. Not since school, at any rate."

"I didn't say I *like* to paint. But I do paint, whether I like to or not." Ella looked at her shoes and then at Herr Schuler's great big ones. She saw her little feet on the bicycle's pedals, pumping behind Professor K.

"That's curious. I suppose you've taken some art classes at one of the Ladies' Academies, then?"

"I began there," Ella said. "But the classes were stupid."

"Ella!" Emmy rose.

"*Stupid.* Now why would that be?" Herr Schuler leaned forward, his long torso angled like an arrow over his thighs.

Ella tidied her skirt over her knees. "Do women paint differently from men, do you think?"

"My goodness, yes," Herr Schuler said. "I'd expect a woman might want to decorate the house with her pictures. That's the good thing about the ladies classes. I've seen some of their pictures in a little shop near the plant, the nice flowers and such."

"Ella," Emmy interrupted. "Will you show Herr Schuler his seat at the table? I'll just go and bring in the veal."

Ella stood up, glad to move.

At dinner, Georg and Herr Schuler exchanged anecdotes and gossip. It was rumored that Herr Müeller from purchasing had gotten himself badly in debt. Herr Gass's wife had given birth again. Georg, himself, had seen the boss snoozing with his head on his desk in a heap of papers. Herr Schuler had heard that the company intended to take on a new client—an advertising newspaper that would pay handsomely for four-color pictures.

"Which four colors?" Ella looked up innocently.

"You see, they work together and make the rainbow." Herr Schuler lifted his head from his plate. He winked at Georg.

"The rainbow! Isn't that lovely!" Emmy refilled his glass.

Georg laughed.

Ella resisted the impulse to smirk.

Herr Schuler turned to Ella.

"Fraulein Münter, I hope you will permit me to ask. You said you did not like to paint. I find that odd." Herr Schuler was bent over his plate, eating big forkfuls of the cucumber salad Ella had prepared. Juice from the vegetables ran down the tines of his fork into his sleeve.

"It's not a question of liking. I like this cucumber salad, as do you, I see. For me, painting is a matter of necessity. Art is something I *need* to do." Ella squirmed a bit as she said the words. Emmy could well question Ella's "need." For months she had not so much as opened her rucksack. Whence this strong defense of her "art"? She pursed her lips, on the edge of something high and steep, higher than Kochel or the mountain. She moved the veal around on her plate.

"Well, I must object, Fraulein Münter. And first of all, please reconsider. The cucumber is hardly trivial. In fact, I can think of nothing more important just now." He looked at Georg and winked again. "People need cucumbers a great deal more than they need paintings, I should think. Oh, I do understand about brightening things up—paintings in the parlor, and so on. And religious art. Glory to God and all." Herr Schuler leaned over the table. "But you say that you *need* to paint? How can that be? Painting is—well, like Georg and his concertina. A pastime. Unless, of course, there is money to be made. I know some artists do rather well for themselves, but I wouldn't expect that from woman artists." He looked around the table.

Emmy stood up noisily and began to clear the plates. Ella rose.

"No, Ella. You sit and talk. I'll be right back with coffee. We can take it into the sitting room."

Ella sat down heavily. "Only a few artists actually earn a living by selling paintings, Herr Schuler. In any event, the necessity to paint is unrelated to income. Art is an expression of the soul, and the soul needs no compensation." Ella clamped shut her mouth. She might well laze away the days with the Schroeters, but in Herr Schuler's presence, she was an artist with convictions.

"But if there is no financial advantage—well, I would have to have a good reason. I would certainly need to *like* to do it."

"I think I have a very good reason." She got up from her chair. "I'm coming with the glasses, Emmy. Don't make the trip in for them."

Never in her experience had Ella felt compelled to explain herself. Her family had always accepted her desire for art lessons as her right to do what pleased her. No one but Professor K had ever talked about the need for art, about its relationship to soul or spirit. It seemed that in no other presence but his could she own the ideas she voiced tonight, and suddenly it became important to own them.

Emmy returned with strudel and coffee, settling the men in the comfortable upholstery of the sitting room, plates and cups on their knees. In the corner, a pair of chartreuse budges hopped from perch to perch, chattering, scattering seed into the tray Emmy had installed beneath the cage. Ella visited the birds, putting her finger between the bars to be pecked, addressing each bird by name. "I hope *you're* having a nice time," she whispered to the birds. She sat herself as far away from Herr Schuler as the furniture allowed. She listened wearily to the male voices talking about accounts and costs and suppliers, images racing through her mind—the church choir, rabbits dead on the table, Georg with his concertina. When Ella saw Herr Schuler's long, long legs crossed at the ankle above his large, large feet, she looked away and lay her head back on the tall cushioned settee.

A picture took hold of her, and her eyes turned backwards in her head so that she could see it clearly. She was seated before her easel, painting, Professor K standing at her side. She had sketched her scene, something outdoors with trees and water, and she was applying bold, rich colors in strong strokes. Just as the scene came to life under her brush, she felt a fluttering of wings in her breast and she turned her head. Professor K had put his hand on her shoulder.

Galerie

"The Village Church," 1908
Gabriele Münter
Oil on canvas-covered cardboard
$13'' \times 16^{1}/_{2}''$
Milwaukee Art Museum
Gift of Mrs. Harry Lynde Bradley

A plain church, bluish-white with a red roof, sits on a grassy slope. We see the church primarily from its side, a rectangle punctuated by two small arched windows. Next to the modest front door of the church, two large green trees take up nearly a third of the canvas and form its leftmost edge. Along the right side of the painting, the tall bell tower of the church provides an opposing vertical form. The forms of the church, the tower, the trees, and the slope all suggest solidity, simple and enduring. The scene is unadorned with either architectural detail or a suggestion of human life. The planes of the painting are nearly flat, with just a suggestion of depth between the foreground and the background horizon.

The palette of the painting is soft, and the dominant colors are greens and blues, highlighted by the deep red of the roof and a strip of sky in rose-orange at the horizon line on either side of the church. A spot of deeper red-orange shines on the top of the bell tower, suggesting that it is sunset, a quiet time in the life of the church and its parishioners.

This unassuming little painting is deeply satisfying in its calm depiction of the strength and reassuring presence of the church as a staple of village life.

J. Eichner

Chapter Three

Curvilinear

Munich
Fall, 1902

SHE HAD TO make a success of this. No more running away. This time had to be different.

Though Ella had sent her bulky things by cart, burdened as she was by her carry-all bags, she would need to catch a tram from the Hauptbanhof out to Schwabing where her modest pension lay just north of the university near the Englischer Garten. Had she not so much to lug, she would have preferred to walk the distance, feeling the streets with her feet and legs, inaugurating herself once again as a citizen of the city.

Munich was, after all, where all the best artists of the day gathered, and Ella determined to be counted among them. Here she would begin again to paint, to establish herself as an artist of the first rank, if it were possible. As she climbed the stairs out of the Hauptbanhof and walked outdoors to the tram, she felt her chest expand with pleasure. Social propriety and artistic convention might surround her like bricks around a deep well, but she would keep afloat and see the sky above her. Still, it was a risk to be so bold, so independent. Emmy hadn't approved, but Ella had gone anyway.

The Munich tram tracks traversed the city with a clear sense of line. The car on the edge of the Maximiliansplatz made a broad stroke around the open area the way a thick pencil line transforms a blob of blue or green into a house or a tree. From her seat inside, Ella couldn't see the shapes the tram made, but she could feel forms in space each time they swerved on a curve or turned a corner, her body leaning into the arc. When she got back to regular classes, she would immerse herself in such concerns and set aside all that distraction of the summer. The Phalanx classes were a privilege for a woman, and she would prove she had the right to be there.

She settled into her room, folding her underthings in her drawers, seeing the contrast of black stockings against white silk chemises and flesh-colored underdrawers. She hung her skirts in the chifforobe by tone: black, dark grey, dark blue, dove grey, blue-grey. Her shirt-waists she grouped by design from solid color to pale stripe to bold stripe to tiny figured floral pattern. Next to the chest, she lined up her shoes by size—tall boots, short boots, white shoes, house slippers. She busied herself about the room, keeping up a running exhortation: *Get back to work, get back to work.* If she didn't resume serious effort, her talent might wither in the inhospitable climate most female artists experienced. Her gift was a tender shoot, and the dry tolerance for women artists Ella had experienced at the academies of her earlier years had nearly desiccated her ambition. But Professor K—his teaching, his thinking about art—had been like rain. She was alone here, true. Her only family was far away in Bonn, and in any event, they could not understand her desire to leave them and settle here. And it *was* a little frightening to be so alone. But she wasn't like most girls. She surely wasn't like Emmy. She was going to be an artist, and she would put her mind to that pursuit.

When she was finished unpacking, she looked at her image in the mirror on the wardrobe door. Just what part of herself she would find when she stepped inside the workrooms where Professor K presided she could not guess. But she would not stay away. She would think only of the tin box of paints and brushes she carried in her rucksack.

‡

She had arranged to be late to her first class, an evening drawing studio, preferring to step into the room while the others were at work. He would be among the group, and she would not be obliged to single him out, excepting the deference owed any teacher. She imagined the greetings, the surprised welcomes, her own affable and impersonal replies. Almost certainly Olga would be among the students, and she could imagine her friend's excited welcome, her warm embrace. The two had exchanged a few letters in the last weeks, and Ella might refer to them. Ella would be a tardy, even wayward student returning to her lessons somewhat abashed at having been absent so long. It was a role she could play, another kind of lie. She slipped down the dark stairs as quietly as she could and silently pushed open the studio door to the picture she had framed for herself. At the far end of the long room, a half-dozen students sat in a semi-circle around a model, wooden easels on their laps.

The model was a female nude.

Ella stood in the doorway stunned. She knew that the class was to employ live models, but she had not anticipated that the models would be unclothed. Involuntarily she lowered her eyes and studied the floorboards. In her chest stirred a small uprising, an inner skirmish. To enter the room called for an openness she was not bred for. Not even in the gymnasium when the girls changed into exercise outfits had she seen a naked body. Even on the steamship to America in the cramped quarters she shared with Emmy, each girl averted her eyes when the other dressed or undressed. No stranger to nudity in art, Ella recalled the sculptures she had admired in Berlin, the paintings and the picture galleries the sisters visited in Bonn and New York. But those statues and pictures stood at a distance, both spatially in the crowded galleries and also emotionally, diminishing her discomfort by their stature as great works, immobile, fixed in time and repute. She had never looked boldly, critically, at a live, naked person. And this model was no Venus de Milo. Sitting in a golden halo of light provided by the gas lamps, she had flesh and hair; she took breath; she moved. Ella wanted to flee.

And yet to complete a fully articulated nude drawing was a rite of passage, a signal that the artist had matured past the stage of dilettantism, a challenge no amateur could attempt. The model's shapes were organic, not structural, and the task went beyond formal design, using line and form and shading to suggest the weight and muscle of the body. To leave now was to divorce her artistic dreams from those of more accomplished students, more committed artists. Could she admit that she was not one of them? Could she abandon her vision of herself?

Standing in the dark outside the studio, Ella could neither turn away nor enter.

Silently she drew further into the shadow of the hallway, averting her eyes from the model. She could sense the woman shift position, and she saw the students turn over the papers on their easels to capture the new shape of the figure. Ella listened to the rustling of sketchpads, the scrape of gritty pencils on coarse paper, the squeaking of wooden benches. She heard Professor K murmur something to one of the boys as he walked quietly behind him.

Grateful that she had opened the door so softly, she stood still. Once more she studied the floor, its vertical slats pointing inward toward the group and the model before them. Facing the nude model would be a victory of artistic ambition over the staid, the shamed, the provincial, the conventional. She yearned to find the power within her to achieve that victory, but she trembled at the thought of looking. Then the sound of a voice caught her ear. Professor K. Ella raised her eyes to look inside the room once more. His back to Ella, Professor K bent over Olga, gesturing onto her paper, suggesting a line, a shadow. Ella saw his bare forearm extended toward the paper, and over this arm, she saw the nude facing him.

She forced herself to look. The woman sat on a chair angled toward the easels with her legs slightly open and bent at the knees as they stretched out toward Ella at the door. She was neither fat nor thin, neither old nor young. Her hair was dark, her face oval and plain. Her shoulders rounded into soft arms bounding a pale torso with white breasts like the balls of fresh cheeses farmers kept in pans of water on their market shelves. Her belly folded in a small pouch below her waist, and her hips spread modestly on the hard chair. Between her legs was a dark triangle of hair, thicker and darker than Ella's own. Her legs were plump, foreshortened, small feet pointing outwards. And yet as much as it shocked her even now to see her nipples and pubic hair unconcealed, her buttocks widened fleshily on the hard chair, Ella saw line and curve, shape and volume, a figure to reproduce in its individuality and variety, an artistic problem to solve. Far away from the model as she was, she saw the white sculptural forms of limbs, trunk, breasts, and belly and smiled to herself. What fun to try to get it right, to work out the difficulties with pencil and paint, to see what the model presented and express it honestly. She watched greedily for some minutes, unnoticed.

A draft of warm air she'd pulled across the long room when she'd opened the door gathered speed and swooped up the stairwell behind Ella, rustling the paper on some easels and causing Olga, the lone woman, to turn. "Someone is at the door."

"This session is closed," Professor K called out, striding to the shadow where Ella stood. "No one can enter now."

"I'm late. I'm sorry." Ella stepped into the room. "I'll just put on my smock."

For a moment he looked as though he had not remembered who she was. Then he reached behind her to lift the rucksack from her back.

"Ladies and gentlemen." He turned to the students at their work. "Fraulein Münter is with us once again. The talented Miss Münter is here."

The Kochel students had all signed up for a dual program at the Phalanx School—a night course of drawing live models with Professor K to follow a related afternoon sculpture class taught by Wilhelm Hüsgen, whose plaster masks Ella had admired at an exhibit the winter before. They were all there—Olga and Kleuver and Doncker, Schneider, Wuest, and Muehlenkamp, and Palme, whom Ella had defamed so shamelessly to her sister. The first night they bustled about her, asking after her tooth and her family and what painting she had done since they were last together, and after a few replies they went back to their own concerns, content to have her among them, noticing her no more nor less than she asked of them. Professor K seemed to have forgotten that he had ever kissed her.

Within a week, Ella fell into a pattern. Each morning in her room she sketched small still lifes set up on her bedside table, quick little studies she mostly crumpled into her waste can the moment she filled each page. At noon, she made herself coffee and warmed soup over the kerosene burner she'd secreted into the pension. Then she set out for the studio, put on her smock in the sculpture room, and joined the others as they shaped and patted and carved. Between the sculpture class and the evening drawing studio, they all stopped for tea and sandwiches, taking turns providing bread, cold meats, and sweets, chatting and laughing together. Afterwards, they walked down the wooden stairs to the drawing room warmed by a wood stove in the nights so that the models might sit in comfort as the students worked. At the end of each class, Ella walked home with Olga, whose pension was near her own.

"Do you not think Professor K is quite brilliant?" Olga slipped her arm in Ella's. Their summer separation had not diminished Olga's pleasure in conveying confidences.

"That's hardly the word I'd use."

"When he talks to me in the class, my hand, it begins to tremble. He makes me shiver."

Ella laughed. "You've got to start wearing your heavy shawl. I told you it was a mistake to come out in just your light jacket."

"But she is so lucky, Miss Chimiakin! Do you not think? To live with him. To hear his wonderful voice very day. And then, at night..." Olga paused. "But it is strange, don't you think, that we never see her?"

Almost as though Miss Chimiakin herself were holding her sleeve on the Kochel hillside, Ella felt the undulations of the mountain surface under her feet. She stumbled, catching herself on Olga's arm.

"My goodness, Fraulein. You have not hurt yourself? But it is true, the pavement is uneven just here." Olga leaned in close, her lips brushing Ella's ear. "So now you must be very, very steady on your feet. I am going to tell you something you must not say to another soul."

Ella pulled away. She would so much prefer to walk in silence. As little desire as she had to discuss Miss Chimiakin, she had even less patience with Olga's confidences. They were of the most juvenile sort, and Ella rarely had any response to these little intimacies that Olga seemed bent on sharing. Still, enduring them was the price of having a companion on the dark walk home after classes. "My portfolio is slipping," she murmured, fussing with the large parcel under her arm. "What would I say? I barely talk to anyone but you." It was true, but immediately, Ella regretted her words. "I mean, I don't gossip."

"Then this must be your secret too." Once again Olga drew near. "So, that night walk we took on the Kochel mountain, the night Miss

Chimiakin turned her foot?"

Ella grimaced in the dark. Must she relive that night? "Oddly, I've just been remembering it—with horror, if that's what you mean."

"You see—but you mustn't say a word—something else happened. My partner and I did not follow the stones quite as Professor K ordered."

"Well, my partner and I got lost ourselves, as you recall. It was easy to do."

"I do not mean that. I mean...Jakob Doncker and I took a little...well, a little...*detour*, as you say."

Ella stopped. She turned to look at the Russian's round face. "What are you telling me?"

"Only that I am not now what I was before." Olga covered her mouth with her hand.

Ella drew back in amazement.

"You mustn't be shocked. Please, Fraulein. I am telling you something from my heart. I am afraid you will disapprove. But he is so wonderful, Jakob Doncker. And I am thinking Herr Doncker and I might step out together in time. When he has a prospect, I mean. After his school days are over. Then it would be all right. Can you not see?"

Ella tucked her paper portfolio tighter under her arm. Olga and Jacob Doncker? Not as she was before? Plump Olga?

On and on Olga went. That night was only the once. She dared not see him like that again. But she might be falling in love. She thought she was. It was the most mysterious feeling. Could it be love? What did Ella think?

It was not for her to say, Ella replied. Love, she imagined, would announce itself. She didn't know. She didn't know much about love. She hadn't been in love, herself. She said not a word about Professor K. Not a word about the 25 kisses.

It was so much better not to think about him that way. Better to concentrate on her progress. And what a distance she had traversed! In only a few days, drawing the female figure had become her passion. Since the night she had first come upon the model, she had ceased to recoil from the sight of the naked woman. She had begun the dual program itching to sculpt, but the evening sessions with Professor K quickly became her focus. The gesture exercises he directed challenged her as the model turned this way and then that, sometimes sitting, sometimes standing or kneeling or even sprawled on a bench Professor K covered with a blanket. Studying the points from which the body's energy seemed to radiate, Ella wanted to reproduce in pencil the weight of flesh as well as its contours. She listened carefully to Professor K's instructions. She scrutinized him as he demonstrated a movement with a charcoal or the angle of a line, and she held her pencil just as he did.

"It's wonderful," he told her once, tearing a page from her sketchpad. "The breasts have volume."

He could say *breasts* in front of her if he liked. She would not blanch.

Before long, she was astonishing the other students, not only with the accuracy of her drawings but with her speed, able to capture details with a few telling strokes. She was a good sketcher and furthermore, she rarely changed a line. At the end of the session, the sides of her hands might be black with charcoal, but compared to the dust the others raised with their fiddling and fussing, when she packed up her pencils and smock, she was relatively clean. Best of all, though, she knew both from the comments of the other students as well as her own analysis that she was capturing the fullness of the flesh displayed before her.

Then, toward the end of the second week of class, Professor K made an announcement. His news was to challenge her even further.

"We must give our thanks to Fraulein Schuh who has sat for us with such patience and endurance. For her stillness and grace, we are most grateful." He bowed toward the model just now putting on her robe and tying its belt. He nodded at the group, directing them to clap.

"Now, when we begin our sessions next week, we will have a model who will pose new problems for us. Our task will be to find form, weight, and texture in musculature." His eyes took in the four boys as a group. Then he turned to Olga and Ella, looking fixedly at her. "Our model will be a male. To make the most progress, you must spend the weekend doing some preparatory studies."

Ella could not hold his gaze. She leaned over to collect her pencils from the easel shelf, glad to have something to do with her hands.

When they had left the boys behind, Ella took Olga's arm. "I have never seen a nude man," she whispered.

"Nor I. Not...not exactly *seen*." Olga kept her gaze on the ground, as though the street were pocked with holes she must avoid.

"I doubt I'll be able to look at—well, you know—his masculinity."

"I am worrying what Herr Doncker will think when I am looking at...the model...that way!"

It began to rain. Ella stopped and opened her large umbrella before taking Olga's arm once more. "My mother would never let us quit something we had begun," Ella said. "The Germans have an expression: All beginnings are difficult. If you say A, then you must also say B."

Olga chuckled. "In Russia my mother would say, 'You have to dish up what you've cooked.' "

Ella laughed in return. Yet, to come to class on Monday was to cross a border into the strangest country in the world.

‡

In her room on Saturday morning, Ella was out of sorts. Irritable, she set up another still life to sketch. Out of spite, she put onto her dressing table one of her summer shoes, her teakettle, and a small picture in its frame. The grouping was ridiculous, but she felt she had to discipline herself, find order, see possibilities, capture relationships. She tried to draw, but at the back of her mind was Monday evening and a man with his genitals exposed in front of her. Would she disgrace herself in front of Professor K?

A knock at her door came as a relief. When Ella opened the door, Olga smiled at her expectantly, her eyes bright. "I have had an idea. Professor K said we were to prepare ourselves for Monday."

Ella looked at her blankly.

"So, we must go to the museum and look at some men." Olga began to laugh.

Still Ella did not understand. And then she did.

Ella had sometimes walked past the Alte Pinakothek, a massive brick edifice built in the middle 1800's to house the collection of valuable masters amassed by a 16th century duke. Munich's inhabitants revered the museum, but Ella had only once before entered its doors, finding the solemnity of the structure gloomy and intimidating. With Olga beside her, though, she strode into the broad marble foyer. It was something of a lark to have such a mission and a partner to share it with, to roam the high-ceilinged rooms with their old masters and academicians.

Nothing on the first floor was instructive. But as they entered the first gallery on the top floor, one painting caught their attention: *Venus and Adonis* by Hendrick Golzius, done in 1614.

"Well, this is a beginning." Olga held Ella's arm at the elbow, leaning into her ear to whisper.

Adonis, nearly naked, was stretched invitingly toward Venus, whose full body leaned heavily into his.

"She is going to need a very big corset some day," Olga whispered.

"By the time she's thirty, she'll be a cow." The girls laughed.

"Adonis would be a good example of what we want, but Herr Golzius has hidden the very thing we hoped to see." Olga pointed at the green vine and leaves draped across the figure's genitals, looking over her shoulder to be certain that no one was watching.

Ella shrugged. "It won't do. Let's go on." Further down the hall was a painting of the Virgin and Child, a famous Da Vinci. The baby, plump and fully naked, sat on the Madonna's lap. Ella stopped walking. "This is a something, but not quite what we need."

"Not, at least, until he grows up." Olga tugged on Ella's sleeve. "Perhaps a guard can help us."

"And how do you propose asking him?"

"That will be your job." Olga laughed and led Ella down the corridor.

They passed quickly by the landscapes, the portraits, the religious scenes. In the next gallery, they stopped cold. The *Rape of the Daughters of Neucippus*, by Peter Paul Rubens, 1618. Two nude white female figures struggled against the aggression of two darker males, backed by rearing horses and a single putti.

Ella stood back to admire the well-formed buttocks of the captured women. "Look at how firm and dense they are. You'd think they were solid to touch. That's so difficult to do."

"Such fine brushwork. And shading." Olga's eyes were wide.

"Brushwork or not, this piece makes me nervous. Let's go." Ella pulled Olga's arm.

In the next room, the girls passed an aging satyr whose private parts were shielded by a loincloth; besides, the satyr was so thin they were not tempted to stop or speculate. Just beyond, however, was a painting that provided precisely what they had come to see. *Midas and Bacchus* by Nicolas Poussin was a grouping—nine figures plus three chubby puttis and a goat. Bacchus was a frontal nude, a young god lounging gracefully among drunken men and an outstretched naked woman.

"Well," said Ella. "Here we are."

"Exactly." Olga planted her feet. "What we came for. The thing, itself."

For a moment, they simply looked, checking behind them from time to time to assure themselves they were alone.

"Complicated." Ella squinted, leaning her head closer.

"More complicated than I realized," Olga leaned her head first one way and then another. "Difficult to describe. How would you say it? More than just long."

"Not so thick as I might have thought. And not straight." Ella looked at Olga.

"And the pouch hanging behind."

"Oh, dear." Ella moved closer to Olga, grateful to lean against her full, solid body, her reliable humor.

"Something to keep his tram fare in." Olga's shoulders rose to her ears when she laughed.

"Shhh," Ella said. "Inconvenient, in that case. In any event, I thought it might be larger."

"Nothing to be frightened of, at least."

"Well, perhaps. But this is just a painting, remember. Paint on canvas."

"Yes. A lot of red and some white, too, and, well, grays and greens and yellows." Olga moved for a closer look.

"Shouldn't there be some black as well? Lots of black lines to indicate—well, you know." Ella looked at Olga for reassurance.

"For a god, no. For us on Monday, yes, of course." Olga squeezed Ella's arm.

For some minutes in the empty gallery, the girls stood and stared. When a man walked into the room, they looked at each other and left.

‡

On Monday night the class drew from the male. Ella had left her room dreading what lay ahead, but the first sight was less shocking than she had feared. When the model finally seated himself in front of the group, removing the towel he had wrapped around his loins, his genitalia were as Ella expected. The model was bearded, graying, a heavy man with full shoulders, a substantial belly, thick thighs. Ella looked carefully at him, and her eye separated his face and figure into parts, lines, shapes. She picked up her charcoal and began with his form as he sat somewhat slumped on the bench. When Professor K repositioned the model, Ella tried again to see the slope of his body and the proportion of his limbs to his trunk. She squinted at his genitals, trying to capture the angle of his penis as it lay, and sometimes moved, among his thatch of coarse pubic hair. She found she had no need to steel herself against his nakedness. His body had many planes and curves on view. The flowering of his manliness was no more to her than a rosebud among leaves.

Afterwards, she walked home with Olga in bright moonlight.

"I was looking at your sketches tonight," Olga said.

"Oh?" Ella was in no mood for chat. Professor K had kept his distance during the session and she wanted to puzzle out what he might be thinking.

"Were you looking at mine?" Olga put her arm around Ella's shoulders.

"No. Should I have?"

"I was thinking you might be curious."

"No. I wasn't. I mean, I was working, that's all."

Olga removed her arm. She did not speak again, though they walked for many minutes.

‡

The next night Olga, cheerful as ever, winked at Ella while the boys busied themselves arranging their materials. At the mid-session break, Ella glanced at Olga's easel.

"You've done well tonight," she said.

Olga shrugged. "I think Professor K is not so nice," she said.

"What did he say?"

"Nothing. He says nothing to me. He sees only you."

"That's not true," Ella said. "He is kind to everyone, I think." That night she had been bold enough to ask his advice. What she loved above everything was the way he spoke to her directly and without condescension. He treated her as though she could set her own goals and solve her own problems. "Our model's torso is full and curved," he had said, "but his manhood is relaxed and soft. How can you express the contrast?" She could not quite look at him when he said that to her, but she lifted her chin and returned to her drawing. She had taken pains not to look her teacher in the eye, though she watched him when he could not observe her doing so, and she always knew exactly where he was in the room. When he had his back to her as he spoke to another student, she studied it, tracing with her finger in the palm of her hand its strong verticality. She would have liked to draw it. She would have liked to see that back naked.

"He'll probably work with you tomorrow," she told Olga.

‡

One Saturday early in October, Munich bid farewell to summer weather entirely, ushering in a spate of rain and chill. Ella darted from her pension in a cloudburst. For several minutes, she stood in a doorway across the street from the tram stop, sheltering herself from the driving wind and rain, but when the tram veered around the corner, she closed her umbrella and ran for it, crossing the slippery tracks and dodging a keg-topped cart pulling out of the brewery lot just a few meters away. When finally she boarded the car through its rear door, her wet hair had come loose from its pins, and her skirt and boots were muddy.

Inside the crowded, steamy car, she found a seat beside a portly man resting an overstuffed suitcase on his knees. Sitting forward on the bench to give him room, angled so that her knees jutted into the aisle, Ella leaned against the seat in front of her. There, two women bent their heads together, engaged in conversation. They must have entered the car before the storm began, for their shoulders and large yellow hats were dry. The woman directly in front of Ella wore a thick green boa around her neck, obscuring any glimpse of her face. But her accented voice carried well.

"...and I say to him, 'Wassily, you must not to expect for me to stay in the flat by myself when you are working so late!' And do you know what he replies to this? 'You might go back to Moscow if you are uncomfortable,' he says. Can you imagine?"

The companion beside her nodded and whispered something Ella couldn't hear. But the first woman's voice was clear enough.

"Yes, you are right. He was fond enough at first, and I could make him fond again, if I chose." She touched her companion's arm with a small, gloved hand.

The screeching of brakes interrupted this astonishing conversation. Ella shifted still forward in her seat as though to escape the dripping hat of her seatmate, but the women had stopped talking.

Close to the Hauptbanhof, the car emptied most of its passengers, some holding newspapers over their heads to run out into the rain, others hesitating at the door to unfold umbrellas before they stepped out cautiously into the wet. Ella rose from her seat to let the soggy gentleman beside her exit the car, and as she did, the woman in front spotted Ella.

"Do I not know you, Fraulein?"

Ella reddened. Only a stranger would be so forward. But then, *she* wasn't a German. And not a stranger. "Miss Chimiakin. How do you do?"

"You were once my husband's student. Fraulein..."

"Münter."

"Yes. And I would like to introduce for you my sister, Natasha Chimiakin."

Leaning on the side of the wooden bench to steady herself as the car lurched forward, Ella reached over Miss Chimakin to shake the sister's hand.

Miss Chimiakin leaned in to her sister. "Fraulein Münter and I took an adventure last summer. It is one I hope not to repeat." She gave a small laugh. Then she turned toward Ella. "You left us quickly in the summer. You were unwell?"

"Why, no. No, I was fine." For a moment, Ella forgot she had blamed toothache for her sudden departure.

"But Wassily Wassilievich tells me something different." She looked first at her sister and then addressed herself again to Ella. "Perhaps I have misremembered. He may have mentioned someone else. And I had thought you were living in Bonn."

"I was for a time." Ella clutched the seat back, feeling the sway of the car, resisting as the movement threatened to put her in Miss Chimiakin's lap. "And are you quite settled in Munich?"

"As it happens, my sister and I have just been visiting Bogenhausen." She paused. "I am thinking of making some...eh...alterations."

"I know a dressmaker quite close by, if you don't want to travel so far." Ella could feel her hair completely undone on her shoulders, limp strands clinging to her cheeks and neck.

"Not those alterations. I am not meaning that."

The two pretty women sat with their daffodil hats and rosy cheeks while Ella stood wet and bare-headed, her coat damp and clammy, her feet squishing in her old shoes.

"Here we are." Miss Chimiakin rose as the tram slowed. "I would invite you to call on me, but I expect to take other quarters soon. Perhaps I will move to Bogenhausen. I give you my regards."

Ella stepped back to let the sisters pass, studying the tidy feet and ankles of the sisters Chimiakin. When she looked up again, the photography shop that had been her destination was behind her. She had missed her stop and would have to walk back in the wet.

It was still raining the next morning when a note came in a creamy envelope. Miss Chimiakin was inviting her for tea that afternoon. The woman's sister would be in attendance, as well as Frau Kandinsky, *his* mother visiting from Moscow. Ella sat at her table and stared. She couldn't think what the invitation implied.

Why invite her? Nothing of convention or courtesy had demanded such a gesture. Was Professor K to be included in the gathering? Was the address on the invitation even where he lived? Yesterday on the tram Miss Chimiakin had spoken so oddly, suggesting there might be something peculiar about their living arrangements. She'd said "I" might be moving, not "we." Was it just that the German was difficult for her? In any event, why ever had she written to Ella? What could it mean?

Immediately Ella wrote a quick reply. She would be delighted to attend. In truth, by now, everything about Professor K made her curious. What were the relationships between himself and Miss Chimiakin? As Olga had observed, he never mentioned her, nor did the students ever see her. Why was that? And now, at his flat, would Ella see them together? How would he address her? Respectfully? Affectionately? Even his living quarters made Ella wonder. Did they live well or shabbily? Was the flat *artistic* or ordinary? Might there be photographs displayed or an article of clothing left lying about, some clue to the enigma of their situation? It was all so odd, odd, odd. If only she could see beyond the forms of names and roles and expectations.

She spent an hour laying out her wardrobe, trying on options. Her suit made her feel dumpy, her dresses flat-chested, the weskit too girlish. She settled on a heavy white blouse and her best blue skirt. She might not feel confident, but she would present herself as dignified, self-possessed. Anyway, it occurred to her, the invitation might be entirely innocent, gratitude for a service rendered months before. But the thought gave her little comfort.

Fully dressed, her pocketbook hooked over her elbow, Ella paced up and down her room. By the time she left the pension, she was in a state.

A maidservant escorted Ella into the parlor where the two Miss Chimiakins graced a blue settee in their black silk gowns. On a green-and-white striped sofa, a handsome matron in a lace cap tilted her head and extended a bare hand. Presumably the woman was *his* mother. Ella made a little half bow, her own palms moist with anxiety. "I am pleased to meet you," she said. The sentiment came rather from her upbringing than her heart.

But Anja Chimiakin seemed completely at ease. "Thank you for coming, Fraulein Münter. Please, will you sit?" She resumed her place before a low table and released hot water from a silver samovar into a brown English teapot. Madame Kandinsky gathered in her skirts to make room on the sofa, while Miss Chimiakin poured. "Sugar?"

Nodding to both the Miss Chimiakins on the settee, Ella settled herself next to his silent and inscrutable mother.

"Did you get wet the day after we saw you on the tram?" Natasha

Chimiakin was younger but a fair copy of her married sister. "My sister and I find this Munich weather quite penetrating."

"Yes, I got drenched. In fact, I missed my stop and had to walk in the rain for blocks." Over her teacup, Ella tried to look about her. The parlor furniture was too large for the room as though it had been designed for a grander space, a palace or the apartment of a nobleman. But she must keep her mind on the conversation. "You are moving some distance away?"

"We decided against Bogenhausen after all. A city neighborhood suits us better, we think." Both Miss Chimiakins nodded vigorously.

Who was this *we*? Ella sipped from her cup. "I see that. One can better enjoy the city's attractions and shops. And, of course, you must like to visit the many galleries and museums."

The sisters looked at each other, and Anna Chimiakin gave a small laugh. "We never go to galleries. We are not artistic." The elder Miss Chimiakin appeared to speak for both. "We prefer the study of literature. And languages. My sister is speaking English as well as German, and of course Russian and French, which we all learn in school. For my part, I have studied the Scandanavian languages, including Finnish. But we are so grateful for speaking German with you. We improve with practice."

"Your command of the language is quite splendid." Ella did think so. But they didn't like art? How curious. "Do you read German as well?"

"It is our passion."

The reply gave Ella pause. She turned to see his mother cover her mouth in a yawn. "I am afraid I read less often than I might."

"Then you must let me encourage you. When Thomas Mann comes here to speak next month, my sister and I will go to hear him. You must come with us."

Ella felt she could not object. "That would be lovely." But in fact she had not read the famous writer. She was on safer ground with travel. "Have you visited Norway or Sweden?"

"Only Finland. It was a cold time for me there."

Ella drank from her cup. The story Professor K told the students at the Kochel fireside had not included a wife at his side while he read the *Kalevala*. What else had he not shared? And where was he now?

The tea-table conversation bobbed for some time upon safe waters, all the time without the participation of Madame Kandinsky anchored to the sofa with her hands clasped on her lap. After several minutes, she spoke to her daughter-in-law in Russian and received a reply, but the subject of the exchange included no name or sound that might indicate to Ella that they spoke about *him*.

And then Miss Chimiakin nodded in Ella's direction, speaking in German. "Mama Kandinsky, Fraulein Münter is Wassily Wassilievich's most talented student at the Phalanx."

Ella set down her teacup, astonished. Had he said that to his wife? What else had he said?

Frau Kandinsky merely smiled indulgently and patted Ella's hand where it lay beside her on the sofa. She spoke then, turning her face to Ella's, responding something to her daughter-in-law.

"My mother-in-law says she would be honored to see your work."

Ella blushed. "I hope she will be patient until I am worthy to be exhibited." She picked up her cup again and held on to its sure surface.

After a bit, the maid returned to the room with a plate of cakes, and the conversation revolved around them. Where the best were to be found. Whether one preferred lemon to raspberry. Recipes and occasions for using figs. Another cup of tea later and Ella felt she could leave. She rose from her seat to say goodbye.

Miss Chimiakin, too, left her chair and took Ella's arm. "You and I will be friends, now. It is important for us to know each other better." She pulled Ella to herself, embraced her, and kissed her on both

cheeks. "I want you to visit often. We will talk about German literature. And you will visit Wassily Wassilievich as well. *Mon cousin.*"

At the time, Ella had thought his wife was addressing her, sending
her off that rainy afternoon with an affectionate statement of how
they might be together—like cousins. Later, though, when she went
over the moment as she did again and again, she puzzled over that
last phrase. *Mon cousin, not ma cousine.* Miss Chimiakin had meant
him. She was talking about him. But *mon cousin,* not *my husband.*

Some days later, the rains stopped, and the hillsides burst out in
flame too stunning to be ignored. Chafing at their indoor studies, the
students formed the idea for an autumn picnic. Wuest and Kleuwer,
the ringleaders, selected a destination, a campground near a stream,
wooded and protected by hills on either side. The air would be just
pleasantly cool, they promised, and the picnickers would be out of
the wind, warmed by their campfire and the still-strong autumn sun.
Professor K seemed happy to join in as they planned the excursion.
He approved the location and suggested the travel arrangements. He
almost seemed like one of the students, sitting cross-legged on the
studio floor as the boys bantered back and forth, besting one another
with the creativity of their plans.

On Sunday morning, the students loaded a horse-drawn wagon
with paints and easels and food. Ella borrowed two large thermos
bottles from her landlady and filled them with hot coffee and milk.
These she brought to the wagon early in the morning along with
some lemon cakes and fall apples in a straw basket from the market
at Elisabethstrasse, and just at the last minute she put in two large
chocolate bars. Olga, staggering under the load, brought a picnic
cloth for the ground, several flat cushions, and blankets should the
weather turn uncomfortably cool. Doncker and Muehlenkamp had

purchased a thick stew made of pork and potatoes needing only to be warmed and ladled onto tin plates. Professor K's contribution would be to build the fire and to provide his expertise as they painted *en plein air*. He looked forward, he said, to being together as they had been in the summer.

The early morning air was cold and clear, the rising sun a rosy promise. Fully supplied, Wuest and Kleuwer gave a wave and set off in the best of spirits, driving the horse and wagon into the countryside while the others, wrapped in coats and shawls, walked in pairs to the train station.

Ella was enchanted by the entire enterprise, full of the confidence of her recent drawing successes, happy to be headed out to the country in an outing that included Professor K. She sat with Olga on the train. Behind them, Schneider and Palme discussed football, but as hard as she tried, Ella could not catch the conversation of Doncker or Professor K, who shared a seat.

"Perhaps Herr Doncker is boring Professor K with all his talk of motorcars." Olga inclined heavily against Ella, whispering.

"Oh? I didn't notice." She let her weight push back against Olga's shoulder until the Russian straightened herself.

"But then Herr Doncker is so amusing. He makes every subject entertaining." Olga turned around in her seat and looked behind her.

Ella leaned now against the window. She loved the way things that you couldn't see far down the track got clearer and clearer until they almost jumped in on you. A farmer's cart up ahead, for example. A swath of saffron was hurtling toward her, a field of wheat it seemed. She followed it with her eyes and then—whoosh—it was gone.

The morning was ripening when the group reconvened at the village train station. Everyone squeezed onto the wagon bed for the short ride to the picnic area, laughing and joking, proud of themselves for having arranged such a party. They were outdoors again as they had been at Kochel, the whole group, all but Miss Chimiakin.

He had come alone to the picnic dressed like a Bavarian out-
doorsman, knees bared in short trousers, calves covered in tall, thick
woolen stockings tucked inside short, stout boots. He wore a woolen
sweater buttoned up the front, a thick scarf about his neck, and he
used a tall walking stick as they climbed to the campground, his
complexion bright with exertion, his eyes glittering with health and
strength and vigor. As much as she had tried to distance herself from
his person during the nighttime classes, Ella felt pulled inexorably
toward him now.

When the wagon reached the site and the horses had been tied
and watered, everyone helped unload, happy to set up the campsite and explore the region. The sun, climbing toward its zenith, had
pulled the day behind it scoured fresh and bright. Wooded hillsides
in the distance gleamed copper and polished amber, and the trees
bordering the campground snagged bits of gold from the air and let
the shards fall dappled on leafy cushion. Hungry as they might be in
an hour or so, no one wanted to sit.

"Professor, Kleuwer brought his fishing nets. He has challenged
Wuest and Palme: who will snare the largest fish. Will you join us?"

"No, you go along—all of you. Enjoy yourselves. But bring back
your catch—we'll cook it." Like a woodsman in a fable, he stood with
his legs far apart, his hands on his hips. "I shall stay behind and build
the fire." He turned to Ella. "Fraulein Münter perhaps will help me
warm the stew and set out the plates." His voice rose. "I have my
Kochel whistle, students, so be listening. When the food is ready, the
whistle will be your signal to return."

So they all set out on their own pursuits. Olga and Doncker
walked together along a path winding around the wooded hillside.
Schneider and Muehlenkamp carried their easels to the far meadow.
Wuest and Palme and Kleuwer removed their shoes and rolled up the
legs of their trousers to run light-footed down the slope toward the
fast-moving stream. The bustle of the group dissipated, and the hill-

side quieted.

Alone now with Professor K, Ella felt her shoulders tighten. Words she might have spoken fled like woodland creatures in a blaze. She busied herself with the pile of blankets Olga had brought, unfolding and shaking them, refolding and positioning them for the picnic lunch. She arranged her thermos bottles and her basket of fruit on the grass. She smoothed her hair and brushed her skirt, and then she could think of nothing else to do nor anywhere to go but toward him.

He was occupied in arranging the rocks disturbed by an earlier camper and stacking them to provide a stable base for the stewpot near where the fire would blaze. He sang quietly as he walked about the fire ring, his voice deep and resonant and true. When the bed of rocks met his liking, he stood straight and called out, "Come, Fraulein, let's gather the fuel we'll need." He gestured toward the leafy grove.

The maples were just turning, the canopy both green and golden, and beneath lay a carpet of dry brush. For some minutes they collected wood, and Ella was grateful for the distraction of stooping and gathering. Would he not address her now? Even strangers would exchange pleasantries. But she, herself, could not find the courage to talk, and he seemed preoccupied with his task, tossing stick upon stick in a pile. Then, back straight, knees bent, he hoisted the whole heap into his arms and headed back to the campsite. Ahead of her by several paces as he walked toward the clearing, he began to sing again, his tune melancholy and sweet. "How quickly do the days of summer fly." Though her silence weighed more than the sticks she carried, Ella could not sing, yet she wanted somehow, somehow to begin.

"My family liked that song," she started. To her own ears her little statement trumpeted like a moose bashing about in a thicket.

He stopped and nodded. "I learned it from my grandmother." His voice was gentle and low. "I am, perhaps, not the stranger to your country that you may think." He set down his armload of wood near one of the large logs that made an amphitheater around the fire ring, and sitting, he motioned to Ella to join him there. "I may have told you—my grandmother was German, and she read and sang to me in German, too." He picked at bits of leaf and wood that clung to his sweater. "I sometimes think I feel at home in this country because I learned your language from someone who loved me." He pulled in a deep breath and stretched out his legs and rubbed his hands on his bare knees. "You once teased me that I'd been spoiled as a child. I hope I have corrected that fault." He smiled at Ella.

She looked down at her hands and saw that she was clasping them tightly. She unfolded her fingers and brushed her skirt. So, he hadn't forgotten their talks, their jokes. Sitting at his side, she could smell the faint aroma of tobacco clinging to his wooly sweater. Once, on the mountain, he had let her try his pipe, she coughing with the bitter smoke in her throat, he laughing and patting her back. She glanced up as he took off his glasses and polished the lenses with the tail of his shirt, humming his tune, his eyes vague and near-sighted. For all that she had turned him around in her head, alternately adoring and castigating him, he was just a man. She dropped her shoulders and took a breath. "I never knew my grandmothers. Nor barely my father."

"I'm sorry to hear it." He put his glasses on again and rubbed the flats of his fingers along his short beard. Beside him on the log, Ella felt his movements rather than saw them.

"All of my grandparents are gone now, of course, but I think about them fondly. And Moscow, too. The blare of the long, white nights and the flaming skyline over the Kremlin and the onion churches. These images have burned themselves in my mind's eye. But one always misses one's native land, I think. One misses home." Then he got up and walked back to his pile of wood. "Perhaps I should begin my task. It takes a while for a fire to flame up and then burn down to coals."

"Do you ever go back?" Her body softened, and she spread out her hands on the firm log beneath her, glad for its support. She watched him enter the fire ring.

"Oh yes. I return each year to see my father and my mother and my many old friends. I suppose one never leaves one's mother entirely—neither country nor parents. At any rate, I have never left mine. Not in my heart. Not in my soul."

Ella thought of Emmy and her grief at their mother's death, her convulsive crying. She did not miss her mother that much. She tucked her long skirt about her legs to make a smooth surface. She was embarrassed that she might be discovered to be so wanting in feeling, something else *wrong* with her.

"My mother died when I was twenty." She raised her voice so that it would reach him where he crouched at the fire pit, sending a bit of herself toward him, wanting to share his mood, his openness. "I don't think I suited her. She needed a daughter who liked to talk and laugh. My sister, Emmy, was better at that." She picked up a long stick and tapped it against her boots. "Emmy's married now to Georg Schroeter in Bonn. And I have cousins in America and a brother, Carly. He's married, too. They wanted me to stay with them in America, but I didn't." Her voice grew louder, the words quick, tumbling out like a runaway horse, bold and reckless. "I didn't want to be like them. They're quite nice, but they're ordinary. I want to do something different with myself. I don't want to be ordinary. I want to be an artist." She broke her stick in half and flung the pieces in front of her.

Professor K looked over to her where she sat. "I am glad of that." For a moment, he held her gaze.

Ella looked down. She had shared something of herself she had never said before to anyone, something nearly wild. He was making her that way, rash and wild. His wistful air had opened up something in her. He understood her. He was like her. He thought like her, saw things the way she did. And he, too, was alone in his life, away from his home. She started up from the log and then stopped herself.

But of course he was not alone. There was in his story a missing character, one who just recently had reached out to her, odd though the circumstances had been. Ella would not ask if his wife, Miss Chimiakin, also missed her country, her home. Stupid Ella. She was in danger of slipping again into the old fantasy. She would say nothing more. She would go no further toward this man nor look at him. Pulling the fabric of her skirt tightly around her legs as she sat, she made her lap a table and distracted herself by making alphabet letters upon its surface, her fingers trembling as she piled the twigs on top of one another, fixing her eyes upon them, afraid of words that might now pour out.

Just inside the fire ring he propped the heaviest logs to let the air circulate and draw the heat up through the fire's core. When he saw that she had separated the sticks into small and large, he took the thicker ones for the center of the fire cone. She watched him stretch forward from his kneeling position at the fire ring and reach into its interior, his figure extended from his hips along his lean sides to his muscular shoulders. When he had secured the base, he came back to her side. He said nothing, but he reached for the wood she had placed on her lap, brushing her skirt with his hands to find the piece he wanted, breaking up her "M," his fingers touching hers before he returned to the fire. At last, when the cone of wood was high and firm, he came back to the log and stood before her.

"Miss Münter, may I speak frankly?" His voice was solemn, portentous.

Please no, please no, she wailed inwardly. She could not bear what he would say. She brushed debris from her skirt and shifted position, folding her legs to one side. She could not raise her eyes to see his face.

"I must tell you how much it pleased me to see you return to Munich, to the Phalanx. When we parted—when you departed from Kochel—I regretted that our acquaintance terminated so abruptly."

"You asked me to go." Her voice creaked like a nail driven into wet wood.

He moved closer and crouched before her, leaning in as though he would share a confidence. "I would not have suggested that you leave the group were it not that I felt an obligation to protect the honor and feelings of one whose innocence is undisputed." He paused and then began again. "I had no wish to part from *you*."

For some moments she let his words lay uncontested in the air. She lifted her eyes. "Miss Chimiakin."

"My *wife*. I say that word to you. I would not humiliate her." He paused. "Permit me to say again how I regret that I deceived you. I apologize for my behavior, for my dishonesty with you. It was unforgivable." He rose and stood in front of Ella on her log. "But, Fraulein, some things have changed for me. Anja Chimiakin and I live apart, now. Legally, our marriage continues, but emotionally—spiritually—we are quite disengaged. I must have told you, the marriage was the union of two families, two fortunes." He stopped and cleared his throat. "I assure you, the marriage was never a union of love, never of spirit."

What should she say? That she was happy to learn of his separation from his wife? Happy that his marriage had been a failure? Was he opening a door for her to enter? Would that be wise? She had no experience in these things. Ella picked up a twig from the ground and spun it with her finger and thumb, her throat and tongue and mouth dry, words withering inside her.

"Well, perhaps we should begin our fire. Time out of doors increases the appetite." He returned to the work, slowly assembling the final cone of kindling with the softest of hands. "Fraulein Münter, I must say another thing, and I beg you not to distrust my words." He stood and brushed his short trousers. "I begin with my most fervent admiration for your talent. Your expressiveness quite humbles me. I find you not just my equal, but my superior." Without stopping for a response, he reached into a pocket along his hip and drew forth a packet of matches. Striking one, he knelt and teased the dry leaves, whispering, coaxing the fuel into smoldering, then into flames.

Crouched before the fire bed, he began to speak again, his voice full and throaty. "But my feelings for you go further. They are more personal." Pursing his lips, he blew steadily into the growing fire. Then he stood, his face red and wild. "Both my body and my soul seek yours. I told you once that you blinded me. My feelings have not changed."

The silence of the campground gave way to the crackle of burning wood and the rush of air, a tremulous ovation in Ella's ears, and as though she had been called to witness, summoned to testify to something grave and mysterious, Ella rose from her seat on the log. She walked to his side and stood beside him and let her shoulder touch his, facing the fire. She could not have said whether the warmth she felt in her body originated in the heat before her or from some other source.

"You say nothing." He reached for her hand, holding it in one of his own. "You don't speak or smile or suggest that you grasp my meaning." He lay his fingers on her cheek.

Ella did not dare look at him. The flame tongues caught her eye like flares at a railway accident and she pulled her face away. A girl risked such a lot if she let herself accept the attentions of a married man, even one separated from his legal wife. If she gave herself to this man, she would be derided, shunned. Every door would shut. And there was her family to consider, too, their expectations of her, their shame and disgrace.

She had run from him once. She should do it again.

"Fraulein Münter, when we return to Munich, I hope you will allow me to visit you in your rooms. I can say nothing about the future, only that I should like to see you alone. I must be with you. But I promise you that I will do nothing to injure you. You have my word in this." He grasped both her hands and drew them to his lips.

The fire popped, and a damp log sizzled and smoked. Standing close to him, Ella's taut skin bore the impact of his every syllable, each fine hair on her arms and legs alive to his voice. She needed to get away, but her movements felt heavy like those of a dreamwalker as she slowly pulled her hands from his. A larger Ella had climbed inside her, stretching her skin, pushing up into her chest and throat and eyes, forward and insistent. She seemed taller to herself, her limbs fuller. Unused to this ample frame, she stumbled toward her perch on the old log. Crouched there, she sat silently and watched the flames reach high and still higher, as though to singe the sky itself. When the fire ceased its initial blazing and the flames set the larger logs glowing, she watched him carry a thick grate from the wagon to brace across the stones, leveling it for the heavy stewpot he would set upon it. She listened to the crush of twigs and leaves under his feet. She watched the movement of his hips and legs as he walked and turned and bent and knelt beside the fire.

Ella rose from her seat and joined him there, kneeling, leaning on her heels beside him. She felt the heat on her face and chest. Putting her right hand upon his lower back, she lifted up his woolen sweater and burrowed beneath his shirt and singlet. She held her hand on the warm skin of his back and kept it there, feeling the curve of muscle, the arc of rib, following the boney spine with her thumb. She listened to the roaring in her ears.

‡

Years later when she recalled the night she gave herself to Professor K, the night she earned the right to address him as Wassily, Ella remembered the scene as though she had painted it, fixed forever in time and attitude and emotion.

When she answered his knock at the door, he had stood in the entryway in silence for a time. He smiled at her. "What a solemn little person," he said. And he embraced her, his strong arm in the small of her back pulling her flat against himself until she felt his manhood rise. His face against hers, he breathed in deeply as though to pull her soul from her, and as he kissed her, she lost the sense of time and place. It might have been daylight outdoors or night. Minutes might have passed or hours. She thought nothing but rather released herself into his mouth, and arms, and hands. She let him lead her, direct her movements, teach her her own naked body, find its curves and forms, its swells and hollows, the sources of its pleasure. Lying on her little bed, his warmth and weight upon and in her, she heard an unfamiliar music, faint and far away as though some rare and distant melody were being sung in the depth of her being. Gradually the mere quiver of a soft note deep within her grew louder and clearer. With his taut body hovering above hers, she held herself still, attentive, calling it forward, the music of her soul made manifest.

Galerie

"Yellow Still Life," 1909
Gabriele Münter
Oil on cardboard
$16^1/2'' \times 13''$
Milwaukee Art Museum
Gift of Mrs. Harry Lynde Bradley

Breaking with the classical tradition of the still life as an expression of *momento mori,* in this little painting Gabriele Münter presents a departure in subject matter, form, palette, and meaning.

Form first. With no attempt to provide a realistic representation of space, the objects sit on what must be construed rather than observed to be a table. The edges of this "table" are neither parallel nor perpendicular nor even straight. Nor do the objects "sit" on its surface. Rather, the objects appear almost pinned upon it, as one might affix notes to a bulletin board, higher or lower than each other but sharing equally the vertical plane of the painting.

Objects next. One might be a plate in the conventional sense. It is circular for want of a better description, but it is hardly round. On this plate-like shape a few other round-like shapes adhere. Only one of them has a suggestion of volume, perhaps a piece of fruit with a fruit-like stem. Knowing that, the other round shapes must also be fruit or perhaps nuts. Directly above this plate is what might be the base of a lamp or a candlestick. To the right of this vertical shape is a curious object done in blue. The object suggests nothing to this viewer. To the left of the lamp is a toy done in blue, red, and white, perhaps a figure on a horse on wheels such as a child might roll across the floor.

Colors. Yellow, yellow, and more yellow. The plate is orange, but the fruits are mostly yellow. The table is yellow. The lamp is yellow. The background wall is yellow. Of the two peculiar objects that flank the lamp, both have touches of yellow amidst their primary reds or blues. With subtle highlights of green and black, the colors of this painting shimmer almost like stained glass. The painting glows.

And so meaning. The objects in this still life are outlined in black as though to say, "This painting is a depiction of a reality that never was. Each one of us must have a place in the world of this picture, but we do not exist like this in any other world. We have a life of our own here in this space, but in no other space."

J. Eichner

Part Two

Chapter Four

Postcards and Snapshots

Tunis
January, 1905

SHE WASN'T so much lost as muddled. The souk of copper pots
ended in a blind, and rather than retrace her steps through the
labyrinthine Medina, Ella turned to the right off the covered alley
into a still narrower lane closed in on both sides by merchants. The
street, itself, was a jumble, Arabs of different ages and sizes wrapped
in woven shawls crying out into the crowd. Stalls jutted into the passageway leaving no clear thoroughfare, and the more Ella tried to
push through, the hotter and thirstier she got. Carrying the large
two-handled tray she had bargained for, Ella struggled to make her
way, sorry that she had been too lazy to turn around along the copper souk's wider lane. She stopped to rest her purchase on the edge
of a stall of fresh mangos and pineapples and released the straps of
the string bag wedged into the crook of her elbow. She pulled out
her money purse from the pocket of her skirt, thinking to buy a stick
of cut fruit to slake her thirst, and while she fumbled through the
unfamiliar currency, she felt a jolt on her left shoulder. She turned
around, and as she did so, a claw picked her coin purse from her fingers as swiftly as a sea bird snatches a fish from shallow water. The
thief dove into the sea of shoppers, leaving not even the smallest of
wakes. Ella was too startled to cry out. She clutched the tray to her

chest as though it, too, were vulnerable. She berated herself. Wassily had told her not to come alone.

Distressed by the speed with which the thief had taken her purse and disgusted with herself, by the time she got to the hotel, she was parched and perspiring.

"Is there no cool water?" She trudged up the steps toward the first floor sleeping chambers and pantomimed to the barefoot servant girl crouching in the dim hallway that she should bring in water from the earthenware vessel the hotel kept packed in straw in a ground hole under palm fronds. When the girl turned down the hallway, Ella entered her room and collapsed onto a wooden chair at the table. Everything about this country was hard on her—the humidity, the food, the language, the money, the smells, the effort of shopping, the distances to walk, the difficulty of telling the housegirl what she wanted, the impossibility of not getting robbed.

Only the light was worth staying for. Indoors might be dim and close in the humid day, but outdoors one's eyes were bathed in ineffable light, clearer than the summer noon of Bavaria, whiter than the gold of Paris, brighter than the wet Amsterdam horizon, cool light in warm air. It was a miracle, and it made the inconveniences of daily life worth it.

These she had in abundance. First of all there was the rigor of packing and unpacking and their restless wandering since Wassy insisted they leave Munich. Even with the formal separation from Anja, he felt uneasy with Ella at his arm in the city where his wife lived. And so they traveled: Kallmünz, Nuremberg, Regensburg, Würzburg, Rothenburg ob der Tauber, Düsseldorf, Cologne, Frankfurt. And they had made a special trip to Bonn, where, in the spring, Ella introduced Wassily to the Schroeters.

Emmy had pursed her lips and sent the cook to the back garden to harvest peas. Alone with Ella in the kitchen, she had voiced discontent. "Like him? I like him well enough." Her sister's lover had comported himself impeccably, patrician in his bearing and demeanor, and there was no denying the force of his intellect. "But it's not right for you to live with a married man."

"I told you he's applied for a divorce. These things take time. There's the whole hierarchy of the Orthodox Church to go through as well as the state."

"But a married man. Ella! What would mother say!"

Ella set her pouty mouth and hardened her eyes. "You and I are very different. I'm a modern girl, and this is what I want."

Emmy turned from her potatoes. "I suppose the wife is asking a lot of money."

"She has a name. Anja Chimiakin. I know her. I visit her. We're almost friends, actually. And she's not sorry about the marriage. But Wassily doesn't want scandal."

"Scandal! Really, Ella, can't you see how painful that must be for her? You call yourself her friend?"

"Can't *you* see that divorce takes time?" Her sulky face slid off. "Oh, Emmy, you mustn't worry. We'll get married right and proper. You'll see."

When the kitchen door banged, Emmy rose from the table. "Thank you, Annalise. We'll enjoy these tonight. Isn't it lovely to have our Fraulein here with us?" The cook nodded, her hands twisting her apron skirt. "You know, Annalise, my sister is a most talented artist. She's brought a painting with her I think will remind you of your father's farm." The woman smiled and gave a little bow in Ella's direction. "I feel like cooking tonight, Annalise. Why don't you go home, have an early night." Emmy waited until the door closed again, her knife tip plunged in a potato's eye. "It's not respectable. You weren't raised to live like a gypsy."

Ella stroked the surface of the wooden table. "I don't live like one now, Emmy."

"Well, I know this. A woman who lives with a man she is not married to is in for trouble. Things are hard enough between men and women without that."

"How can you of all people say that? Besides, I live like an artist, not just some common woman."

"And just what do you think is the difference? Honestly! You've got to look ahead. Supposing he never does marry you! There are things you don't understand, Ella." Her knife blade flashed.

"You don't know him."

"And another thing. You live like nomads. Can't you settle down *somewhere*?"

Her sister had hit upon a sore spot. For months now, Ella felt like a seedling dug up and set down over and over, root growth inhibited, leaves imperiled. And yet, how could she speak disloyally about her lover?

"Well, Anja Chimiakin keeps an apartment in Munich and Wassily won't humiliate her by living too near. I think it's noble of him. He's a good man, Emmy—trust me on this. Besides, things are changing for everyone. As soon as he's free, we'll get married and you can introduce me to as many pastor's wives as you like."

But they didn't settle down. Hungry for new images to imprint on the back-plate of his vision, Wassily took Ella to The Hague, Haarlem, Zaandam, Strasbourg, Basel, Lyon, Marseilles, Paris, and now Tunis. Ella was, herself, an eager and intrepid traveler, but she was weary. And she'd endured nothing so challenging before as this complex culture with its ancient roots. There was, in addition, the awkwardness of registering in the hotels. Even here, a continent from home, they rented separate rooms, though she knew people eyed her with suspicion. It mattered to her that they did: In every way but one, she was his wife.

‡

Ella opened the casement window overlooking the hotel courtyard just below. "I'm back, Wassily."

"Are you coming out?"

"I'll just have some water first." She closed the casement window. She placed her new copper tray on the wooden table, centering it. When she next went to the market, she would fill the tray with fruit and perhaps some lime leaves. She would make the room her home.

Downstairs, Wassily sat in the shade before a small picture. He was fully dressed—tie, vest, his trousers pressed. He could paint in a smoking jacket, he said. Messiness was merely lack of discipline.

"Look at this, Ella. I'm doing something new." He dipped a rag in solvent and with his forefinger wiped a small section of his canvas between the pale blue of a sky and the deeper blue of a sea, his finger transcribing minute circles against the blues until they commingled. Ella stood at his side, watching. Taking care not to crush his brush-hairs, he whisked the paints together along the border into a curved shape, tight and contained.

"There, now."

"Well, it's not quite a seascape any longer." She walked away from the canvas a few steps. "I wouldn't know where you were if it weren't for those areas on the left—boats, perhaps, or rocks?"

"Hmm." He was careful with his brush, exact, persuading the blues now into waving arcs.

"People won't recognize the scene." Ella squinted, bending her head from side to side.

"No. Not with their eyes."

"Are you going to keep the boats?"

"I think not." He dipped his brush again and went back to the canvas. "But something of a suggestion, an encryption."

"Well, I can see the movement, the sailing. But they're still almost boats. You might try flattening the foreground."

"Yes. Yes, you're right. Exactly. And contrast with yellow along the edge." He loaded his brush with more paint, blurring the areas Ella indicated. "What do you feel when you look now?" He stopped his brush to look up at her.

"I feel the energy, but I don't see the setting at all any more. There's no depth. People won't know what to think, you know."

"People will learn to understand. Of course some will never understand, even if we tell them where to look and what to see. But—" He took his notebook from the ground at his feet and penciled a few quick shapes, trying out sizes, positions, angles, perspectives. Frowning, he sat still for a moment and took a deep breath. "This is so very different from music, perhaps even harder."

"Music?"

"Think about this, Ella. A composer's idea doesn't stay his own." He took up his brush and worked his sketches onto the canvas, his hand steady. "Orchestra, instrumentalist, singer—it doesn't matter the piece. The performer transforms the idea." He sat back on his stool and peered at the canvas. His right hand with its brush moved slightly in the air, as though to test out a line before it danced upon the canvas. Bending forward, he let his hand copy the phantom line. "The composer leaves directions—*adagio*, crescendo, etcetera—and then the performer executes the idea. It's a collaboration between them." He stood and stretched, rolling his shoulders forward and back, then sat again before his easel. Concentrating, he dabbed a stiff brush onto his palette, mixing pigment bold from the tube with white until it swirled in a graceful ballet for two colors. "But the painter has the entire responsibility. He conceives the idea, but he must also interpret it. He does not give the *impression* of the subject so much as the *expression* of himself."

Ella folded her arms, her brow furrowed, listening. He often tried out his theories on her like a fashion designer dressing a model. If she stood still, he might take off this robe and put a different one on her. She could partly own his thoughts, then, when he had gowned her in them.

"Those who can really see will feel the picture. They'll walk around in it, live in it." He looked up at Ella. "You've helped me understand that."

Ella flushed. "I understand nothing." Better just to stand by his shoulder, following his hand with its brush, breathing along with him and seeing the work unfold with her own artist's eyes. "But the blue moves me." When she painted, she often thought of his colors.

"Blue is...spiritual." He spoke quietly and cast his eyes upwards. "I have always heard blue."

She looked intently at the canvas, entering its space.

He turned back to the painting. "I hear flutes in these blues, a flute duet, pure and clear."

"Parallel sounds."

"Exactly." He reached for his palette knife.

"I like it." She put her hand on his shoulder.

"My partner." He lowered his hand from the canvas. "My dear, little friend. My best eyes."

Ella stroked the back of her hand along his cheek and short beard. He took hold of her hand and held it against his lips.

He set down his knife, turned on his stool toward her, and put both hands low on her hips, nestling her between his knees. He closed his eyes and put his head against her breasts. "Shall I pack up my paints? Shall we go up to your room?"

She followed the slope of his shoulders with her palms, drawing him to her, soaking in the scent of his skin, tasting its fragrance. As always, she abandoned her separateness only to find herself bettered in him. "I want you to see what I've bought."

"Yes, later. I will want to look at it."

After dark, they lit the kerosene lamp and sat at the table in her room. He was writing an essay. She called him Wassy now and smiled to think he was once Professor K. And how much she had learned since she'd earned the right to call him by his name.

Not all was about love. Some time ago, in fact, he encouraged her to make woodcuts, and for weeks on end she sketched images on paper and then transferred them onto wood, gouging out the images in reverse and then inking them. Late one night he rose from his bed to find her bent over the table.

"I've been up all night grinding and mixing paints and then bumbling. All I've done is make a mess. The ink is too thick to absorb evenly. You've got to help me." She leaned her head on her hand.

And so he directed her to another medium. Linocuts yielded to her knife and small hand more agreeably and gave up the ink less temperamentally. They became her specialty, and she found she could capture even delicate nuances in the bold and streamlined portraits she made. Each project was a foray into new materials, new images, new efforts at understanding how to see, what to center on, what to discard. Wassy took each piece into his hands, turned it over and around, considered its form and color and concept, entered her thinking. But as much as she loved to work side by side with her teacher, her lover, her mind must be her own. Of that, she was sure.

Yet she gave of herself to him each time he spoke or wrote or painted. When he began a project, she waited for him to find his subject. When he paused to consider a next step, she offered questions and considerations. When he got frustrated with a piece, she agreed he should stop. When he was hungry, she found herself ravenous. When he was tired, she slept. The few times she left his presence, she regretted it, lonely for his company, his probing reflections on everything they saw together, lonely as well for his scent and the pressure of his hand on her arm.

But she hated her uncertain condition, hated the looks, the sneers. "Must we always and forever take two rooms? Why can't we just register as husband and wife?"

"Be patient, my sweet," he said. "When I am divorced, I promise we will marry and go everywhere as one. But for now, this way is the best. There must be no public disgrace. We must be able to hold our heads high in the world."

But nevertheless she longed to make a home of her own with him, and she dreamed of the day when he would make good on his promise.

Rapallo
April 1, 1906

My dearest Emmy,

I have sent you (or rather, Friedel) something by separate post, but you must be careful not to tear or bend what you find. The doll in the picture is Gertrude. If I remember being six (and I do!), you spent the whole of one Christmas dinner with "my Gertrude" on your lap. Tell your perfect little daughter that story, and be sure to give Friedel several birthday kisses that come exclusively from her Aunt Ella.

Wassily and I have a whole villa to ourselves, excepting

for our frequent guests. Wassily's father even came for a
<u>second</u> visit. (I am promised that I will soon be able to
call him my "father-in-law.") We socialize with so many
artists, and Emmy—I am one of them!

Please give my love to Georg. The next time I visit you,
you will have moved to Berlin and I will have to get used
to a whole new living arrangement.

Your peripatetic sister,

Ella

Paris
November, 1906

"*Mon dieu*! But you must do better than this. You have no texture,
here, Fraulein. Use your pencil on the side—like this. Here, give it to
me, give it! Like this—shade the figure. Make the figure rounded, a
life form."

"But I don't care to make it real. That is not important to me."

"Preposterous. It is not important what you care for. You Germans! *Mon dieu*!"

"But I can give the essence with my pencil."

"No. No. No. No. You must train your eye to see what is there."

"But too much is there. I want to draw just what is essential."

"That is for children—the house, the window, the tree. Bah! For
the artist, the pencil sees everything."

"Not everything. I use the pencil to find the line of the picture—its
movement in space, the importance."

"You are being clever. I detest clever women. This is not the studio for you, *peut-etre*. If you will not take my direction, you should go
home. I have no time for amateurs. For women amateurs. You said
you were a serious artist. But this? Preposterous. I won't have it. Not

in my studio. You cannot draw. Like a child, you draw—squiggles and lines. You do nothing I tell you, nothing. You waste my time. Bah!"

Sèvres
February, 1907

Dear Carly and Mary,

Brother Carl, may I impose on you to authorize the Bonn bank to send a double payment to the affiliate in Paris? I've run up some extra expenses of late—a sadly futile drawing class, a room in Paris for a few weeks, and some expensive framing. I'll save the details for when I see you. Wassily sends his regards.

Much love,

Gabriele

Sèvres
February, 1907

Dear Olga,

I'm so sorry I didn't respond to your last letter right away, but now let me congratulate you on the birth of your baby. You mustn't worry about not painting. You have such very important things to attend to!

No, we don't have plans to return to Germany for the present. I can't explain why. Things are not as simple as they once were. We are both busy, but that is not an excuse. Some days, actually, I am very lazy and don't do a thing.

Please excuse this brief letter. I think of you often and remember how much we shared when we were girls.

Those were precious days for me.

Your friend,

Ella

Sévres
February, 1907

"Help me choose, Wassy. Which ones, do you think?"

"Well, surely *Path in the Park of St. Cloud.*"

"Yes, I think so, too. It's quite like yours, you know."

"In some ways, perhaps, though mine is bolder. But then I am older than you, and a man. And also, I used more red."

"Tell me, then. Which ones?"

"Put all six paintings in the Salon des Indépendants show. You might then send the woodcuts to *Les Tendances Nouvelles* to publish."

"You always know what to do."

"Do I? I think not. Certainly not. You must not say that."

"Take me with you to Odessa."

"You know it is not possible. When the divorce is final, you will come with me. You must be patient, Gabriele."

"When we go home to Germany, can we take Waske?"

"He would hate the train. He would cry even more than you do."

"I only cry when you leave me."

"But I must attend to business, Ella, as you well know. In any case, I don't think we should take Waske. We'll give him to the landlord."

"He has a cat."

"All the better. He can have two cats."

"I want to go home and have a house and a cat of my own and a garden and a studio and twenty-two children that all look like you."

"Another time I would laugh at you for the way you talk. If you have twenty-two children, you will never paint even one picture and no one will take you seriously. I thought you wanted to hang your work in a gallery."

"Yes, I do. And I am going to do it, too, six of them. I am going to have six paintings in the Paris exhibit, just like you. I am going to be famous just like you."

"I cannot match your mood just now. I have a headache."

"Another one? Shall I darken the room?"

"Yes, if you will. I think I should lie down. Leave me alone for the time."

Eagelhaus, Bad Reichenhall, Austria
July, 1907

The road to the top was so steep in places that at one point Ella had to climb out and walk a hundred meters while the wagonmaster led the horses to the crest. By the time I get there, they'll have to let me stay as well, she thought. I'm exhausted, too.

"Will there be more?" Ella seated herself behind the driver once more.

"That was the last." The stout man swiveled his whole body on the bench to look at her. Perhaps it was unusual for an unaccompanied woman with a suitcase to be headed toward the sanatorium.

As the wagon creaked slowly upwards, Ella, its only passenger, looked about. The view was spectacular, snow-capped peaks vying with a deeply azure sky for dominance of the landscape. Down closer to the train station, they had passed picnickers and hikers along the roadside, gripping their walking sticks or seated in small patches of mountain laurel. If things were different, Ella thought, she might have liked to be among them.

"Do many people make the trip up this high?"

"Aye, surely. It's not usual for me to have just one passenger in the wagon. Mostly the wagon is full. And I come up four, sometimes five times a day in summer, two even in winter."

"So many patients!"

"Those who can afford to be sick," he grumbled.

Inside the hospital, she waited on a hard chair to see the doctor. She had already decided she would call herself Frau Kandinsky. Wassily would not approve, but the hospital administration would not allow her to visit him were she to tell them she was merely Fraulein Münter. The name would mean nothing to the doctor or his staff. Such people would have no knowledge of the Paris Salon des Indépendants and her own accomplishment in showing her recent paintings there. No, all that would matter to these hospital people would be to think that she was *entitled* to visit Herr Kandinsky, patient of the eminent Herr Doktor Zimmerman.

He addressed his remarks to the papers in his hand. "The diagnosis is a mild neurasthenia. Your husband's nerves are exhausted, compounded, as I am certain you will have observed yourself, by his acute sensitivity and tendency toward introspection." Herr Doktor Zimmerman was tall and bald, and his cheekbones gleamed in the cold light from the window behind him. At no point did his eyes find her face. "Complete rest is required."

"May I see him now?"

"One thing more. Specialists in the treatment of melancholia of this type regard the self-accusation we have observed in Herr Kandinsky as a symptom of a more significant condition."

"A symptom? Of what? What condition?" Ella sat straighter in her chair. Wassily was, indeed, hyper-critical. She, herself, had occasionally taken the brunt of his withering assessments, but she knew, too, that he was harshest on himself. He was struggling with a vision he could not execute, a vision only partly formed in his mind, a concept new and troubling. And he wanted perfection.

"The specialists, as I say, see the fatigue of which Herr Kandinsky complains as an assault of the nerves. The cause may be the consequence of non-complete coitus." Herr Doktor folded his hands on his desk and studied his thumbs.

Ella cleared her throat. "I see. But he—"

Herr Doktor interrupted. "Here at the clinic we are addressing the problem with the best of scientific information. The cure involves regular immersion in our brine springs, ingestion of milk twice each day, and complete rest from labor of any kind." Her rose from his desk to walk to the window. Tapping one finger on the glass, he craned his neck as though to see someone just out of view. "But, madam, until the cure is entirely successful in alleviating the fatigue, the treatment cannot be said to be complete." Returning to his desk, Herr Doktor gathered up his papers. With a brisk nod, he made his way toward the door. "In short, Herr Kandinsky must not be disturbed. Upon his release, I am certain he will want to regain contact with his family."

On the ride down the mountain, Ella sat with her hands tight atop the pocketbook on her lap. How stupid it had been to lie like that, how humiliating. And if Wassily ever discovered that she had appeared at the sanatorium calling herself his wife, he would be furious with her. Besides, Herr Doctor was wrong. *That* was not what had caused Wassily's depression. It was that he struggled with his work, wanted something he had not yet achieved. He'd gone back to painting figures, Moscow's onion domes, women in folk costumes, horses and riders done with little dabs of paint like tiles from a gold mosaic. The work was good but he felt embarrassed by it. Neighbors of theirs in Paris, an American brother and sister named Stein, had visited her and Wassily in the studio at Sèvres. The woman, a rather mannish individual, had sniggered when she saw Wassily's latest Russian images and themes. It had turned out that she was a patron of some of the newer artists and had touted their brilliance. She had bought one of Matisse's window paintings from the Salon des Indepéndants show and was said to own several others along with some new and bold things by the Spaniard Picasso.

Calling himself a failure, then, Wassily had fallen into a tirade of self-castigation and had stopped painting altogether. His head throbbed and his sleep was disturbed by nightmares in which he felt himself frustrated and choked like a man whose message is vital and urgent but whose throat has been slashed. His work was his problem, not his ability to love. Inside his being, an idea germinated inchoate, and he could neither clear his mind of its insistent swirling nor execute his incomplete vision. And when he saw the work of the Paris artists, he became jealous. Only Ella knew that about him. Only Ella knew how much he suffered.

Lausanne
September, 1907

Ella put the leftover bread into a napkin and tied its four corners together in a knot. Before the sun slipped behind the mountain each night, they liked to walk to the lake and take out one of the small boats tourists could rent there, rowing out toward the cove where a colony of swans nested. The mature birds floated beautifully white, and even the babies in their ragged grey coats looked lovely with their little white bottoms.

"They mate for life, you know," said the man who let the boats.

"Is that so?" Crouched and holding the gunwales, Ella stepped down into the boat.

"I've been watching that pair out there for years." The old boatman stood on the pier. He wore his thin white hair long in front, and it lifted gently in the breeze. Wassy climbed in and situated himself, lifting the oar handles from their locks, raising their tips. The boatman let loose the rope and shoved the rowboat with this foot.

Released from the dock, the boat drifted slowly away from shore. Then Wassy dipped the oars and turned the boat around, rowing silently toward the big swans bobbing about on the clear water, invisible rotors turning their legs and floppy feet.

"When I was little," Ella said, "my mother read us *The Ugly Duckling*. I always thought that was me."

"But you were never ugly."

"I thought so." Ella loosened the strings on her bonnet. White sun was dissolving on the dark mountaintop like foam spilling over the rim of a pewter tankard.

Wassily lifted his oars above the water and let them drip. His eyes were bright and his skin taut and tanned. Ella smiled to look at him. He was more himself after his stay in the sanitarium. He'd gone back to work. The exercise of rowing did him good, he said.

"In the *Kalevala* there's an immortal swan in the land of the dead." He leaned forward again and let down the oars, his back and shoulders the center of a broad arc spanning the boat. "The legend is that if a man ever does kill the swan, that man will die. But the one who saves the swan becomes immortal."

Ella threw bread hunks into the water and watched them sail whitely on the clear layer topping the green depths. "Oh? I'd be afraid to be immortal." She trailed her fingers through the water. "Wassy, look at the babies! Aren't they funny looking? I want a swan hat, I think."

'You mean a costume hat for Fasching?" He raised the oars and hooked them inside the boat.

"No, I want a real hat, a beautiful big white swan hat. Could we catch a swan?" She liked to tease him, now. If she could make him laugh, he would love her more. It did him good to laugh.

"No, but we could steal your feathers from the swan's nest." Wassy frowned and rolled up the sleeve of his shirt and leaned over, putting his arm into the water nearly to the elbow. "I would never kill a swan."

"Wassily, don't lean. You're going to tip us. No, I didn't mean killing anything.

Wassily straightened. "My grandfather knew, though." He shook his wet arm and rolled down his sleeve. "He used to talk about the Tsar's soldiers tearing through the villages."

"Don't talk about that. Let's just be here now. Let's be right here in the middle of the swans, and let's lie down in the boat and be swans ourselves. Come. You do it, too."

"This kind of thing is difficult for me." He returned the oars to the water. "You are a little foolish tonight, I think. It is getting dark. We had better bring the boat in."

Ella removed her bonnet and placed it under the prow. "All right. You row. I'll lie still and be a swan." Slowly she lowered herself until she could lie on the flat wooden floor, her legs tucked between Wassily's. The sky was the color of the deep water, the early evening star just visible, the world above her endless and immortal. She felt the boat rock.

Bonn
Late October, 1907

Ella was truly lost. At first when she got off the tram, she turned left and walked parallel to the tracks, sure she could find her way. She checked the address once more on the scrap of paper she tucked into her glove and made her way east, away from the Rhine. Recalling that Elizabethstrasse veered, she expected to see the publisher's office just below. Wrong again. The street was entirely given over to small houses. Retracing her steps northwards and then west, she walked toward the riverbank, and when she reached the next street, she found herself just opposite the Rose Garden entrance to the Rheinaue Leisure Park. She would certainly be late, now.

"What a nuisance," she muttered. Five years out of the city, and she couldn't find her way around. She'd been on her feet since morning wearing new shoes in the bargain, a little tight and stiff. The strap of her leather portfolio dug into the shoulder of her light coat, and she felt her hat sliding forward on her forehead, its grey plume brushing her eyebrows.

She thought of walking to the shopkeeper at the corner to ask for directions, but her feet hurt. "It won't matter," she told herself, and she crossed the street where the path led into the rose garden. Just outside its little gate, she found a bench. Ten minutes, she promised herself. She lay the thick envelope beside her on the bench and then bent and loosened the ties on her shoes. Someone had left a newspaper behind, one with a large fuzzy photograph of the Kaiser in military dress, and she studied it for some minutes. Was there some kind of war? She glanced at the headlines. A Belgian had been slain by Congo natives. Nothing to do with her. She folded her hands over her pocketbook on her lap. Ten minutes. She closed her eyes.

"I don't want to listen. I don't want to listen."

Ella woke with a start. She'd been dreaming she held a cat on her lap and the cat had tried to bite her.

"We'll just read a little. Then we can buy some chestnuts. You'd like that, wouldn't you?" A stout woman hoisted a small boy onto the bench across from Ella.

"I don't want the story. I hate that story."

"You hate *Little Suck-a-Thumb*? You didn't use to hate it. That used to be your favorite story."

"No. No. No Suck-a-Thumb!"

"Well, shall we read *The Story of Fidgety Philip*?"

"No, no, no, no, no." The child began to cry.

"Here, why don't you just sit on my lap for a bit, and we'll just watch the world go by, shall we?" The woman lifted the boy onto her lap, and he leaned his head back against her. "There, there. You'll feel better soon." She folded her arms around his small tummy, rocking and humming softly in his ear.

Ella could almost feel the weight of the little boy on her lap, sense his warm, sticky cheek against hers as though she, too, had a little boy to hold. Her nephews were grown by now, and while they were polite, after the pleasantries they shared each morning and evening, they went about their own activities.

After years of wandering with Wassily, Ella had come back to Germany ready to establish a household for the two of them. She was thirty years old. A woman had to be careful how long she waited to start a family, she'd told Wassily. By the time he returned from Moscow, he should have the divorce papers in hand, and then her real life could begin. She would only allow herself a few weeks in Bonn, just long enough to visit her family and also to prepare her exhibit for Friedrich Cohen. And now that she had finished the pieces, she was ready to deliver them to the publisher. If she could find his office.

Ella got up from the bench. The idea of chestnuts appealed to her. She strolled down the path away from the rose garden, following the scent of roasting nuts. Just beyond a growth of spirea, the vendor stood, stirring the brazier under his copper kettle.

Ella gave the man a coin and then, paper cone of hot nuts in her hand, walked back to her bench across from the cranky child. He had fallen asleep against the stout woman. His nanny? She was too old to be his mother.

"You've gotten him to take a nap, I see." Ella whispered across the path.

"Yes. Thank God. He's had such a long day." The woman spoke quietly, bending her head away from his. She smiled at Ella. "I've had him on my hands since five o'clock."

"This morning? Why so early?"

"His mother's gone into labor. They needed to get him out of the house. But I've no playthings at home, so here we are."

"Ah." Ella smiled. "A new brother or sister."

The woman nodded and stoked the child's head. "My grandson. My son's oldest."

Ella peeled a chestnut and ate the flesh. She leaned back against the bench and crossed her ankles. She really was weary. She'd been working non-stop since she arrived, not even taking an occasional afternoon to re-acquaint herself with the city. In the evenings, Carl and Mary had invited guests in to meet her and had taken her out to concerts and meals in restaurants. Carl seemed to want to show off his prosperity. Everything had to be just so—the wine, the waiter. Ella liked Mary well enough, but she was so absorbed in her children, the two women had little to share. Ella barely got a sentence out before one of the family interrupted with a concern. When was the tutor due to arrive? Would the music lesson be rescheduled? Could an outing be arranged to include a school friend? Why had the housekeeper hidden a notebook? Ella felt like an audience to the domestic drama. She was getting restless, tired of being the houseguest. When they got back to Munich, Wassily would rent a large apartment they would share. She'd made it clear that was what she wanted.

When she finished her snack, she crumpled the paper cone and put it in her coat pocket. She still did not feel rested. The child, though, was waking up.

The grandmother took a handkerchief from her pocketbook and wiped the boy's face. "There, now. Shall we take a walk and find the chestnut man?"

The boy climbed from her lap onto the bench beside his grand-mother.

"I want the ABC's."

"All right. Let's see." She reached into her bag and retrieved the child's book. "Here's an 'H' for 'Hans.' That's you, Hansie. Just like your Papa. Big Hans and little Hans. Can you see? A stick and another stick and a little seat between them. That's 'H.' "

"I want 'P' for 'Papa.' A stick and a bump."

"That's quite the clever boy. You know 'P' for 'Papa' then, do you?" She began to turn the pages.

"Yes. And 'S' for 'Schuler.' "

"What a fine boy. Yes. 'H' for 'Hans' and 'S' for 'Schuler.' Very good!"

Ella sat, stunned. The child's father was Hans Schuler, Georg Schroeter's colleague. The man Ella might have gone round with. Might have married. It was possible. She scoured the child's face to see if the father lurked behind it, but she couldn't tell.

"Is your Papa Herr Schuler, the printer?" It was a bold thing to do, to ask so forward a question. Had she been out of Germany so long she'd lost her reserve? But there in the park on this fall day, what difference did it make? If the grandmother, Hans Schuler's mother, was offended, Ella could just leave.

The child looked at Ella and then up at his grandmother. He kicked his legs on the park bench. "I want my chestnuts now." He tugged at his grandmother's sleeve.

"Come, little Hans." The woman gathered up her parcels and helped the child from the bench. "Good afternoon, Fraulein." Taking the boy's hand, she nodded at Ella, and the pair walked up the path toward the chestnut vendor.

Ella swung the strap of her portfolio onto her shoulder. She slipped her arm through the straps of her pocketbook. Hans Schuler was about to be a father for the second time. If she had married him, well....But she couldn't have. Not even for a child of her own. Yet, she could still feel the sense of a child on her lap. Ella rose from the bench and took the path out to the street. She caught the streetcar home to brother Carl's house, and when she got there, she went into her room and took off her coat and hat and lay on the bed until it was time for dinner. The portfolio with her linocuts for Friedrich Cohen lay on her bedside chair.

Unter den Linden 58
Berlin

January 18, 1908

Friedrich Cohen
74 Elisabethstrasse
Bonn

Herr Cohen:

You should expect delivery of twenty-four wood and linocuts within the week. As I mentioned in my last letter, the series devoted to toys, bears, dolls, children, etc. is the most new and ought to be displayed last, if you insist on a chronological order. The portraits I made in Italy over a year ago (including the woodcut of W. Kandinsky) are, perhaps, more finely done in the Jugendstil style. I leave it to you, then, to decide on the arrangement.

Sincerely Yours,

Gabriele Münter

* * * * *

And yet, he was not ready after all. In Munich, Wassily and Ella rented separate rooms, separate studios. They met daily, sent notes and letters back and forth at intervals throughout the day, ate, socialized, and loved. He had returned from Moscow without the divorce, and she had to make do with that.

Galerie

"Portrait of a Young Woman," 1909
Gabriele Münter
Oil on canvas
$27^5/_8'' \times 19''$
Milwaukee Art Museum
Gift of Mrs. Harry Lynde Bradley

Had she expected to be flattered in the tradition of the Dutch por-
traitists of the Renaissance, the subject of this painting (sometimes
referred to as "Young Polish Woman") would certainly have been disappointed. While she is fashionably attired, the position of her head,
her downcast eyes, and the set of her lips characterize her as stiff,
possibly imperious, and decidedly unhappy.

It is a three-quarter portrait, capturing the woman from the
crown of her flat-brimmed hat to just below the waist of her skirt. The
artist has been attentive to the style of her jacket, which has a double lapel—a layer of deep yellow-green atop the jacket's main color,
a rich, rosy pink. Her mustard-colored blouse sports a white collar topped with a soft pink necktie, knotted like a gentleman's. Her
skirt picks up the green inner lapel and the jacket's green buttons.
Stylish certainly, but what might have further discomfited the painting's subject is the color of her hair, taken directly from the mustard
and green of the artist's palette. The figure's right shoulder and arm
droop away from her head as they might if the wearer were to remove her jacket and drape it casually about her. The woman holds
her left arm away from her body, though, and although the viewer
can see only a portion of that arm, the form of the sleeve has convincing volume. Behind the sitter are two vertical panels of blue, the
larger one deep and rich with vertical brushstrokes, the smaller one
lighter, streaked with pale yellow and white.

All of the major forms—hat, hair, face, jacket—are outlined in
thick black, a style of compartmentalizing color areas reminiscent of
cloisonné.

The viewer cannot help but admire the woman for her beauty and style, but she is difficult to approach. She will not gaze at us as we do at her. Communication is prohibited, and we cannot tell whether to sympathize with her distress or resent her rejection of us. The artist, it seems, is ambivalent, and so must we be.

J. Eichner

Chapter Five

Murnau in Five Movements

Solo

Murnau
Late August, 1908

Eʟʟᴀ ᴄʀᴇᴘᴛ out the inn door. She hoisted her rucksack onto her back and walked south. When she got to the end of the small street, she turned around, the mountains looming behind her, the sun still climbing behind the houses to her right. Just off the lane that delimited the town, a farmer led three cows along a path, their neck bells a distant music almost clerical in its sober purposefulness. Aside from the rustlings of rural life in the outlying lanes, the town was quiet, just beginning to acquire the day's traffic. Last night's rain had tamped down the powdery grey dust of the streets, and moist freshness rose into the cool Alpine air stream, whooshing across the plain like a hausfrau rinsing off her sidewalk with clear water. Featherbeds began to pop out of windows like smooth button mushrooms, their sporey gills tucked neatly away from sight.

Could anything be more charming? Ella felt she could roost in this town, itself firmly planted where the moor edged toward the hills. Colorful houses stood with their legs spread wide, shoulder to shoulder like laughing brothers posing for a camera. She smiled at the family resemblances of the houses—the blond one and the redhead sharing their father's bulk, their mother's grace, the slope of roofs, the

style of chimneys, the window placement passed along from genera-
tions past.

Looking for a place to settle outside Munich, Ella and Wassily
had found this most delightful town splayed out before the foothills
of the Bavarian Alps, a little market village on the Murnau moors.
Its streets boasted a harmony of architecture as well as a purity of
light that captivated them, and they persuaded their Munich friends
Alexei Jawlensky and Marianne Von Werefkin to join them here for
a summer's painting jaunt. In Murnau, Wassily had said, they could
redress the restlessness that had taken them to so many cities. Ella,
at least, was famished for permanence, tired of trains and wagons,
sleds and sledges, packing and repacking, cities and soot, negotiating rents, lowering her eyes against the inquiry of innkeepers. How
welcome this repast, this sweet respite. In Munich, she still felt the
burden of her awkward position, Anja continuing to keep rooms just
streets away from where Wassily had rented his new apartment. Here
in Murnau, though, Ella felt free.

And besides, she was learning to subtract. After years of experi-
menting, both she and Wassily had discarded their palette knives and
thick paints in favor of stiff brushes and thin, flat colors. And rather
than try to reproduce images realistically, they had evolved something truly revolutionary. Wassily particularly had moved in a bold
direction. In fact, some of his paintings were nearly abstract, quick
movements of color and form and gesture, only the merest suggestion of landscape or objects grounding the colors in scenes, in places.
Though he hadn't yet succeeded in achieving it, his goal, he said, was
to paint "absolutes" with nothing of the real world depicted on the
canvas, nothing but true, pure color and form. Though not quite
so bold as he, even Ella abstracted, getting to the essence of scenes
rather than copying their details. It was that she would do today.

With her back to the mountains to the south, she set up her easel
and her stool, not because she would paint sitting down but because

she needed to look and think. Getting the vision was the important thing, finding its essence. It helped if she put an imaginary basket on the ground at her side next to her stool. She thought of her basket as big and tightly woven with a wide, gaping mouth. Into it she threw things she didn't want in the scene before her, the extraneous distractions that confused the eye and cluttered the core of the picture's expressiveness.

First to go in the basket today were the people on the early morning street—the farrier in his leather apron, the sleeves of his blue shirt rolled to the elbow, a milkmaid carrying pails on a rack across her shoulders, the innkeeper's daughter rounding the corner toward the cheese merchant, a boy with a pocketknife, a washerwoman. It was a very big basket. Then went encumbrances—droppings from the horse the mayor rode on his way to fish in the nearby stream, shutters on the upper windows of the green house, a hand-carved wooden sign outside the beer hall, the brewer's splintered wagon, a broom left overnight in the rain, a bicycle leaning against a wall. After that she scrutinized the houses themselves and picked away at them. Some lost their doors. Some doors lost their latches. All of the houses lost their chimneys. When she had the street denuded of inessentials, she fixed the sun in the sky—9:15 a.m. Into the basket would go 9:30 and 10:00 and 10:30 and later. Now she had just the forms of the houses, the slant of the street, the feel of the morning. When, in her mind's eye, she had subtracted the scene to its essentials, she could begin to paint.

First she sketched out the lines—the slight left-leaning diagonal of the street lined with vertical rectangles and inverted V-shaped roofs. She smiled to herself as she brushed in the partial structure on the very far right of the picture as though she were next to that house, seated so that she could get only a bit of it in her peripheral vision, as though she could not turn her head to take it in, as though this street were so present, so alive that human alertness could not grasp it all.

Next, the colors. The street was colorful already, but not colorful enough. Her stiff brush pulled bright sun out of bed to poke among spotty clouds in a sky of blue promise. Then came the street drying from rain, grey with brown powder emerging with the daylight heat, the very feel of an early morning after a wet night. Flanking the street, houses and more houses popping out of an Easter basket— pastel green, yellow, blue, pink, colors that would surprise their owners. Roofs bright red and orange and brown and black, intense colors and more varied than the roofs, themselves. A few strokes for windows, but not justice. No curtains. No frames. No featherbeds. No old men leaning out to wait for the post. Just the abstract of a village on a quiet summer morning. Just the essence of its calm, true reality.

Today Ella was in love with this street, these walls, these windows, this moment, this air, this painting life with Wassily and Alexei and Marianne, this clear, cool summer morning, her strength and youth and sexuality and the breath that went into and out of her. This picture would sing a full-hearted aria to life, to the joy of being an artist and painting what one felt and saw and knew. For the moment, for today, for now, just happiness and peace that she could shape with her brushes and own.

Duet

Murnau
August, 1908

"Higher, higher, Gabriele." With the flat of his left hand over his head, Wassily made a platform for the note. "You can reach it. Try again, now. Breathe. Come again. We start at bar twelve." He played the notes, taking a deep breath to signal Ella's entrance.

"Better. Much better. Shall we start again? I begin." He played the introduction, two measures of instrumental lyricism before his rich baritone entered: "O do not weep."

When Wassily returned to Murnau the week before, he brought back some sheet music—mostly Schubert songs. The Schroeters were expected in September, and the plan was to hold a night of singing. And now that he and Ella had installed his harmonium, he was eager to play. If the tone of the harmonium was not quite suited to the songs, well, so be it. The purpose was the family gathering, after all.

Ella looked forward to entertaining the Schroeters and her adorable little niece. Now that she had purchased this charming yellow house of her own tucked away in the Alpine foothills, she wanted family life, the easy sociability of kin and kind. And she welcomed the chance to show off her Wassy, to let her sister see the domestic comfort of their life, to appreciate Wassily's excellence in every way. Proof, if it came to it, that she was right to wait for him, right to wait this long, long time.

Yet Ella was not always at ease here in Murnau where the local residents had little experience with artists or foreigners, not to mention an unmarried woman who, like herself, owned a bit of Murnau property. They held their heads high and stiff when they saw her on the village streets, and the merchants handled her money as though she had soiled it. No one called her by name. No one greeted her on the street or acknowledged her *Guten Tag*. Once, when she left the bakery, stopping to shift her string bag on her elbow, she thought she heard a customer whisper *whore*. Alone sometimes in the Murnau house, Ella saw herself nested high in a precarious tree, the villagers below swooping up the hill to gawk and gossip, unwelcoming, suspicious. She felt freakish then, a woman like no other, belonging to no group but the little ones she made herself—Ella and Wassily, Ella and the Schroeters, Ella and a handful of other painters. Wassily might travel and talk and be a man among others, moving back and forth between Russia and Germany, citizen of the world, but for Ella, living with Wassily placed her outside of other people's lives, citizen of no country but the tiny municipality they made for themselves.

In the music room on Kottmüllerallee tonight, they sang "Selma and Selmar," a languorous duet between parting lovers. The accompaniment featured slow chords, so Wassy could both play the keyboard instrument with its pump pedals and sing his part. Or would Ella prefer to play? But though she kept a piano in the Munich flat, she had abandoned her singing and piano lessons. "No, you do it," she said.

Whenever Wassily played his harmonium, Ella knew she had made the right decision to buy the house. They could retreat here, ignore the world, gather a few others like themselves for music and late-night debates about art. Here, with its several rooms for sleeping and eating and working, they could live together for periods of repose and regeneration while they waited out the divorce. But how slow it was in coming! Month after month, the conversation circled, a rondo of words, repetitious and abrasive.

"How many times have we examined this matter, Ella?"

"You told me you were going to finalize it when you were in Moscow. And then you didn't. You have everything on your mind but me."

"Ella, Ella. I have already put rubles in the right hands. You do us no good with your nagging."

"I sometimes think you only care for me when you're here. In Russia, your thoughts fly in different directions."

"Nonsense. I love you in every country. Come here and kiss me. My little Ellchen must be more patient."

It was a theme and variations, over and over.

Tonight, Wassily sang the first quatrain, ending with Selmar's plaintive line: "I shall return, a happy man!" He played out the bar and nodded to Ella to begin:

> *Aber in dunkler Nacht ersteighst du Felsen,*
> *Schwebst in täuschender, dunkler Nacht auf Wassern!*
> *Teilt' ich nun mit dir die Gefahr zu sterben:*
> *Würd ich Glückliche weinen?*

> But in the depths of night you climb crags
> and float on the waters in the treacherous dark night!
> If I now shared with you the dangers of death
> would I, a happy woman, weep?

Ella's tune was low and solemn. Selma's lament made her tremble, and the *Aber* brought up a sickness in her breast. Her voice caught, and she almost thought she would have to stop lest she break into tears. She had to ask Wassy to begin her part again. The song was their own. They, too, were lovers parting.

Wassy had arranged to move into a new apartment alone in the fall. He was adamant that they maintain separate residences in Munich where people knew him and where they still could pay respects to Anja from time to time. But worse, his plans were to leave Germany altogether in October and travel again to Moscow for several months. He must supervise, he said, the traveling exhibit of the Neue Künstlervereinigung München, the new art organization he headed.

Ella finished the line without crying, but when he suggested they sing another song, she demurred. The soup needed stirring, she said, closing her songbook.

Trio au Table

Murnau
February, 1910

It was like hearing *War and Peace* read aloud. When Ella stepped out of the cold into the grey cellar room, she heard two voices above, each braiding French and Russian. Alexei Georgewitsch Jawlensky must have come to see them after all. What good luck. The bear was her greatest supporter, after Wassy, and her biggest inspiration. And it just so happened that she had a painting to show him right there in her arms. Wassily would approve it, but Alexei would love it.

She stomped on the stone floor to shake off the snow before she sat on the narrow bench to untie her boots.

"Gabriele? *Ist, dass sie?*" Wassily moved from Russian to German as though his Slavic tongue had always twisted itself around the German language, two yarns knit together, indivisible.

"Coming."

"I have been eating your nut kuchen," a deeper voice called down. "*C'est magnifique!*"

The moment she stepped into the cozy sitting room, the bear lifted her quite off her shoe-less feet.

"Wassily Wassilievich says you are leaving him behind. You are the painter, he says. You have become a master, the expressionist extraordinaire!"

"He's teasing you." Ella settled herself back on the floor.

"Impossible. He would never." Jawlensky took the painting from her hand into his large one. "Well, what have you here?"

"Will you want tea?" Wassily kissed her cheek. "Fanny has gone back to town to see to her mother. I am playing servant for the time." He tucked a small towel into his trousers and walked to the stove.

"My goodness. But yes, I will have tea. And cake, too, if Alexei Georgewitsch has left me any."

"A crumb or two." Wassily scooped out wet leaves onto a plate and rinsed the brown pot at the kitchen washstand.

"I've been painting in the cemetery with Olga Archádina." Ella breathed into her cold hands. "My fingers got so stiff, I kept dropping my brush. If you want to know why the paint is thin,—it's mixed with snow!" She rubbed her hands together and slid onto the bench at the table.

"Fantastic." Jawlensky held Ella's cardboard over his head, squinting and adjusting his head to catch the light from the kerosene lamp on the table. "I love it. A thousand marks for your picture!" He brought the painting close to his face.

Wassily laughed. "You've never earned a thousand marks in your life, you hussar."

"True. But I love this, nonetheless. Look at it, Wassily Wassilievich." Jawlensky carried the stiff board to the steaming samovar. "You see, this is what I mean. The bold expression of the leaning crosses, the brushwork on the wreath and snow—this is magnificent, a real *Synthés* of outer form and inner feeling. She has the essence, the extract of the scene. So expressive I could weep!"

Wassily set the teapot onto the table and put a hand on Ella's shoulder. "Ella has made a leap these last months. She copies my sketches to good effect."

"Wassily, I don't *copy*!"

"Fraulein, please consider. You live with a master. I, too, would copy from such a man." Alexei sat against the wall, his bulk squeezed against the table. "Your Herr Kandinsky has just been showing me his latest Improvisations. *Mein Gott*, as you say! Is the world ready for such things! Even the little landscapes—the summer one, the one with the locomotive, the blue mountain—my heart bursts to see them."

Ella removed Wassily's hand from her shoulder. He wasn't right. She didn't copy, ever. True, they sometimes stood on the same hill, looked at the same church steeple, felt the same light shift under their brushes. But copy? She hadn't been his student for years now. He should not have suggested it. Ella shifted in her seat to face Jawlensky. "And you, Alexei Georgewitsch. Synthesis has become your motto, I think."

"It should be everyone's. Your Wassily has converted me." Jawlensky took the last slice of nut kuchen onto his plate with his free hand; the other held fast to Ella's painting.

Ella nibbled at the walnuts fallen from his slice. Had he really eaten all the cake? Now that she had warmed up, she was hungry. And she did not copy. She was sure of that.

"Gabriele worries that she doesn't progress. But I tell her that her pictures are wonderful." Wassily returned to the kitchen and cut an apple on a wooden board.

A paw patted Ella's. "But so much art remains in this little hand." Jawlensky smiled beneath his mustache. "Now tell me, how goes the glasswork?"

Here Ella really could take the lead. She had been the first to try the new technique. "We've made dozens. And we've even been teaching Fanny when she has a moment after the washing up. Wassily thinks she has good color sense. A little primitive, but a steady hand."

Jawlensky stroked his beard and smiled.

Ella grew animated and rose in her seat. "Look there, behind you—you see? Wassily's St. Georges are the very best." She pointed toward a row of small glass paintings arranged on the ledge. It *was* a pleasure to show off Wassily's work. She paused a moment to allow Alexei to take in the wonder of the colorful saints astride their rearing horses, heroes poised above threatening dragons, lances aloft. Wassily's hinterglasmalerie seemed almost to deserve veneration, almost like icons. Ella sat again. "So, Alexei Georgewitsch, isn't Wassily looking splendid? A little fatter, I think, from all those Russian blinis, and quite wonderful. But the brute—he made me endure all of the holidays, even New Year's Eve, without him."

Wassily leaned against the table. "It was a lonely time for me, as well. There I sat in the ruins of my former life while progress toward the divorce proceeds but slowly. Ah, Alexei—the rubles one spends to grease the wheels! When you see me pulling at my hair, you will know why." He placed cut fruit on a saucer. "And then, I am trying to sell a property, and it goes badly."

"Well, my friend, you are returned to the bliss of Bavaria and your esteemed Fraulein, so you must regain your good cheer. Besides, you opened the Neue Künstlervereinigung München exhibit in Odessa, am I right? Tell me—do our countrymen appreciate the bold new art of Munich?"

Wassily poured Ella's tea. She watched him, curious. He *had* missed her.

"I took my mother and Anja Chimiakin, if you can imagine such a grouping." Wassily sat and cupped his hands around the teapot. "But the exhibit was a gorgeous spectacle. Men and women wrapped in furs, sleighs night and day, the rooms lit end to end. We are a sensation in Odessa, I assure you, much appreciated." He glanced at Ella. "Unlike these blockhead Germans at the Munich Secession, the Russians understand the life of the spirit."

"Wassily, you are too harsh. Besides, the Secession rejected me, too." Ella folded her hands in her lap.

"But, Fraulein Münter, he has something here. We Russians have been raised to see beyond the material life of Europe. We have this in our hearts." Jawlensky thumped his chest and then turned back to Wassily. "But in Munich we were admired this fall, so you must not despair. You were right, Wassily Wassilievich, to write our manifesto. With it, we will change the world." He rose from his chair holding Ella's painting above his head like a banner and strode up and down the small room pacing to an inner military march. "This is beautiful—a new level of spirituality, outer and inner worlds in harmony."

"Alexei, Wassily and I painted side by side all fall after we saw you," Ella said, calling after him. She would have to correct Wassily. She had *not* copied. "Sometimes you cannot tell which is his and which is mine."

"Well, I would not say so much." Wassily looked straight at Ella. "Why would you say that? My palette is brighter, Gabriele, you admit yourself. But the forms—I suppose—though my forms are more complex than yours."

Ella shook her head. Now what did he mean by that? Was she to conclude that he thought complex forms superior? But simplicity was what she was working for. Alexei Georgewitsch understood that she wanted the essentials of the scene, not its complexity. It was a question of philosophy, of aesthetic principle. It wasn't fair for Wassily to suggest she was wanting in depth. It was he who had taught her to extract the core, its most immediate force. "Wassily," she began. But then she could not think how to say what she felt, could not use the word *belittled*. She crossed her ankles under the table and held her elbows in her palms.

Jawlensky, panting, resumed his seat at the table. "My countryman, you are brilliant and you lead the way. But Fraulein Münter— ah, she too is magnificent. These shapes speak of the objects, but they do not reproduce them." He held the canvas before Wassily's face.

Wassily turned in his seat and crossed his legs. "I have been teaching Gabriele the voices of colors. That is where her spirit excels."

Ella toyed with her cup, tracing circles with her index finger on its china rim. She would have liked to discuss the picture, herself, but Wassy did it so much better. He disassembled and named what she had not even realized was there. And yet, he need not have taken credit for her color sense. She had always been good that way, even before they met. Some nights as she teetered on the cliff above sleep, colors vied for preeminence in her mind, a certain rich red bumping against a marine blue, two shapes yielding and molding like amoebae seen under a microscope. She'd watch the colors tussle, expanding and shrinking, moving forward, retreating. She'd fall asleep her head abuzz with color.

"Alexei, we have not visited you and Marianne in ever so long." Ella fixed Jawlensky with her eyes. "Not since we hung the exhibition at the Galerie Thannhauser. What work are you doing now?" She poured more tea for herself. She picked at the crumbs on the cake plate.

"Ah, my work. Well, I am still in love with the French. I will always be in love with the French, I think. But since the fall, I have taken on a new mistress." His eyes twinkled. "No, not another woman. I have already too many women. But another love—Monsieur Gauguin."

"The man has been dead over five years, Alexei Georgewitsch," Wassily said.

"All the easier to love him. He will never desert me."

Ella smiled. "Did we tell you we saw Matisse when we were in Paris? Or at least some of his work—not the man, himself. Wassily admired it very much."

"I did, indeed. If he were nearer, Alexei, he would be a friend, I think. He thinks freely, as we do."

"And the Spaniard, too—Picasso. We saw his work, too. But I'm not sure Wassily liked it so much." Ella looked up for confirmation.

"His imagination is boundless, I understand." Alexei Georgewitsch folded his arms across his round belly. "They say everything he attempts has a new look. Did you think that, too, my friend?"

"I do not remember. I may have done. I cannot recall." Wassily rose from the table and brushed crumbs from the tabletop into his open palm. "Perhaps."

"What is it you love about Gauguin, Alexei Georgewitsch?" Ella watched Wassily leave the room. He would never have forgotten Picasso. He was quite struck at the time, and besides, he never forgot anything he saw. And it was uncharacteristic of him to take the domestic role, making tea and cleaning up. Was he slipping again into one of his moods?

Alexei, though, was cheerful, ready to smile and appreciate everything. "Those things Matisse does with flat planes of color—do they seem similar to yours, Fraulein? I would see them again, if I could. Ah, there is so much to understand and to express. So much, so much. But we will discuss this later." Jawlensky slapped his palms on the table. "I must go. I must catch the evening train back to Munich." He began putting on his coat and wrapping a scarf around his thick neck.

"You will give our kind regards to Marianne?"

"Of course."

"Why didn't she come with you? She might have gone snow painting with me and Olga Archádina."

"The boy. His throat again. She stayed to assist the nurse."

"Ah, yes. Well, they say a mother's first love is her child."

"Gabriele..." Wassily's voice was a warning.

Ella looked up, puzzled.

"Wassily Wassilievich wishes to remind you that Marianne is not the mother of Andreas. He need not have mentioned it. She loves him like a mother."

"Marianne is not the mother of Andreas!"

"This is a story I have neither the time nor the strength of character to reveal to you. I leave it to my countryman, here, to provide the glorious and ignominious details."

"I beg your pardon, Alexei Georgewitsch." She flushed. "And I say again that we must see you and Marianne again. Now that we have this house, we must have guests. Come in the summer, and bring Andreas." Her faux pas troubled her so, she barely heard Alexei taking his leave.

"I will talk to Marianne. Fraulein Münter, your house here will be a paradise for Russians!" He took Ella's hand and kissed it. With a wave to Wassily, the great bear trundled down the stairs to the boot room. In his absence, the small room contracted and the air thinned.

"Wassily, do you agree with Alexei about this thing he calls *synthesis*?" Ella stood in the kitchen doorway, a stack of saucers in her hands. It helped, sometimes, if she asked Wassily for an opinion. Expressing his thoughts often lifted his mood as though his emotions had to find words—and sometimes paint—to be realized.

"Alexei is a naïf, and I love him for it. But his attempt at identifying a system for painting is simplistic." Wassily moved to his desk and began trimming a pen. "He is a wonderful painter, but as a theorist— well, he should leave the thinking to me." He opened a bottle of black ink and took a fresh sheet of paper. "In some ways as a painter, Alexei is by far the most advanced of our set. But he is like you, Gabriele— intuitive, *incapable* of theory or constructing principle."

Her hands in the wash basin, Ella stiffened. *Incapable*? Months of comradeship lined up like apprentices found wanting. What happened to their partnership? And now Wassily was in the other room, writing an essay, doing what men do while she tended to the cups. "Well, I like Alexei Georgewitsch very much." Her mouth and jaw were tight. "And I must say, he appreciates my work more than you do. He actually *looks* at it."

"Gabriele, my Ellchen, where does this talk come from? You know I see everything you do. No one could be kinder to you than I am."

"Oh, you! You write and paint, but you don't even know what I think." Once she'd spoken them, her words convinced her.

"This is not healthy talk, Ellchen. It should not be." He bent over his paper and began to write.

Ella rinsed the plates, water from the shallow basin sloshing over onto her skirt. There was something else. "And if Andreas is not his son, who *is* the boy?"

"Andreas is the son of Jawlensky. But Baroness Marianne von Werefkin is not the boy's mother." He did not look up from his paper.

"You might have told me that! You said they were a family."

Ella emptied the washing water into a pail in the corner of the room and dried her hands on her apron. She pared four red potatoes and set them to boil as her mother had always done. Her mother would have sniffed at Jawlensky and von Werfkin. But how different were they from her? She sliced onions, her eyes on her hands, the knife. She watched her fingers as they worked. Perhaps Marianne was like herself, an impermanent accoutrement to a great man. She and the other women who circled Russian painters had become citizens of a country unto themselves. But what were its laws or freedoms?

"Who is the boy's mother?" She tried to sound disinterested, merely curious. When he did not answer, she raised her voice. "Who, Wassily. Who is the child's mother?"

Wassily continued to write. Ella slipped the onion circles into a heavy pan with thick strips of bacon. His silence smothered her clatter, the pouring water, the scraping and slicing, the spit of fat, silence channeled through the megaphone of his refusal.

"Wassily, you don't answer my question."

"Gabriele, I am writing, now. Will a meal be ready in half an hour, do you think? Perhaps we can discuss these matters as we eat. Will six o'clock do, then?"

His response hissed in the air like thunder in a snowstorm. With her back to him, Ella could not see that the pen trembled in his hand. She was so far away.

Boating: Quartet plus Dog

Murnau
July, 1910

Ella could see from the beginning it was not a good day for an outing. Marianne had brought only her red silk hat, and if there was rain, the hat would be ruined. And she would not leave the hat behind, protesting that the wind would darken her skin. Andreas had brought his black dog, and the animal, sensing both atmospheric pressure and human tension, was restless and jumpy.

And then there was the matter of the boat on the Staffelsee. Wassily climbed aboard without examining the number of seats along the cross thwarts compared to the number of their group and stood obstinately while the others shuffled for position, as though probity demanded that enough seats materialize for any excursion to which he was party. But there wasn't room for everyone. Alexei Georgewitsch behaved gallantly, though, insisting that the others get in the rowboat while he waited for them on the shore. He would stay with Hunter, he said, who would not like the rolling of the craft on the water. The dog might even get sick, he said. Besides, the boat was too small and he was too large, he protested, when Ella and even Marianne offered to stay behind. "*Mais non.*" He bowed and waved his straw hat. "I will take a picture of your nautical adventure with Fraulein Münter's camera. That will be my excitement for the day. And when the picture is ready, we will all enjoy to look at it." He, at least, was always generous that way, joyous for others. And so the boy and Marianne took seats on the center cross thwart with Wassily in the bow, leaving Ella, the smallest of the adults and least able rower, by the oarlocks. And in the end, Hunter jumped aboard, and no one could lure the dog back to Alexei Georgewitsch on the shore.

Furthermore, Andreas said he did not like to be in the boat without his father, and he did not regard Marianne as a suitable substitute for a parent. No sooner did the boat scrape off the mucky bottom, forced with a jerk into the deeper water by Alexei's strong push, but the child rose from his seat and tried to climb back ashore to his father, both rocking the boat and terrifying Marianne who only managed at the last minute to grab hold of his blue jumper and pull him back.

The little farmhouse on the opposite shore was the designated object of exploration, and the passage should have been short across that narrow tongue of lake, but they made slow progress. Gabriele was not an adequate oarsman, Wassily accused. She pulled too hard with her right oar and sent the boat at a diagonal to the shore. She dipped her oars too deeply and sent showers of water into the boat, wetting their clothes and Marianne's red hat and startling Andreas who sat with wide eyes and narrow shoulders, refusing to touch Marianne's hand or accept her comforting assurances. As the water grew black and the sky yellow under a dark cloud, tempers thinned like whispers.

"You should have allowed me to row," Wassily complained.

"You should have taken the rower's position when we entered the boat," Ella retorted. "You should have thought ahead. You should have thought of others. And now it's too late." When would they be there, Andreas asked, and would it be soon. And could she be more careful with the oars, Marianne said. Her hat would be ruined. And could Andreas please stop his dog from whining and drooling on her dress. Agitated, Wassily got up from his seat on the bow cross-thwart to take command, only upsetting the skiff's delicate balance further, worrying everyone.

"Sit down, Wassily," Ella said. "You're rocking the boat."

"I am looking out for rocks and snags. You must not row us into trouble."

"You are the one who is causing the trouble." She was warm with the exertion of rowing. "You are making things worse." Ella, too, was in a good hat, blue with a black band, and a heavy blouse.

The outing had originally been planned as a stroll down the long tree-lined Kottmüllerallee behind the house toward Oberammergau, a cool, leafy path protected from sun and wind. But then without consulting the others, Wassily engaged a wagon to take them all to the lake, insisting that his idea was more grand and therefore more worthy than the idea of a mere walk which they could do any time.

When they reached the opposite shore, they all disembarked and walked quickly up the meadow to the farmhouse, only to discover it empty and abandoned. The clouds dropped even more heavily above them, and without speaking, they reentered the boat, Wassily assuming the rowing position now, and quickly returned to Alexei Georgewitsch. With his huge hands, Alexei grabbed hold of the rope on the bow and pulled the boat ashore, but seeing him, Hunter jumped over the gunwale into the reedy water and got thoroughly wet and muddy. When they climbed out, the dog greeted them with a dirty shower as he shook himself dry. What's more, the wagon driver, expecting the boating excursion to last much longer, had taken himself off, so the party had to assemble under a tree, taking what little shelter from the wind that it offered, worried that the rain would come down in earnest. For the most part, they were silent, waiting for the wagon to return. Andreas, when he spoke at all, addressed his dog.

And when, later, Ella discovered the photograph that Alexei Georgewitsch had taken just as they reached the middle of the lake, she laughed. And she painted a picture of the day as she recalled it and as she felt it was. Wassily she represented standing in the bow, dominant, imposing, unyielding, the leader facing the viewer and herself with judgment in his heart. Marianne and Andreas she made look frightened and unhappy, their eyes round and impersonal. Herself, the rower, she painted from behind, a woman at work with no face at all. And when the painting was completed and Wassily looked at it, he was offended. "As a painting," he said, "of course it is excellent. But I do wonder what you were thinking to present me as such a ridiculous figure." But Ella could neither laugh nor protest. To herself she had captured the essence of the scene, tense and discordant. The grouping only appeared to be a family, but not one of them was related to another. Wassily was in command, and she was rowing where he directed. But it was nowhere. She was rowing nowhere.

Trout Quintet

Murnau
Late August, 1911

The early sun had just begun harvesting gold from the wheat fields, fattening itself with cereal hues, when Wassily cycled to the village to buy milk. An hour later, packing cool bottles in the cellar bins of straw, he called to Ella on the floor above.

"Has Fanny left for market yet?"

"What did you say?"

"Fanny," he said, leaping up the stairs into her studio. "Has she gone?"

"Well, look for yourself. Can't you see I am working?"

"The Marcs are coming. They'll be here for dinner."

"Today? Tonight?"

"I just met Franz in the village. We've arranged it."

"You should not have invited them without consulting me. I cannot change my evening plan because you have met a man in the village." Particularly that man, she did not add.

"What evening plan did you have?"

"That's not the point. The point is that you didn't consult me."

"Ella, be reasonable. Marc and I are onto something very exciting. I would have thought you'd be pleased at our progress."

"I'm only saying that you should not expect me to stop what I am doing. You know I have a September deadline. You think the Thannhauser Gallery will wait while I entertain your friends?"

"The Marcs are your friends, too, Ella. We'll all be part of this together."

"Oh?" Why would he say that? Just because they sometimes came for dinner?

"Think, Gabriele. *Der Blaue Reiter* almanac will speak to the whole world."

"China? India? Move, Wassily, you're in my light. I'm trying to look out the window."

"Why are you being so difficult? I am saying that we can be a group now. *Der Blaue Reiter* stands for the future—art, music, theater, philosophy."

"It's too ambitious."

"No, not at all. The old barriers are gone. Don't you see that, too?"

"Fine. Fine. What do you want from me?" She put down her brush.

"I simply want to tell you that Franz and Maria Marc are coming here this afternoon, and we will eat something together. My God, Ella, things should not be so difficult."

"And I suppose you want me to entertain Maria Marc."

"And why not?"

"Because she is not one of your Blue Riders, and you know it. You and Marc have gone your own way in that. You expect me to stay with her. How can I be part of it if I am entertaining Frau Marc?"

"If you and she want a role in *der Blaue Reiter*, you both may have one."

"So Maria Marc and I are in the same category, then." Ella folded her arms across her chest.

"I did not say that. Frau Marc is not an artist, I realize, but she might have a role to play, nonetheless."

"Like preparing her marvelous coffee, for instance."

"I would be glad to have her coffee, if you must know. But I am not suggesting that her role would be your role. Perhaps you will submit a woodcut. Or you might like to edit the almanac."

"Edit? That is what you see for me? Editing? Why would I do that? And what about a painting?" She craned her neck to look once more out the window.

"I cannot say now what the almanac will hold. That is the discussion we are about to have. Look, Gabriele, you can do whatever you like. I only ask that you not be disagreeable. As you are right now."

"You are not making it clear what you want from me."

"Ella, can you not just prepare yourself to sit with us and talk? You may play any role you like in the almanac. Or no role at all. For today, I am only asking you to be pleasant and cooperative and to take part in this discussion which is important to me."

"And sit with Frau Maria Marc as well and talk about our households."

"No, and *be* with everyone, sociable with everyone, with Franz Marc and me and Maria Marc—and Fanny, too, goddamn it, if she wants. Just sit at the table and talk. That is what I am asking. I cannot say before the talk has happened what role you or I or Marc or the man in the moon will have in *der Blaue Reiter*, for God's sake."

"Fine. Fine. I will speak to Fanny about the shopping. But you really should not be planning parties without consulting me." She capped her tube of vermillion, then cerise.

"Parties? Ella, two people do not constitute a party."

"I beg your pardon. I thought four people at the table made a party. Five, if Fanny joins us." She capped an umber.

"Oh, for Heaven's sake. Yes. Fine. I am sorry I brought the world to your door. Go up and talk to Fanny, and may the markets have enough food for the multitudes who will appear before us. Honestly, Ella, you wear me down."

In truth, Ella never felt as at ease with the Marcs, as she did with Jawlensky and even Marianne. Despite the fact that Marc had actually purchased one of her snow paintings, in his presence she felt inept, incompetent, superficial. He once praised Wassily for his *spiritualized and dematerialized inwardness of feeling*, but afterwards when Ella looked at her own paintings of roads and barns, villages and flowers, she could not see in her work the spiritualized element Marc admired in Wassily. Why, then, had he purchased her *Village Street in Snow*? The painting as she remembered it was quite figurative with buildings and a street. She tried to identify its spirituality, but she could not. Marc was so odd, his language so...she didn't know what. When she listened to Marc theorizing on a "Utopian art world devoid of materialism," she felt small, and along with his lofty voice she heard Emmy's long-ago question: "Is there something wrong with Ella?" She could not look Marc in the eye for fear he would discover her to be wanting. And yet he came to dinner.

What Fanny had brought home from the market was spotted trout, five of them. Potatoes. Asparagus. Onions. Peaches. Cream. She had bread baked yesterday. Jam from last summer. Tea.

Marc was kind enough, praising the tender asparagus and the trout. These Fanny had cooked in butter until they were brown and crisp, and she had poured the brown pan juices over the fish when she served them. The aroma was lovely, and Fanny sat with the group at the table as she felt free to do after so many years of housekeeping for Wassily. With no home of her own to repair to as she followed the restless couple from Munich to Murnau and back again, Fanny seemed like a distant relative come to stay.

"Delicious." Marc nodded to Fanny, clucking under his breath. He bent over the table and used his knife to push the delicate white trout flesh from its slender bones, his elbows jutting from his sides like bony gills.

"With all your interest in painting animals, I don't suppose you've tried to paint a fish." For Wassily's sake, Ella would throw out the opening gambit. Others could move the pieces.

"Why not?" Marc paused, his eyebrows raised, his fork in the air.

"I know you want to express the spirit of animals. But fish—well, one hardly sees them. Unless, of course, the fish is on one's plate. A still life of trout?" She was trying, wasn't she, getting the guest into the game?

Maria Marc laughed. "Franz loves to go fishing, but I have never caught a single one! Isn't that so?" She turned toward her husband, but he was looking at Ella and frowning.

"Fraulein Münter, as you know, it is not necessary or even desirable to fix a precise image of the animal," he said, soberly. "One need not see the creature so much as perceive its essence—its swiftness or strength or wiliness."

"And our favorite, the horse," Wassily said. "Endurance? Speed?"

"Nobility, I should say. The horse must be our symbol, don't you think, Herr Kandinsky? St. George upon his horse as he fights the dragon of evil." He paused. "The dragon of evil," he repeated, his voice tremulous. "Do you agree? The blue horse, as we were saying? Can we agree on the blue horse?"

"The blue horse and the blue rider." Wassily held his fork just as Marc did, suspended. "They represent us quite well."

"Oh? You mean you've decided that already?" The two of them, Ella thought. Where would she fit in? Could she work with Franz Marc? "When was that?" But she could not catch Wassily's eye.

"Herr Marc," Fanny said. "I'm not so fond of horses. I've had a run-in or two I shouldn't care to repeat. But if I did paint a horse, I'd make it grey or brown or black. You say blue, though. Nobody has ever seen a blue horse, have they?"

Marc had sliced a peach in half and was struggling to dig out its crenellated pit, his thin fingers fumbley on his knife. "Maria," he said. "Tell Fraulein Dengler about blue."

"Oh, no." Frau Marc smiled with her eyes, her voice sweet and caramely, a second violin in its middle register. "I wouldn't presume. Here, let me cut your peaches. You tell the Fraulein about your blue horses." She took the peach from her husband and removed the pit with her spoon.

"Now, Fraulein Dengler." Marc rested his elbows on the table and leaned in to the housekeeper. "Have you never admired the fluid grace of a colt, one who has mastered its legs and finds that it can nearly fly?"

"Well, I grew up cleaning out the stalls, you see. I had to shoo them away from where I needed to get." Fanny pronged a small potato and ate it whole.

"A horse in nature is never blue, of course. Ah, yes. Yes, but if we want to capture its spirited movement, we can do better than reproduce its external aspect." He looked away from Fanny to address the whole table, and he stretched out his arms high above them, one hand clutching a peach half, the other a napkin. "Colors give us feelings." He pulled in his arms and turned to Wassily. "I was just writing this to Macke a few days ago," he said. His voice dropped nearly to a whisper. "Blue is spiritual and male. Yellow is the female principle, don't you agree, Herr Kandinsky? Yellow and blue complete each other, like man and woman, the marriage of hues and the complement of spirits." He ate his fruit noisily. When he had finished, his wife wiped his chin.

"Yes, definitely." Wassily nodded. He appeared not to notice Marc's dramatics. "The white yellows might rise to a higher spirituality, but not the darker ones. These are the female ones, grounded, like the earth. But one uses such a yellow sparingly. Too much yellow grates and irritates."

Ella rolled her eyes. She picked up the empty pitcher of cider and rose from the table. It irked her that Franz Marc addressed himself to Wassily. And that Wassily should reply to him so directly, almost exclusively. Was she not a part of the discussion? And Maria Marc with her fishes and peaches. Hausfrau.

"So your assumption is that women are creatures of the soil?" Ella returned to the table with a fresh pitcher and sat heavily in her chair.

"It's the men I've known who've been the dirty ones of the lot," Fanny said. "That's a certainty. But I suppose you have your reasons." She rose and began clearing the plates and glasses as though she had given up discussing such foolish matters. Women, she seem to say with a grunt as she left the table, have better things to do. Ella watched her tug at her dress as she left the room, a stack of plates braced on one hip. Fanny was plain, uncomplicated, unflappable. She had no more use for artist talk than the man in the moon. But then, she had nothing to prove. Lucky in that way.

"Well, in a way, yes," Wassily said, "women *are* a kind of soil, I think. Clearly all infants are rooted in their mothers. This is a wonderful thing, a woman's life's purpose."

"*If* having children is a woman's life purpose. But that's not every woman." Ella tapped her spoon in her palm.

"The nature of men, though, is to grow beyond, to seek a higher plane." He turned toward Marc.

"Exactly."

Wassily pushed back in his chair and took out a cigarette. "So to continue, freeing art from its bonds is our mission. *Der Blaue Reiter* will be our statement, we agree. But also it must lead the way and demonstrate our principles."

"We will include the best men of our time." Marc licked his fingers. He wiped his hands on his napkin. "All of the arts. Poets. Composers. The French, too, Matisse, Picasso. The best men."

"Men?" Ella said.

"Herr Marc, you think by invitation only, correct?" Wassily took over. "Only those whose vision is along our lines. Idealists. Revolutionaries, if necessary. Yes, of course, the French. You will recall that Picasso is a Spaniard. But him as well. We will leave the Academy and its stifling principles behind." He flicked ash into his hand. "What I have in mind—excuse me, what I think we both agree, is that the new thinking of our generation should tie us, should reveal our ties, to the ancients. These will be the ideas of the future."

"Your thought, then, is that the almanac will be a collection of essays about art? Not pictures?" Ella folded her napkin in half, then quarters, then eighths.

"Macke will write a piece for us," Marc said. "He is one of us."

"*Us,*" Ella repeated. She unfolded her napkin and began again, her fingers agitated on the cloth. Half. Quarters. Eighths. And again.

"Good. We want him, then. And Schoenberg, too. You've heard his second string quartet? He is like us—breaking free of the old stories. So from him, a piece of music, perhaps. Or else an essay on music."

"Not a painting? Should we ask him for that, too?" Marc sat back in his chair and crossed his legs.

And again. Half. Quarters. Eighths. Ella folded quickly, slapping the cloth on the table.

"When we exhibit, Schoenberg will give a painting, certainly. But we'll see. First the almanac, then the exhibition."

"And will his painting then be blue?" Ella shook loose her napkin. "And is his music blue? Perhaps his music paper is also blue, and his ink. I suppose you may want a yellow painting from me? Or perhaps Frau Marc and I shall simply wear yellow dresses."

For a moment, no one spoke.

"Ella, will you see if Fanny is preparing tea." Wassily frowned. "Herr Marc and I will take our tea outdoors, if that can be arranged. You ladies may prefer to stay here. The insects are sometimes bad at this hour." He stood up from the table and gestured that Marc should follow him. Maria Marc planted her eyes on her plate. Ella sat beside her in a silence that expanded into blackness.

Galerie

"Listening (Portrait of Jawlensky)," 1909
Gabriele Münter
Oil on cardboard
$19^1/2'' \times 26''$
Städtische Galerie im Lenbachhaus, Munich
Gabriele Münter Bequest

Rather than a portrait in any conventional sense, this piece is more the expression of an idea.

The setting is a social one. A figure sits at an eating table lit by a large lamp. Foremost by virtue of size and centrality, a white lampshade dominates the composition. Beneath the bright shade, a red rectangle hangs, suggesting light emanating from the lamp or perhaps an ornamentation of the lamp. The central human figure is, in fact, not central at all but rather placed in the far right quarter of the painting, leaning precipitously as though to catch every syllable of the unseen speaker just off the edge of the painting. The angle of the listener's head as he leans and of his body, curved dramatically to suggest attentiveness, communicates total engagement. Balancing the sweep of the listener's pose, a large plate in the bottom left of the painting holds two long items, sausages, perhaps, or cigars. So from the bottom left corner, the lines of the painting point diagonally upward to focus on the arched eyebrows and wide round eyes of the listener in the opposite corner.

The painting is flat, both in composition and brushstrokes. The table edge functions as a horizontal bar behind which the figure sits outlined by a completely black background. Neither lamp nor figure has depth or proportion. The figure's round head and simplified features provide more a caricature than a depiction of a real person, more comedy than individual personality. What is clear is that the figure is fully engrossed in the act of listening and that all other elements in the painting support the meaning of his act.

J. Eichner

Chapter Six

Sweets and Sours

Munich
April, 1912

Elysestrasse 16
Cologne

March 21, 1912

Dear Fraulein Münter,

Please to excuse me for address you by the name I called you when we were girls. I presume you are now Frau Kandinsky, but I fear old habits of thought must remain. In 5 years many things must have changed. My husband Jakob says to recall to you when we all painted together and then we thought that the future of art would be our future.

We live now in Cologne where my husband is a doctor. We are happy here, with our son Wolfgang, almost 6 years old, and our daughter Silke, who just became 4 years old.

I am writing you because we are this afternoon returned from an exhibit of *Der Blaue Reiter* painters at the Gereon Club in Cologne. We were excited to see four or five paintings by Fraulein Gabriele Münter! I must congratulate you on your success! We liked to see, as well, the pictures of Professor K, although some of them are a little difficult as it is hard to see the picture. But Jakob admired especially your painting of the Russian Tablecloth, but then I enjoyed to see all of them, and I hope this letter reaches you.

As it happens, my husband and I are planning a visit to Munich on 1 and 2 April, as he will attend a medical meeting there. I would enjoy to meet you for coffee and to catch up on all the life details. I will go to Dallmayr's at 4:00 in the afternoon of 19 April and hope that you can join me. It would be so nice to see you once again!

Your good, old friend,

Olga Stanukovich Doncker

Ella kept the letter in her drawer for nearly a week before she replied. How could she possibly correct her old classmate on the issue of her name? Eventually, she dashed off a quick note accepting the invitation to coffee, signing simply "Gabriele," an informality she deplored. Perhaps the Russian would not attribute to it the degree of intimacy the Christian name would have signaled to a German, still for some days after, Ella squirmed inwardly, berating herself for her cowardice in failing to clarify her situation. But she could not explain it to herself.

Her hands clasping each other inside her muff, Ella waited just inside the door at Dallmayr's. She had arrived early enough to browse through the shop's polished cases—ham on toast topped with egg and pepper, commas of shrimp covered with clear jelly, oysters shivering on ice, veal shanks like horns of plenty in a mushroom gravy— and the trays of golden pastries topped with custards, jams, and crystallized sugars. She had bought Wassy a quarter-kilo of Dallmayr's good coffee and a bag of the fruit chocolates he liked especially. It was to be a peace offering, one sorely needed.

Outdoors in a light sleet, the street was the color of stone. She pictured the shades of the day washed out of the air, pooling sadly in the cobbled streets, rivulets of mud catching in the crevices. Were she to try to paint the atmosphere itself, she'd need grey and white and nothing else. The drear suited her mood. She had very nearly skipped the meeting. She had work to do. She had not felt well. And where *was* Olga? Wasn't she late? Likely she would never come. Why should she? Ella had rarely returned her letters, had just as rarely read the ones addressed to her. The well of her affection was dry. She was no good.

Then there she was—Olga, Frau Doncker now, beaming and effusive, a broad fur collar framing her broad red face. Emerging from a nimbus of lavender scent, the matron embraced Ella and kissed her cheeks, right and left. She took Ella's elbow and steered her inside the coffee room to the visible dismay of the waiter whose authority she had preempted. "Let's have coffee *and* chocolate and a slice of cake each," she whispered across the table as they sat. "What a fine thing to see you again! You are as young as I remember."

With Olga, the distance of years was irrelevant; standing on ceremony was forbidden and good riddance to it. Once she had declared herself your friend, she remained your friend. Suddenly Ella realized how much she had missed Olga, her open generosity, her steadfastness, her simple acceptance. With such a friend, she might find solace for the growing anxiety and distress nettling her. Pieces of herself she'd left scattered about seemed to collect in her, damming up holes and patching cracks. Why had she let this friendship slip? She knew the answer, of course. She had changed her social set. The companions of her life now were artists who exhibited, argued, theorized, experimented, artists people talked about, artists whose paintings people bought. Their companions were competitors, artists vying for gallery space, patrons, collectors, museum approvals. She and Wassily and their friends dickered over gallery percentages, agonized about what to charge, fearful of rejection, stubborn lest their work be devalued. Ella had thought she'd moved up in the world, become sophisticated, found her true self. But Olga came from a time of simplicity and freedom. In their student days art was a gymnasium in which they sported for the exercise of their growing understanding. But after the games, the other students made different lives for themselves, normal lives. They all did—Olga and Schneider and Kleuver. Probably Palme as well, though he was among the gifted ones. Olga and the others were all amateurs. In some way, Ella envied them.

Seated on a cushioned chair, Ella looked around. How pleasant this room, how inviting and richly furnished. How attractive the other diners in their furs and fashionable hats. How fragrant the coffee and sweets. Her shoulders loosened, and the din inside her head gave way to the arpeggios of the harpist just beyond the case of cakes and tortes. Wasn't it enough to eat and drink and laugh? Must one be forever striving and straining? Did one need always to be creating, finding life's meaning, again and again?

She smoothed her skirt. "Olga, do you remember the time we tried to embroider shirtwaists?" Could she once have been like other women?

"Mine was as lumpy as bad gravy!" Olga laughed, throwing open the folded napkin at her place. "And so my embroidery goes into the fire!"

It was so easy for Olga. She cast away her effort as though she were discarding old newspapers. *She* was not nailed to a singular ambition that required her to invent herself over and over.

"I wish I could show you my two beautiful children. Such joy they give me. And such trouble! But I love all their tricks and little ways." She stopped to order apple tart with cream, assuring Ella that the treat was hers. "This talk of children must be to bore you. Children are not of interest to the talented Miss Münter, I fear. But for me, it is the life itself." She leaned forward and smiled. "And you. You must tell me your news."

Ella swallowed. Must it be one or the other, family *or* art? Painting *or* children? And was she so unwomanly that her friend, her *friend* assumed she would not want children? What to say? "I suppose the latest is that a very fine gallery in Berlin is showing *der Blaue Reiter* exhibition now. Herwarth Walden is the owner, very avant-garde in his taste and very important, too. Wassily and I are quite pleased."

"*Wassily*. This is so sweet that you say his name. I remember being so frightened of the great Professor K. Ah, our youth was a treasure! And now we are no longer young, and I have my Wolfgang and Silke to care for."

"And your husband."

"Ah, Jakob. Well, he is up before the light and then all day with patients. He is most important to the committee meetings and the club of doctors."

"You must get lonely."

"Yes, of course. But also no. I must do the shopping and supervise the housekeeping. And so many hours with the children's lessons. I am quite exhausted!" Olga put down her fork. "But I think I disappoint you."

"Quite the contrary. I envy you."

"For me, the art is over. But you must smile for me." Olga reached across the table and patted Ella's hand. There was the children's school and sports and music lessons; her house and garden, the friends who visited, the concerts they attended. While Frau Doncker spoke about her happiness and her orderly life, Ella began to dread the moment when the conversation must inevitably turn again to her. When it did, it took her by surprise.

"And so my mother brings to me so many newspapers from Moscow." Frau Doncker signaled the waiter and held up the empty cream pitcher. "Mama returns home to see her sisters, and when she arrives back to Cologne, I must read for one week to catch up all of the events. Some of the politics—so distressing. The Tsar and the Kaiser quarreling. You must know about that as well. And, oh my goodness, just this week—the terrible big boat." She leaned forward, pink elbows on the table.

"Boat?"

"What is it—gigantic? No, no. The *Titanic*. Such a tragedy."

"The what?"

"The English boat. She sinks. You have not read?"

Ella stirred her coffee and took a sip. "I've never been much of a paper reader."

"No matter. Then comes the good news from Moscow—Professor K is granted a divorce. Every paper reports it. In Moscow he is the célèbre!" Olga's eyes became crescents with glee.

Ella felt the blood rush to her cheeks. That his divorce had become final she knew, of course. But announced in the Moscow papers for all to see? She plunged her fork in her pastry. The news would churn up even more public speculation about her. So he married his mistress at last, the tongues must be saying. Ella groaned inwardly.

The irony was—now that he could, Wassily was taking no steps to marry. He was conflicted and disheartened, he said. The tension between them would need to be resolved, he said.

"What tension?" Ella had demanded.

"You know what I mean. In any event, I wish to go on as we are for the time. The legal institution should have no authority over our freedom to live as we like. We hurt no one."

But, of course, there *had* been rows and silences, for how could it be otherwise? Any couple fought from time to time, Ella reasoned. Even Olga and her Jakob must sometimes disagree. She and Wassily would find their peace, their pattern together. Marrying would speed up the course of harmony, she had told Wassily, but he had turned away. He had not acquiesced.

Ella put down her fork and folded her hands in her lap under the white tablecloth. Seeing Olga once more, she had thought she might reveal her life gradually, a tale of delay and decision-making, of philosophy and liberality, of artistic temperaments and misunderstandings and jealousies. She had hoped to invite support and female commiseration. But when Ella looked across the table at her happy friend, no words would come. There was no story she could tell to encompass all that had passed, no way to confess the remove between Wassily and herself, his sharp daytime words and his cold nighttime distance, her own sarcasm and bitterness and resentment. Their lives, instead of converging as they had once promised, seemed more now like the network of walking paths behind the house in Murnau. There, religious icons nestled in peasant-built grottos at the head of each crossroads as if in warning, as if to say, "Separate at your own risk; you might not meet again along the path." She'd gone a different way. Or he had. And it wasn't just their personal lives that had splintered. Even her sense of her own artistic merit had been compromised. Wassily had moved boldly toward full abstraction. In his work he had soared beyond her, a Daedalus, while she remained in the maze below.

"There is still some paperwork to do before we marry—nothing important," she said. "I am as I was, Gabriele Münter." She tried to smile. "My name means something now—I've been exhibited all over Europe." Skirting the truth, not facing it.

At Dallmayr's door, Olga described the route she would take back to her hotel, hopeful that she might arrive before her Jakob, a box of cakes in her hand. Take me, Ella thought. Take me with you. Teach me to be someone else, someone like you. But when the old friends kissed goodbye, Olga walked away alone. Ella hastened to the tram out to Schwabing, her hands cold in her muff, Wassily's coffee and sweets left behind on the cafe floor near her chair.

‡

"I met Olga Stanukovich for tea," she told Wassily. "You remember her?"

"Hmm," he said. "Russian. Fat." He was writing a letter.

Ella winced at his dismissal. No friend of hers could possibly please him. She raised her voice, the words clipped and brittle.

"You *would* say that. Well, she's married to Jakob Doncker, now. He's a doctor, and they have children. Of course I wouldn't bring her here. It would be too uncomfortable." Her eyes attacked him.

"What are you saying? You could surely have invited your friend back. I would never object. We have people here nearly every day." He put down his pen to light a fresh cigarette.

"Artists, yes. None of them my friends, of course. But respectable people, here? Never."

"Stop it, Gabriele. Don't be ridiculous." He looked up at her. "Alexei Georgewitsch adores you. And everyone we know is respectable."

"You don't believe me, but I tell you Marianne absolutely turned away from me at the concert. When you are not with me, these Russian friends of yours are no friend to me, I can tell you."

"I am quite certain that you mistook what happened. You deliberately misunderstand people. You deliberately provoke me." He returned to his writing.

"It's not just here in Munich. When we're in Murnau, the townspeople actually *mock* me, you know."

"I know nothing of the sort. We hardly even see the villagers, except in the shops."

"Exactly. We live in splendid isolation. At least I do. But do you know they call our yellow house the *Hurenhaus*? They mean me, of course, the *whore*."

"You are mistaken. The word they use is *Russenhaus*," he insisted. "It's understandable. Our Russian friends come often. I'm glad of that."

"And 'whorehouse,' too. Don't deny it. They also say that." She was shouting now. "You are responsible for that."

"Gabriele, you must compose yourself. You exaggerate. No one is calling you a whore. Is that what this outburst is about?" He put down his pen, sat back in his chair with a sigh, and drew on his cigarette. "I remind you. We have agreed that marriage is a mere formality. This is enlightened thinking. You understand that as well as I. Of course, if you absolutely insist, I will marry you. I leave the decision in your hands." He leaned forward and crushed his cigarette into a saucer.

"But you don't...you don't *want* to marry me."

"I have made it perfectly clear, Ella. I am in your hands."

"That is a cold thing to say. All that talk of love! You've used me for your purposes, and now you've made me a woman without a home."

"You try my patience with these charges. And as for the idea of love, I am certain that I love you more than you love me, if it comes to that." He lit another cigarette, drew deeply, and exhaled a long column. "But if you do not feel at home, it can only be the result of your attitude. I encourage you to reconsider it. Now you must excuse me. I am working. Come talk to me when you have regained your balance."

Still wearing her coat and boots, Ella went to her room, crawled into her bed, and rolled onto her side in a ball, pulling the covers over her head. She drew her furry muff up to her face and let her tears fall into it. She could not say who she had become or what darkness prowled about in her. She had met a setback she couldn't master by sheer will. Crazy with early love, she had written in her diary: "I yearn to be beloved in a cozy, domestic way. All I really want is to be the center of another's life and to make him the center of mine."

The years, the cities, the travels, the exhibits, the friends, the talk, the painting, the lovemaking—none of it had changed her in that way. All that had happened was that her heart grew heavier, her temper more raw, her speech less guarded, her pride more vulnerable to attack. When the days were worst, her head was full of damp, and it rained in her heart.

Why then did she not insist on the marriage? What demon ate up the request before it formed in her mouth?

Often now, she fell into spates of indolence and restless agitation, alternating between lassitude and reckless ill-conceived action. Bored, she sat at the table and opened letters, tossing their envelopes on the floor beside her chair. Herwarth Walden would accept her collection for his Berlin gallery but only conditionally. Hans Goltz would exhibit but demand 18% of each purchase price. Reinhard Piper required a second editing of Wassily's *Klänge*. Could she send the changes within a fortnight? It had been so kind of her to entertain Franz and Maria Marc the previous evening. The tomato soup had been particularly flavorful. Anja would call on her later in the day. The Munich landlord would be replacing a window on Thursday, next. She should be at home to receive him. The dressmaker had found a flaw in the fabric she had selected for a new white dress. Would she stop by and choose another? The letters, too, went on the floor.

Shortly after Olga's visit, Wassily returned alone to Russia to arrange an exhibition. Ella developed a cold and sore throat. No sooner had she recovered than she complained of toothache. Frustrated and impatient, she let a dentist remove the offending tooth, but afterwards, she felt disfigured, aged and ugly. In letter after letter to Wassily, she cried out that he should not have left her, that she should not have had the tooth removed, that she had acted impulsively, that she hated what she had done. He wrote back that she should be patient, that the gap in her mouth would close. Self-conscious, she turned down opportunities to join the Giselists at concerts and exhibitions, later complaining that his friends excluded her. She was a barnyard fowl pecking in the dust, plagued by mites, squawking, an irritant to all. She could not help herself. Her status of his not-wife was to blame. It worked away at her, a grinding drill on her spirit, an ache that worked through her nerves from her groin to her jaw.

Soon after Wassily returned, the Marcs and some others visited the Ainmillerstrasse flat. How had the exhibition gone? Marc, particularly, probed for details. Theirs was the art of the moment. Wassily was leading them all into the future. Ella gathered the group on the cold, grey terrace to take a photograph. Later, when she looked at the print, she saw it all—*she* was not present, not among them. *She* was on the outside, recording the gathering without participating in it, an adjunct in the drama and not a central character. Approaching middle age, she feared she had lost some critical concept of herself, had broken something she could not make whole again. Yet she could not compromise. *He* must initiate the marriage. *He* must want it.

Love, it seemed, was a mere glancing shaft of sun against a window pane, darkening to shadow, a ray of light but for the space of an hour.

There was, however, one action she could take.

The day after Olga's visit, Wassily left the flat after lunch.

"I'll see Nolde at his hotel," he said, bundling up his portfolio, sliding sketches and small studies into its folds. "He's brought *The Prophet* printed on some special Japanese paper."

"Is he here for long?"

"A month or so, he says."

"See if he'll show with *der Blaue Reiter*, then."

"Yes. I'll take him round with me to Alexei's. I'll be home late." He secured his scarf with a pin. He placed his hat just so and checked his profile in the mirror. "Will you be up when I get back?"

His question was a code. No matter the tension between them, from time to time, he made his way to her bed.

"If you like," she said.

When she heard the door latch, Ella went to her room and stood in the doorway, listening to his light step on the stairs to the street. From the top drawer of her bureau, she took out a small round case and sat on her bed cradling the box on on her lap. Wassily called it her "little lady's hat," though he saw it only once, the day she came home from Herr Doktor. She had been shy about showing it. From then on, when he was feeling loving, she excused herself and put it in. He rarely spoke about it, but on occasion he might rise up on his elbow in the bed and whisper softly in her ear, "Perhaps you would like to get your 'little lady's hat.' " If he noticed it afterwards, he never said.

Ella opened the case and took out its contents. He didn't have to know. It would be her secret. She would excuse herself as always, but when she returned, the hat could still be in its case. But then she had a better idea. She could tear it a little, just enough. She took a hairpin from her bureau drawer and punctured the device in the center. The hole gave her hope. When the day came that she had special news to give him, she could say that something had gone wrong. It sometimes did. He wouldn't ask to see. He would never deny her, then. She would have what she had always wanted, and by the time she had to reveal herself to him, he would want it, too.

Months passed. Often, the hat remained in its case. In any event, she never had the news to share. Their course remained unclear, their mode together tense. The two kept their distance like boxers circling, wary, testing each other, ready to strike, and from that posture of antagonism, they decided to separate, she to Berlin, he to Moscow. The summer apart would reveal whether their futures would call them back together, or not.

September, 1913

After a lengthy stay with the Schroeters, Ella let herself into the empty flat in Munich as though she had entered the wrong door, slipped off her shoes in the wrong vestibule, sat on someone else's divan. She passed the first hour reacquainting herself with the furniture. Was she to live here alone after all? The significant pleasures of active family life with Emmy, Georg, and Friedel had stood in notable contrast to her own situation. One afternoon, as she and Emmy sat picking through gooseberries, Emmy put down her paring knife. "You could stay with us, Ella. If you like. You could give Friedel art lessons. You'd find your way here. We have room."

"No," was all she said. "I've already bought my ticket." Reliable and loving, the Schroeters were a rock, but though Ella felt fragile and unmoored, she could not stake her anchor with her sister's family. She must have her own harbor.

Wassily would be returning to Germany in a few days, this she knew, but he might not return to her at all. She could not think what she would do if he didn't. She lay awake most of the night hoping to hear his key in the lock.

He did come back to the flat, though, tired and sick from his lengthy journey. He went almost immediately to his bed, claiming dizziness and nausea and woke up the next day with a headache, his night clothes damp with sweat. Unshaven and groggy, he stood in the parlor as though he were a stranger deposited there and waiting for instruction. True, Munich was hardly refreshing. The hot September days lingered like a guest with nowhere to go, rummaging about the rooms with sticky fingers, unwanted. Perhaps, Ella suggested, they should retire to Murnau for a week of rest. They both could recover their strength there before work began again in earnest. Fanny could stay behind and put the Munich household in order after the summer of neglect. Mightn't Wassily like that? He did not object.

They spoke little the next morning, but the long habit of travel moved them out of the flat and onto the morning train to Murnau. They sat lightly touching on the narrow seat, soothed by the swaying movement of the car. When they arrived, the yellow house was breezy, fragrant with late summer roses and purple phlox outside the polished windows. Wassily drank deeply from the clear well at the back of the house and splashed water over his head and neck while Ella tidied up the kitchen and put away the sausages and cheese she had packed.

They napped in their separate rooms and woke to burnished light and the calls of children playing in the fields just below. Wassily found his spade and staked out a new bed for tulips and hyacinths, trying to estimate where the snows would melt first and where the sprouted bulbs would best catch the spring sun. It felt good, he said, to work. They'd spoiled him in Moscow. He'd gotten fat. It felt good to touch the soil.

They ate a simple dinner from the basket Ella had brought on the train and then walked together to the village to drink beer, coming home silent in a black night punctured by fireflies. They went to their separate beds and slept.

Early the next morning Wassily tapped on the door to Ella's room. He curled his fingers around its edge and poked his head inside. He was feeling better, he said, and hungry. Should he fry some eggs? And he was thirsty, too. Which reminded him. His Odessa relatives had served him a sweet concoction of whole plums and vodka bottled for years until it took on a rich amethyst color and an aroma like the Garden of Eden. Wouldn't they like to make some for themselves? He and Ella could cycle out to Emil Bauer's farm where the small Italian prune-plums would be ripe. He'd brought down vodka, in ready supply since his trip to Russia, and there was that fine crystal decanter from his mother's house going to waste. Would that be nice?

Ella rose onto her elbows. He had not entered her bedroom for months. "Shall I pack a lunch?" The tease of a cycling trip was more than she needed for motivation. Wassily's good spirits were refreshment enough.

"We soak the plums in vodka and sugar," he continued. "The vodka extrudes the flavor from the fruit and makes a rich liquor. They say it lasts forever."

"I see," she said.

"And grows a glorious purple."

"That does sound nice."

"It takes time, of course." He stood at the foot of her bed. "But we have that, don't we, Ella? Time?"

Young Herr Bauer was accommodating, generous. The Russian man and his woman had bought his fruit often before, and if he knew how some of the villagers felt about what went on in the yellow house, he did not appear to set much store by such thoughts.

"The Spitzenbergs make a good sauce, but they're not ready. It was a dry summer." He strode on strong legs past a stand of well-established apple trees. "I'm trying my hand with some new stock. But if it's plums you're after, that one over there is a nice variety." Bauer pointed down a slope toward a grove. He found a ladder for Wassily to climb and gave Ella a slatted, wooden box for the small purple fruit she scooped up under the trees. When they had collected all they could carry home, Bauer ushered them back toward the road, talking about the storage addition he had built onto the old farmhouse and the field he was preparing for fall planting. Over in the kitchen garden, his rows of chard and beans and onions prospered, and they could take some of that off his hands, too. "I'm glad of the sale." As he spoke, a fair-haired woman came out from the house, a toddler on her hip, and she spoke to Bauer in another language. "My wife, Aniela," Bauer said. "And our son."

"We have happiness to see you," the farmer's wife said and nodded. The Pole went back to the house, coming out again with an armful of burlap sacks. The farmer poured the plums from the wooden box into the sacks and transferred them into rucksacks Wassily and Ella strapped on their backs, supporting Ella's with his broad hand as she climbed onto her bicycle.

"And when you've finished with the plums, I've taken a stall at the market at Elisabethstrasse Wednesdays and Saturdays." He waved as they pedaled off.

Ella cooked Herr Bauer's vegetables for their dinner. Together she and Wassily washed a dozen canning jars and filled them tightly with sweetened plums in a bath of Russian vodka. Wassily lit the kerosene lamp at the table and sat quietly while Ella finished up, taking the last few jars to the cellar shelves. But he did not take out his book or his writing papers. When she returned to the sitting room, he called her over to him and pulled her gently onto his lap. "Come. Sit here as you once did." He wrapped his arms around her and pressed his face against her breasts. "My Ellchen, we must begin again and be as we were."

On his lap, Ella, tentative at first, softened her back and encircled his head with her arms. She breathed into his hair, letting it brush her cheeks and eyes. So much was grey now. She lowered her head to kiss him and found his face wet with tears and added to them with her own.

And so she took Wassily to her room, and for a time they held each other quietly in her little bed, holding not just to the bodies they had grown to know but to the selves they had been once, selves they might be again. Ella found the tight bands she had drawn around herself loosen and the agitation, the crankiness, the fear, the disappointment dissipate in the warmth of his skin on hers, his breath on her neck and shoulders, his low voice loving her. And then the old pleasure flickered and flamed. They shed months with their clothes, and felt the familiar shapes curve and mold to each other as they bent and arched. Later, as he lay along her length, spent from the eruption of his pleasure, she felt his chest rise and fall on hers, pressing and yielding until at last they lay apart in their quiet separateness.

Munich
November, 1913 to August 3, 1914

Work restored equilibrium to their days. Ella covered her canvases with images she might have seen through her camera lens—a still life, a landscape, a village street, a pair of lovers languishing on a hillside, a child holding a doll. She simplified the images, to be sure, setting out blocks of color, removing extraneous details, expressing herself in the only way she knew. Her paintbrush led the way, heedless of anything but her inner nature. For her, painting was a way to lose touch with words, to enter a world stripped of everything but visual expression. She could neither explain nor defend her works— they came out of her unawares.

Wassily, though, had changed. While she trod the ground beneath her, he had soared into spiritual realms, parting the clouds above. Deep into expression of the symbolic and spiritual, some of his painting was visual music, entirely abstract, only the merest gestures suggesting the vestige of an onion dome, a boat, a horse and rider, a mountain, a waterfall. He took risks Ella didn't dare, and while she admired his forward thinking, the hairline crack that once had separated their styles deepened and widened in a crevasse, exposing a fault in the bedrock.

Yet she still thought of herself as his helpmeet. Her careful Handlist recorded his every piece, its size and composition. She even argued on his behalf when, as sometimes happened, a gallery owner took advantage of him, underpaying or over-keeping his works. In the disputes that came inevitably in the wake of his pioneering ideas, she devoted herself to his defense, speaking up, walking out, entering in.

In the next weeks, Kandinsky prepared studies for a magnum opus, a work of unparalleled energy, imagination, and wonder. When it was all over, Ella wrote in her diary, "And then he flew still higher, an eagle brushing wings with God, Himself." In the morning light, she felt embarrassed at her sentimentality and ripped the pages from her book. Even she saw the danger of such a comparison.

He had long ago categorized his paintings according to the preparatory effort that went into them. The *Impressions* were quick representations of images. The *Improvisations* conveyed spontaneous expression. But the *Compositions* were symphonic in their complexity, thematic significance, and energetic movement. He worked for weeks preparing them, making pen-and-ink drawings, watercolor and oil studies, clarifying details of design, coloration, symbol, motif, meaning.

Composition VII consumed him all fall. Rising at dawn, he paced through the rooms, drinking coffee and smoking. When the weather was kind, he took fast walks along the Schwabing streets or in the nearby English Garden. On rainy days, he stood in the back courtyard and huddled near the building with his pipe. Back in his studio, he shut himself off from every noise, directing Ella to dismiss Fanny for hours at a time. He barely ate. He let his beard grow. By November, he had completed over thirty preparatory studies, some of them finished works, completed fragments. Ella tracked the progression of his thinking as it evolved in abstract forms and symbols. There in the preparatory sketches, the watercolors, the oils, she saw ideas that had been germinating for years, large and resonant of disaster, the apotheosis of the unthinkable.

By late November he was ready. He announced his intention to begin in the morning, and Ella prepared herself by loading her Kodak to record the process. In the next four days she witnessed the birth of an offspring every bit as remarkable as a human infant in its individuality and the inherent presence of the Divine. And she photographed the process, several plates each day.

The canvas was enormous, 200 × 300 centimeters, considerably taller than either Ella or Wassily. From side to side, she could stretch her arms out to their fullest and still not measure more than just over half its width. It took, in fact, substantial ingenuity for them to prop up the painting for the photographs she took each day, some negotiating of chairs and easels and one breathtaking moment when the canvas threatened to topple.

On the first morning, Wassily drew in the major forms and sketched in the central section and some of the movement on the right edge, studying his pen-and-ink and watercolor drawings for the general placement of the shaped areas. By late afternoon, he stretched out on the sofa and fell into a deep sleep. On the second day, he moved from the center of the canvas toward the upper right, and he used his oil studies to adjust his palette and contrast colors, squinting his eyes and taking off his glasses to polish them over and over. On the third day, he filled in the left side and added calligraphic lines, some of them arrow-like in their directional thrust, others curved and sensuous. That day was his most productive, and he painted until well after nightfall, his lower back aching with the effort of standing, reaching, crouching. And then on the last day he completed all the forms, referring often to his glass painting of The Last Judgment for symbols and final motifs. The finished canvas was a riot of color and movement so vibrant it almost roared with its expression of apocalyptic transformation.

For Ella, it was like being at the Creation, a process, she remarked irreverently, that took Wassily only half the time it took God. The painting felt like the Almighty at work, too. Ella could recognize ideas of destruction and redemption, his themes from earlier paintings, but had she not lived with his ideas as they developed, she could not have identified the forms he used to represent them. What used to be boats and oars, symbols of the artist as progressive, he had now abstracted into curves and black moving lines. The trumpets of his earlier paintings now appeared as imagined sound waves, lines wavering. Years ago when she and he seemed, she felt, to walk in a perfect paradise of united beings, he liked to represent two lovers in his paintings. But these figures, now, were totally abstract, merely ovals nearly touching. No one would think they were people. His signature blue horse, the visionary symbol from *der Blaue Reiter*, was now just a swath of color, nothing one could point to and say, "See, here is a horse."

He had transformed color, line, and form into pure idea, something really new in the world. From a small central area of circular forms cradling one another, a vortex projected pulsating waves, an inferno of reds, greens, and oranges on which rays of intense gold and lakes of white and black took the eye around, color clashing like cymbals. If the first day of Creation had produced a seismic crack as the world struggled to be born, this painting, Ella thought, seemed like God's representation of the event, spinning, whirling, dizzying, bedazzling. She would keep the photographs in her drawer of treasures for safekeeping.

Within a week, the Giselists came to view the masterpiece, as did the Marcs. Ella instructed Fanny to set out cake and oranges and make tea for the visitors, and everyone who came stared, looked away, stared, walked away, and stared again. No one encounter with the painting was sufficient to register its impact. Maria Marc seemed embarrassed before it as though privy to an explosion either too private or too cataclysmic to be allowed her. Franz and Marianne stood arrested before the piece. "*Mein Gott,*" Marc uttered under his breath. "*Mein Gott.*" Jawlensky took Wassily in his bear's embrace and wept. He sat backwards on a wooden chair too small for his bulk, interpreting aloud. When he prepared to leave, he took Wassily Wassilievich in his arms and embraced him again. "You are a sensation," he said. "But no one will love you as I do."

Lowering her voice when she addressed him, Ella watched him recover as he lay on the sofa and smoked. He spoke little. Visitors came and went. Ella tidied the house around him, putting aside the ink studies and laying out the oils carefully, handling them the way an archivist puts on gloves in the library print room, breathing as little as possible. And as the days passed and his energy returned, he nodded to Ella as she put away his sketches in a file, and he reorganized his paints. He let Fanny clean his work area, and he went through all the papers on his desk. He returned his glass painting of the Last Judgment to the collection he and Ella had hung over the table and took *Composition VII* from the pair of easels on which he had set it and placed it on the floor against a wall. He wrote gallery owners that the painting was finished and promised that he would send more information on how it should be shown and priced. "The critics will say I've gone mad," he said.

While the snows blew and the ice cracked on bare branches in the back garden, he wrote essays and letters to publishers, rarely leaving his desk until nightfall. When the first warm winds encouraged open windows and a small pot of primroses on the table, he went to the barber to shave off his beard entirely, and he ordered a new suit. His friends flocked to see him. For a few weeks, it seemed to Ella that they went somewhere every night—concerts, exhibits, lectures. Standing in a crowd, Ella overheard Marc tell a new friend that there was "no one more charming than Kandinsky." But Wassily's good cheer had little to do with her. The summer mood they had bottled in Murnau had cooled. Even in his moments of sociability, he withdrew from her, and she could not reintroduce the subject that lay behind her every thought. Their conversations were like pieces of a jigsaw puzzle fallen to the floor. She saw bits of her life but not its picture. Her mood slid downwards, a hiker on a loose and pebbled slope, and she could not keep herself from slipping again and again into gloom.

July was hot. Disquieted by the political situation, Wassily's Russian compatriots von Hartmann and Jawlensky came to take him with them to a Schwabing cafe where Russian emigrés smoked and drank and argued about the Kaiser and his aggression and how the Tsar might respond. Wassily came home agitated. In the morning, after coffee and the newspapers, he walked through the apartment, restless and silent.

"You've got to write to Herwarth Walden, you know. He's waiting for a reply." Ella was sorting letters, a pile for him, a pile for her.

"Are you offering to take on my correspondence, now?" He snatched up his pile and took it into his studio.

"I'm only reminding you. You asked me to remind you." Ella followed him into the studio and crossed to the window.

"Well, so you have done." He stood with his back to her.

"After lunch, can you help me with that stretcher?"

"I told you, there's nothing wrong with it." He snapped his letters onto his desk like a man dealing cards.

"It's loose. You're the one who discovered it."

"Just leave it, I said."

She changed her tack. "You know, I'm thinking of submitting to that jury-free show in Leipzig. What do you think?"

He turned suddenly and left the room without speaking.

Ella retreated to her bed. It seemed to her, then, that Wassily had no interest in her, no patience with her. He neither looked at nor touched her. His attention had turned frighteningly elsewhere—the newspapers, the streets and cafes, the Russian ex-patriots. On a steamy July night when Alexei Georgewitsch was visiting, Wassily took him aside and insisted that he read an article.

"Ah, my countryman," the bear sighed. "The Tsar is beginning to roar."

"You realize," Wassily said, "you and I will be enemy aliens here."

"I do," Jawlensky said.

"The Tsar will defend the Serbs if it comes to that."

"Surely the Austrians will retreat."

"Alexei Georgewitsch, the point is this. Germany will lean with Austria against Russia and the Serbs. Germany will fight Russia."

The bear rubbed his eyes. "This is a complex situation for us."

"Worse, Alexei. You and I—and Marianne and my mother and Anja, and all of us Russians in Munich—" Wassily did not continue.

"I understand, Wassily Wassilievich. We must consider."

When Ella skimmed the newspapers, she could see from the headlines that the news was grim, the articles strident and alarming. But though the Russian community debated and worried, smoking and drinking far into the night, none of the talk seemed connected to her. Back in the apartment after a night with his Russian friends, Wassily hunched his shoulders and paced in the rooms. He left his paints in their chest and a new roll of canvas propped up in a corner, unopened.

Ella suggested they go to Murnau. She could use a change, she said.

"Have you nothing better to do with your time than think about pleasure?" He scowled at her.

"You needn't criticize me. I only thought you might like to rest."

"Rest? What do I do but rest? All Europe is talking war, and you want to go to the country?"

"Why are you angry with me?"

"You are like a child. A serious situation is developing. The papers are full of most distressing news, and you want to go to the mountains. Well, go then. I would not stop you. But really, Gabriele, I must ask why you have so little respect for the affairs of the world outside this apartment."

And so she did not go to Murnau. Europe's tension moved into Ainmillerstrasse and took up all the room for loving.

On August 1, while Ella groped for direction in a miasma of antagonism, the bad news came, spreading like cholera among the Russian ex-patriots. Russia and Germany were at war. The announcement brought people to the streets where they waved newspapers in each other's faces and gesticulated with cigaretted fingers. A course of action emerged through the agitation, the fear, and eventually the mandate. The Russians had to leave Germany immediately.

"Leave? But why? You're no one's enemy." Ella stood with her hands on her hips.

"In the eyes of the state, I am an enemy. Could you pack a case for me, do you think? I have to gather my papers and see about getting money. And Fanny. Call her, would you? I want her to go to the station and buy me a ticket to Moscow. Others will be leaving, too, and I want to reserve a seat."

"Do you mean you're going by yourself?"

"Of course. You are not an enemy in Germany."

"But I don't want to stay without you. I'll go with you to Moscow."

"Gabriele, why do you not understand. You would be an enemy in Moscow, as I am in Munich. Our countries are at war. You can come and go in Germany, but you cannot come to Russia."

"Then we will go somewhere else together. If you're leaving here, I'm coming with you."

He was pulling books from a shelf. "All right. If you like. We can go first to Switzerland and then decide. But you will have to hurry.

Get your things together."

"But what about the apartment? Are we leaving everything? All our paintings? There's a fortune here."

"It can't be helped. Perhaps at some time later you can return and pack up the flat properly. You might store everything or take it all to Murnau. I, certainly, am never coming back to this apartment. Hurry now. Get Fanny and then pack a case for each of us."

Within forty-eight hours, Wassily and Ella closed their Munich household, notified the landlord, settled up with Fanny, and ordered a cart to carry them to the station. They left Ainmillerstrasse in the dark of night and traveled by train to Mariahalden, in neutral Switzerland.

Aboard the hot, crowded car, Ella twisted her handkerchief in her hands. This was not just another trip, another holiday or escapade. Wassily was officially in exile, and she had no confidence that he welcomed her beside him, no assurance that they would continue together in any capacity. She felt as though she had been thrust out of a high window, and she could sense neither the speed of her descent nor its duration.

As the train pointed its nose at the future, Ella looked backwards at the years unrolling behind her. What had she gleaned from her labors? A few dozen exhibits? Some reviews? A few purchases? The pleasure of work, certainly. But she was thirty-seven years old, unmarried and childless, and the tenderness and passion that had promised a loving life with the man who had meant everything to her had dissipated. Perhaps even more importantly, the hundreds of paintings and drawings they'd abandoned in Munich waited behind, vulnerable to the caprice of war.

Galerie

"Section 1 for Composition VII (Center)," 1913
Wassily Kandinsky
Oil on canvas
$34^1/_2'' \times 38^1/_8''$
Milwaukee Art Museum
Gift of Mrs. Harry Lynde Bradley

The explosion of color, form, and movement of this canvas belies the careful control that went into its composition. Let there be no mistake—for all the abstract energy emanating from its surface, for all its disparate forms, there is nothing random in the work. Indeed, Section 1 for Composition VII (Center) is a fully-ordered, complete, coherent piece of the highest order.

But it is not easy to grasp. It might be useful to compare the work to the most modern musical composition with all its irregularities and dissonances and surprises. Major and minor, perhaps. Rhythm, certainly. Repetition, of course. Even lyricism. But such a piece does not revolve around a central chord. It does not take the listener on a melodic journey or resolve in a cadence. Instead, the listener foregoes time and expectation, responding instead moment by moment, phrase by phrase, anxious perhaps for want of an anchor, but stimulated by the richness of sonority or the thrill of tonal transformations or the delight of bold contrasts. This approach to modern listening has an analogous benefit for the viewer of Composition VII, of which Section 1 is a carefully executed, complete study, one, in fact, of over thirty studies which the artist prepared.

Let us think, then, in visual moments, phrases, if you will, as we peruse "Section 1." One dominant phrase revolves around a rough circular shape bounded by lashes of black paint and crossed with lines as though shot from a bow. A smaller phrase nearby echoes both the color and form of its neighbor. A third stretches vertically nearly the height of the painting, imposing on the canvas a solid blue

form whose depth recedes as one gazes, providing a boundary between the left collection of diminutive forms and the larger area to
the right where we begin a shoreline edged in orange. Further to the
right a large softly-edged rectangle takes up the cry of orange and is,
itself, crossed by slashes. And below, a deep red oval with its black
halo, its pricks and sticks. Moment by moment we travel through the
world of the painting, experiencing a gentle phrase here, a momen-
tous clangor there, singing lines amidst the rat-a-tat-tat of percussive
color, shape, and form.

Some of the phrases appear to have evolved from the private
iconography of the artist. What we have seen before as mountains
are tipped on their sides. Boats have lost their shapes along with
their oars. What may once have been a horse, even a blue one with a
rider, is now a galloping shape easy to interpret as a lake or a cavern.
Pieces are stitched or pierced, overlapped or belted to other pieces.
And while there is neither narrative nor subject, there is, undeniably,
coherence, force, and expression.

Words fail. And yet, this viewer, at least, leaves the painting completely satisfied.

J. Eichner

Chapter Seven

Contacts

Copenhagen
1916-1919

4 December, 1916

My Wassily,

Many, many good wishes for your birthday. May the next 50 be as abundant in blessings as this first 50. I wish you had, after all, come back here as you thought you might, but in any case, I think of you on this special day and wish you happiness.

People here are saying that Moscow is in total upheaval and I worry about your safety. I tried reading the papers for a while, but I was not very good at it. You know how I am. I was wrong to be cross with you, my dearest one, and I promise to be better—not so selfish. Anyway, we were not as bad together as you say, and right or wrong we still mean a great deal to each other. Come to me here. I have done quite a lot of exhibiting, and you can do even more. Herwarth Walden's sister-in-law can arrange it. The money doesn't matter.

I don't agree that we must wait until the end of the war to marry! Marriage is the way to <u>endure</u> these dreadful times. You said you would do what I asked, and now I am asking you to come to me. Please!

Your Ella

P. S. I did go back to Ainmillerstrasse and empty it, as you suggested. I've put the paintings etc. in storage. (Getting there and back on the trains was terrifying. I won't return, now, until the war is over—if it ever is!) I assume you have heard about Marc at Verdun. My heart breaks for Maria.

1 July, 1917

My dearest Wassy,

I am in despair. Over and over I write you. Why do you not respond? Send me something. I will be grateful even for your bad wishes. Write me that you are alive, at least!

In all love and kindness,

Your Ella

Copenhagen
December, 1917

Ella knocked on a black door. She took off her coat while two fair-haired boys in blue jackets elbowed each other and vied for control of a tennis racket. Their mother watched them from the gold brocade of a settee. "Eckhard, you have the violin. Let Lars hold the racket."

"He is an abominable tennis player."

Ella took the older boy by the arm and led him to stand in the curve of the grand piano.

"Let Fraulein pose you, now. Remember where you were last time?"

"But why should he get to hold the racket when I am the superior player?"

"Lars is younger than you. He'll improve." The mother stroked a white cat on her lap.

"I am not abdominal." The younger boy's eyes flashed. "I beat father last summer."

"Father let you win. You know you can't play."

"Lars, the word is *abominable*." The mother began paging through an illustrated magazine.

Ella angled the younger boy next to his brother so that the two appeared engaged in conversation. She removed the tennis racket from the boy's hand and set it on the fold of the piano so that its handle formed a line joining the two brothers. She positioned the violin under Eckhard's arm and smiled inwardly. Young Friedel would be just his age now. Until the war, she'd been taking violin lessons, too.

"Stop fidgeting, Lars. Fraulein cannot paint you while you are moving around. Be good, now, and when Fraulein is finished, we will see if Cook can prepare something special."

Ella set up her easel and her folding stool.

"I'd rather have a chocolate roll," said the older boy. "Cook hasn't any, has she? Can we go into town?"

"Yes, can we?" asked the younger boy.

"Lars, be still. Eckhard, you should smile. Can you ask Fraulein if you should smile for the portrait?"

The boy spoke to Ella in her language. It comforted her to hear German. Danish exhausted her. She shook her head. Then she clapped her hands and motioned to the boys to hold still. Now, for fifty minutes, she would paint these scions of the Danish shipbuilding industry in its capital city. Without such commissions, she could not eat or pay her rent.

Ella adjusted her chair, lowering its legs. If she painted from be-low the boys, looking up, the diagonal could still draw movement from her baseline point of view through the figure of the smaller brother, the line of the tennis racket atop the piano, and then on to Eckhard's head. She could still see, could still paint. Yet even a good portrait could jeopardize her worth as an artist. "Serviceable," she could hear the critics say. "Workmanlike."

In truth, Ella must provide her patron with a picture that a mother could admire. The younger boy was handsome, so Ella shaded the lines of his eyes to catch his merriment. The older boy had a narrow face, so Ella softened the lines of his cheeks and shoulders, so that his form appeared more elastic than she saw it. It pained her to know that her name would lay on the painting while so little of her own truth was in it. Those days of self-expression were all gone, now. Her talent was fading like pencil sketches left near a window. But Ella must eat.

When the sitting was over for the day, Ella packed up her paints. She would return tomorrow. She left the unfinished canvas in the fine home, assured by the mother that no harm would come to it. She would not house the canvas in her pension where she might look at it and see evidence of her plight.

Afterwards, Ella walked down a narrow street through icy slush. She knew to the øre what she had in her purse. Eckard's mention of chocolate roll was tempting, but she could do without. She had some bread left from the breakfast she paid for with her rent. That would have to do. If she got another commission, she might treat herself to something. A pair of shoes? Not yet. Certainly not a new coat. Probably just paints and canvasboard, investment in another commission or even an exhibition. But who bought anything these days? In Germany things were much worse. Emmy wrote her about the rations, the privations, the challenges of providing for her family with wartime shortages of meat and milk. "Don't come here," Emmy wrote. "We've nothing to feed you. I am so worried about Georg. Pray, now, Ella. Even if you don't want to." Ella longed to see her sister. Some nights, the dream of being in her sister's embrace warmed her to sleep. She dared not dream of Wassily. He was surely dead. Her heart contracted to think it.

Back in her room she kept her door slightly ajar to hear the murmur of conversation between her landlady and the woman's grown daughter. She could catch only a few words at that distance, enough to know that there were people in the house carrying on ordinary relations, moving about with chores and concerns. She lit her kerosene burner and spread the leftover roll with a bit of soft cheese. She swept the crumbs into her hand and ate those, too. She drank her tea black, although she had a can of milk. But she could do without. Its small comfort might be more necessary tomorrow or another day when she had not had the reassurance of being employed, if only temporarily.

After more than a year in Denmark, Ella had few friends she could visit. Her nightly routine served as companion and confidante. She cleared the small table and took out her ink and pen for another letter to Wassily, a note detailing her day and beseeching him to write her, to be alive in the world. Writing to him was making him live.

Yet, she had not received a reply from him in over eighteen months, and she knew he was dead. Surely he would write her if he could. No, likely he was dead. They all were dead. Still, she couldn't be sure. Her thoughts frightened her, but she could not stop them. Over and over, the same thoughts.

She put away her things and readied herself for bed. What she did best was sleep.

For Ella these were days of biting snow and wind, nights of bitter starless skies, her heart as grey and contracted as the chunks of ice that lined the roadways. Time was plentiful but money in desperately short supply. Fear she had in abundance. Every day in which he did not write, and that was every day, her heart shrank.

‡

The final sitting with the boys went well enough. Now she would take home the canvas and complete it on her own. The mother did not offer to give Ella an advance on her fee, nor did she offer her coffee or a meal. Ella would have been glad to have it, but she packed up her things and left the fine house. She had no wish to try to be sociable, struggling through the clumsy interpretation of the older child. She had no wish to talk at all.

Thankfully, the walk back to the small pension room was not long. Buffeted by wind, clutching the canvas, she stopped to adjust the strap of her rucksack when she heard a familiar voice calling in German,

"*Frau Kandinsky. Ist, dass sie?*"

Ella turned, astonished to hear *his* name. It was Anna Roslund, sister-in-law of Herwarth Walden, the Berlin gallery owner. Frau Roslund had given Ella a bed when she first arrived in Copenhagen. Clutching the matron's address in her hand, Ella had introduced herself then as Frau Münter-Kandkinsky, convinced that her situation would quickly be resolved, for he had promised to come and marry her. But now, more than a year later, how could she tell the truth of her name? She had deceived Anna Roslund, and to admit it now would be to expose her vulnerability to additional assault. She was Gabriele Münter still, and a liar.

Better not have met up with Frau Roslund at all, she with her rich Danish husband, her small dogs, her large house, her self-assured generosity. Ella was not good company these days, if she had ever been. And today, with the portrait of the two boys still fresh in her mind, she was especially depressed. But Ella must be civil for Herwarth Walden's sake if not her own.

"Frau Roslund," she said. "Good afternoon. The wind is strong today."

"Why have you not come to see me?" The woman kissed Ella's cheeks, right and left. Her dark coat had a thick fur collar, and her soft hat was made of black seal. "I did not know how to reach you. I have missed our chats. It must be a year or more. Will you come for coffee with me now?"

Ella fingered the øre in her pocket. She had not eaten since her modest breakfast.

"Please, let me treat you. I am famished, myself, and the best place for pastry is just at the corner. Even in Denmark there are shortages, don't you notice?" Anna Roslund took Ella by the sleeve. She was a tall woman, broad without being stout. "Come. You must."

Ella had lost her will to protest. She nodded, but when they were inside the cafe, she hung her wool coat on a hook and set the canvas against the wall near her feet where she could not see it. In the warm, steamy room, fragrant with pastry, her limbs softened.

Anna Roslund ordered for them both, real coffee and a small tray of sweets. At the last minute, she selected a large open sandwich, too, ham and pickle, and cut it into four pieces, offering Ella a share. "Has your husband found work in Copenhagen?"

Husband nettled the air about her head, stinging the back of her neck under her knot of hair. Ashamed of her dishonesty, Ella lowered her eyes. "He has not arrived."

"After so long? You thought he would come to you right away." Frau Roslund spread her elbows wide on the white cloth, leaning in to Ella, inspecting her. "I assumed he was here with you all this last year." She sat back in her chair and picked up her fork.

"He stayed in Moscow. I—I can't reach him." Ella bit into her sandwich, glad for the portion though she had no sense of its taste.

"Moscow. You must be worried. We must hope he is safe from the Bolsheviks. One fears the violence will spread still further." She poured cream into Ella's cup and nodded at her. "You will be strong, yes? The war will end in Europe, and these revolutions in Russia will straighten themselves out. Your husband is not a soldier, is he? No, of course not. So, be patient. You must." She drank from her own cup, looking at Ella over its rim. "And you—you are doing well? You are painting?"

"Just commissions, portraits and such. I had an exhibit or two, but the war—" There was no need to say more. She took a second quarter of the sandwich.

Anna Roslund poured more coffee into Ella's cup and moved the sugar bowl toward her.

"Frau Kandinsky, I must return to this difficult topic. Your husband. Do you fear the worst? I can't help but ask."

Ella turned her head away. "I do sometimes think it. But I have no information. I know nothing." Outside the windows of the coffee shop, men and women bundled against the cold wind walked briskly along the streets. People seemed to have somewhere to go. Everyone was alive but Wassily. She, too, must be dead. Wassily was dead, and Gabriele Münter was nowhere, and Gabriele Kandinsky had never lived. She put down her fork and folded her hands in her lap.

Anna Roslund looked at her. "Frau Kandinsky, I have no wish to offend, but have you thought about contacting your husband?"

Ella looked up. "Of course. I have written and telegraphed, again and again. But I receive no reply."

"I was thinking of another means, a spiritual means. Through a medium. Frau Kandinsky, pardon me, I do not wish to distress you. I only suggest this course to relieve your anxiety. Certainty can be a comfort of its own."

Ella took a deep breath. She wanted him alive, but he was not. What other explanation was there, this silence from Wassily? She sipped her coffee, unable to reply.

"Not everyone agrees, I understand. But I feel so certain that those who have passed on before us are with us still. We walk among them without knowing it. But there are those gifted persons who can bring the other world to us. Have you considered it, Frau Kandinsky—contacting your husband through a spiritualist? To assure yourself, to give you comfort?"

Through the window, Ella watched a newspaper flattened against a pole, flapping in the wind like a pinioned bird. She turned her eyes back to the room and Anna Roslund. "My sister took me to a medium just after our mother died. They'd been close, and my sister grieved quite hard. But it didn't work. Not for me. My sister—she's—quite different from me."

Frau Roslund leaned forward. "Frau Kandinsky, perhaps the time was not right. Let me introduce you to Frau Anagret. What harm can it do?"

Ella took the last section of sandwich onto her plate. "You have been most generous, Frau Roslund." But now she could not eat. She put down her fork and placed her limp hands in her lap. Her eyes lowered, and she glimpsed the portrait on the floor near her feet. It was the not-knowing that was wearing her down. If she knew with certainty that Wassily was dead, she would go home to Emmy. The longer the war dragged on, the worse things grew in Germany. Her individual grief would go unnoticed there. She could die, herself, there. She raised her eyes. Certainty would send her home. "Thank you. I would be glad to accept your help."

‡

Frau Roslund's medium met Ella alone in a small, dark room, just large enough to accommodate a round table no larger than the tray Ella had left behind in Tunis, and two soft chairs pulled up to it. The room was bordered on one side by a thick curtain that sometimes moved slightly, Ella thought, as though her breath gave it life. But the room was quiet, excepting for the murmured conversation between herself and Madame Anagrete.

The medium was a slow-speaking woman well past middle age, dressed simply in a dark dress and warm shawl. She had a motherly air, her white hair pulled up in an old-fashioned style. She was kind, patient, inquisitive, and Ella found herself pouring out a tale of loss, a Russian husband gone missing, an eminent man taken up, perhaps, by the waves of history transforming Russia from its feudal past into something quite new, a statehood she did not understand but one, said the papers, that promised a kind of spiritual hope. She had to assume Herr Kandinsky was dead there. No other explanation sufficed. Ella called him her "husband." Madame Anagrete could know nothing other.

"And was he well when you last saw him?" the medium asked.

"Yes," Ella said. "But angry with me, I'm afraid. I wasn't nice to him. He blamed himself for...for not loving me enough." Her throat swelled up. She had never said these words aloud before. She sat with her head bowed, her gloves on her lap. She rubbed the woolly fabric between her fingers.

"Are you sure he was angry?"

"I think he was. We...we quarreled. He knew he hurt me, but he couldn't help himself. It wasn't what he wanted, but it took a while for him to know that."

"My dear," the medium said, "are you quite sure you want to speak with him now? What he says might cause you pain."

"I just—I simply don't know where else to turn."

Madame Anagrete reached across the small table and placed her hands palm up in front of Ella. Ella put her own hands in the soft ones of the medium.

"My dear," she said, her voice a quiet thrum, a cello bow quavering on the strings. "The dead *can* speak to us if we listen carefully.

Let me suggest a way for your husband to reach you. Close your eyes and let him come to you in your spirit. He will find himself in you. Sit here with me, and let him speak to your soul. I cannot say that he will come, but let us sit quietly and softly together, and we will ask him to join us. Let us ask him to enter your spirit and speak to you of his heart." Madame Anagrete covered Ella's hands with her own, keeping them warm like a hen in a nest.

In the dark, still room, Ella's heart found its way into her eyes. She cried and cried, and when her convulsive emotion was spent, she wiped her eyes with her handkerchief and lay her head against the padded chairback, exhausted from the violence of her outburst. She listened to the breathing in the room and the pulse of blood in her ears. Tears came more slowly, now, and she let them fall down her cheeks. Then, out of the thick black stillness, her loneliness and grief took form, his form, his presence. Her eyes were closed, but in her mind, she could see him coming towards her, his light, lithe body, his fine face, his bright eyes. She could feel the warmth of his skin, his taut muscles, the way his shoulder curved under her hand. Inhaling, she breathed in a whiff of cigarette smoke, a haze of which nearly always enveloped him. And then she could hear him, his voice low and aching. He was talking to her in that measured way he had, that formal gentleness. *Ella, my wife*, he said. *My own wife. My love.* Over and over he said it. Ella, my wife. She breathed in his voice with the smoke, down into her throat and chest, his voice trembling in her breast. *Ella my wife, my love, my own. Ella, my wife.* The tears dried on her cheeks, but she could not raise her head for fear he would cease speaking, for fear she would not hear his voice say again and again *Ella, my wife.*

And gradually it was over. The darkness thinned. His voice grew quiet, and his form faded from her, seeping away. Ella found her damp handkerchief and wiped her face. She felt empty, hollow, a carapace left to dry in a hot room. And yet, he had said it. He had said she was his wife. And she could say it, too. She was Frau Kandinsky, and she could say it openly whenever she wished.

Galerie

"Grave Crosses in Kochel," 1909
Gabriele Münter
Oil on cardboard
$15^7/8'' \times 12^7/8''$
Städtische Galerie im Lenbachhaus
Gabriele Münter Bequest

Five simple crosses emerge from a flat plane, but rather than sitting neatly in a still-life display, the crosses mix with suggestions of snow and watery puddles. Positioned alternately further and nearer the viewer, none of the crosses addresses the viewer directly, but all sit at slight angles to the front of the painting, avoiding our direct confrontation. Reading left to right, crosses two and five are large, taking up well over half the height of the painting. The remaining three crosses are less than a quarter the height of the larger ones. Cross two is ornamented with a hanging wreath-like circle done in black and dark orange. Three of the crosses display a Christ figure. The backdrop to the crosses is suggestive but imprecise. Perhaps there is a wall behind them. A bloc of deep green ornamented with suggestions of a figure provides most of the background along with areas of white, yellow-white, and blue.

The crosses are disembodied, absent of other conventional grave markers like tombstones, flowers, angels, or urns. They seem to relate more to each other than to any realistic setting. The strong upward vertical shafts of the crosses are at odds with the horizontal cross-pieces and the waves of blue and white that drift at diagonals. The brushwork is quick and imprecise. Smears of color overlap. Edges blur. The beauty here is in contrast – contrast of bright colors and dark ones, wet and dry, soft and hard, horizontals and verticals and diagonals. There is movement among the stillness.

At once both anxious and ambiguous, the graveyard scene is eerie and disturbing.

J. Eichner

Murnau
April, 1921

Ella sat down on his bed, smoothing the blue cover on either side of her. They had always kept separate bedrooms, even at the height of their intimacy, a carry-over, perhaps, from the years of renting separate quarters, meeting at one place or the other for long evenings and longer nights. But the times of her brightest happiness had been in this yellow house on the Murnau hillside. Here a fragrant breeze swept up from the valley and into these rooms where she and Wassily had eaten, slept, and worked, carrying his spirit through the house like a runner with a torch. Here they had entertained, debated, and loved each other. Here, she thought. Here is where I was most complete. If only he had not squeezed himself into that small space in his head where there was no room for her. But that was over now. He was hers forever.

Sheer curtains at the open window of his room blew inward, gesturing her into the place where he had slept alone but where also sometimes he had undressed her and covered her with his naked body, warming her inside and out. He was everywhere here, in the colorful washstand with the folk motifs he had stenciled, in the chest of drawers he had painted a bold yellow, in the red bookshelves and the knobs of the headboard, in the walls and the floor and the ceiling, in the curtains and in the window from which they hung, outside the window where the church tower looked over the garden and the horses in the fields, in the rain and the sun and the wind. Everywhere. He was everywhere.

Fanny was due to arrive on the afternoon train with Wassily's black fancy dress coat. Ella's idea was to lay it out right here on the bed, as though he were about to slip it on for an event, a concert or maybe the opening night reception of an exhibit where there would be champagne. She had his good shoes, too—funny that he hadn't taken them to Moscow, though now that she thought of it, they'd have been wasted there, ruined. She would place them so that the toes would just peep out from under the bed, ready for him to sit down and put them on. He'd been a little vain about his feet and legs, and with good reason. Lovely legs, well-muscled, shapely. Perfect feet. She'd never minded when he put his feet on her flesh, even in the winter. In fact, she loved every part of him that she could touch, and she'd loved his mind and his principles and his dignity and his ambition.

The underthings she had saved for last. The shirts and neckties were in the lower drawers already, but she had been reluctant to put away the things that lay closest to his body. She could do that now, though. Better to touch them one last time before Fanny arrived, maybe put them up to her face and see if there was anything left of him in their scent. She took two pairs of his summer underdrawers from the stack she had placed on his bureau, stroking her cheeks with them as she sat back again. When Fanny came and arranged the coat on the bed, she'd be finished with his personal effects. Piece by piece, Ella was bringing him back to life.

She hadn't decided on what to do with the books. Put up some shelves in the cellar? He had been a scholar as well as everything else. So few people knew him as she had. When she felt up to it, she might write a little something about him. An article about life with the great man. Nothing intimate or coarse. Appreciative. "The Artist As I Knew Him" she could call it. She could look into her diary to remind herself of things. And people would want to come here to the house, too, to see where he had done his best work, where *der Blaue Reiter* had been born. She wouldn't think of charging an admission fee. Certainly not. The point was to venerate his memory. She would be putting him away for safekeeping in this house where he belonged and she could watch over him. Others would share her view. And as Frau Kandinsky, his watchful protector, she could shape their appreciation.

She looked up at the boxes lined up against the wall. It had taken her trip after trip to get them all here. Oh, but his top hat! That could go on display, too, along with the fancy coat! Yes, that would be just the thing. But not now, not yet. As long as Fanny hadn't come, Ella could stay a while here on his bed, fingering his clothing.

She stretched herself out on top of the cover, his underwear covering her eyes and mouth, feeling the familiar contours of the soft mattress under her. None of it smelled like him, though. Too many years ago. Still, he was hers entirely, now. That was for sure. His death had fixed him, the elusive butterfly secured with pins. Death was like that—it caught a person in the midst of life and held him there, positioned forever as he had been known, kept just so by the people who lived on. As a child, she had played statues. You skipped and danced and made silly faces and then someone called "Stop" and you froze in place. Wassily was her statue now. But since she didn't know how he died, or when, or where, Wassily was not fixed in a way that settled her. That was why she was putting him together. That was why she was building a memorial.

Returned to Germany years after the war, Ella came to Murnau as soon as the back of winter had been broken and she could close off the main sitting room, a fire in the stove keeping her cozy enough in the evenings. She wanted to arrange things as he would have liked. At first she had worked in the garden, preparing it for planting in the wet, cold spring. He had loved the vegetables, the berries, the roses in the circular bed. They both had. Her back hurt more now, though, when she stooped to dig and hoe the heavy clay. Of course, she was doing it all alone. You'd expect that, a little discomfort, if you were doing it alone.

She had expanded the sitting room display of *hinterglasmalerie* with some they'd had in Munich, and she was laundering all of the linens, a few each visit. She did all of the chores alone. She had to. Fanny didn't come to the house any more, now that Ella could no longer afford to pay her salary. Still loyal though, she stopped by Ella's pension in Munich from time to time and shared a cup of tea, catching up on the latest, relaying stories from the war years. "I'd like that," she had said when Ella suggested Fanny visit her in Murnau for a little holiday. "And if you want me to carry anything down there, Fraulein, why, you just tell me."

"It's Frau Kandinsky, now, Fanny. I told you. It's hard to get used to a new name, but you should try to remember."

In fact, it was Fanny's offer that gave Ella the idea of restoring the yellow house to its rightful sense of order, the way it would have been if he had lived and they had married. Well, no one had to know that they hadn't. She had introduced herself to her new Munich landlord as "Frau Kandinsky," and the butcher, too, who put aside her chop and the nice sausages, and also the woman who colored and dressed her hair from time to time. "Frau Kandinsky" was what she answered to. She had the right to, now. He had made that clear.

Fanny, of course, sometimes forgot, and when there were just the two of them, Ella let her say "Fraulein" as she had done before the war. As for the agents and the artists from the old days, how could they dare object? In any event, she wasn't in touch with most of them. The last time she'd seen Jawlensky, they'd all been in Switzerland together before Wassily had left for Moscow and she for Scandanavia. And as much as she'd counted on Alexei's friendship a decade ago, she wasn't sure he would contact her again, now that Wassily was dead. Marc, of course, was another one dead, along with his friend Macke, both soldiers. Tall Franz Marc, whose language and principles had so discomfited her. And Maria Marc? Ella didn't know what had become of her. Perhaps she had gone back to her mother to live out her days a widow.

Ella wore black on the streets, herself, and since a great many of other women now did as well, she attracted no attention at all. She had bought a suit with a new straight skirt, not an expensive one, but fresh, stylish. She had cut her hair and changed the style. She looked modern to herself, not the old Ella, mousy, dependent, desperate. A widow, now, she had a new stature, a better way to present herself in public. When she went into town, she felt she bore a settled air, a stability of demeanor that marked her as a woman of renown almost as much as if she had been the wife of a burgher. And then there was the matter of her own paintings, her own exhibits. Hers was a name people knew from the old days. She had rarely felt better.

Outside, a wagon rumbled up the hill. Ella got off the bed and patted the cover smooth. She folded his underdrawers and gave them a last kiss before putting them all in a tidy stack in the top drawer. It would be good to see Fanny here again. Fanny would remember some of their parties and the long nights arguing about art and principles and what to do next. Yes, it was a good idea to invite her down. But a little awkward, in a way, since Fanny was neither friend nor servant. Ever since the war, it was harder to keep the social distinctions, the old formalities, except in language, of course. Fanny would be forever *Sie*. Still, she was a tie to Wassily and important for that.

"You'd think the whole of Bavaria was going someplace else," Fanny said, climbing the stairs to the sitting room, setting down her bundles, unpinning her hat, slipping off her shoes. "I saw a man with one leg and the other trouser folded up at the knee. Another man was worse. His nose was kind of gone, I suppose you'd say, and he had to keep wiping at the hole where it should be. I almost couldn't look. Still, everybody moving. There was a group of scouts going down to Garmish-Partenkirchen. Lovely boys, they were, still peachy-cheeked and sweet. One of them got up and gave me a seat as we was pulling out. I wouldn't of taken it but for the packages. You wouldn't believe what that old coat of his must weigh. My arms was busting."

"Give me the coat," Ella said. "I'll just lay it out on his bed, and then we'll rest for a bit. Have a cup of tea. I've not got any cake, I'm afraid. But we can have a sit. I've been working, too, you'll see. His room is just as it used to be."

"Oh, and I have some letters to give you, too, ma'am. Your landlord give 'em me when I went to get Herr Kandinsky's coat and such. Here, I'll just carry the coat to where you like it, and then I'll get your letters for you. And I would like a cup of tea if it's not trouble."

It was morning before Ella got to the letters. First she and Fanny had set to admiring his room and the care she had taken to call his spirit back. And then they'd had some tea and fixed a simple meal. No trout or meat or cream such as they had had before the war, but a loaf Fanny had brought down from Munich and a wedge of cheese Ella had bought in the village with some early radishes and green onions. For a dessert, she had brought up one of the jars of fruit in vodka that she and Wassy had prepared so many years ago. Fanny and Ella each ate a few of the plums, and they toasted each other with short glasses of the liquor. They admired the deep purple and the rich aroma and tried to like the sweet, thick drink, but the taste was unfamiliar and the alcohol potent. The treat had sent them to sleep early, fuzzy and a little sick.

Next morning, Fanny was still abed when Ella thought to look through the mail brought down from Munich. She sat at the bare wooden table, the pale light puddling onto the floor as though a yellow ghost had toweled itself off after a morning wash. The Schroeters were good correspondents. The letter from Friedel made her smile. Her niece had a beau, her first, and she went into some detail about a moving picture the young man had taken her to. Emmy's news was mostly about shortages and losses. Georg, at least, was fine, but thin and shaken. He was looking for work since his plant had been destroyed. Most of the other letters were bills. Ella sighed. She really didn't know how she would pay them. She would have to sell something soon. Only a few of the old galleries had reopened. Walden in Berlin was still standing, she thought. She might have to do portraits again, or flower paintings. Selling herself made her head ache, but when she got back to Munich, she must try. There really was no alternative.

The last letter, though, was a puzzle. Ella did not recognize the handwriting or the return address in Berlin. She slit the envelope and in so doing slashed open a part of herself as well.

She thought for a moment that the letter was written in a language she hadn't understood and that if she showed the paper to someone who read that foreign tongue, the meaning would make sense and not shatter her so. The empty teacup on the table began to rattle uncontrollably in its saucer, and she didn't know why. The brittle sound bothered her, and she looked at the cup crossly, irritated, until she realized that she was holding the cup and that it was her hand that shook. She dropped the cup onto the floor, and she held the letter out from her body like a soiled cloth or the bloody inner vestment of a man who had been knifed. Her bare feet on the floor beneath her began to shuffle, but she did not feel their movement. She could not sense the hard chair under her or know for certain where she was. She might have been floating above the room, looking down on a middle-aged woman with frightened eyes. She might have been the wind that shook the paper in that woman's hand.

"Fanny," she called. "Fanny!"

"I'm just coming, ma'm, putting on my wrap. Are you hurt?"

Ella bent in her chair and began to moan.

"Fraulein, are you all right?" Fanny ran in, barefoot.

"Read it." Ella jerked the letter from the length of her arm like a something sticky she could not loosen from her flesh.

Fanny pried the paper out of Ella's hand.

March 30, 1921

Dear Fraulein Münter,

This letter comes to you from the law office of Ludwig Baehr on behalf of Wassily Kandinsky and his wife, Nina Andreievskaia Kandinsky, who direct that you return to Herr Kandinsky the holdings entrusted with you in August, 1914.

Herr Kandinsky is now returned to Germany to begin a professorship at the Bauhaus in Weimar and once again is in a position to resume his artistic career. The paintings, drawings, sketches, letters, and personal effects belonging to him may be sent to him in care of the Bauhaus, Weimar. The shipping charges are payable by the deliveree.

Please direct any questions regarding this request to the law office of Captain Ludwig Baehr, who remains,

Your servant,

Ludwig Baehr

By the time Fanny finished, Ella's spirit had slid from herself entirely.

Galerie

"Houses on Wintry Road," 1910-11
Gabriele Münter
Oil on canvas
13″ × 16″
Milwaukee Art Museum
Gift of Mrs. Harry Lynde Bradley

It is a wintry day, snow on the ground, on the road, on the roofs and walls, the artist's palette pale as the bleached-out wintry sky. We sit at the corner of a hamlet, able to identify houses both to the left and to the right along a wide V-shaped line. With color and form, the artist identifies eight structures, some with pointed roofs, others with sloped or curved edges and planes. The houses are softly shaded, rose, pale blue, mustard yellow, white. Each building is indicated less by architectural detail than by suggestion—swift, rough dabs of paint implying windows, doors, chimneys, roof-lines. Strong diagonal brushstrokes in the lower left corner of the painting suggest the hilly topography of the snowy road along which these houses sit.

The artist, as she has often done elsewhere in urban, rural, and natural landscapes, keeps the viewer at a distance by erecting a fence or wall between us and the structures she depicts. Here, a low wall separates the viewer from the major house at the painting's center. We may not walk along with her to the painting's right, either, as a brown picket fence bars us from the path to the blue and green houses. To the painting's left, shut doors, walls, and angles keep us out of the interiors of the hamlet. The scene is peaceful but lonely. No one walks along this road. No one leans out a window or opens a door to reveal a warm interior.

This is a scene we may admire but not enter.

J. Eichner

Part Three

Chapter Eight

The Blackness of Coal

Berlin
Summer 1921

"I T'S ALL RIGHT, Ella. You're here now. Shhh. Come on. Let's get you into bed. Shhhh, now. Here, use my handkerchief. Shhh."

Ella lay on her side, knees pulled into her chest, her back flush against the wall behind her. She arched and banged her head against its unyielding surface. She wanted to enter the wall, crush her body within it. When they pulled the bed away from the wall, she turned so that her back was to the door, and she rocked back and forth and plucked at the dark grey blanket and closed her wet eyes, dissolving into the grey where there were no words.

Darkness presses against the body, invading the orifices, pushing into the creases and craters of the mind. Rivulets of molten coal co-agulate the will, sealing the self inside, mummified, fossilized. Pain cracks and splinters and crusts.

Only the unspoken is safe.

Voices snake into the room, slithering, coiling.

* * * * *

"With all due respect, you and your family are not specialists. The science of psychiatry is quite advanced in the treatment of maladies. In situations like this, hospitalization is the usual course. Surely you understand that patients with melancholia as severe as hers are known to harm themselves. We have a responsibility here. I cannot state too strongly the dangers of her situation."

January 18, 1922

Dear Carl and Mary,

I've only got time for a note. I couldn't do it. We'll keep her. He'll come to the house to treat her, not that I'm optimistic. I'm not sure we'll ever get our old Ella back. That man Kandinsky has hired a lawyer to get his paintings from Ella. I'm prepared to fight him tooth and nail.

Think of us, when you can. Life here is pretty hard.

Love,

Emmy

February, 1922

Out behind the rabbit hutches, Ella used her bare hands to dig a shallow gully in the pile of snow left where last night's raging wind had blown it. From here she could not see the dark house, though the moon was bright and the stars piercing, battering her head with their sharp points, digging into her skull. She yanked the canvas tarpaulin over her shoulders against the wind, and she burrowed into the snowy pile. She pulled her arms from inside the sleeves of her thin gown and crossed them against the bare skin of her breasts. She waited for the bitter night to turn her into stone.

March, 1922

"You know I've always liked your sister, my love. But isn't this asking a lot?"

"What? To save her life? It's not that much to ask."

April, 1922

Dear Carl and Mary,

We're all sleeping better now that I've moved my bed into her room. It's a little cramped, but at least I know where she is at night. I have to admit, she's strong as an ox. Not even a headcold after that crazy episode last month. Oddly, it seems to have done her some good. She looks at me from time to time, now, though she hasn't spoken a word.

Love,

Emmy

June, 1922

"How were things today?"

"The same."

August, 1922

She was corroded metal left out in rain. She had not used her voice for so long that she could not, as the sun beamed down upon her bed, find the mechanism to move her vocal cords and the muscles in her tongue to place against her teeth. She had forgotten her mouth entirely. In her brain was a name, and she had to keep that name from her mouth. She had to forget her mouth entirely.

She lived in a black cave where pain lurked in a dank corner. How she ate or what, how she bathed or dressed, if menses came and went she did not know.

She badly wanted to relieve herself and wished she could let the bedding soak up her effluence and with it the rest of her liquid will. But this morning, she could not let go, could not abide the warm wet, and she rose, her legs thin and white, the soles of her feet soft on the firm floor, and she sought out the toilet.

Hearing the flush, Emmy came running.

November, 1922

"Of course you should go to University."

"But won't you need help here?"

"Not so much. You can see she's coming around."

January, 1923

"I don't like lamb."

"Well, that's what we're having. I'm not making a separate meal for you. And you'll come to the table, too. No more of this dinner on a tray business. You're well enough."

Ella sat at her place. She ate potatoes and cabbage and carrots. Afterwards, she went back to her room and sat on the side of her bed and listened to the sounds of the household going on without her.

August, 1923

"Ella, dear, Friedel is just about to leave. She really wants her Tante to come with her."

Ella lay like a blue mummy, her coverlet wrapped tightly around her, a loose flap covering her mouth and nose. She looked at the ceiling.

"Time to get up, Ella." Emmy pulled open the curtains. Silver foil unrolled across the window. "It's a grey day, a good day to take the tram downtown. Come on, now, Ella. Friedel wants you to help her. You have the best taste of all of us, the best eye." Emmy shook the side of Ella's bed with her hip, rocking it from side to side. "I'm bringing you some coffee, and I'm going to see to it that you drink it. You might as well get up before I spill it all over you." She pulled back the quilt from Ella's face. "My God, you've got this thing tucked completely *under* you." She tugged at the quilt with a firm jerk. Ella lay fully dressed, stiff, unmoving. "You'll have to change your blouse. It looks like you've been sleeping in it. Up, now."

Ella swung her legs over the side of the bed.

"That's good. I'll be right back. You put on your shoes."

Ella reached over the side of the bed. She put her shoes in her lap. These, she said to herself, are shoes. This is my lap.

Emmy returned with the hot drink.

"Can you take this, or shall I spoon it into your mouth?"

Ella took the cup in her hands and drank the sweet coffee.

"Which blouse do you want? The blue one, don't you think? You can look nice when you try."

Ella put down her cup. She unbuttoned the wrinkled shirtwaist.

"Now, don't let Friedel buy something shabby. She's coming out in the world, and I want her to make a good impression. You have the artistic eye. Take care of her, now, Ella. I'm trusting you."

"You shouldn't."

"Well, I am. Now move along. Friedel has been very patient with you."

Ella tucked her blouse into her skirt. She fastened her belt. She left the house silently, Friedel on her arm.

Closing the door behind them, Emmy called out, "Watch her, Friedel. Watch her every minute."

"It was actually amusing—or would have been if it were somebody else's crazy relative. When the shopgirl showed us something she didn't like, she grunted and looked away. "

"Your Tante Ella is not crazy." Emmy sorted through the pile of mending.

"Papa said she was famous." Friedel set down her packages. "Was he right, or was he just being Papa?"

"There's all kinds of fame. Tante Ella has some piece of it." Emmy cleared her sewing from the round table and motioned Friedel to bring her purchases closer.

"It's called a 'sport suit.'" Friedel took the garments out of their box, shaking each one and holding it against herself.

"See how long the jacket is?" She passed the jacket to her mother. "Look at the skirt, too. It's quite slim and well above the ankle." She held the skirt close to her body, taking mincing steps. "I love this look. It makes me look tall, I think."

"And your Tante approved of it?"

"She didn't grunt, at least. What do you think?"

"Well, I can see I'll never fit into that style in this life," Emmy said. "It's a good thing you're nice and slim. Don't be like me. Watch that you don't get fat."

"Well, that's what Tante said, too."

"Did she?"

"Yes. And she told me to buy this blouse with the huge collar. I wasn't so sure, but she held it out, and when I tried it on, I thought I might as well."

"So she was paying attention." Emmy snapped black thread between her teeth.

"But she went right back to her room the minute we came home."

"That's all right. Every day a little progress." She moistened the thread in her mouth, picked up her needle, and inserted the thread's wet end. "She's never been the easiest person to get along with."

"Maybe *he* had his reasons."

"Not in my book, he didn't. Married behind her back! I'm telling you, if I so much as see that man, I'll strangle him. Don't even say his name." Emmy set down the sock she was darning and picked up Friedel's jacket.

"Whatever happened to his family?"

"Disappeared, I guess." Emmy folded Friedel's new jacket on her lap. She sat stroking the fabric, her eyes gone from the room.

"Oh, come on. You can't mean that."

"Lots of people in Russia disappeared around then. Millions. Your papa heard that Kandinsky nearly starved. It might be true."

Friedel took her new jacket from her mother's hands and placed the garments back in the box. "I can't be angry about him, mother. Just think what it must have been like."

"Well, I can be angry even if you can't. If you knew how many times he promised her. At the very least, he could have told her he was alive."

"Do you think she'll paint again?"

Emmy picked up her mending. "I'm glad you mention it. Go up to the attic, Friedel, and bring down that big box of paints. There might be a box of charcoals, too. Right near your old dolls. I've been meaning to get her set up. Remind her of what she can do."

October, 1923

"Friedel— where is she?"

"I didn't hear anything."

Emmy ran to the back garden. The new snow was undisturbed. She looked up and down the front street. No one. She ran into every room. "Ella. Ella." No one. "Get me some light." Emmy headed down the cellar steps. Friedel arrived with two lit candles. "Come with me now."

Mother and daughter entered the low-ceilinged furnace room. In the near corner on the packed earth floor, Ella sat on a pile of soft coal. She held a chunk in each hand. Her face was smeared, black everywhere, thickest on her closed eyes. Deep wet runnels scored her cheeks, thick drips darkening her neck and the collar of her blouse.

"Ella, dear, don't open your eyes. You'll hurt yourself. Hold onto me. I'm going to take you upstairs and wash your face. Were you wanting more charcoal, Ella? Don't cry, now. Don't cry."

June, 1924

Traveling on the straight track across the moor and then sloping upward toward the mountains, the train neither swerved nor swayed. Ella and Emmy sat in first-class, looking out the windows, the fields swishing past like the strokes of a palette knife.

"Oh look, Ella. Some early edelweiss. Can you see just ahead?"

Ella nodded.

"There's some blue, too. Violets, do you think? Or gentians?"

"Forget-me-nots."

"Oh, yes. I think so too, now. A lovely field of them. When we get off in Garmish-Partenkirchen, we'll walk out and find some. Forget-me-nots used to be your favorite."

Ella nodded.

Christmas, 1924,

Dear Carl and Mary and the boys,

A most happy Christmas to you all! What a fine idea to take a skiing vacation just now!

We look forward to your visit in the spring, and I think you are going to be pleased. Ella still has her moments, but she's much improved. We've taken an excursion or two (You remember how much she used to like to travel?), and from time to time she works at a drawing or some sewing. By the time you get here, you may even be treated to a conversation—or at least some words.

Enjoy the slopes for us, and have a happy New Year, too.

Love,

Emmy and Georg and Friedel

March, 1925

"Take my arm, Gabriele. The traffic is heavy." Georg Schroeter looked both ways into the street. "Just a few more streets. Do you see the spire?" Georg pointed with his finger at the end of his long arm. "You'll like the music, Ella. But be patient—we'll start and stop quite a bit."

Ella saw two black shoes kicking under Georg Schroeter. Georg tipped his hat to a woman walking alongside of them. "We're not walking too fast, are we now?" Georg looked down at Ella. "So then. There's two choirs." Georg Schroeter put his hand on Ella's back and moved her around a corner. "Remember when we visited you in your house in Murnau and we all sang?" Georg patted Ella's hand. "It's all right if I talk about that, isn't it, Ella?"

Ella tightened her hold on Georg Schroeter's arm.

"Just a little further, now. We've worked hard all winter, I'd have to say. They've brought in the soloists from all over—Dusseldorf, Cologne, Dresden, Munich. One sings Jesus, one Pontius Pilate, Mary, Judas—all of the main people in the story."

They reached the church's stone front steps. Ella planted her feet.

"Judas." Ella said.

"Yes, Ella. Do you remember who he was?"

"The Betrayer."

"Yes, Ella. That's Judas."

"I remember," she said.

10 November, 1925,

Captain Baehr,

As far as I am concerned, those art works are mine. Believe me, I earned them. You can tell him that if he

wants those paintings back, he can come and look me in
the face.

Gabriele Münter

31 December, 1925

In the high attic room, afternoon sun whittled saffron dust motes
into spears. Lest they pierce her eyeballs, she closed her eyes and
stretched out her palms, skimming the dry walls with her hands, feeling her way to the huge cedar box Emmy used for storage. Bumping
its side softly with the toe of her slipper, Ella took its measure, running her hands around its open top, following the edge of the wood,
smelling its spicy aroma and the faint ammonia of old clothes—her
girlhood middy blouse, the skirt Mama had made to match one for
Emmy, Friedel's baby dresses, Georg's wedding tie. Rummaging un-
derneath the soft things, she found what she knew would be there,
flat between two cardboards. She had kept one print for herself and
Wassily, but the second she had mailed to Emmy. She separated the
stiff outer covers from the slick paper between. Then she opened her
eyes and looked.

They'd worn their best things, it being a Sunday, and had gone for
a stroll along the river, stopping at the crest of the bridge to watch
the lazy skiffs float beneath them. When a friendly man walked near,
Wassily, always the more outgoing, had asked if the gentleman would
mind. Ella would set up the camera, he had said, and the gentleman could simply operate the mechanism to photograph them. Ella
would show him how. Then they leaned casually back against the rail
and posed, near each other but not touching, he fingering his cane,
she holding her closed parasol. He wore a boater hat and tucked one
thumb into his vest. She wore a vest as well, tan and white striped to
match her skirt. Her blouse had impossibly puffed sleeves. Ella could

not help but smile. The couple looked so innocent and young. They looked familiar. Perhaps she had known them once.

Memories lay in her brain attic loosely wrapped, accessible and harmless. Her brain cellar, though, housed an immutable presence, threatening and dangerous.

14 January, 1926

Dear Fraulein Münter,

I am responding to your letter of 10 November, 1925 stating your demand that Herr Wassily Kandinsky appear before you personally to reclaim the collection of paintings, drawing, sketches, letters, and personal effects left in your care in August, 1914. You must understand that Herr Kandinsky will make no such accommodation. Under no circumstances can he be induced to meet with you. I speak as his representative in this matter.

The collection heretofore referred to belongs to none other than the artist Wassily Kandinsky. Professor Kandinsky is the sole owner and has not transferred rights to these works to any party. He requests that you return said items to him at his place of employment, The Bauhaus, Weimar. I urge you to reconsider your demand and to prepare the items for shipping as soon as possible. The shipping charges will be born by Herr Kandinsky.

I repeat, Herr Kandinsky will not meet with you in person.

Yours,

Ludwig Baehr
Baehr and Gastright
Attorneys at Law

10 March, 1926

"The last thing we need is a lawsuit around here." Georg stoked the fire with a pointed prong. "How different is it from stealing? If they're his and she won't return them, isn't that stealing?"

Ella sat on the stairs out of his sight.

"She's offered to meet him there with a key." Emmy turned her page and looked up.

"So? What's the problem?" He swept ash from the hearth and replaced the screen.

"He won't see her. And she won't have it any other way."

"What a pair. *Mein Gott!*"

Bent forward, her knees to her chest, Ella felt her jaw clamp shut, long screws in its hinges driving upwards into her thoughts. Liquid brain tissue dripped into the verandas of her ears, drooled out onto her neck and down her chest, moistening the tender flesh of her nipples, pooling in her lap. Thoughts like puddles wetting her dress.

28 March, 1926

Fraulein Gabriele Münter,

Acting with the authority of Wassily Kandinsky, I must repeat, under no circumstances will Herr Kandinsky meet with you. My client is unmovable in this. Your responsibility is to ship the art works and effects of Herr Kandinsky to him directly, and legal action must accompany your refusal to do so.

Ludwig Baehr
Attorney at Law

June, 1926

Herwarth Walden's gallery rooms were on her route to the doctor. She found that she could pass them comfortably enough if she held her breath, much as she had done when Papa took the family for a country drive and the horse walked along the lane behind the village church where the cemetery leered at her with its broken-tooth grave markers. This walk was very like that. Very like.

8 October, 1926

"Here's a letter from Georg, Ella. Do you want to read it?"

"You do it."

"You remember what he's doing in Munich, don't you?"

Ella sat in the chair with her arms folded tightly over her chest.

> My dear Emmaline,
>
> We've packed them all up and mailed off one carton of paintings and some letters to Weimar, but the rest (It's quite a lot, really) is with the Munich Transport Company. That's what she said, isn't it? We have to hope he'll be satisfied with the one box. Friedel thinks her Tante's worth a fortune, but I wouldn't know. Truth is, they're really not hers to sell.
>
> Gave the studio key to the realty company. It was sad, poking through all those old things. Photographs all over the place, too. I'm bringing one or two home so you can see. I liked him, you know, in spite of everything. A serious man.
>
> Will you tell Ella it's all over? Give her a kiss for me.
>
> Friedel and I are going to a picture show tonight. We've earned it.
>
> We'll be on the late Sunday train. Might walk in the Englisher Garten tomorrow, if it's not too cold.

Love,

Georg

"There, see. It's over, now. Forgive and forget. That's what you should think about."
"Is it?"

February, 1927

Yellow electric lights dangled above the heavy library tables. Draped over wooden dowels, the week's newspapers hung like laundry on the line. She rarely read newspapers. Never read them, in fact. But there was a review, she'd heard, with illustrations, photographs, an account of a faculty exhibit at the Bauhaus with a party following.

She held the article beneath her chin, looking hard. In his hand he held a hat, a fedora. His hair was thin. And the little woman beside him with dark bobbed hair wore a shimmery dropped-waist dress with a fringe at the hem. She was young and pretty. His wife.

When the librarian left the room, Ella slipped the page from its layers and folded it between the leaves of her sketchpad. At home, she cut the page in shreds and stuffed the confetti in Emmy's rabbit hutch.

April, 1927

The Chinese birdkeeper sat among wooden cages stacked higgledy-piggledy along the riverbank. Ella waved as she passed him. She'd never heard him say a word to anyone, but he smiled and nodded to his regulars, Ella among them. If a customer wished to buy a bird, first the Chinese calculated on his abacus and then wrote the price in Deutschmarks on a paper. Ella had witnessed such a transaction, though she'd never made one. She liked just to come and look on her walk home from Herr Doktor each week, a pleasant stroll along the river, calming, reassuring. The scritch and scratch of claws, the whistles and the warbles made good company, good distraction from the beetles that sometimes burrowed through her brain when she was alone. When she first started coming, the dartings and hoppings about, the occasional flap or flutter would startle her, and she would draw her shoulders in, holding her pocketbook close against her. Now she talked to the birds, clucked her tongue to them, had names for the few the birdkeeper kept as his own and hung in a white wire cage on the thick branch of a low-slung tree.

Ella had her favorites. Not the carrion-eaters, black behind bars, or the carrier pigeons with tiny capsules affixed to their legs, not the doves or the tiny hummingbirds or even the songbirds. She liked to see the fighter birds, though. The Chinese kept a fierce-faced sparrow hawk, an osprey, and a peregrine falcon, each tied to its perch, the birdman's leather glove on a crate beneath. She visited the showy plumage birds, too, the red and green and blue and black ones, and the ones with oil-on-water heads. She liked to look into the floating cages that housed the ducks and geese, squawking madly, and the adolescent swans with their great reserve. And always, she turned up the row to the cage of hospital birds, the fledglings that toppled from a nest too soon or the grown birds stunned and felled by a dangerous swoop into a window, the weak and injured birds kept warm by an ancient hot water bottle wrapped in flannel. But today when she reached the cage, it was empty. She caught the birdkeeper's eye and pointed. He bowed and grinned and began to flap his arms. No wounded birds today.

December 31, 1927

"You look nice, Ella. You've stayed slim. These new dresses with the dropped waists look good on you."

Standing before the dressing table mirror, Ella watched her hands fumble with the sash at her hips. "It doesn't matter when you're old."

"Fifty isn't old, and anyway, that's not the point. Some of the people you knew before the war will be at the party."

Ella strapped her shoes. They were new and tight.

"I'm proud of you, you know."

"Because I'm not dead, you mean? Or crazy?" Ella picked up her hairbrush from the vanity. She put it down again.

"You were ill for a time. There's no shame in that. But you're better now, and you'll keep getting better." Emmy crossed her arms over her belly.

"I don't know why." Ella brushed her hair, short now and wavy. Grey hairs caught in the bristles.

"Because life wants life. I know that. But don't you think about it. Have some wine tonight, Ella. And stay as long as you can."

"I'm a throw-away person." Ella looked at herself in the mirror. Her face looked back, unsmiling. "I doubt I'll stay until midnight." She swiveled to look at her sister. "I never asked you for this— bringing me back. I can't say I'm glad."

"But *I* am. Now go. We'll talk in the morning. Get a taxi afterwards." Emmy pushed herself up from her chair.

"You sound like mother."

"I know." The corners of her mouth lifted. "You could have a whole new life."

"Ridiculous."

"So you say now. Give it a chance. You might be ready. Life could happen to you all over again."

Part Four

Chapter Nine

The Future is in the Lead

Berlin
Feast of St. Sylvester
December 31, 1927

Her head in a haze of potent *Feuerzangenbowle*, Ella stumbled toward the only open seat in the room. She needed to sit, even if it meant sharing the settee with a gnome.

Herwarth Walden, her host, had roamed through his lavish house topping her glass each time he neared despite her protestations that she had been ill, could not take alcohol, might embarrass herself, might be sick.

"But after such an ordeal, it is necessary to let the spirit free," he had said, his own red face emanating the rotwein, rum, and spices infusing his prized punch.

And for a time, just holding the etched crystal had been sufficient to help her navigate the waves of chatter, as though the glass were an astrolabe and she a lone boat on a dark sea. But then she had taken a tentative sip, and then another. And now, well, she needed a harbor, and quickly.

She grasped the padded arm of the small sofa and lowered herself, her eyes fixed upon her punch glass, woozy. What would be worse—that she might spill the red wine on her new blue dress or that she might stain the yellow brocade of Walden's furniture? Or that she might accidently touch the elbow of the little man seated on the couch? He had made himself as small as possible, folding his arms over his chest, crossing his thin legs. Hips? He had none.

"*Glücklich ist, wer vergisst, was doch nicht zu ändern ist...,*" he hummed under his breath.

"I beg your pardon." She was afraid she had, indeed, nudged him when she sat down. He did not look like a man who would wish to be disturbed.

"Happy is he who forgets what can't be changed...."

The melody was familiar.

"I can't place the tune." She let her eyes rove to the side, just catching him as he sat. What a strange little man, singing alone in the noisy room. Even she could tell that.

"*Die Fledermaus,*" he said. "Strauss."

"Oh," she said. His head looked too big for his body. Or perhaps it only seemed big as she sat close to him on the narrow couch. She would get up, as soon as the room stopped moving.

"All of Vienna attends *Die Fledermaus* tonight," he said.

She had to be careful with her eyes, but she found that she could still converse. "You are Austrian?" His words required a response, and she could provide one.

"Of course not," he said. "But one yearns for culture in Berlin. It is a city of crass revelry."

Ella drank again from her punch glass. She felt steadier, now that she was sitting. She could look out onto the straining paunches and the slim haunches, the imposing bosoms and the corseted derrières of Berlin's art cognoscenti as they bumped and swayed and shifted position in a buzz of conversation. A string trio in the corner of the large room set out a tight quickstep, and two couples twirled on the wooden platform Walden had laid atop his Oriental carpet. One of the dancers looked familiar. His hair had greyed, to be sure, but she could have sworn it was Jakob Doncker, her old friend Olga's husband. She must be wrong. This man had his arm around his slender partner's waist, pulling her body close, her hips in the cradle of his.

"Fraulein Münter." The man beside her, again. Was he calling her name? Ella heard him as though through a congregation of insects. Careful not to take her eyes from the dancers, she raised her voice. "You know me?"

"I have reviewed your paintings."

He might just as well have said he'd known her father, had fished in the Isar, had brewed beer in her cellar, had mined diamonds, had kissed the Kaiser. Amazed, Ella turned her head to look at him, but the sudden movement unsteadied her, and she had to grasp the arm of the settee. "Please excuse me." She rose. She needed the toilet.

"Let me escort you," the gnome said. He was still singing, or perhaps she only thought he was singing. The sound might be coming from her own head.

When he stood, he was not so very small. He was just taller than Ella as he curved behind her, guiding her through the crowd. As for the size of his head, she dared not look. She let him steer her through the rooms, his hand firm on her elbow. How did he know she was headed for the Ladies?

She did not know how long she had stood before Walden's toilet, but when she finally emerged, freshly splashed with cold water from Walden's tap, she felt somewhat better. The man was waiting.

"You will eat," he said, neither pronouncing nor instructing, simply predicting a certainty.

He seemed a kind of shepherd dog, not exactly touching Ella but shouldering her toward Walden's great dining table with its vast assortment of meats and salads. She had the sense that if she were to walk too near a cliff, he would throw himself in front of her.

"Herring and cabbage, for the New Year. Cheese and bread and butter for your stomach." He might have been naming foods, but he was not. He was choosing for her, putting spoonfuls and slices on her plate.

He guided her toward the small tables set out in the conservatory. There, with a dozen white snowflakes drifting carelessly through the black world outside the glass, they sat under steamy ferns and bearing fig trees. Coffee appeared, and the blurred lines around people's heads sharpened into focus, delineating features. It seemed he was not a gnome at all. He was a tidy, precise man, grey-haired and clean-shaven, grey-suited and immaculate about the neck and hands. Ella found she had an appetite. He ate beside her, spooning fruited custard into his small mouth.

When she sat back from the table and had drunk her second cup of coffee with cream, he rose.

"Please come," he said. "They are pouring the lead."

Guests clustered around a small alcove in the passageway back to the drawing room. A tall man in a white apron held a long silver spoon, and under it he waved a lit candle. From time he time, he dropped the contents of the spoon into a wide pewter cup of water. Then he fished into the cup with his fingers and gently grasped the form that swam there. "Ah," he told the large woman in black lace at his elbow. "A journey. You will be taking a long journey in the New Year."

"Oh, yes," the matron cried. "We're going abroad. To America! How splendid that you knew."

"*Mais non*," the man replied. "It is the lead. The future is in the lead."

"And will you pour for me and this lady?" The grey-haired man had his hand once more on Ella's elbow.

The tall man bowed.

It was a ball for Ella. And another ball for the man at her elbow.

"My luck will change," he said. "And yours as well. Perhaps we will have luck together."

"I don't know you," Ella said.

"But I know you," the man said. "And so my luck has already changed."

After the lead ball, the shepherd guided her to watch the fireworks, removing his suit coat and draping it around her shoulders as they gathered with the others under Walden's shallow portico. Bursts of primary colors hung like spiders of light against the night sky before they fell and someone cooed "Ahhhh." But some of the guests grew uncomfortable with the rat-a-tat-tats, the pops and frizzes and flickering lights. One man turned to go inside. "Too much like Verdun to suit me," he said. The smack and spatter of the colorful sprays unnerved Ella, too. She tensed her shoulders and covered her ears. And she was cold. Jacket-less, her companion circled behind and moved her back inside, away from the raucous clapping and the gaiety. There, he found once more the secluded alcove, deserted now, and nodded to Ella, directing her to the padded bench. She sank onto the cushion, then moved to make room for him as well.

"You said you'd reviewed my painting. Here? In Walden's gallery rooms?"

"Yes. And in Cologne. And earlier, in Paris."

"That was years and years ago."

"Yes."

"I am embarrassed to have forgotten your name," Ella said. "We must have met."

"No."

"But you knew me."

"Yes." Beside her on the bench, he crossed his legs at the knee. Loose jointed, his foot in its gleaming shoe hung limp but graceful. The knobs of his ankles were covered in black silk.

"And could I have read your reviews? Were they published?"

"In many places. I can let you read them, if you like."

"Then, will you tell me your name?" Ella said.

"Johannes Eichner is my name."

But she could not call it up, could not say she'd seen or read or heard it. Squeezed beside him on the bench, she could not easily turn to face him. "It seems silly to shake your hand now."

"There will be time for that later."

Wassily had said something like that, something about having plenty of time.

"My time is running out," Ella said.

"Then I will drive you home," Johannes Eichner said. He stood and offered Ella his hand. She took it, and he helped her onto her feet.

It was past three when Ella opened the Schroeters' door. The house was dark. She removed her shoes and went quietly up to her bedroom, glad that the household was asleep. She was feeling something, something she could not name. She had sat in Johannes Eichner's Audi, the motor purring into the empty street, and talked for hours. She told Eichner she had been ill for half a decade, delirious, frightened, shaken, depressed. She wasn't certain she could re-enter society. Tonight had been an experiment in being in company.

And he had sat beside her, his hands clasped softly in his lap. "I understand illness of that kind. Recovery can be slow." He appreciated its perils, he said, the setbacks, the uncertainties, the demons. He, too, had experienced suffering, had witnessed it intimately, even to the grave.

She spoke about painting, about the satisfaction of losing oneself in the work, of elapsing time, of forgetting where one's hand stopped and the impulse to draw or paint began. He nodded at that. He wished he knew more. He admired painters, he said, had written about several in Berlin and elsewhere over the years. He, himself, was a journalist and a scholar of art, an historian. He did not create; he criticized. Or if that seemed too harsh, perhaps she might say that he interpreted.

She didn't know, she said. She didn't read reviews. She had been advised not to, she said, by a man who had meant a great deal to her, a man to whom she had been attached, a man who had taught her everything.

"And was that man Wassily Kandinsky?" Johannes Eichner had said.

Ella found that she could still breathe.

When he walked her to the door and she offered him her hand, he bowed, instead, his own hands behind his back. Courtly, he asked if he might call upon her. She nodded, looking over his shoulder into the silent, black night.

Inside her sister's house, she sat at her small desk. Forgive and forget, Emmy said. Easy to say. But, perhaps. She found her journal and wrote in a trembling hand. "I think, perhaps, that life may come again to me. Am I ready for it?" She ripped the page from her book and folded it over and over. Before she turned out the light, she put the paper in the drawer and shut it firmly.

Galerie

"Still Life with Saint George," 1911
Gabriele Münter
Oil on cardboard
$20^1/_{16}'' \times 26^3/_4''$
Städtische Galerie im Lenbachhaus, Munich
Gabriele Münter Bequest

Knowing the Christian iconography of St. George and the dragon provides little help to the viewer who wishes to understand the meaning, if there is any, of Gabriele Münter's "Still Life with Saint George." In Christian myth, George, a young Roman soldier under the command of the emperor Diocletian, was tortured for his unwillingness to persecute Christians. He survived his ordeal and went on to earn the gratitude of a Libyan king for rescuing his daughter from the ravages of a terrible dragon. With such heroic deeds ascribed to him, one wonders at George's presence in the painting Fraulein Münter has named after him.

First of all, the icon is represented not centrally but, in fact, encircled in the upper left corner of the painting by two irregular smears of color, one orange, one black. The figure, himself, is drawn the way a child might execute it, the face a blur, the steed stiff and unproportioned. If anything, St. George floats, disembodied, above the other figures of the still life who haunt a mysterious tabletop rather than impose their weight upon it. The largest figure is an image of an Eastern Madonna and child, looking like a simplified carved statue, the face of the seated Mother a scrawl, the figure of the infant awkwardly placed on her lap. Before this figure sit two folk objects, both statues of a human form. The larger of them might be a bearded woodsman carrying a hunting horn. Closest of all to the viewer is the image of a carved, wooden hen seated in a brooding posture before a completely indistinct figure and a vase of indistinct flowers.

Gone are the expectations of realism, flowers and fruit in harmonious composition. Gone is the coherence of like objects, reflected forms. Gone are the expectations of *trompe l'oeil,* the buzzing fly upon the rose, the worm upon the peony bloom.

Instead, we have discomfort. Muddy colors, suggestive forms, shadowy appearances, visible brushstrokes play with the way our eyes travel about the canvas. All is flat—but wait, there is depth. All is still—but perhaps not. We are in a room. No, we are in a cave. The figures are toys. But perhaps they are malevolent beings. Nothing evokes what it is. Everything evokes an inward sensation of discontent and unease.

We are perplexed by the painting, but we dare not leave it. Fear and magnetism propel us inward where paradox and ambiguity predominate.

J. Eichner

Chapter Ten

Snakes

Murnau
June, 1932

JOHANNES WAS undoubtedly right. "There's no question it's a liability," he had said. "Any asset you don't directly benefit from becomes a liability. That's an economic fact, Gabriele. And if what you say is true—that the locals don't like you—well, then, isn't it best just to get out?" He was right about a great many things—Ella's finances as well as his own, how the two of them could travel together companionably, how they could socialize without raising eyebrows, how Ella might regain her strength and confidence in herself. But when it came to the house in Murnau, she would have to take action alone, no matter how difficult, no matter how she suffered in doing it. If Johannes were right, she would have to sell the house.

The thunderstorm had blown over, the rain lightened to a drizzle when she stepped into the weeds below Kottmüllerallee. From the cover of her umbrella, Ella looked up the grade. The house was losing its yellow skin like a sunbather who has fallen asleep and wakes to find herself burned, the thin, transparent ectoderm crackled, lacy fringe outlining peeled places of raw flesh. One of the shutters had fallen off and had blown into the bushes at the bottom of the hill.

She turned to the path beside the house and crossed over into Wassily's strawberries. But the patch had turned its back to the cultivated flowerbeds and run off to the mountain slopes behind the house. Wild grasses and goldenrod infiltrated the raspberries, the roses. Beneath one bush, a length of snakeskin.

"So you think I should get rid of it," she had said.

"Think of the unnecessary expenses—the taxes and upkeep."

"I could try to get work again."

"Painting portraits?"

Of course Johannes wasn't serious. Even assuming she could bring herself to go back to that demeaning work, no one was commissioning anything in this economy. As Johannes liked to joke, the Reichsmark wasn't worth a pfennig.

"In any case," Johannes had continued, "your family money appears to be run through. You can thank your brother for that. And your brother-in-law."

"Please don't be sharp about them, Johannes. They rallied around me when I needed them, sure enough. Besides, you haven't even met them."

"Gabriele, my dear. The fact remains, you have no money. While I am perfectly delighted to treat you well here in Munich, that place of yours in Murnau is your responsibility."

"You don't know what it meant to me." She hadn't brought him down in the four years they had known each other. For her it was a decade. "I suppose I'll have to go and take a look." The thought gave her no pleasure. Fanny, a letter in her hand, walked across her brain.

"Do you want me to come along?"

"Give me a few days. Then drive down. I want you to see it at least once."

Johannes agreed. An excuse to test the Audi on the new road, he said. "You've more than one bedroom, I suppose."

"I'm not suggesting anything untoward, you know."

"I should think not."

And so it was arranged.

She struggled to open the cellar door, ducking to stay in the shelter of her umbrella as she jiggled the key and rattled the doorknob. When at last the lock gave and she pushed in, stale air fled out the open door like a burglar caught in the act. She propped her umbrella in a corner and began the climb to the upper floors, mindful not to see Wassy's horses galloping alongside her on the painted side of the staircase. She would have liked to close her eyes everywhere.

Upstairs, she sneezed. "Good God," she said. The rooms were a museum of dusts, balls of fuzz, cloudy surfaces, the tables receding through jellied air. The glass paintings on the eating room wall looked out through cataracts. Dead flies littered the windowsills. It was just as well that Johannes had not come with her. Sensitive as he was to all things unseemly or disagreeable, he might have turned and left on the spot.

Gingerly, she walked into the sitting room, startling herself over and over with the air she disturbed, the creak of her feet on the floorboards. Worse than the dust was the lacuna of memory. Ghosts of conversations climbed out from the walls like mad clowns snatching at her hair and dress, their features exaggerated and horrifying. Their words banged away at each other, Russian, French, German, grammars, dialects, idioms, laughing, nonsensical. The hinterglasmalerie stood sentinel, little Saint Georges riding off, dragons cowering, each one brandishing a spear in her direction as though laying to waste some hope she had harbored. She put her hands over her ears. Her own paintings on the walls seemed unfamiliar, images and objects she couldn't recall seeing, landscapes she might never have visited, portraits of strangers. Somebody else must have made them. What she had failed to be flashed up into her face. She had failed her own talent. She had thought that if she walked with the gods, she was one of them. Wassily and Marc and Jawlensky had all stood on the edge of a cliff together, but when the others flew into the ether, she could not follow. She was suspended still, hanging between the past of all her promise and some indifferent future where what she might have been and done was unknowable, unacknowledged, and irrelevant.

Ella set down her pocketbook and carryall and circled warily through the living area, the kitchen, the music room, fearful of something she could not name. She crossed the studio area to stand in the doorway of his bedroom. His dusty dress coat sprawled across his bed where she had put it a decade ago, flattened and splayed out like the skin of an animal that has been hit on the road and left to disintegrate.

She returned to the sitting room and sat there for a bit, listening to the dust settle around her. For all that she had been flattened for a time, she was here now, taking stock, assessing. Johannes had blown some breath into her as though she had been falling like a leaf and then caught the wind and fluttered up. She had supposed that without that breeze, she might drift down to the earth, be ground against it by the heel of a boot. She had felt herself that thin, leaf thin. But here in the midst of the decay, she was still breathing. It was not killing her to sit in this house, at this table, among these memories.

In fact, she kept a cheery, little album in her mind, pictures fixed in place. Wassily, proud with his shovel in the garden. Fanny peeling potatoes, apron tied behind her back. His mother at the tea table. Alexei and Marianne laughing. Maria Marc with her soft, white skin. Herself at her easel, dissolved in the surface, colors announcing themselves, black lines finding a path through the picture. Life going forward.

And other things. At first, when they were young, she had loved the yellow house for the way the air moved through it. They would throw open the windows, and the breeze tumbling down from the mountains would whoosh through the rooms. In the early days, she had run up and down the floors barefooted, talking as though the house were a friendly dependent. "I'm curling your hair," she had said to her bedroom window the time she sewed white curtains and hung them so that she and Wassy could close themselves in at night. And everywhere the smell of paint—wall paint, oil paint, whitewash, thinners, solvents, brushes bathing in amber glasses, rags crisping as they dried.

Ella leaned against the eating table and drew a cup and saucer in the powder on its surface. She supposed she should do as Johannes suggested—tidy the place up and then go into the village and engage a sales agent. Put the pain of that past behind her. Well, she would make a cup of tea and think about it. She forced herself out of the chair, ran water at the kitchen tap until it was no longer brown, and used her handkerchief to wipe down the sink, rinsing it over and over. She poured water over the tea kettle and then filled and emptied it and filled it again, and again. If you were going to drink tea made from that kettle, the interior had to be clean, even if you couldn't see it. You wanted where a thing came from to be true. Make your inside match your outside. If you'd be embarrassed to show your thoughts, don't think them. Be one with yourself, clean inside and out. Tell the truth of yourself to your own heart.

She unpacked the bread and cheese she had brought down from Munich. In the cupboard was a jar of Fanny's raspberry jam, still unopened. She unscrewed the lid and tipped the wax disc covering the jam to reveal the dark, preserved fruit. So, not everything decayed while she was gone. She went back to the eating table with her wet handkerchief, cleared a spot for herself, and laid a place—plate, knife, spoon, cup. When the kettle whistled, she poured the boiling water into the familiar brown teapot and carried it to the table.

After she had eaten and drunk, she looked about her once again. The house was dusty, true, but it was also dry, even after today's heavy rain, and nothing appeared moldy, nothing broken but one shutter. And perhaps her pride. "Well, let's see," she said aloud, silence gulping down her words. How old was she now? Fifty-four? Not an old woman, but a damaged one. She took a deep breath and blew at the dust on the table. She stood up. Even a leaf had a spine. If Johannes came to the house now, there would be no question she would have to sell. But perhaps, if she could spruce things up a bit, he might see things differently.

She rubbed her hands together, bringing herself back. "Too bad Fanny's gone," she told the silent room. "She'd have put things to rights." She left the tea things on the table and went down to the cellar.

Tucked and low under the stairs was a wide, shallow closet, its door cut into the grooved panels lining the walls. Easy to miss this closet, she thought, Fanny's domain, scrub brushes and buckets, brooms and mops, cleansers and solvents. She'd once thought to build a darkroom there. Another failure. But there was still time, wasn't there?

She unfolded a worn table-cover Fanny had stored there, shook it loose, and tied it around her waist. She found an old, thin dishtowel to cover her hair. She combed cobwebs from the bristles of the scrub brush, the straws of the broom, the fibers of the mop. She filled the bucket with bottles of vinegar and ammonia and a cake of lye soap. Armed like a laborer, she climbed the stairs on the back of Wassy's galloping horses. Art elevated you, and then you trod on its back. It didn't hold you aloft. You didn't stay up. You weren't a bird. You didn't fly. You fell to the earth and smashed things. You had to clean up after yourself. That was your life. But perhaps you could live it.

Beginning with the ceilings, she whacked at webby corners with her broom. If Johannes could see her now, he'd run. Best to do the dirty work without him. Generous as he was with her, he was not a man who dirtied his hands. Cerebral, he lived in a world of scholarship and business, and he liked to see his female companion dignified. When he suggested she paint him a portrait of herself for Christmas, he directed her. "Wear your dark dress." Everything about him was orderly and even a little prim, but his sense of righteousness gave her something to lean against. When her eyes sought out the future, she could see nothing clearly, but she could feel him at her back. She did not ask what else she might feel.

She pulled down the sad curtains and gave the soft furniture a vigorous brushing, sending up clouds of dusty memories. How Alexei had sprawled about this room, larger than the sofa or settee, too big to seat or settle. And that odd Franz Marc. If she had known he'd be killed at Verdun, still a young man, she'd have made a greater effort to learn to like him. She swept him up on the wooden floor, forming volcanoes as Fanny used to do, whisking them into the ample dustpan. She was pulling down all the dust, all the accumulation of years.

She'd have to go through the rooms all over again with vinegar-water and rags. You cleaned in layers, down and down, an archeologist, until you reached the thing itself, the thing beyond which you could not go, the window sills, the tables and chairs, the floor. You were subtracting to elements, essentials. She was getting down to it, down to the bottom of things, down to the hard surfaces you could touch and brace yourself against. And she hadn't even tackled his room yet.

Johannes would have to sleep there, she reasoned, in Wassily's bed. That meant she'd have to enter the room, move *his* things, empty the chest, strip the bed. She recalled his underthings, folded in the drawers. She would have to touch them, lift them out one by one. She pinched the thin handle of the dustpan, then set it down

and stood the broom in the corner. Back in the kitchen she poured
out more tea and sat with a second cup. Well, that's how you managed. You had a thought. You fortified yourself. You might not like it,
but you made a plan. You saw yourself doing the job, cast yourself in
the role you'd written. And then, you put yourself to it. Well, down in
the cellar there used to be boxes. She did not need to sit and weep.
She would not.

The cellar was surprisingly dry, the boxes firm and usable once
she'd blown the dust from their tops. She climbed the stairs again
with a stack of containers, the horses galloping under her, and she
stood before his room. For a moment in the doorway, she tried to see
him lying there, leaning up on one elbow, reading. But the bed was
just a bed, small, anonymous. And he was nowhere in it. He would
be 65 years old, now, certainly grey, balding perhaps. And nothing
smelled of him, only of the dust that settled over everything. She
looked at his black coat. Johannes could wear it, though he wouldn't.

Ella walked to the painted chest and opened the drawer in which
she had folded Wassy's things the day before her world collapsed.
Nothing had been touched. She took out a set of his summer underdrawers and held them to her chest, fingering the thin fabric, burying her face, inhaling deeply. Cotton, just cotton. She bit at one edge,
gripping it hard between her teeth, and tugged until the cloth began
to rip, an aching sound close to her ear. She tore the garment in two.
Good. She reached into the drawer and pulled out all of the things
she'd stored there, tumbling the knitted union suits and the newer
lightweight sets onto the bed. She bit another one, and another. Very
good. She ripped and ripped again. What would he think of her now?
She began to laugh and laugh. She wiped her eyes with a handful of
torn cotton. Yes, it was comical. She'd need plenty of rags for cleaning and scrubbing. And here she had a drawer-full of them, perfect
for mopping up the detritus of those days and securing for herself a
place to live once again. When Johannes arrived, she could tell him

she had cleaned the house with Wassily's underwear, and if he didn't find that funny, she would laugh anyway. She was done with it all, the pain of it. The yellow house in Murnau had been her sanctuary, with or without the men in her life, and she would find a way to keep it.

"You say there's no heat in winter? That's rather limiting, don't you think?" Johannes sat in an armchair, legs crossed, taking in the bright room, the light, the space, the breeze, watching Ella bustle about.

"It's a summer house. A getaway."

"Mind you, I'm not opposed to getting away. I don't like what's going on in town. People are all nerves these days, and I do hate all the crowds and the demonstrations. The economy is a mess, and I doubt these National Socialists can do what they say."

"It's not as though the house is costing a great deal. I own it free and clear."

"The Kraftfahrtstrasse could make a difference, I suppose" Johannes said. "Tourism. Skiing. That sort of thing. If the Reichsmark ever buys anything again, that is. But it will. Real estate down here will be worth something if government ever gets a hold of this inflation. It wouldn't be bad to have a place here, away from the cities."

"Is there a way to economize? I hate being a burden." Ella was setting the table for their dinner.

"You might, of course, give up your Munich flat. Save on rent that way."

"And move here permanently? We just discussed the problem of heat."

"That, of course, could be changed. I could look into it. But no, I was rather thinking you might move in with me in Munich. And we might both come down here from time to time."

Ella turned to him, stunned. His crossed leg swung from his knee, keeping time to a rhythm only he heard. She leaned against the eating table, forks in her hand like a small clutch of steel flowers.

"I have lived with just one man in all my life." She measured each syllable. "It nearly killed me."

"Yes, but I'm not your Russian lover."

Ella winced. "No, nor my German husband either."

"Let's just say I'm your *lebensgefährte*. We could leave it at that for now."

Ella turned back to the table. She pressed the sharp tines of the forks against the palm of one hand. *Lebensgefährte*. Could that be it, then? A life's companion. Johannes Eichner, writer, scholar, partner. Not a passionate attachment such as she had known before, but not a loveless one either. Or rather a different kind of love. A friendship. A loving friendship. A man who cared about her, protected her. Could one be content with that? Did she have a choice?

"Yes," she turned to look at him. "We could."

By winter, Johannes had installed a heating system, and they spent the next two years motoring back and forth between his Munich flat and the yellow house, taking respites from the mounting tensions of the city during the more clement months, taking part in the intellectual life, what there was of it, when they were in town. The subject of marriage proper asserted itself infrequently. *Lebensgefährte* seemed sufficient. Better than sufficient. The yellow house had its attractions for them both, and their intervals there grew longer and longer. Had they realized how furiously the political electricity bristled in the Munich air, they might not have returned to the city at all.

The event began with plumbing. Fastidious in his personal habits, Johannes insisted on replacing the outdoor facility with the latest in indoor accommodation. "It's long overdue. I'll motor down to Garmish-Partenkirchen in the morning," he announced one evening. "I've a lead on a contractor there." Ella looked up from her beadwork. He had such energy for improvements. Even as he talked, he roamed around the room, repositioning a chair, adjusting the angle of a painting on the wall. She had no taste for such plans and preferred to stay back, building a small fire in the stove, lighting a kerosene lamp. Johannes had plans for that, too. "I'll see to putting in some electricity while I'm there. Are you sure you won't come?" No, she said. She looked forward to silence. The house in his absences suited her. She could reacquaint herself with its ghosts. "No," she said. She'd spend the day indoors. There was this purse to finish. Or perhaps she might look through some seed catalogues. They could plant a garden before long. That, too, was a ghost.

Johannes returned by nightfall, exhausted. The contractor he'd been advised to hire wasn't available. With all the government buildings going up in the cities, skilled men like Klingenberg had bigger fish to fry.

"You're lucky you caught me here," he told Johannes. "I spend most of my days in Munich. I've had my hands full with a big renovation."

"What's that?" Johannes said. He knew, himself, that Munich was jammed with cranes and demolition equipment. One could hardly drive through the center city, so many streets were blocked off.

"Enlarging government offices—Union, Marienbad. The SA High Command outgrew the Brown House. Ernst Röhm's moved his quarters, and my men have done the work. I've been careful to do things properly, you can imagine." He laughed thinly. He couldn't be bothered with Johannes's little domestic project. But he knew a workman who might take on the job, so Johannes drove out to a cluster of small properties outside town to find the man and arrange for him to assess the plumbing for the yellow house. He hadn't had time to engage an electrician.

"In any event, you're going to need to make some choices," he told Ella. Fixtures, basins—that sort of thing. "We'll drive up to town for a few days, and you can shop. Besides, I've not read the news for weeks. This isolation down here is fine for a bit, but I want to check in at the paper and talk to Berger. His last letter was odd."

A few days turned into a fortnight. As infrequently as they visited the Munich flat now, there were errands to run. Johannes made day-trips, attending to family business in Augsburg and Nuremberg, consolidating loans and collecting rents on some properties he owned there. Ella visited her dentist and had her hair colored. She made some preliminary sketches for a three-quarters oil portrait of Frau Hartmann, an old friend, and she sorted her stockings and under-things preparatory to giving away the soiled and worn ones and re-plenishing her supply from the Munich shops. She had intended to order a new frock from her dressmaker as well, but found that Frau Silverstein and her family had left the city, suddenly, the neighbor said, and without leaving a forwarding address. Such an inconve-nience to find another seamstress, Ella grumbled, and she found her-self complaining to Johannes the minute he arrived home.

"And something else, Johannes," Ella reported. "I hear that Herr Doctor Cohn is no longer seeing patients."

"It's this thing with the Jews." He sighed and bent to remove his shoes. "Cohn has relatives in Haifa, at least. Presumably he'll join them."

Ella walked to the stove. "What *thing* do you mean? I have tomato soup with potato fritters. Will that do for dinner?"

Johannes sat back in his chair and stretched his legs.

"Well for instance, Rosenblaum had to prove he did front line ser-vice in 1918 to keep his post at the University. Luckily for him, his wife kept his discharge papers."

"Well, that's not so bad, is it? He *did* have the papers."

"Yes, but now the Reich teachers' organization is asking for proof of Aryan status, and, of course, he can't come up with *that*. But it's not only that business."

The telephone rang. It was Berger, himself. Jelsky was to have reviewed the new Riefenstahl film opening tonight. Could Johannes do it instead as a personal favor?

"You don't mind, do you, Ella? You'll want to come as well. It's a documentary from Nuremburg."

"Aren't you exhausted? You just got in. Why can't Jelsky do it?"

"He was let go. I'm all right. I'd like to see it."

Ella frowned and looked up from her cooking. "All right, then."

"They're saying this film will make history."

"Jelsky's Jewish, isn't he?"

"Yes, and out of work now."

They took two seats on the aisle as the first credits began to roll.

"Leni Riefenstahl." Ella pulled Johannes's sleeve and whispered. "I thought she was an actress, but look, she's the director."

Johannes nodded and took a small pad of paper and his pencil from his breast pocket. "That's why Berger wanted a review."

Just as the opening swells of Wagnerian majesty were subsiding, the film reel stopped and the house lights came up. The crowd murmured puzzlement and discontent. There to Johannes's left, two SS hulked in the aisle while the portly theater manager reached over Johannes and Ella with a cane and poked at a man sitting just to Ella's right. "Jews are not permitted in this theater."

"I have a ticket," the man replied.

"Jews are not permitted in the cinema. You must leave immediately."

The two SS stood with their hands behind their backs, wooden truncheons tucked under their arms.

The crowd grew silent. Then from the back of the house, a loud voice: "Get the filthy Jews out of here." From the balcony, "*Kotzbrocken*" and "*Drecksack.*" Ella drew up her shoulders.

Again reaching across her, the manager wielded his cane, prodding the shoulder of the grey-coated man at Ella's side. "Get up. Get out."

"Stand up, Ella. Let the man out." Johannes rose and clasped Ella's arm.

"Yes, of course."

The Jew said nothing as he passed before them, but his eyes flickered left and right and he pulled his coat collar high around his neck. As he walked up the aisle, another loud voice from behind Ella shouted "*Heil Hitler,*" and a small, disjointed chorus echoed the words from the seats nearby. As suddenly as it stopped, the movie reel began again. The lights dimmed, and the rustle of the audience was drowned in a leitmotif from *Die Meistersinger von Nürnberg.* On the bright screen, a mass of party members assembled for the National Socialist Party Congress in Nuremberg, and beneath them glowed the film's title: *Triumph of the Will.*

Ella returned to her seat next to Johannes and was swept away for a time by the rousing martial music, the multiple camera angles, the aerial photography, the cheers of the assembly as they gathered to listen to the *Führer.* Still, sitting in the crowded, dark theater, she could feel the press of a cane across her chest into the shoulder beside her, and when the film was over, she had no taste for chatter. Nor did Johannes speak, excepting to hail a taxicab and pay the fare.

As the car pulled up before their apartment house, Johannes leaned forward to release the door handle when a cold, sharp wind yanked the door out of his hands and slammed it open into the wet night. Startled at the violence of the gust, Ella climbed clumsily out of the taxi. Trembling, she looked up and down the dark street as though she were being watched. She ran for the flat, her heart pounding.

Munich
August, 1937

A dessicated beetle fell from the thin curtain.

Out in the wild wind, it had flown to the sill, found a fine fissure in the old wooden window frame, and descended into the dark cave from whose ceiling hung the heavy glass pane. Under the weight of roof above, from storm to sash, it had wormed its way forward into the glowing inhospitable room where it had died.

Unremarked upon, it was swept away.

Then, too, if a butterfly wing in a dark, still forest trembles, fluttering a wisp of air to rise and grow and push the moon-loving sea toward some apocalyptic upheaval, how much more so the trail of a single stiff hair on paper? Or a whole brush upon canvas? What then? What whirlwind rises from that moment of stroke upon surface? What vortex ensues? What civilization shudders?

Johannes put down his pen. He wrote for himself, now. *The Journal of Art and Philosophy* that had published his essays for twenty years had dismissed the staff and closed its doors. The directive came directly from Josef Goebbels: the publication was "Bolshevist," elitist, corrupted, untraditional, un-German.

"I hardly think that's fair," Ella had said. "You haven't attacked anyone. You may be more refined than some, but who could be more traditional? And as for *un-German*—well, what's that supposed to mean?"

"Look, it's better not to raise a fuss. Better to stay out of their way."

"You can't mean me. I'm not the least bit political."

"Perhaps not, but every image is a comment on the values of the time and place."

"I don't think that," Ella said. "I just paint the way I feel."

"Your feelings have a context, Gabriele. They come into being as the child of your experience. The thing is, if the National Socialists can get away with burning books the way they did in '33—well, you know what they say about living in *interesting* times. We need to be careful how these people see us."

Ella frowned but said nothing.

"Look, we're going to see it for ourselves on Sunday."

Some days earlier, Johannes had promised to take Ella to the new state-run art exhibition. The Nazis wanted to teach a lesson. She should expect to be shocked. The *Entartete Kunst* was not for the faint of heart. And Kandinsky would be hanging there, too. She should steel herself.

Ella stroked her crossed arms. "Why should I care what they do with Kandinsky?"

"I think you underestimate yourself, my dear. I'm telling you, this won't be easy."

A tense and impatient crowd moved slowly forward through impos-ing August heat. Standing on the bright sidewalk in the line that wound along the Galeriestrasse toward the broad entrance of the old Archaologisches Institut and up its narrow back stairs into the sec-ond floor exhibition rooms, Ella felt a snake wind round her neck. With each wave of movement toward the door and into the airless stairway, her throat constricted further, cutting off any possibility of a scream. Halfway up the dark tunnel, she tried to turn back down the stairs, but the crowd pushed forward, admitting no deserter. "Keep in line," she heard. She scanned the heads above her for a glimpse of light as the crowd crawled upwards.

At a landing in the stifling stairwell stood a huge and horrible sculpture of a wild-eyed Jesus crucified at a tortured angle on a wooden cross, a mad savior, a statue placed so threateningly that the throng of viewers had to sidle past its sharp wooden knees thrusting into the passageway. It frightened her less than the green-shirted Orpo looming beside the door as they passed, jeering. Behind the sculpture, over the arch that led to the exhibit, a heading in thick black print proclaimed *"Ausstellung Entartete Kunst"*—Degenerate Art Exhibition. As Johannes had said, nine rooms of madness and insults authorized by the Third Reich.

Men and women in their summer Sunday best pushed and shoved past her. A large woman rammed against Ella, her shoulder hitting a painting, rocking it on its nail. The painting depicted a tortured head hovering over slashes of a cityscape. "This stuff is garbage," a man said, "more of that Jewish-Bolshevist filth." Ella flinched. She forced her swollen feet across the worn floor past a label reading "An Insult to German Womanhood." When she entered the room marked "Nature As Seen By Sick Minds," the snake shuddered just slightly tighter, dry scales scratching her neck, a busy tongue licking her ear. Johannes, craning his neck above the crowd, took her arm. "It's all right, my dear, we're almost there. I think I can see him."

The room smelled of urine, of feces, as though in the night the guards had relieved themselves in the corners and on the walls where the paintings hung. Straight from rehabilitation classes in the prisons and madhouse, some of the artists had actually employed excrement, thick brown paste smeared heavily along with carmine and ochers from tubes. People in the crowd were gagging. The guards in the corners looked on with amusement.

Ella pushed on. She spotted him, too. Wassily was hanging at a crazed angle, the parallel lines of the frame sliding awkwardly in diagonals from the horizontal of the ceiling, the balanced energies of his exuberant reds and spiritual blues askew like the drawings of a naughty child sent to his room angry and left to cry and kick the furniture. The label over his *Improvisation 10* read "Modernism—A Conspiracy By People Who Hate German Decency." On either side of him were ragged burlaps chewed on the edges and smeared by brown fingers dipped in chamber pots and anuses. Filth was his neighbor.

Ella turned away, sickened. It was so blindingly stupid. He had never been interested in producing art that made social commentary. His paintings were transcendent expressions, spiritual, even Biblical in their themes. Now his work hung defeated, a man on a rope in the public square. The degradation would have saddened him. For all his stature in the art community, how little the general public understood him. "I'd like to spit on that one," a man said. Another gentleman nearby ducked his head and lowered his eyes, though his companion surveyed the painting with interest. Yet when Ella caught her glance, the woman looked away. Ella felt dizzy. Johannes took out his pocket handkerchief and offered it to her.

On the anterior wall hung a friend, flanked by black graffiti careening up and over the canvas. The word "*Entartung*" scrawled beside the painting pointed out its "degeneracy." A swastika painted on the wall approved the term.

"Johannes, look," Ella said. "It's Beckmann."

"*Die Bettler*. I remember it."

"They make him seem mad. And after all he's been through."

"That's Franz Marc on the left wall."

"He's dead twenty years. What is the point?"

"My God. They've got him upside-down."

Ella felt like dissolving, memory thieves stealing her resolve to face the exhibition boldly. "I've got to sit." Her feet had grown puffy in the heat, her shoes tight. But there were no seats, no benches for viewing.

"Hold on to me." Johannes led the way. "We don't need to stay long. But surely you want to see all of his."

Ella gripped the exhibit program, her fingertips moistening its pages. The Nazis had hung fourteen of Kandinsky's altogether in this crazy display. So far, though, she had only found *Improvisation 10.* That one she knew. She remembered it. The rest of his came from much later after he'd left her for Russia and later still the Bauhaus. Seeing them would be like being abandoned again.

Where was Johannes? In the crowd she could not find him. She listened to the murmurings around her. "This so-called 'art' is a disgrace to good German people," a woman said. "These people ought to be shot." The woman who had seemed interested in Wassily's painting was nowhere here.

And then Johannes appeared at her back, shepherding her along. "Several of the others are in this next room. Let's see them, my dear, and then we'll go." Over the entrance to the gallery, the sign read "Crazy at any Price."

Two of his later abstract works were dangling on ropes from the ceiling, and Ella and Johannes had to stoop to avoid hitting the paintings as they swung. The Nazis had strung them up like criminals.

Written on the wall behind the paintings was a caption: "Method is Madness."

But it was all mad—the guards, the burlaps, the lines of disgusted people, the stench, the perverse and hateful labels, the ropes and angles. Ella felt a hiss in her ear as she stumbled gasping toward the street.

‡

They fought their way against the incoming crowd lined up to enter the Archaologisches Institut and walked into heat assaulting them from stone and concrete buildings where steam rose along the gritty tram tracks. Heat from the pavement blew up Ella's loose dress, wooling around her thighs, rising into the thin fabric under her arms, making her cross and irritable. She yearned to suck in clean, cool air, but each breath felt dragged through a blanket. She couldn't shake the odor of excrement. If she were younger, she might have run, but her legs felt like columns. If she were younger, she might have shouted out profanities.

The tram came too slowly. When it did, she climbed aboard as though she carried a sack of rocks on her back.

"I don't know who these people are." She clutched a seatback to keep herself upright.

Johannes, standing beside her in the car, jingled the coins in his pocket. His summer trousers fell loosely about his lean hips, his thin legs. "Hold on, dear. We'll talk about it, but not now, not here."

Johannes bent down to peer out the window. "Look, Ella."

She shuddered. In the next square a phalanx of soldiers in high boots kicked their way toward a grandstand draped with flags. Hundreds of people stood on the grey curb and watched admiringly.

Back in Schwabing, the crowds had thinned. Sunday strollers sought deeper shade under the tall lindens in the parks and boulevards. Seated in a sidewalk grove under a blue awning at the Törbrau Cafe, revived by hot food and strong coffee, Ella felt the serpent loosen round her throat.

"To call it *degenerate* is totally off the mark. They've gone too far." Johannes ate slowly, deliberately. "They somehow think abstraction is unnatural." He cut a bit of fat from lamb and pushed it to the side of his plate.

Ella flicked a spoon on the table. "For God's sake, Johannes, a chair is not only a chair, that specific individual chair. Every chair is all chairs, the essence of chair. We wouldn't even know to sit in a chair if we didn't know that." Reaching, she tore a piece of bread and dipped it in his gravy so forcefully she caused a splash onto the blue tablecloth.

Johannes lowered his voice. "You know Beckmann lost his position at the University, don't you?"

"Max Beckmann?"

"And Ernst as well."

"Good God. How will they live?"

"I saw it coming. Look what they did to Grosz."

"Why stick their noses in art? Why don't they just leave us alone."

"Shhh. We're in public."

Johannes gestured to the waiter for more coffee. "Are you having something else, Ella?"

"Another coffee." She tapped the table with her fingers.

"And what about Kandinsky?" Johannes took her hand and held it quietly. His fingers were slim and soft on her blue veins. "Does he know?"

"I don't know what he reads or who he talks to. He's in Paris, after all."

"Do you want to write him?"

"Of course not."

"He'd be outraged."

"Well, *I'm* outraged. But I have no intention of contacting him."

Ella removed her hand from Johannes's. She toyed with a smear of gravy on her plate. She drank her coffee. An elderly couple took seats near by. Ella watched them settle themselves awkwardly on the small chairs. The waiter cleared the plates. Some months after Olga's husband left her, she'd written Ella, pouring out her heart. But Ella had had no advice, no consolation to offer. After so many years, the distance between the women could not be bridged. With Olga as with Wassily, there was nothing she could say to the past. The old days were a magnet that sucked up your energy. It was hard enough to be sixty and alive.

"How did they even get the paintings?" Fury forced its way deeper into Ella's throat. She watched the old woman fumble with her eyeglasses. How long before that woman was *her*?

"The Reichskammer. Ziegler can authorize confiscations." Johannes leaned forward and lowered his voice. "He gets his orders from Goebbels, himself."

"You mean they *stole* them?"

"It's nothing new. The Nazis take what they want. When I saw Walden in Berlin last month, he told me a story." Johannes leaned back in his chair and looked around him. "Goering fancies himself a connoisseur, you know. Last year, he helped himself to a half-dozen masterpieces from the Kaiser Friedrich museum. Rumor has it he's installed a genuine Rubens in front of his home movie screen. He's on the lookout for a Vermeer, too. Believe me, if he finds what he wants, he'll help himself."

"How in heaven's name can they get away with it?"

"It's been in all the papers—under the name of 'protection' or 'national security' or some drivel. What they don't say is what they'll do with the paintings. Likely they want to sell them. Make the money."

"When did you read that? Where was I, Johannes? Why didn't I know?"

"You must have been in Murnau."

"And you didn't tell me? You know I get no papers in Murnau!" She banged the table and turned sideways in her chair. "For God's sake, Johannes, you should have told me! I count on you for that!" She folded her arms across her chest.

"Gabriele," Johannes whispered. "Not so loud." He looked around. A pair of young men, hats pulled low over their foreheads, passed near the cafe groupings on the sidewalk.

Ella leaned over the table, her voice quiet but intense, a hiss across the chasm.

"Why didn't you tell me they were confiscating paintings?"

Johannes stirred his drink.

"Why, Johannes? Tell me."

"Come, come, Gabriele. Don't make me say it." His voice became careful.

"Say what? What won't you say?"

"Only that they didn't confiscate yours. That's all."

"Mine. I don't know what you mean." She tapped her fingers on the table top. "Mine. Oh, I see. If mine had been worth it, they would have taken them, too. Is that it?" The veins in her neck bulged.

"Only in their eyes, Gabriele. Be reasonable. Be grateful they don't see you as a Modernist."

"You're the one who wanted me to back down. Be more commercial, you said, paint what sells. 'Adolf Hitler's Streets in Art'! What a piece of trash that was. I'm ashamed to think I painted it. I sold out and what good did it do me?" She crossed her arms.

Johannes began again. Lowered, his voice had authority. "Ella, it's not a question of selling out. Your work is just not their aesthetic. That doesn't mean you aren't good."

"Not good enough to confiscate."

"Don't be stubborn. You don't offend them. They don't see you like the others—like Beckmann and Ernst and Kandinsky. Look, take it as a compliment. Or at least be neutral. Be glad no one turned you over to them."

The snake's tail flicked at her throat. His words hammered behind her eyes. *They don't see you like that.* For a decade, she and Wassily thought they owned the air they breathed. They were the vanguard of art in Germany, and artists came to be with them where they worked. Now all the Blue Rider were being confiscated. Except for her. She was not even worthy to steal.

Ella took a long breath. True, she *was* glad not to have attracted the attention of Ziegler and the Reichskulturkammer. It was a danger to be singled out. But in a perverse way, it would have been an honor to be confiscated, a privilege to be shown along with Wassily and the others. The men. Taken that seriously. In the eyes of Goebbles and Goering and that whole hideous lot, she was Gabriele Münter, *woman* artist, safe to ignore in the minor cities but not one of the avant-guard group after all, not a real Modernist, not one of the giants. She exhaled slowly.

Just this year, Johannes had organized a retrospective for her birthday. And when the Bavarian Nazi Minister of State attacked it for its simple forms and unnatural coloration, Johannes had stood by her. She was too free thinking for Bavaria, he'd said, but he encouraged her to prepare some more realistic things, for the Great German Art Exhibition to ingratiate herself with the Nazis, and she had done it, too, wincing as she wrapped the paintings, nearly propaganda they were, nearly illustrations, banal and soulless. She shuddered at the disgrace of it, the toadying degradation. The dreck she had painted to please them! To humiliate oneself with that bad art— and then to be denied! For that, she had sacrificed her integrity. The Nazis didn't see her as modern or offensive—they merely thought her incompetent, unskilled. The day she learned the National Socialists had refused her work was black. To be denied there, too. Rejected there, too. Even there!

The sun was lower, now, a giant ginger lozenge caught in the tangled hedge beside their table. For a moment, a shaft blinded her, then shifted its angle as the leaves stirred. A breeze brushed overhanging branches onto the canvas awning over their heads. Ella listened to their mild shushing, shushing. What were they saying? Indignation drained out of her, pooling under the cafe table at her feet. She was simply tired of walking, talking, fighting, tired of the heat and wearing tight shoes, tired of being no longer young. Better to let it rest, count her blessings. And, on the good side, she could breathe again. She drank her coffee.

"Gabriele, there's another thing. Quite apart from the issue of 'degeneracy,' the Nazis want to get their hands on paintings they can sell abroad. They want to raise cash. It's hypocritical, I know, but..." Johannes leaned toward her, his fine, clean face nearly touching hers, his thinning hair as grey as her own. "I don't like to bring it up, but what about those things you have in storage? Gabriele, listen to me. If Zeigler and his thugs get wind of what you have, they'll take them the way they took those others. And think about this—they'll presume you're protecting Kandinsky. Besides, we haven't even begun talking about what the paintings are worth. It's likely to be a fortune." Johannes leaned forward. "How secure is this storage space?"

"I've no idea. I've made it my business not to go there."

Johannes rose from the table, waving to the waiter.

"Have you a key?"

"Ach, Johannes. Why do this to me?"

"We'll go now."

"You can look, if you like—just leave me out of it."

"You've got to come."

"Believe me, Johannes, those paintings mean nothing to me but pain."

"You can't just ignore them."

"Indeed I can. And I will. Let Ziegler have them. I'll burn them, myself." She forced her feet back into her shoes.

‡

The stripe of horizon, fractured in a forest of tall buildings, shaded from coral to salmon. Beneath, the taxi plodded steadily forward along the broad streets into an old neighborhood populated by small factories and storeyards. Just off the broad expanse of Landsbergerstrasse, Johannes signaled that they should stop. He preferred they walk the rest of the way. Better not even the driver should know where they were headed.

The row of storage lockers gave off the air of a mausoleum, deadly quiet and airless. Ella gave Johannes the key and turned her back, leaning against the doorframe to look out into the evening. What a ridiculous escapade. No one was going to go poking about in these remote little rooms. Johannes could do his sleuthing about without her. But she stood quietly and listened to his movements.

"What do you see?" she asked after a bit, her arms crossed on her chest. In the hot August air, she felt she might shiver.

"Well, it's quite dry in here, to start." He stepped quietly around the dim room. "You really should come in. There's nothing to be frightened of. It's like a post office, rather, like giant envelopes ready for mailing." He walked among the paper-wrapped packages, wiping a fine film of dust from their tops.

Ella felt heat from the chamber sweep out the door. "Are the big ones there?"

"Yes, I'd say so. Listen, Gabriele, I can't really say if these things of Kandinsky belong to you in a legal, financial sense. But at the very least, Kandinsky is likely to last—you have to admit that. This situation goes beyond you and your former lover. You can see that, can't you? Isn't it time to see it that way?"

Ella looked out at the horizon behind the cityscape. The sunset, opal and eternal, faded before her, while behind her the brilliant colors of the new generation sat in the dark. Truly what right had she to keep them? If she could accept Johannes' words, the locker was like the storage room of a museum, not the symbol of her wound. She could be free like a patient released from care. She could decide to be free.

She stepped inside.

Many of the pieces stood wrapped in brown paper along the side

walls, with smaller works leaning against them. Several huge paintings topped with a light tarpaulin rested against the back wall. Ella
fingered the brown packages, leaning the smaller canvases with their
stiff boards against her legs as she counted, first on one side of the
room, then the other. She moved under the tarp sideways through
the stack of large paintings, the "Compositions," the "Impressions."
She felt each one. She remembered the hard planes of his collarbone.
There had been a time when she would not have been able to keep
her composure as she felt his firm musculature, breathed in the smell
of his skin, the odors of oil, pigment, athleticism. But with Johannes
holding the door to let her see, touching the paintings was more like
rifling through a row of wooden hangers in a closet one had emptied
of its gowns, the scent of parties packed away.

"So, it's something over eighty just here."

"I had no idea you had so many." Johannes stood beside the doorframe looking out at the street, his hands in his pockets. "I think
we ought to get them out of here."He reached in his pocket for his
cigarette case. "Listen, Ella, I hope I'm wrong, but supposing the
Nazis come after them in Murnau. I wouldn't put it past them."

"Johannes, really. I *own* the house in Murnau. Nobody's breaking
into a private house. You exaggerate things." She reached around to
rub the small of her back. She was getting too old for all this bending
and stretching.

"I wish I had your confidence. At the very least, you've got to get
them out of the city. But I'm just saying that even Murnau is not a
guarantee." He lit a cigarette and looked out the door again. "Hurry
up, can't you? We need to get out of here."

Ella felt uneasy, like someone who had roused sleepers from their
dreams. A light wafting of linseed oil rose from the surfaces of the
larger canvasses. Might the oil soften in time? She stared at a large
unwrapped painting. In the dim light, immense swirls curvetted
across the canvas. For a moment, she was inside the painting, lost

in rounds of motion, snagged in brief explosions of energy. Dark reds and blues competed like wrestlers on a mat, their limbs intertwined as they rolled. For a moment, she almost thought she heard music in the room, discordant phrases, soutaches of sound surrounding her, drawing her through a coda of remembrances and feelings, a melody far, far away.

"It's not just a question of taking them away, Ella. We'll have to hide them."

Sulfur from the match Johannes struck brought her back to the quiet room. It was clear—they must take them all to the yellow house. She was resolved. "It gets dark in the cellar. You never did get that electricity down there."

Johannes looked out the door into the street. "Let me see if Hans Berger can loan us a delivery truck on Sunday." He pulled on his cigarette, craning his neck, watching the street.

"Johannes." Ella touched his arm. "Not just any man would help a woman protect her old lover."

"I'm no hero." He stubbed the butt of his cigarette against the door frame. "But he's Kandinsky."

Munich was in indigo twilight, only a few electric lights punctuating the scrim of dusk. Johannes and Ella walked side by side along deserted streets toward a major thoroughfare where they might hail a taxi. The central city with its glittering concert halls and theaters looked emptied. People seemed to have gone indoors as night fell, abandoning the wide streets where armed Orpo patrolled and soldiers conferred in shop entrances under dim streetlights.

"Not much traffic, tonight," Johannes said to the driver as they climbed in.

A line of trucks and military vehicles rattled down the broad avenue. By the time they reached their flat, they stepped into a Munich gone dark.

‡

Early in the morning, the heat wave broke and the city drank in heavy rain. Still, Ella's mood deteriorated. That night, she dreamed she held a cat that scratched her face and arms. She moved her head left and right to avoid its paws, but she could neither evade the scratches nor release her hold on the animal. When she got up at first light, she coughed incessantly, as though her airways had narrowed.

She was sorry to have seen his paintings again. They weighed on her, less because she missed those days with Wassily than because something nameless in her was dead now. The woman she had once been had sat enthralled while a ground-breaking genius poured his soul into pulsating prongs and horns of color. That woman had served as consultant, assistant, muse, and that woman had been, herself, an artist of stature. But for years now she had not completed a single work she would be proud to show. The old Ella was nearly gone. She had been a disappointment to herself, had squandered what should have been hoarded.

Late the next afternoon, she walked through neighborhoods made unfamiliar by tension. Martial music and declamations rang raucously in the central squares. Trucks and lorries on the side streets bore down like thugs in alleyways. A woman she sometimes visited looked at her crossly when they met by chance at the launderer's. The garrulous butcher whispered to his assistant behind the sausages. The headlines of the newspapers seemed to scream from the kiosks, but Ella couldn't determine what she should think. "Shall we go down to the rally?" Johannes had asked. "Listen to the speeches?" But the crowds frightened her, and they stayed in the apartment.

That evening Ella sat at her piano and picked through a simple melody. "We need to have this tuned," she said. "It's gone flat in the heat."

"Rosenburg's gone, though."

"Out of business?"

"Just gone. The shop is empty."

"Well, can you get Goldstein to come?"

"The Jews have all left. At least anyone who could get out has gone."

"I don't blame them." She pulled down the lid over the keys. "I wouldn't mind leaving, myself."

"But you have a choice."

Hans Berger was out of town. Johannes said they must wait to see if they could use the paper's truck. Ella said she didn't care. There was no hurry, was there? For several days, they ate their meals, listened silently to reports on the radio, and went to bed early.

One afternoon Ella picked up her camera and looked through the eyepiece. At the other end was an image of her sofa, manageable, the world brought into a scale she might control. For some days afterwards, she took her camera to the Englisher Garten, framing the beds of scarlet monarda and purple phlox, tracing the curving paths and the edges of the pond, centering the swans. Images seen small were unlikely to threaten. For a time, looking at the world through a camera lens seemed the only thing she could do without fear.

Galerie

"In Schwabing," 1912
Gabriele Münter
Oil on canvas
27" × 20"
Milwaukee Art Museum
Gift of Mrs. Harry Lynde Bradley

Gabriele Münter situates few of her paintings in urban settings, despite the fact that she lived and painted in Paris, Stockholm, Copenhagen, Bonn, and Berlin as well as Munich, where for many years she made her home. Of those paintings whose subject is at least partially a city, many share a common characteristic—that of putting the viewer at a decided remove from the scene. Most often in these paintings, we are behind a window or sometimes inside a door or passageway looking onto a street.

In the colorful painting "In Schwabing," we are once more prohibited from entering the life of the city she puts before us. This painting has depth, perhaps not so much as to provide a Renaissance vanishing point, but certainly there is the suggestion of space between the viewer and the central structures. We may be behind a window here where we look out through the fronds of a green plant, or perhaps the plant is outdoors near some kind of barricade. No matter. From our vantage point, we are at a distance from Schwabing where tall apartment buildings reach up to penetrate circular, white clouds.

The structures, themselves, are unadorned rectangles outlined with thick, black lines. They are yellow and orange and blue, with red and blue and yellow roofs. Green trees and bushes nearby soften the strong vertical thrust of the cityscape. Between us and these simplified houses, a pair of parallel lines, perhaps a street, sets us further away from the city. And also as is the case in many of Münter's paintings, human life is not visible on the canvas. No people walk the streets of this Schwabing, which in Münter's day was a busy district home to many artists. Yet, the scene is cheerful, its atmosphere generated by the brilliant colors and regular shapes that make up the buildings.

Sharing the simplification of form and the intensity of color, this urban setting projects the stability, calm, and joy of some of Münter's most exuberant country landscapes.

J. Eichner

Munich
September, 1937

Ella stepped under the broad awning. The current window display of Heinrich Hoffman's shop in the large office block on Amalienstrasse featured photographs of the Führer congratulating members of both the Hitlerjugend and the League of German Girls for their work with the new box cameras. Hoffman really was an excellent photographer of a type, though it pained her to acknowledge it. Besides that, he was also the government-appointed director of the Great German Art Exhibition, and she could only hope never to see him again.

Still, she had to concede, Hoffman was gifted at the pose and the angle of light on the human face. Just look at that particularly fetching young girl, her fair braids hanging down over her cleverly tied bandana. Thank God Friedel had grown out of that stage without being drafted into the BDM. And it would be years before Friedel's own little daughter would have to be part of a Nazi girls group, singing, marching, saluting. Perhaps that day would never come. One could hope.

Ella lingered over the display. The Führer with his hand on a boy's shoulder. The Führer smiling as he pinned a badge onto a girl's collar. The Führer posing as a boy took his picture, a group of men and women looking on admiringly. Every face smiling. No wonder Hoffman had become Hitler's official photographer. All of the photos were crisp, balanced, the depth of field flattening the background, controlled to emit just the right air of mystery to frame the faces. You could do that with the new cameras. She had longed to own a Leica like the kind Hoffman had undoubtedly used for these pictures, but the 35mm cameras were costly, and she had settled on a 127. With cameras as with so many other things she had learned to compromise. Still, she was planning to transform the dim little housekeeping closet in Murnau into a darkroom.

Ella opened the door, breathing in the familiar smells, the winey emulsions and chemical fixers, the resin-coated and the acid-free papers. Well-stocked shelves lined the walls like padded ribs. Hoffman was a good businessman, and the Reich appreciated him. Suddenly, from a dark hallway that led to the interior of the building, a voice startled her.

"So you grace my shop after all." The man himself appeared behind a counter. Now that he was famous, she hadn't expected to find Hoffman minding the store.

"Herr Hoffman. Good afternoon." Ella set her pocketbook on the counter. She lifted her chin. "Why wouldn't I come here? I've been patronizing your shop for years. I need contact paper, please."

"And yet it has been some time since I saw you last. I thought perhaps you were disappointed not to be selected for the Great German Art Exhibition." He was a handsome man, well into his middle years, the kind who held his head down, coyly looking up with cold blue eyes focused directly into yours.

"I suppose you had your reasons. I don't hold a grudge." Ella looked away to the shelves on which Hoffman had displayed an assortment of wooden picture frames. She felt like spitting.

"That's not what I hear," Hoffman said. "People say you've been quite vocal. They say you've criticized the new exhibit. I don't think that's wise, Fraulein Münter. You should be more careful."

"Many artists have criticized the new exhibit in the Haus der Kunst. I'm not alone." She turned to the counter and faced him. That such a toadying fool should feel free to give advice!

"But not every critic is one of your standing. Your former standing, I should say." He glanced at Ella's hands resting on the counter.

"Will you sell me contact paper?" Her jaw hardened; her face become a beak.

"That I can do, of course." He turned his back to her, his hand on the knob of a cabinet door. "You remain Fraulein Münter, am I right?

Many years ago now, I thought I heard it said that you had married the Russian." He fumbled with a set of keys. "Wassily Kandinsky, was it not? Quite a famous man, but wrongheaded." He dropped the keys, bent to pick them up, and tried again. "These abstract artists undermine the spirit of the German people. The Fatherland needs loyalty from its artists. You worked together with the Russian, I recall, side by side. And then, I'd heard he'd married you." Hoffman opened the glass door. "But it seems the rumor was wrong."

"Just the contact paper, please."

"Six by nine, is it?" he said. He pulled a stack a paper from the shelf. "I did hear it that way, though. Years ago, of course."

Ella tried to keep the words inside, tried to swallow and contain them, but they flew from her mouth, landing wetly on Hoffman's countertop. "Have you also heard it said that the art you have chosen for the Haus der Kunst is trivial and banal? That is what I have heard." She could not make herself breathe or pause or hold back. "That your idea of art is sentimental and trite? That your entire exhibition is a travesty, an insult to the true nature of art?"

"I might say that, too, if I had been denied entrance." Unruffled, Hoffman locked the cabinet door. "If I had tried to submit paintings to a great exhibit and been refused. If my art were thought degenerate, or, as in your case, perhaps simply inadequate." He turned his head over his shoulder and eyed her.

"No one has said that to me," Ella said. She was panting as though she had been running.

"No, of course. But then, the Reich has not seen much value in your work."

"I hardly think the Reichskulturkammer enlightened." She frowned and hooked her purse over her arm.

Hoffman looked hard at Ella, a nerve at his temple pulsing. "I'd advise you to hold your tongue, Fraulein Münter. Times have changed. Your kind of art is not, shall we say, 'fashionable'? And your new escort, Fraulein Münter. He's not a Jew, is he?" His eyebrows raised and his eyes brightened.

The sheer audacity of the man! His newly-minted arrogance provoked her. "I don't know who you mean. How dare you!" Ella turned on her heel and left the shop. Heinrich Hoffman watched her go, smiling, a stack of contact paper in his hand.

Ella closed the door into their flat, locked it, and fell against it, trembling. How could she have been so cheeky and impudent to a man of Heinrich Hoffman's prominence in the Reich? God knows who he talked to.

"Ei," she called into the rooms. "Where are you? I've done something bad, Papa. Don't be angry."

"In here. What's wrong?"

"I went to Heinrich Hoffman's store, and I quarreled with him. I said some very bad things." She supported herself against the doorframe. "And he asked me if you were a Jew."

Johannes put down his book. "I think this is what they talk about behind closed doors—who is Jewish, who is loyal to the Party, who needs to be brought aboard." He ran his fingers through his thin hair. "Hoffman wants to throw his weight around, Gabriele. In any event, he's simply wrong. But you were wrong, too, to insult him."

"He frightened me, Papa."

"Come here, Mü, and let Papa comfort you." Johannes patted the cushion next to him. "Come. Sit here."

"Johannes, we should leave Munich." She felt her knees grow weak. "We should go to Murnau where we have no radio and no newspapers and no one to bother us."

"But first, Mü, we have to deal with those paintings in the Munich Transport Company. We have to take care of your Kandinsky."

Ella settled herself in the crook of his arm. She thought about Heinrich Hoffman and his leering grin as she left the shop. "Then do it, Johannes. Find a way, Papa. I'm frightened."

On Friday evening, Johannes returned to the flat, his tread heavy. Ella was cooking supper.

"Things are very bad." Johannes slumped at the kitchen table. "Beckmann is gone."

"Gone where? Why?"

"Amsterdam. Exile. Werner says he was running for his life."

"You can't mean that literally!" She wiped her hands on the towel tucked into her belt. "Max Beckmann? Why? What's going on?"

"Goebbels is calling avant-guard artists *enemies of the state*."

"Well, that's ridiculous."

"*Threats to German culture*, he says. He's ordered a second wave of confiscation. Paintings, books, anything they want. The people at the paper are saying the Nazis have stolen thousands, maybe tens of thousands." He rubbed his temples. "Werner heard from Nolde that he's not been allowed to purchase paint or brushes."

"Nolde? He's a Nazi, himself. Nazis *bought* his art."

"Not any more. Apparently he defies them now—uses watercolors so no one can smell that he's working."

"Good God!"

"I've heard talk of artists being sent to work camps, too. It's hard to imagine, I know." He paused, looking up at Ella. "But people are leaving if they can. Dix is gone. I know that for certain. Beckmann must have thought he was in trouble, too."

Johannes poured himself a glass of beer and sat down again. Ella turned away from the stove.

"All right, then. We'll get out too." She hesitated, then leaned over the table and took a drink from his glass. "Murnau is safe."

"I'm not certain of that by any means. But for the time being, perhaps."

"We could drive down tonight, if you're worried."

"Listen, Gabriele, there's something else. No one can know we have these paintings. There's danger aplenty in just possessing them. I hate to think how the Orpo might react. They tend to strike first and ask questions later."

"Did you ask about a truck?"

"It won't work. Berger's trucks all belong to the Nazis now." He took a long drink from his glass. "But the Daimler certainly can't hold everything. It could take us weeks, not to mention what to do with the very large ones."

Ella returned to the stove. She was frying liver, putting the brown slices on a plate, covering the meat with heaps of tender onion. Why not just let them all go? What did *he* mean to her now? Just a bad memory, an ache in her spine. Why should she put herself in harm's way for him? She was no hero. Let the Nazis have them, if they must. Be done with the lot. And as for the financial loss—well, it's not as though the paintings were really hers, if you told the truth. "I'm sick of it. Let's just unlock the storage unit and leave the doors open. Let them take what they want. We'll go somewhere else." She scraped up crusty bits at the bottom of her pan and poured in a slash of beer to make a sauce, earthy like the scent of linseed oil. *Composition VII* flashed past her eyes, brilliant, vital. Oh, no. No, they mustn't. No. They must not have them.

"I didn't mean that, you know." Ella put liver, onions, and potatoes on two plates. She leaned against the stove, the plates in her hands, the steamy aroma reaching her face. "Onions. Bauer." An image was forming. "He brings in vegetables to the Elisabethmarkt. I was just there Saturday."

"The Murnau farmer?"

"Supposing we ask him to haul the paintings back to the house?" She rummaged through a cabinet for mustard. "He'll be at the market tomorrow. He'll have a truck."

Johannes piled onions onto his fork. "What makes you think you can trust him?"

"To what? Run off with the paintings? Turn us in to Goebbels himself? Not likely." She poured beer for herself and more for Johannes. "He's a good man, Bauer. Married a Pole, but his wife died a year or two ago, I think. You drove me there for plums once. I'd have thought you'd remember. Wassily and I bought fruit from him too."

"If he says no?"

"Farmers always need money."

Yes. Now it could happen. Once she got a picture in her mind, she could believe in it, could act.

Johannes ate steadily, his gaze far from his supper. "You realize if the Reich finds out, they'll call us thieves and Bolsheviks."

"Then they mustn't know." Ella stood up from the table, carrying plates and glasses to the sink. "Let's get the ones from the studio tonight." She gestured toward the door. "There's quite a few there. They'll fill the Daimler."

"You're counting on Herr Bauer to cooperate."

"I am," Ella said.

For the second time in just days, the paintings stirred inside her, a living part of her present life, not just detritus from long ago. She had vowed she'd never look at them again, but then she had. Just days ago she'd thought them to be a burden, but in the face of the imminent danger, they felt like her own limbs, lungs, liver—personal, vulnerable. The part of her that loved them recoiled against the idea that they might be handled by brutes who called them *degenerate*. The image of some green-uniformed Orpo touching them made her skin crawl.

‡

In the warehouse district where Ella rented a studio, the empty streets unrolled like funeral ribbons. The old building loomed above them, the windows black, though sometimes, Ella knew, a painter might work well into the night, sleeping on a makeshift bed or heap of canvas. She held her key tightly. Cloaked in caution, she crept to the warehouse door while Johannes scanned the street.

The old wood door resisted like an arthritic knee. Ella froze and, hearing nothing further, tiptoed inside. Removing her shoes, she made her way quietly down the dark stairway to the basement closet, afraid to turn on the light or make a sound. Up and down, down and up the hard back stairs she padded, her feet bare on the cold concrete, carrying stack after stack to fill the Daimler's trunk with Campendonks, Mackes, Marcs, and her own Kandinskys, three or four in a load. Each descent terrified her. Unused to covert activity, the blackness of the building with its shadowed planes of walls and halls, even the sound of her own hard breathing—everything alarmed her.

Outside, Johannes packed the sketches, prints, and woodcuts into the car. They worked until the basement closet and the studio were bare and the spacious trunk of the Daimler was filled with Ella's personal stash of the Blue Rider movement.

"That's it," she whispered, shutting and locking the warehouse door. She got into the car and shrank into the seat, her hands jittery in her lap, her feet pressing the floor as though she could speed it forward.

"Thank God," Johannes said, locking the gears in place. "Thank God."

Back on Keferstrasse, they parked in front of the flat, the trunk locked, its silent contents a contrast to their pounding hearts. They were well past their youth, well past the years of risk-taking and saber shaking. Not since the Great War had they felt outright fear. Not since then had they taken such extreme measures. It remained, still, to see if farmer Bauer would help them protect what must be kept safe.

Chapter Eleven

Road To The Birdhouse

Munich
September, 1937

DETERMINED to look the housfrau, Ella arrived at the Elisabeth-markt just after dawn, her old net marketbag swinging from one elbow. She had not slept a wink and jittered with the coffee Johannes had made her drink before she left the flat. "Watch who hears you," Johannes had cautioned. "Orpo prowl around that place looking for free food." Working her speech over and over in her mind, she set her sights on Bauer down at the far end of the alleyway where motorized trucks and horse-drawn wagons lined up so that farmers could unload their wares directly onto the open-air shelves. Aware of the daylight brightening along the packed-earth lanes, she swiftly picked her way among empty stalls that by mid-morning would be laden with the bounty of an early Bavarian harvest. Nothing could tempt her, though, but the sight of Emil Bauer.

The farmer had already laid out onions and beets on a rough wooden board held up by sawhorses. A white apron tied around his waist, he faced away from Ella, his sturdy legs spread wide as he hoisted a slatted basket onto the ground. Ella could see where his small truck stood, the back gate lowered to allow him access. Would it be big enough? She stepped up to the counter, looked behind her and to each side, and took a deep breath.

"*Guten Morgen*, Herr Bauer." Ella greeted him with an out-stretched hand. First was that he remember her.

"*Grüss Gott*," he said, accepting her handshake, his speech thick with Bavaria. He began laying out tied bundles of blood-stemmed chard.

"Herr Eichner and I are still enjoying the onions I bought from you last week. Very good. Very sweet." She might have been Maria Marc. "And I see you have some nice greens, today." She looked behind her, but the row was empty. She lowered her voice. "Herr Bauer, may I speak with you in private?"

The farmer looked up from his counter. He frowned a question. Then he edged one end of a wooden board off its sawhorse, careful not to jostle his produce, and gestured Ella through the gap, impatient like a man who distrusts interruption.

"Herr Bauer, I've come to ask a favor of you, one I am willing to pay for."

The farmer eyed her under his straw hat and reached into the truck's interior, retrieving a small thermos bottle.

"Could you carry a load of items down to Murnau when you leave the market today?" She spoke quietly, her voice a mixture of importunity and fear.

A lone early customer came to the stall and riffled through the bundles of chard. Having handled each one, she moved down the lane, purchasing nothing. Bauer watched her leave. "You were out to the farm a year or so back," he said. "Didn't your gentleman drive an Audi?" He unscrewed the top of his thermos and poured coffee into it, steam whispering in the pale light.

"He has a Daimler, now," Ella said. "But yes, we came to see you. We bought some Rome apples, a bushel of them, and made apple-sauce."

"What do you need taken?" He looked at Ella as though she might offer him something sour. Her heartbeat quickened. She was going to have to convince him.

"Some paintings. Rather too many for us to fit into the car." She tried to laugh pleasantly.

A woman carrying a small child in her arms stopped to look at the onions. She set the child on the wooden board, saying, "Now hold on to my skirt while I pay the man" and put two pfennig on the counter. "Will this do?" she asked. Bauer nodded and turned his attention back to Ella, who stood against the side of the truck tying a scarf about her head, adjusting it as though she were the farmer's wife come to help with business.

"I remember you used to bicycle out to the farm," he said. "Met my wife a time or three. Was a many years ago. You had a different gentleman with you in those days, a foreigner. He painted pictures, I recall." He folded his arms in front of his broad chest, holding the steaming cup just under his chin.

"Yes. It's that man's pictures I'd like to take to Murnau. Can you help?"

Bauer turned and leaned against the truck. He took a drink from his cup and shook his head. "I won't be going right away. I take my time getting back on a Saturday. I've got no reason to rush. I'll be tired by nightfall and want my dinner. You'd do well to ask someone else." He looked down the lane as though he might call for help.

"Oh, that's quite all right, Herr Bauer. Actually, we'd rather not leave until after dark." Ella tried to catch the farmer's eye, but he seemed fixed on a pair of young women standing before the neighboring stall.

"Oh?"

"They're valuable, you see, the paintings. It would be best if no one saw." Ella lit her eyes as if she had a pleasant prank she might play at any moment.

He drained his cup and screwed it back on his thermos. "Ach, that's not for me, then. I don't like trouble. I'm a widower now, not the man I was." He looked down the empty row. Farmers were still pulling up and unpacking.

"Herr Bauer, please don't say no. We'll make it worth your while." Ella began to pant. He must help them.

"Yah, but a man has to be careful. Like I say, I don't like trouble. Orpo everywhere. You've even got Gestapo lurking about."

"Herr Bauer, there is no problem here, nothing illegal. These paintings are *mine*. I simply want to take them to my house in Murnau, near your farm. It wouldn't be out of your way." She stepped closer.

The farmer shrugged.

"Here." Ella folded a paper in his hand. "My address and some money. There'll be more when the job is finished."

Bauer looked at Ella and shoved his hand in a pocket beneath his apron.

"You wouldn't take my money and not come, would you?"

He shook his head, walked toward his counter, and started to stack his chard bundles, handling them as though they might contain prickly thorns.

"We'll be waiting for you—me and the man you met with the car."

"I'll come by when the market closes." Bauer slid his countertop so that Ella could pass through to the lane. She looked up and down the rows, thickening now with shoppers. No Orpo. She caught the farmer's eye and nodded to him. Off in the distance, a siren wailed. She shifted her string bag to her other arm and quickly left the market. Bauer had to come. He had to.

Morning crawled toward noon, noon toward evening. Ella packed her traveling case with blouses and skirts, shoes and stockings, undergarments, a sweater. Johannes and she might become permanent residents of Murnau, she said as she scooped up her paints and set her brushes in their case. The quiet market town suited them better now than the city with its strident voices, its harsh criticisms, the smashed windows, the firings, merchants one had known all one's life sent away or worse. Best to be far away from the banners and slogans and speeches, the noisy rallies, the snide remarks of newly important people, the new museums one couldn't exhibit in or the old ones that still retained the power to haunt and discomfit. Johannes agreed. Get out of town and tramp along the lakes. Let the parades and loudspeakers go on without them. If the Jews could leave, so could they.

Ella climbed into the attic storage room and brought down two paintings. In one hand she held Marc's faint horses emerging in fractured pastel forms, angular and overlapping. Both cubist and romantic, the painting reminded her of the man she remembered, sharp-edged but softly colored. She had several more of his, too, and they must all come. In the other hand she carried a brilliant portrait she'd watched Alexei Jawlensky make when he visited them one summer, an aged gardener, red in the face, lime hair fuzzing out. She had a picture of her own in the attic, and she'd bring that one, too—Alexei and Marianne lounging on a sunny hillside, Marianne in her big hat. Remnants of an easier time.

"This is a lovely one." Johannes held out the splintered horses with its diagonal planes of pink and peach and gold.

"He was a genius," Ella called, halfway up the stairs.

Worried that Bauer might not come, Ella busied herself with packing and sorting until she saw the farmer drive up, the motor on his truck rumbling. Grateful, she ran to the street. "Won't you come in for tea?" They had hours to wait until dark.

The farmer turned off the engine and let himself down from the high seat. He looked up and down the street, tall apartment buildings fronted with gardens and flowered entryways. Though he had hardened and thickened with the years, Ella saw the young man showing them through his orchard, proud to show off his wife, babe, crops.

"Nah, not for me, missus. I'll find myself a brewer. Now that I know where you are, I'll be back. You needn't to be worried—I'll be sober by dark. I'm not one for driving back to the mountain with my head all beery."

Ella returned to the flat to wait. The angelus bell in the corner church rang six o'clock. The light goldened in the room. Ella cut some ham and set it out with bread and tomatoes and the green onions from Bauer's stall, and she called Johannes to come and eat. But she could only nibble at her plate. She sat at the table and watched the light fade. Afterwards, she freshened the blue cloth, brushing crumbs into her hand. She took down from the walls of the parlor the last of Wassily's works she had kept for herself from the old days—two woodcuts, an etching, a drypoint engraving, an oil on cardboard, and she set them on the small table where they put the post. She'd wrap them now, but the wonder of it was that she and Johannes had walked by them every day for years, never once thinking either of their value or their menace.

Bauer admitted to being proud of his truck. Not every farmer could afford one, and as they pulled away from the locked storage rooms and headed out of town in the black night, he kept up a running commentary on the virtues of the engine, the gears, the chassis, the bargain he had driven to purchase the vehicle. Ella, sharing the front seat with him, bumped along in silence, listening only enough to murmur from time to time and keep him talking.

The ordeal of securing the contents of the locker onto the truck had left her spent. She had not been able to watch while Bauer and Johannes stacked the paintings and prints and covered the high load with canvas roped to the rails. She had sat shivering on the running board, scanning the dark narrow street, listening with every cell in her body for any sound that might signal discovery. The political rallies, the shouting through bullhorns, the burnings and lootings, the takeovers and mysterious disappearances that for years had seemed far in the distance had become real and personal, affronts and dangers she had never considered her own until now. It was not just a question of confiscation, of their value, though certainly the paintings had increased tremendously in worth in the twenty-some years since Wassily left them behind. No, it was not their worth in Reichsmarks. The stakes for her were much higher than that.

She sat in the truck cabin and rubbed her hands against her lap, brushing the fabric of her dress over and over as though she could wipe away from her person the threat inhabiting the city and now herself. Emil Bauer glanced over at her. "You can ease your mind, now, missus," he said. "The load is a little high, I guess, but plenty of trucks drive along like this."

"Not *leaving* the Saturday market, they don't."

"No, but nobody has any reason to look at us. You just relax."

She couldn't, though. Bauer had introduced a danger she hadn't even considered. In the tense political atmosphere, a small farm truck with an oversized cargo between its wooden sides might call attention to itself, undermining their caution. She slumped in the seat, her spirit contracting. There was too much to worry about, too many things to grieve. She closed her eyes and listened to the wheeze and rattle of the truck, trying to time her breathing to the click of the tires on the concrete seams of the pavement. It was not the size of the load on the truck that wrung her soul. It was her tortured relationship to the paintings. She had to admit that they weren't really hers at all. They were Wassily's, and she had held onto them out of spite. Anyone would say that. But now she had a public and not merely aggrieved responsibility to them. She owed it to the art itself, to the impulse to create that brought the paintings into being, to the expression of the human spirit that they represented.

And then there were Johannes and Emil Bauer whose risk in the enterprise was as great as her own. She'd dragged them both into something perilous. If the SS or Zeigler or Goebbels himself got wind of what they'd done, they might all be branded as Bolsheviks and arrested. The art was not merely "degenerate," not merely even the work of Kandinsky, a man they called "insane," his works a jumble of dashes and darts. No, they could be in trouble for more than protecting art the Nazis despised. The real Nazi motive had become political—power, possession, control, loyalty to a twisted ideology. The Party wanted compliance, not defiance, and they struck out at resistance to their will. Worst of all, the police were unpredictable and erratic in the way they lashed out, in the objects of their violence, in their lust for intimidation. There was no telling what could happen. People had disappeared; lives, and not only Jewish ones, had been crushed. Ella looked over at Bauer driving the truck. Supposing the heist were uncovered? Then what?

Ahead of them, Johannes led the way. Ella watched the taillights of the Daimler as they snaked through the back neighborhoods and finally onto the new road that went straight south past the Starnbergersee to Garmish-Partenkirchen and then northwest toward Oberammergau.

"It's a good road," she said, trying to steady herself. She wished she could uncoil the tightness in her eyes.

"A lot of people got jobs building this road." Bauer leaned forward in the seat, the bulk of his belly grazing the steering wheel.

Ella looked at the farmer. Supposing he was a patriot, a sympathizer, a Nazi, himself. Had she misjudged him? Might she have him to fear, too? Just outside her window was a dense crop of wheat, tall, nearly ready for harvest. If she stretched out her arm, she could almost catch a handful. "They say these new building projects have stopped the inflation." She would have to keep him talking.

"Yah, but I'm no fan of these National Socialists."

"Because of the road?"

"My wife—you met her once, I think—she was Polish. I met her when I worked the shipyards in Gdansk. We married young and then came back here to farm. But this crowd has no use for the Poles. *Kotzbrocken.*" He looked over at Ella. "Pardon me. I'll watch my language."

"You lost your wife, didn't you?" she said.

"Not but a year since." He cleared his throat. "At least the kids got a chance to grow up with her. My daughter, she's having a hard time. My wife, Aniela that was her name, suffered quite a bit towards the last. She was glad to make an end of it."

"I'm sorry to hear it." Ella looked at the farmer, his thick shoulders sloped, his large hands firm on the steering wheel, a man who had married a woman, raised a family with her, lost her early.

Bauer cleared his throat again. "Well, we'll get your load home soon enough now. Been no trouble so far."

When the truck bore left around a bend, Ella let her body list toward him, her shoulder grazing his. A good man. She wished she could do more.

The truck jounced along for a time, its occupants silent. It was after midnight, and the road south was empty. A knife of moon cracked open the black sky just enough for a leak of light to dribble down, illuminating but distorting the hillocks, the scrub brush, the swells and gullies, the neat fields, heaps and shapes in grisailles, ghostly and imprecise. Small houses and outbuildings stood away from the road at a distance as though they disapproved of the way the paved layer sat upon the land.

Ella's eyes were heavy. The golden wheat heads that edged the road bent sleepily, the papery hulls brushing each other in the night breeze. She folded her sweater into a pillow and held it against the window, her head bouncing against it, lines from an English poem she and Emmy had both learned in school.

> The wind was a torrent of darkness upon the gusty trees,
> The moon was a ghostly galleon tossed upon cloudy seas,
> The road was a ribbon of moonlight looping the purple
>   moor,
> And the highwayman came riding—
> Riding—riding—
> The highwayman came riding, up to the old inn door.

She shivered, and the lines came again and again until the road before her stretched out like that ribbon and she thought she heard the highwayman's horse coming after her. But it was only the engine and the muffled tap of her head on the window as she dozed.

Ella woke when the growl of the engine diminished to a purr. Emil Bauer had pulled the truck over to the weedy shoulder of the road, parking it behind Johannes in the car. Across the road was an old brown inn, low to the ground, dimly lit, sounds of singing seeping out the door and open windows.

"Ella, we need to eat something, Bauer and I. You, too." Johannes held the door open.

"But we're almost there. Shouldn't we go straight home?"

"We've nothing in the house. It's well past one o'clock, and we've still got to unload."

Still groggy from her muddled dream, Ella eased herself from the cab. She smoothed her skirt and hair and shook her head to wake up.

Crouched with its entrance just meters off the highway north of Murnau, the small inn smelled of stale beer and smoke. Half a dozen long tables sat at intervals along the rough board walls, a place as dim and charmless as the barman bent over the counter. Hunched at the tables, half a dozen laborers sat, caps pulled low over their foreheads, their women buxom and thick-waisted in their coarse dirndls. Opposite them, seated with his back to a long table, a grizzled man squeezed and pulled an accordion to accompany their drunken, lugubrious songs. And in the far corner sat four soldiers, Gestapo, eagle-and swastika patches on their sleeves, death's heads grinning on their collars.

The barmaid, her apron stained and limp, took their order. One of Hoffman's photographs of the Führer hung above the bar. Ella caught Johannes' eye and motioned him to look.

"I wonder where that came from." Johannes sat forward, his hands between his knees.

"Thirsty work tonight." Bauer held his stein with both hands, drinking in gulps, but Ella could only bring the glass to her lips and wet them, her eyes fixed on the black uniforms swaying. She eyed Johannes. They would need to get out quickly and not draw any attention to themselves.

While Johannes stayed behind with the barman to settle up, Ella felt her way to the outdoor toilet in dark broken only by the spill of light from two small windows on the inn's north side. Bauer stationed himself near the truck, choosing to relieve himself on the road's grassy shoulder out of Ella's sight. Just then, the inn door opened, and the four Gestapo stumbled out onto the roadway. The first out the door careened over to Bauer and struck at him with the butt of his gun.

"I order you to stop!" he said, a young man, fair-haired and very drunk. "In the name of the Fatherland, stop!" He sneered. "Stop squirting on the new road!" His voice grew loud and mean.

"Show us your pecker." The second soldier swaggered closer. "Is it all there, or have you been stripped like a Jewboy?" He grabbed his crotch and hopped, squealing.

"Ah, let him alone," the third youth said. "Your Uncle Dieter pees out here every day. His beer's that sour, too." He unfastened his trousers and urinated powerfully into the ditch beside the Daimler.

Buaer buttoned up his overalls and walked to the truck door.

The officer of rank, older than the others, moved in close, examining the truck bed. "What's this?" He carried a stick and dragged it slowly along the length of the vehicle, tapping at the canvas from time to time. "Contraband, perhaps?"

"Leave it alone. I'm helping my friends move to the country." The farmer spread his legs and crossed his arms over his broad chest.

"You do not order us," the urinating man said over his shoulder.

"Perhaps you are carrying guns." The officer's voice was dry, uninflected. "Headed for Switzerland, I think, and arming the Swiss?" The officer stroked the heavy canvas as though he might divine its contents through his palms.

"Let go." Bauer put his fists on his hips and spread his legs still wider. "I told you. I'm helping the gentleman move."

Crossing the road from the inn in the dense darkness, Johannes joined the group. "What seems to be the problem?" He smiled at the officer.

"Show us what you have in this truck." The fair-haired soldier stepped onto the running board. The officer pulled himself to his full height, his shoulders gaining width with his air of command. "Untie the rope." He was terse, sober, un-amused.

Johannes looked at Bauer. "Herr Bauer, you can show the officer what we have." Johannes stepped away from the truck, his right arm extended as though welcoming guests. "As you have heard, my wife and I are moving to the countryside."

For a moment, the farmer held his ground. He shook his head from side to side as though to say it was not his party. First on one side of the tailgate, then the other, he loosened the thick cords that secured the canvas cover to the side rails of the flat bed.

Johannes continued, the gracious host. "You see, here, some of our furnishings, the paintings and other artwork from our home. Nothing dangerous. Nothing illegal."

Ella, seeing the group, came up behind Johannes and took his hand. "These are mine, officer," she said. "I paint for a hobby." Her voice grew girlish, flirty. "You are most welcome to look. Are you fond of art? Perhaps you would like to buy something. Many people buy my paintings."

The three drunken younger soldiers climbed aboard the truck and began rummaging through its contents, holding canvases up, tearing off their wrappings, peering at them.

"It's all art up here."

"Some of them are huge."

"Why do you have these paintings?" The officer addressed Johannes, his voice more accusation than question.

"As my wife said, she is an artist. It is a great hobby of hers." He put his arm around Ella and drew her close. "Unfortunately, she does not sell as many as she paints." He smiled broadly, looking at Ella with fond eyes.

The officer pointed his flashlight on the load, moving the beam onto one painting and then another, illuminating the ghostly images on the top of the load, still lifes, landscapes, abstractions.

"I'm sorry to say it, but these things are not very good. Still, if it pleases you to paint this way, you may take your truckload and get along. It is late. We are sorry to detain you."

Emil Bauer retied the ropes fastening the canvas to the rail on either side.

"Come, get in the car, my dear," Johannes said.

Ella made the rest of the trip in the Daimler, hearing the truck rumble, feeling its lights shining on her shoulders as she trembled in her seat. Over and over again, she looked behind her, watching for another vehicle, listening for another motor. Only when Johannes turned up little road alongside the yellow house was the night black and still enough for her to fully breathe.

‡

"Will you have another cup?" As tired as she was, Ella hoped the farmer would decline. The sun had just touched the horizon, and it had taken nearly all their strength to unload, carrying armfuls into the cellar and stacking the paintings on the floor against the walls.

Johannes and Emil Bauer agreed that the incident was not over.

"They'll be back," Bauer said.

"Those Gestapo won't know how to find us." Ella felt she might fall asleep as they sat. "We might have been anyone."

"That bartender saw everything." Bauer stood and stretched, rolling his shoulders and cracking his neck.

Ella put her head on the table, her eyes cradled on her forearms.

"Dieter Jaeger, he was. Begging your pardon, Missus," Bauer said, "the truth is, the whole village knows the Russian's House."

"Supposing they do." Ella turned her head to the side and rested her cheek on the table. "This isn't Munich. No one cares about a load of paintings down here." She was so tired. "Besides, who would remember Kandinsky? It's been over twenty years."

"Gabriele," Johannes said. "It's not so simple." He cleared the table, carrying the cups into the kitchen. "Have you forgotten Beckmann and Ernst and Nolde? When those men report what they saw tonight, the Gestapo will come looking."

Ella and Johannes woke feeling heavy, lead in their stomachs. Each of them separately went down to the cellar to look at the stacks of paintings, half hoping they had disappeared or at least righted themselves into an order. Neither could see quite what to do with the load, many small works on paper, but several large canvases on wooden stretchers well over six meters tall and even wider. "We may have made a mistake," Ella said. "We've nowhere to hide them."

But Emil Bauer had promised to help and they waited for him, anxious. Johannes said he heard an engine, but it was only water boiling in the kettle. Ella thought a car door had slammed, but it was Johannes closing the gate after he had made a tour of the garden, looking about for footprints or the butts of cigarettes.

In late afternoon Bauer arrived. He'd had chores to attend to, he said, watering, feeding the animals. He stood in the cellar, arms crossed, surveying the lot. "What's in the little closet under the stairs?"

"Brooms and such. I can barely stand up inside." Ella opened the door, demonstrating the impossibility of fitting in the large paintings.

Bauer stooped to look in. "The little things could go on the shelves, at any rate." He stood back up and ran his fingers through his thinning hair. "Those big ones are the problem."

Johannes crouched in the dark closet, feeling its width and depth with the palms of his hands. "Actually, the paintings, themselves, aren't so bulky," he called out. "The canvas gets nailed to a stretcher, a kind of interior, wooden frame." He came back to the cellar room. "They could be un-stretched, I should think. Gabriele?"

"Well, I don't know." Ella leaned against the wall. It was all so much responsibility. Supposing the canvases ripped when they were removed from their stretchers? Supposing the paint cracked or flaked off? She put her head back and closed her eyes. Against the back-lit screen of her brain, she saw herself walking through Herwarth Walden's gallery rooms and on toward the dark spaces behind them, rooms like the butcher's cold storage, canvases coiled like sausages on shelves. She opened her eyes and walked to the closet. "Will they fit if we take them off the stretchers?"

"I'd say so." Johannes held his arms wide, measuring the space against himself. "Bauer? What do you think?"

"I'd leave it to the Missus."

"This is your decision, Gabriele. Shall we pull the canvases off and fold them?"

Ella walked once more through Walden's back rooms.   "Roll them," she said. "Roll them gently."

Ella spread an old bed sheet in the center of the room. Bauer and Johannes upended the largest painting first, *Composition X*, and carefully lay it onto the floor, paint side down. With the forked end of a claw-foot hammer, Bauer worked the nails loose from the stretcher board, yanking the stiff canvas free with his hard, thick fingers. Johannes knelt beside him with pliers and twisted out the sharp tacks left in its tight threads, his boney knees on the hard cement. Barely breathing, Ella watched, listening to the painful squeak of the wood as it released the nails, wincing as though her own skin had been flayed. Holding the huge, heavy canvas by its corners, Bauer and Johannes took the painting to the adjoining cellar room and lay it on another sheet. In the failing light, let loose from its supports, the painted canvas lay flaccid, its edges curling.

"I hate this." Ella braced herself against the wall. Johannes and Bauer returned to free a second canvas, and then another. They carried each painting to the floor and lay it down on top of the last one.

"Johannes." She stood before the stack, her two hands clutched at her chest. "Johannes."

When they had finished with the largest ones, as though they were rolling up a heavy carpet, Bauer and Johannes formed the flat pile into a tube, struggling to bend the unyielding layers, each stiff painting backing its neighbor in a rigid confederacy. The two men dragged the tube on its bed sheet to the floor of the low, wide closet, and Bauer leaned his weight to push the heavy form into the narrow space, grunting, the veins in his thick neck bulging. Wrapped in its shroud, the roll of paintings lay inert, a corpse. They set the works on paper and the smaller paintings on the shelves. They filled every inch, and then they shut the door.

"Fine." Johannes stood beside it, massaging his lower back, panting. "But if anyone opens the door, there they'll be, like Bluebeard's wives."

"Johannes!"

But Johannes was already unloading the storage unit on the opposite wall. "Herr Bauer, if you could remove the metal latch, these shelves could sit flush against the door." He was readying the wooden structure to stand flat before the little closet like the warden before an above-ground interment.

In the end, a heavy shelving unit obscured the tomb, and on one shelf sat canned tomatoes, beans, spinach, pickles, and six jars filled with Wassily's plum liquor, twenty years aged and purple as a priestly vestment.

Bauer built a fire outside the yellow house to burn the stretchers, smoke from cremated rectangles thickening the night sky.

How would it occur? How would they act? Supposing the paintings were discovered? Were they, themselves, in danger? For their lives?

They dined on questions, slept on scenarios.

A day passed. And then two. And then a week. And another. The air turned cool. Aspens on the hillside burst into flame, rusted, greyed. For a few nights, there was a frost. Ella harvested brussels sprouts and cabbage, packing them in straw on the floor of the cool cellar, a complement to the innocent shelves of canned produce. The cellar of the yellow house looked ordinary, the house of two aging people, harmless, careful with their money, putting aside food, preparing themselves for the long, snowy days ahead. A fine layer of dust filmed the tops of the glass jars.

And the room with the little closet now also held dozens of her own paintings leaning against the walls among jars, bottles, brushes, solvents, rags, a large roll of plain canvas, her easel. Some of the paintings came from her prime, the days of the Blue Rider, when to take her rucksack to a site was to invite a new way of seeing, of extracting an essence, conveying an impression. But others featured more common images—the roads and flowers and hillsides she had attempted for the Great German Art Exhibit that had been such a failure, paintings she had done in the Murnau house during these last summers, merely decorative, not artistic, paintings it pained her to own. They all added up, though. The Gestapo had not been thorough that dark night, had not done a count. They might, Ella hoped, mistake her paintings on the walls and floor for the far more dangerous ones that lay just beyond the shelves.

The knock came on a cold, rainy afternoon. Johannes had walked to the village cafe to drink hot lemonade and listen to the radio. He had his reservations about this pact Hitler made with Belgium, he told Ella, and he wanted to listen to the political commentary, even though he knew it was partisan, likely even censored. He'd pick up a paper, too, and be home before dark, he said, and bring something from the market, whatever looked fresh. Ella sat at the table beading a purse, a design of her own making, a copse of gold and green trees fashioned after one of her old paintings. The rap on the door made her jump, spilling the tiny beads onto the floor where they skittered and rolled into cracks between the floorboards. Habitually uneasy now, she tiptoed to the side window. If she stood pressed against the wall, she could glimpse a slice of the road that ran along the hill above the house, the side they never used where the door was customarily locked. Only strangers knocked at that door.

A large, black car stood running under the dripping trees. In the back seat, a passenger. Uncle Dieter. It took Ella a second to realize the moment had come. Everything inside her went soft.

She stood behind the closed door and listened. Two male voices, one heavy and coarse, the other lighter, lilting, refined. The knock came again, insistent. Should she run to the cellar and out the lower level? But her legs barely supported her. She crept toward the steps. Again the knock. Even if she could get down the stairs, she would be seen coming out, intercepted, perhaps even arrested for trying to escape. It was no good. She went to the door and cracked it open, her hand trembling on the knob.

Neither of the two on the stoop looked familiar. Hunched under large black umbrellas, these men wore ordinary dark suits, their wide lapels and shoulders innocent of jewelry, their shirt collars unadorned.

"Yes?" Ella leaned her body into the wooden door.

"*Guten Tag.*" The older man was in his middle years, tall, slim, his straight, dark hair beginning to yield to the flesh and bone of his lean face. He held his umbrella slanted forward as though to shelter Ella from the driving rain.

"*Grüss Gott.*" The younger one, clearly Bavarian, made a triangle of his stocky body, legs wide. He shifted his eyes all over her, taking in her faded dress, her hair, her age.

"*Gnädige* Frau Münter."

The term of address took Ella aback. *Honored* Frau? By whom? And they knew her name. Her breath lay high in her chest.

"Yes?" Her shoulder pressed against the door.

"We have some questions regarding your paintings. May we come in?" Again the older man. Educated. A Berliner by his accent. He clicked the latch on the stem of the umbrella and lowered the loose folds to stand against the wall under the shelter of the roofline. He stepped closer and wedged the toe of his shoe between the door and lintel. The stocky Bavarian shifted his weight forward.

How could she shut them out now?

"Yes, of course. I'll make some tea." The voice coming forward hardly seemed her own. It was too high, too thin, someone else's voice. "I rarely have guests." She opened the door wide.

"No tea, thank you. We just have some questions." The men stepped inside, stomping their wet shoes on the little rug, brushing the wide shoulders of their dark suits.

"*Questions.*" Ella repeated the word as though it were a foreign tongue she was just beginning to speak. "Perhaps you would like to sit down." She gestured toward the sitting room. If only Johannes were here. How was she to manage?

The older man paused in the entryway and looked about him. He took off his hat and bowed to Ella, then took a seat on the small settee under the window and placed his hat next to him companionably. He crossed his legs, and uncrossed them. He put his hands in his lap. The younger man walked boldly in, crunching small beads under his feet. He crooked one knee and turned his shoe upwards as though something had stuck to its sole. "What's that on the floor?" he said. He may have grown up in the mountains or the farms nearby.

All of a sudden, Ella knew who she was. "I beg your pardon, young fellow. Just as you came, I spilled my bag of beads." She spoke slowly, drawing out her words, the cadence of her phrases melodic and slow, a kindly grandmother interrupted on a rainy day. In the space of a second, she aged a decade. "I've been making a purse, but I get so fumbly these days! Oh, but don't bother about them. I'll get down on my knees when you leave and get them all. I've some sticky tape right over there in the drawer, and they'll come right up." A simple woman, she liked craft projects, handiwork, had crocheted the shawl that covered the sofa back, knit socks, might stitch a sampler, might try her hand at rosemaling a table. She was frugal, made jam and pickles, canned peaches, stewed tomatoes. Her husband had walked to the village. He was paying a call on the priest at St. Nikolaus. They smoked cigars together, balanced the parish budget. "Now, what can I do for you gentlemen? You said you had some questions." She clasped her hands together and smiled. Luckily she'd stopped coloring her hair. She walked to Wassily's handpainted chest and took out her oldest cardigan. She draped it around her shoulders and sat down on a hard, wooden chair across from the men. "My, but the air is chilly today. And so much rain! Winter will be here in no time." Whose words were these? What voice had this tune? She'd never been good at small talk, and here she was chatting on about weather.

The older detective leaned forward on the settee, surveying the room, the painted landscapes over the sofa, the *hinterglasmalerie* over the eating table, the prominent portrait of Wassily on an easel in the corner. He rubbed his hands together and cleared his throat.

But Ella kept talking, letting someone's voice give her direction, attitude. "You've come looking for my pictures, you said. Well, I have quite a big collection still. I can offer a good price." It was true. Stacks of her paintings did line the cellar walls. In her ears, Hoffman's judgment banged a gavel, and his cruel words and her sharp reply pecked at her. Watch it, she said to herself. Watch it. She could be pushed, could lose control, could release the hawk tethered inside her. Ella smoothed her dress on her lap. She pulled her voice-cloak over her shoulders. "I'm so glad you've come. So many people want something more realistic these days. My things are a bit out of fashion, you might say. But I do have a following of a kind. And I so much enjoy it, painting, I mean, when I can afford it." She leaned forward from her chair, confiding. "You know, canvas and paints cost a lot these days, and now that I'm getting on, well—but you understand. Do you gentlemen paint, or are you collectors?" She looked first at the Berliner, then at the Bavarian skulking where he stood. Wings worked at her stomach.

"Fraulein Münter, it is not your pictures that concern us. We understand that you know the artist Wassily Kandinsky." The Berliner spoke the name as though he had been practicing its unfamiliar pronunciation.

Deep within her, the sparring Ella rose like a raptor fighting for release. She wanted to say *knew*. Not *know*. She took a deep breath, forcing the bird lower. She looked at the portrait on the easel. In a moment of whimsy, she had painted a colorful parrot on Wassily's shoulder. She had teased him then. That was her, she'd said, watching over him, a guardian spirit. She swallowed. She crossed her ankles in her chair across from the Berliner, holding onto herself, that slow-speaking self.

"Oh, yes. I certainly did know him when I was a girl. He was my teacher. He might not remember me, now." Some things were hard to say. She rose from her chair. "Are you sure you won't have tea?" The Berliner shook his head and drew a small notebook from the breast pocket inside his jacket. He sat looking at her, his pencil at the ready. Ella sat again, remembering who she was just now.

The two men looked at each other. The Bavarian threw his head back and crossed his arms. He tapped the fingers of his right hand against his left biceps. The Berliner rubbed his chin. His voice grown loud, and he enunciated as though perhaps she could not hear so well. "Do you continue to be in contact with Herr Kandinsky?"

"Dear me, no." Ella thought of the corpse in the cellar, her hand on the shroud. She folded her arms over her breasts. "Let me remember. Professor Kandinsky returned to Russia in 1914. He is a Russian gentleman, don't forget. No, he left us when the war broke out. We—well, it was a whole group of us—we were his students. No, I never saw Professor K again." She let her voice trail off. She could smile a bit. She was telling the truth, in a way.

"But I think you were his lover. You lived with him as his wife. Isn't that so?" He thumbed through his notebook.

Did he know everything? Or only some things? Ella coughed a little into her hand. She gave her chest a few pats. "I do know the gossip." She lowered her eyes, modest old grandmother that she was. Could she blush? "But it was never true. Oh, I took his classes, all right. And I followed him around where he taught, before I got discouraged and settled down. But nothing personal. He was married, you know. We lived in the same neighborhood. Do you know Schwabing? Quite a few artists there. You'd run into a friend every time you stepped out the door." The Berliner moved as though to speak, but Ella kept right on, ignoring his attempt to break in. "Romance? I'm afraid not. And live together? No, no, no. There were parties, when we were young, and they sometimes went on and on. But you wouldn't have known him. No, he would never have done the slightest thing improper. He was quite the gentleman. That's the way he was. And besides, Anja Chimiakin and I—that's his wife, you know,—we were friends. Oh, I suppose I did have a bit of a crush on Professor K in the beginning. He was a handsome man. But lover? Dear me, I'd have been so flattered." She gave herself a little laugh. She was riding the currents, now, up and down with the breeze, feathers steady, feeling the flow.

The Berliner frowned. He wrote slowly in his little notebook, his pencil dragging along the coarse paper. The Bavarian crossed to the door, looked out, crossed back to his station near the window and leaned against it. Were they a team? Did they travel around the countryside looking for people to interrogate? Or was this a new assignment? Ella lowered her shoulders and lay her arms across her belly.

"You know, perhaps, that Wassily Kandinsky has returned to Germany. You are aware that he lives in Weimar. Do not deny that. We expect you will work together with us." He looked up from his writing like a man taking dictation, waiting for the next directive, unsure where to begin.

"Weimar." Ella paused as though struggling to remember that the nation of Germany contained a city in its center called *Weimar*. "Well, no. I'm embarrassed to say it, but I haven't kept in touch with things of that nature. I was never able to afford to buy much in the way of art." She put her finger to her cheek. "I know Professor K made quite a name for himself. I gather his things became much in demand. Very expensive, I'm told. And unusual. I do have a few things he made right here in the house. Would you like to see them?" A partial truth could serve.

The Berliner flipped his notebook shut. "You have work of the painter Wassily Kandinsky?" The Bavarian clicked his heels.

"Yes, right here!" She was more than willing to show. Ella got up from her straight chair and went to the eating table. "This is called...now, let me see, just what *is* it called? Well, in any event, it's painting on the back side of glass. We all learned to make these things. Lots of girls did them. Professor K let us have the ones he made." She reached over the table and pulled one of the *hinterglasmalerie* from its nail. "It's an old folk technique. A fellow near Oberammergau has quite a nice collection." She held the picture at arm's length, studying it. "I liked the St. Georges best. Shall I take them down to show you?"

The Bavarian followed Ella to the eating area, ready to find fault. Power lay on him like the broad shoulders of his dark suit. He took the piece from Ella's hand. "St. George and the Dragon, sir." He held himself erect, geometric. He brought the piece to his commander.

"And the other paintings of Herr Kandinsky. You have them. Where are they?" The Berliner spoke just loud enough for Ella to hear him, a low monotone, uninflected, intense.

So many truths flying about the room. Ella felt like ducking, like shielding her head. She steadied herself, her fingers poking the flesh of her thighs, and then she cupped her elbows in her hands.

"Well, I suppose he has them in Weimar, if that's where you say he lives now." She'd become good at selective listening. She tried to make her voice sound collaborative, cooperative, she one of three interested parties solving a puzzle. Just where were those paintings?

The younger man scowled, but the Berliner soldiered on, water rushing over rock.

"Frau Münter, I beg you, do not insult us." He wheedled with his voice. He fiddled with his pencil. He smiled, his lips stiff in his face. "You are in possession of several of his paintings. You must show them to us."

She could do something even better. "That portrait on the easel, there? Now, that's a portrait I did myself *of* Professor K. He didn't really have a parrot." Ella walked to the easel. She talked on. "It's not much good, I'm afraid. He was much more handsome. That picture does not do him justice." She felt she had taken up another woman's person, slipped into her skin. Where had she learned to leave herself elsewhere? Who had she become?

The man returned his notebook to his vest pocket. "Fraulein Münter, I ask again: Are you in possession of the works of the Russian Communist painter Wassily Kandinksy?" He picked up his hat, fingered its felt brim, put it back again.

Communist? Wassily was no more political than that man's hat.

"Are you interested in buying something by Herr Kandinsky? You've come to the wrong place, I'm afraid. I have nothing of his to sell you, if that's what you want." Perhaps she had slipped into Emmy's voice, or her old friend Olga's. Or Fanny, if Fanny had ever been approached in this way. Fanny Dengler.

"Fraulein Münter, you must know that Wassily Kandinsky is an enemy of the National Socialists. He is a Communist and a degenerate, a bourgeois threat to the Third Reich." His voice clicking its heels, he snapped at Ella. "In the interests of the German will to national self-preservation, I insist that you answer the question."

So. He'd picked up their language. Not just water but waterfall. But Fanny would never yield. Ella laughed. "*Degenerate*? My St. Georges? My goodness, I don't think you mean that." She went back to the eating table, sat, and laughed again. No one ever got the better of Fanny.

The Berliner motioned to the Bavarian and nodded toward the sitting room. "And the other pictures you have?" The Bavarian took long strides across the floor.

"*Gabriele Münter* on this one, sir." The Bavarian sidled along. "And this one. And here. They all say 'Gabriele Münter,' sir."

Ella held herself still. Fools. Had she wanted to, she could easily have painted her own name over Wassily's simple "Kandinsky." His paintings and hers had similarities for a time, before he moved on. But the works on the walls were truly her own. The painter was Gabriele Mnter, and she was not under attack. The Bavarian checked each signature, reporting again and again "*Gabriele Münter.*" Ella clasped her elbows. She sat as still as she could, mute. If she spoke with her own Ella's voice, she would ruin the image she had built up this last half hour.

The Berliner stood up. He was taller than she had noticed. Towering before her, he held his large, pale hands in front of his body as he flipped the pages of his notebook. "Fraulein Münter, I must make myself clear. I work under the jurisdiction of special law. My colleague and I represent Josef Goebbels in the search to rid the Fatherland of destructive elements, carriers of the poison of Bolshevism." He stood taller. "If you are in possession of the works of Wassily Kandinsky, you can give them over to us, and we will leave you to your beadwork. But you must understand, if you are found to be harboring the work of an enemy of the state, you put yourself in quite a dangerous position." He fingered the knot of the tie at his throat, and he looked hard at Ella. "A German must not foul his own nest." He put his notebook in his vest pocket, folded his hands, adjusted his fingers slightly, and re-folded his hands. "It would be a mistake to resist. Here is your opportunity to come forth. I state once again, if you have paintings of Herr Kandinsky in this house, you must reveal yourself at once." He lifted his eyebrows. "Unless, of course, you, yourself, are a Communist." He pulled the small notebook from his vest pocket and flipped over the pages as though something could incriminate her there. "You were living, I believe, in Munich during the revolt of the Bavarian Socialist Republic." He raised his eyes from the notebook and looked at her piercingly. "Were you a member of the Communist Party at that time?"

Imperturbable Ella refused to understand. She blinked. If this curious visitor wanted to know all about her, she—Ella, Fanny, someone else—why, she herself had nothing to hide. Only what lay below. She looked at the ceiling. "Let's see." She willed herself to soften, made her stomach loosen, her shoulders slope. Oh, she *was* a bit of a bumbler, now, wasn't she? "When was that? I was never much good at keeping up with events." No woman this simple would consort with Communists. Surely he would see that.

He raised his voice like a man shouting to a crowd. "Were you or were you not living in Munich between November of 1918 and May of 1919?" The Berliner bent forward, the lupine planes of his face straining. He folded his notebook, returned it to his vest pocket, and put his hands behind his back, stretching his chest wide. His voice grew stronger still, and he asked again, insistently. "Were you a member of the Communist Party in Munich in 1919?" He seemed to think he was on solid ground, now. He repositioned himself in front of her.

Ella felt her neck and shoulders grow tense, the hawk fluttering. She might...she might...she felt the hawk rise. She wanted to peck at him with her beak, to shout out at him, to make him leave her alone, leave her house, just get out. Count, she told herself, count quickly. Onetwothreefourfive. Breathe. The raptor quieted. "I don't believe I caught your name, young man."

"Answer the question, please. We know, as well, that your father defected to America." He might have been chastising a wayward child.

Once again, the truth would serve. She pushed the bird down.

"Papa? My goodness. Well, yes, but he came back, didn't he, before I was born. Papa was a dentist in Dusseldorf, but you might not know that. Now, let's see." She played with the buttons on her cardigan, feeling the shelf of Papa's lap beneath her. "As for those Communists you mentioned, I couldn't say for certain what they want. I'm not really the person to ask. Such a lot of shouting. I was never a great reader of newspapers. And I'm not sure why you bring it up." She smoothed her dress on her lap. "But about Munich. Well, I spent the war in Scandinavia, you see. Things were so hard to get here." She lifted her eyes. "In Denmark, we could get meat from time to time, and milk. And fish, of course. And fuel—now that could be hard to come by even there." She crossed her ankles. "No, in 1919 I was still in Copenhagen, living with a friend. I could give you her name, if you like. I didn't get back to Germany until after 1921, and then I went to Berlin to live with my sister and her family. I was quite ill in the 20's." A harmless woman, she was, simple. Who could doubt it? "But Munich. Well, I certainly did live there, but not until 1930. You can check the registration records. You'll see." She took a deep breath. "I do wish my husband were here. He's so much better at dates and things."

"Your husband?"

"Yes. Johannes Eichner. He'll be home soon, I imagine, if you'd care to wait. Now, 1927—that's a date I do remember. Yes, we met on New Year's Eve, 1927, or does that make it 1928? In any event, in Berlin, as it happens. You, yourself, come from Berlin, I imagine."

"We have no record of your marriage to a man of that name." He looked disgusted, as though he might spit.

"No, no, you wouldn't. No. This is a personal marriage. Not a matter of the state or anything like that. Nothing formal. But why would you need a record of me? Just to buy a few paintings?"

The two detectives looked at each other. The younger man made a choking sound. The Berliner shouted. "And are you and Herr Eichner Communists?"

"Goodness, no. I've told you that. Why ever would you think so? My, my. Such a fuss." She took a minute to let the thought sink in. "Oh, I see. That's what this is about! You want to take my paintings without paying! You want me to *give* them to you!" She put her hands on her Fanny hips. The nerve. Ella blinked and pursed her lips and jerked her little sparrow head.

The Berliner nodded to the Bavarian, the perfect gentleman once again, self-possessed. A man in charge.

"Frau Münter, I am afraid that my partner will be obliged to search your house. You will excuse him. He may leave your things is some disorder."

"What are you looking for? If I have something you need, I can get it for you. No reason to make a mess. Just a moment!" She hopped up from her chair.

The Bavarian crossed his arms in front of his barrel chest. "We want the paintings of Wassily Kandinsky, and we believe you have them."

"Young man, I have shown you what I have." She faced the Berliner. "As for the glass paintings, well they really are not for sale. I don't understand this at all." Her voice got higher, shriller, twittering with the indignity of offense. She had been the subject of idle gossip by strangers. And now the other young man was going to go rifling through her things. It was undignified. It was not to be borne. Keep channeling Fanny. Think Fanny's thoughts. If she thought about Ella, she was doomed.

"The pictures of St. George are not of interest to us." The Berliner nodded to the junior officer. "Buckholtz," he said, jerking back his head at the Bavarian. He motioned to Ella. She must sit.

Ella pulled the cardigan tight around her shoulders. She watched the Bavarian leave the room, his thick haunches moving under the thin fabric of his suit. Likely this was his first. He'd have been raised in overalls. She heard the ruckus as he pulled aside the bed from the wall, opened the drawers of her bedside table, rummaged through her soft clothes and the dresses hanging in the wardrobe. She listened while the Bavarian called back reports to his senior officer. The Berliner sat on the settee, twirling and twirling his hat in his hand.

The young man moved into the music room, the kitchen, the other bedroom. It would not take long to scavenge the entire house, the upstairs part. She and Johannes were neither wealthy nor acquisitive. In this part of the house, he would turn up only the paintings of Fraulein Gabriele Münter, paintings clear to the naked eye on the walls of every room. Downstairs, though, was a different story.

Finding nothing to interest them on the upper floors, the Berliner and the Bavarian started down the stairs. When he got to the bottom, the Bavarian turned back, and seeing Wassily's blue horses charging upwards, pointed at his colleague. "This?" But the sight of fanciful horses galloping up a slope amidst flowers and folk motifs did not alarm the Berliner. "Charming," he said and called to Ella. "Did Wassily Kandinsky paint these stairs?"

"Yes, he did. As I said, we were friends. Quite a few of my friends were artists, and they took a fancy to decorate the house." She came down the stairs slowly, holding the rail tightly, settling her weight on each step before she left it for the next. "I've never seen the need to change it."

"Yes, charming." The Berliner stood at the bottom, inspecting Wassily's horses.

But the Bavarian had moved into the cellar room.

"Sir?" he called to the Berliner. "Sir, in here. I think we've found them."

The Berliner took his time. He stood in the hallway just outside the cellar room, dimly lit, rain pouring heavily outside, the sky dark. He looked into the room. "I'll need light," he said. The Bavarian left by the lower door. In his absence, the Berliner began to hum, tapping the fingers of his right hand on his thigh. Ella stood by his side. "I do hope you'll find something you like," she said. "There's a great deal of variety, here. Lots to choose from. Such a lot of memories for me." Her throat swelled. The Berliner looked at her. But she smiled at him. "Yes, I'm sure you'll find something nice."

When the Bavarian returned, soaked, the Berliner took the flashlight. He stroked the long shaft, clicked on the switch, and aimed the beam first at the ceiling, then the floor, skimming the room with his torch, letting an amber circle of light rest on each of the objects he found there. Dozens of stretched canvases leaned against three walls in short stacks like folds of a paper fan. Against the fourth wall stood the shelving unit full of food lined on either side by cans and bottles of solvents, trays of paints in tubes, jars of brushes, bare cardboards, a large roll of canvas. For some moments, the Berliner held himself erect, surveying the lot, letting the beam of light trail from stack to stack, small noises in his throat suggesting disbelief. Then he crouched to the floor and sifted through the paintings. He touched every one. A cluster of trees, gold and green. A village with its church under spotty clouds. Lavender mountains behind some small brown sheds. Round yellow fruit on a plate. A woman seated before a window. A city street. A farmyard with cows. A stiff blond girl in a red dress holding a babydoll. A cluster of shops on a village street. A crooked lamp on a table among some wilted flowers. A woman's portrait. Four people in a rowboat. Houses on a hill. A grouping of toys. A wide blue lake. A snow scene. A graveyard. A woman reading. A bald man at the table. A barnyard. The yellow house in winter. The yellow house in summer. A vase of flowers. A book on a table. The interior of a room. A road. Every one signed *Gabriele Münter*.

When he had inspected the things on the cellar floor, he stood up.

"These paintings. You are the person who made each of them?"

"Well, yes. Is there something special you want? I don't do portraits any more. I did have some from Copenhagen, but they've got lost, I think. I tell you, I don't have anything of Professor Kandinsky excepting my little St. Georges, and they aren't for sale." She would persist in thinking the two men customers. She was not a woman to be put off by the word *Communism*. She could not imagine why they raised its specter. "Was there nothing you preferred? Won't you let me show you some of the things? I have some favorites among them."

"Fraulein Münter." The Berliner stopped. He started to speak, caught himself, started again. "Frau Eichner, I think we have troubled you enough." He looked at the Bavarian. "Buckholz." He turned into the hallway.

"Oh, but you mustn't leave yet." She walked to the Berliner and took his arm, directing him toward the stairs. "Please, stay for just a little something. It doesn't matter if you don't want to buy anything. Won't you taste my plum liqueur? You don't want to go out into the rain without something warming. Go on up, now, and make yourselves comfortable. I'll just get a nice bottle."

The Berliner and the Bavarian exchanged looks.

"We would be most happy to accept." They started up the stairs.

Ella walked quickly back to the cellar room. Lined up in front of where the door cut into the closet sat the row of plums in vodka. She took the jar furthest from the latch-less door. Then, standing on the cellar floor, her foot positioned on the first step, she listened to the Bavarian's low hiss above.

"That Russian fucker was screwing her for twelve years, and she'd like to think nobody even knew? Stupid cow!"

Ella bit her lip to stop the trembling. "All right, gentlemen," she called out. "I'm coming with some of my lovely homemade plum liqueur. I think you'll enjoy it. And then, we'll say goodbye." She clasped the rail and slowly climbed the stairs on the backs of Wassily's horses, galloping higher and higher.

‡

When the long car drove onto the road and out of sight, Ella leaned heavily against the door, her heart pounding. She thought she might collapse, and then she did, sliding slowly toward the floor, the tears coming and coming, her breath halting, chest heaving. For some minutes she lay crumpled on the floor near the door, shivering. Could it be that the moment they feared had passed? That the Nazis had come to her door and tried to intimidate her and that she had fended them off? She, alone?

She listened to the rain on the roof, the silence on the road. Hearing nothing to alarm her further, she rolled herself onto her knees and moved haltingly across the floor, picking up the spilled beads as she crawled, collecting them in her lifted skirt. When she reached the other side of the room, she gripped the sofa arm with one hand and pulled herself up. She poured the beads into a bowl and walked stiffly into the kitchen to make a hot drink. Water sloshed as the hand holding the kettle jittered of its own accord.

Never in her life had she endured such strain, never marshaled her intelligence and resolve so intently, never faced an obstacle so boldly, never mastered her own self so thoroughly. It had taken every bit of self-control she could muster. She had found a spirit inside that directed her and would not give up, a spirit that went beyond her own inclination or individual expression. Love was a giving away of the self. When you fully loved someone—or something—you replaced yourself with that greater purpose. If you were lucky in love, you never regretted your loss.

Later, sitting at the table with her tea, she smiled. She had done well with her little performance, and she would tell Johannes all about it. Furthermore, it seemed, for now at least the paintings were safe. She had been wrong to think the paintings were nothing to her.

She had been known them since their birth and had loved them. And now she had saved them.

Part Five

Galerie

"Road in Multicolored October," 1959
Gabriele Münter
Oil on canvas
$20'' \times 14^{1}/_{2}''$
Milwaukee Art Museum
Gift of Mrs. Harry Lynde Bradley

Bright with primary and secondary colors in large patches and forms, the scene appears to be a curved road heading off toward a great distance marked by mountains. The road is composed of rough horizontal rectangles of red and pink and purple sloping along a hill. We, too, are on the road, not prevented, as we sometimes have been, from accompanying the traveler. Trees provide a partial canopy, protective and cheerful. They are, themselves, whimsically composed of fanciful shapes and color combinations. One maple, it must be, is made up of concentric waves of red and green as though caught in the act of October change.

The colorful patches are worth special mention. Far from being realistic in their depiction of a country road, the color areas are so large they might almost be cutouts of paper or fragments of colored glass such as one sees in modern stained glass windows. The artist, it seems, has been liberated from any obligation to literal truth but indulges her visual imagination in playful expression.

An example of painting at its most joyous, "Road in Multicolored October" demonstrates the artistic distance traveled by this remarkable woman.

J. Eichner

Chapter Twelve

View from the Mountain

Murnau
Winter, 1957

GREYLAG GEESE honk overhead, late travelers south. Ella imagines them skidding to a halt on some sub-Alpine plain in Italy, some warmer place near water. Though she cannot see the geese, she can hear the raucous calling high above the cloud ceiling. Silently she wishes them god-speed. A warm shawl draped over her shoulders, she leans on her elbow at the eating table, her back to Johannes. He sits on the cushioned divan against the yellow-papered wall, his thin legs crossed so as to support on his raised knee the heavy book he is reading. He has read the book many times, Ella knows. It is a history of Chinese porcelain, a subject he tells her he has only been able to forget so much about because he was once, himself, an encyclopedia of porcelain. She understands that he does not want to forget what he once knew. It is a question of pride, a refusal to allow the personality to attenuate the way the calves of one's legs grow stringy.

And so she lets him read quietly behind her while she studies the letters on the table before her. The Post Office system leaves much to be desired. Those who acquire one's address feel free to send letters one wants only to discard. One must not be asked to explain. And then there is the matter of replies. Mostly one does not reply.

First she sorts them, a pile for Johannes, a pile for Ella. Her pile is much larger. When the sorting is done, she tugs at the edges of the tablecloth, running its flat, blue hem under each fingernail, feeling each crescent curve. She uses the edge of one stiff envelope to scrape the cloth in front of her, scattering toast crumbs into new configurations. She has made a little Milky Way of brown bread, she sees, and she brushes the crumbs with the side of her hand to send galaxies flying into space. From her pile of letters she makes a second heap— the mail she will not read—and she places that stack as far away from her on the table as she can reach. Now she will open the letters whose exteriors have not offended her. From time to time, she takes a sip of hot water and lemon, returning the cup to the saucer to turn a page or slit an envelope. One letter invites her to attend the opening of a new art exhibit. She throws that letter to the floor.

After the war Ella visited the exhibitions that Johannes organized, but then she stopped going. Rather than express the passion she once felt, these paintings looked friendly, cordial, open to conversation. Not like her. Not like anybody she would know. In fact, she has stopped attending all of the surveys of contemporary art, most especially those that include her. Last year she saw that nearly no one stopped at her pictures. No matter. She could not look at her own work either, but she was glad no one recognized her as the painter of those neglected pieces. She has no need to attend another such exhibition.

One letter comes from some American cousins, good correspondents. They regard her as a celebrity and boast of her to their friends. In the war years and just after, they sent packages of tinned fish and dry beans, and it was never enough even when the mail got through, and she knew there were things she never received, things she needed, suffered from not having. They did not starve, she and Johannes, though they nearly went mad the time the soldiers swept through the village and raided their little patch of turnips and potatoes. They might have died if Emil Bauer had not come by, then, with a bag of parsnips and some cabbages. He, too, had grown thin and grey, but he had been allowed to stay behind and farm for the Reich. Afterwards there were months of numbing cold when Ella and Johannes hung blankets over the windows and sat huddled together on the sofa wearing all their clothes, shivering and hungry through the dark days and the darker nights. The war years were grim and frightening and horrifying, and Ella knows she will never again look about her in quite the same way.

The letters bring her back. She has a letter from the cousin in St. Louis, Missouri, the United States. Her face is shadowy, now, but Ella has a photograph of her in the drawer, and when she finishes with the letters, she may look at it. A letter in a pink envelope comes from Friedel. Ella raises one lean hip and slides this letter onto the chair seat under her for later. She misses Emmy, dead a few years now, and even Friedel is middle aged. But her niece brings news of the younger generation. Ella cannot imagine what to say to them about their love affairs and the scurrying they do to establish themselves in the world, but she is glad to hear from Friedel, her lone conduit to a world Ella has left entirely behind.

When she looks up from her letters, she sees through the window that snow is falling thickly, and she frets, briefly, about the geese and hopes they have not lost their way in the snow. When she leaves the house, she, herself, will need to wear her boots and scarf and gloves. She will bring her cane and carry the ski pole with the claw Johannes had welded to its end. She plans to take her camera to the gravesite to mark its place behind the ancient Baroque church, a church she has never entered for prayer or worship because that kind of thing does not appeal to her. Many times, however, she has lingered in the gardens on either side of the churchyard gate to look at the tablets memorializing the Murnau soldiers lost in 1943 and 1944. She has read their names, the Ottos and Felixes, Peters and Dieters, Franzes and Gunthers, and she has considered these fallen boys now lying on the Steppe in Russland or in Polen or Jugoslav or another forsaken spot while she stands, an old woman, in their village churchyard and reads the names they left behind. The boys died far from home, young boys, whereas she is still here, letting go of the years a little at a time. That is what she prefers, to say goodbye to things slowly, privately.

She once entered the house of the priest who sold her and Johannes the burial plot behind the church. Like them, he lived through the war in Murnau, but Ella believes he was a Nazi collaborator.

"Don't forget," Johannes had said, "he says Mass out at the camp."

"Well, I should hope so. All those Poles, officers most of them. Someone should look after them."

"I'd say we're lucky they're nearby. The Allies won't bomb the camp, so we're safe, too."

"You'd find the silver lining in a thunderstorm."

But when they sat before the priest's desk, she kept her eyes on her lap and Johannes did the talking and the paying. Ella does not expect to see this priest again, though she does not believe that it is a Nazi burial plot just because this priest sold it to them. In fact now she is photographing the spot they have purchased, to consider from time to time. She is taking pictures in every weather so that they will be able to imagine the future. She has not yet photographed the site in snow on a grey day like today, but she knows she will see, when she gets there later, that the gravesite is on the ridge of a slope sliding softly down toward an open valley. The slope and the valley will be pure white in the new snow, at least to the untrained eye. Were she to paint it, though, she would need blue and yellow and perhaps even black to do it justice, to capture the depth of the white and the lurking shadow. In any event, she long ago dispensed with painting what things looked like. Today she will only photograph the spot where she intends to spend the life that succeeds this one. *Succeeds.* Will there be success in the afterlife? Has she not had enough success in this life to supply her with fame for eternity? Perhaps not. But one must be careful. Might not such a thing get out of hand, like the apprentice in *Der Zauberlehrling*, brooms growing out of brooms? Best not to think too hard about it. Just see.

Some trees will be on the slope as well. Perhaps today the snow-laden branches will be white with black tracings, instead of the other way round, as though she were to paint a white tree and then define it with a black line. She has never painted a white tree, and now she wonders why she has not. A white tree outlined in black against an orange sky might be quite wonderful. She sees herself as such a tree, the whole world ablaze over her head. When she last visited the gravesite, the trees were yellow like a hill touched by Midas, the little gold leaves flickering, catching the sun and winking the light into her eyes. The yellow trees and the hill formed a golden funnel for the wind, sucking it upwards from the valley, and she stood there that day and wished she could unbutton her head-top and let the cool wind blow across her brain and down into her soul. Weeks before, when she went there with Johannes on the afternoon that the grave papers were signed and the money turned over, they could see that the summer winds would cool their festering bodies as they lay beside one another one day. They have lain together these last thirty years now. Just thirty. They had not been youthful lovers, no, but *lebensgefährte*, certainly. And more than that, too.

Even with her back to him, Ella knows that Johannes is here in the room with her, and she looks forward to spending her death years nearby him. As for the time of youth, Ella has never asked Johannes to explain his past, and Johannes has not begrudged her Wassy nor what followed in the wake of loving him. Not at all.

Ella is almost finished with her mail. But when she reads in the last letter of the stack that she will be expected to sit on the dais at the center of a ceremony, she is outraged. Outraged. Walk onto a stage like a showgirl? How could Johannes have allowed it? She turns around in her wooden chair and glares at him and shuffles her feet on the wood floor and makes noises in her throat. She rouses him from his book with her discontent. She will not cooperate. What she has agreed to do is enough. This is too much. She is prepared to back out entirely. Entirely. She had not anticipated this. She tells Johannes that she had never agreed to be made a spectacle of and if a circus pony is what they are after, they will have to look elsewhere. She cannot abide being gawked at. She can certainly not be asked to speak. He will have to phone them and call the whole thing off. Surely he understands her position.

Johannes looks up from his book. "It's only natural that they would want to honor you, Gabriele." He turns his page.

"It's the last thing I'd ever want." She tears up the envelope in which the letter arrived.

Johannes holds his page with a finger and closes the book. He adopts his most long-suffering voice. "I understand. But you've done a grand thing, Ella. I'm not just talking about Dr. Röthel and the museum. The mayor is saying your gift is a civic enhancement. Of course they want to make a celebration. I've been expecting it, in fact." He sighs and opens his book again.

Ella crumples the offending letter and throws it onto the floor. She crosses her arms and holds her elbows cupped in her hands. She throws her words into the basket she has made of her chest. "I don't know what you mean by *a grand thing*. I'm going to die soon, at any rate, and what will happen to the paintings then? So why do they need a ceremony? I won't be part of it."

At first Johannes does not raise his eyes. He is looking at a dragon, greenish with wide eyes and a horrid grin. "You are certainly not going to die immediately. And even if you did, assuming I were here to see to things, I'd go ahead—give the paintings to the Lenbachhaus." Johannes puts his bookmark in place and sets the book on the small table beside him. "It's clearly the right thing. All they're asking is that you sit on the dais and let them thank you."

"You know I hate being looked at!" Ella folds her arms more tightly against her chest.

"Gabriele, it's not such a terror as all that. You'll sit and smile and someone will give a speech and someone else will bring you flowers. Perhaps there will be a dinner and wine. I quite look forward to it." Johannes gets up from the sofa and bends his knees one at a time to loosen them.

"I do not smile on command." Ella nudges the balled letter with the toe of her soft slipper.

"Yes, yes, but you can look pleased. You're quite lovely when you're pleased with something." Johannes removes his reading glasses, folds them carefully, and places them in his breast pocket. "And you should be happy. The city fathers are grateful to you, and I'm proud of you. Everyone is calling you a heroine."

"Nonsense. Ridiculous. Simply ridiculous. An exaggeration. It was all your doing anyway. Why are they fussing about me? It's you who should be on the stage." The corners of Ella's mouth are turned down in a shape she prefers. When she looks at herself in the mirror, she holds her mouth like this.

"The paintings are yours, Ella. That's the simple truth."

"Johannes, read this." Ella bends from her chair and retrieves the letter, though her stiff lower back complains when she moves. "The mayor and Röthel are planning to give speeches. It will be intolerable. I won't know where to put my eyes." She resumes her spot at the table and unfolds the crumpled letter, smoothing its wrinkles against the blue cloth. She reads the page again.

Johannes reassembles his hips and knees and goes to stand behind Ella. He puts his hands on her shoulders and brushes her fine hair with his thin lips. He bends forward and rests his chin on the top of her head. He has not shaved today, which is unusual. In the morning, he has told Ella that he will be on holiday the entire day. That means he will not shave until just before dinner. He does, however, bathe and wear a fresh shirt and a tie, even though he has told her he has no plans to leave the house. His idea, he says, is to reconnect with Chinese porcelain.

"You deserve to be recognized. You mustn't resist it. Don't torture yourself like this." He gives her shoulders a little squeeze. "Here's what I suggest. Treat yourself to a new frock. Why not? Have a little fun. I might even indulge in a new necktie."

"Buy a dress—Johannes, you must be daft!" Ella raises her voice. She moves her shoulders under his hands. "What can you be thinking?" She rubs her palms over the galaxies, asteroids scattering. "There is no such thing as a *frock* for an eighty-year old woman. Are you mad? I've no shape at all. My hair's gone white. I can't even walk properly."

"Nonsense. You know you walk very well. Just yesterday you walked back and forth to the village twice. I can't keep up with you. And your hair is lovely, like strands of creamy silk. I wouldn't have you any other way." Johannes kisses the top of her head and returns to the divan. He picks up his book. "Let's just motor up to Munich on Saturday and see. One of the shops on the Residenzstrasse will have just the ticket. And we'll eat somewhere. I'd quite like some nice tellerfleisch. Didn't I order that last time at Jodlerwirt?"

Ella sits, fuming, playing with the lemon in her cup.

"Don't decide just yet. Think about it. The evening might be just what you need. Put that part of your life to rest. That part of my life, too. You see that, don't you, Gabriele? It's time to lay it all to rest. Then we can go up to the churchyard and have a nice sleep together. What do you say?"

Ella says nothing. The cat, Delphi, rubs against her legs back and forth, back and forth.

It is not the dark that she dreads, that total dark they talk of from time to time, not death, itself. But the men with their speeches are the outward signs that she is already a ghost. She does not want to sit among those men. Their words to her will have only to do with what is already gone and who she was and what she did then. *Was. Did. Then.* She sees already that there is no piece of her that is not already fractured and lying on the floor of a closet. How many selves she has left behind in dusty places. She has molted like a snake. She once found a snakeskin and spread it out on a shelf until it disintegrated and had to be swept away. Bits of her are on shelves, too, and hanging on walls, and collecting dust in museums. Most of what happens to her now, in fact, even she cannot recall. Everything about her is past.

As for her youth, the young face she has seen in the photographs that are supposed to be pictures of her belongs to a sensibility she cannot remember as her own. If life is a heaping up of events and experiences, a stacking upwards from the earth of our birth to the heavens above, surely what's at the bottom of the heap must decay, like fruit and vegetable peels at the base of the compost heap in the garden. So it is not only in death that we become dust, she thinks. Our youth is rot. And who can believe in heaven? So what becomes of those selves we have inhabited? Maybe instead we are a geology of selves layered like the slice of a hill where a road has cut through, limestone and granite in heavy slanting ribbons, bits of fossilized treats pinched in time. Compost or rock, which is it? She cannot say.

The snow has stopped falling. She gets up from the table and puts on her coat. She will get her camera and take photographs of the site on the mountain ridge covered today in snow. She intends to photograph the graveyard in all weathers, imagining that future, that certain one.

‡

Outside, the air is still and wet. No one is about, the silence of the hillside broken only by the swish Ella makes with her feet on the narrow path that winds down to the road to town. She is glad to have the cane and the pole, glad that Johannes insisted she carry them. Both hands in their gloves are occupied with holding on. She wears a backpack for her camera, and she also carries a handkerchief and some money in case she wants to buy a coffee. Since she was a young woman mountaineering, she thinks, she has worn a rucksack. No, she corrects herself. Before that—in that long trip she and Emmy made to America right after Mama died. She and Emmy had watched a rodeo in Colorado. Emmy had shielded her eyes, frightened for the bucking rider, afraid that she would see him trampled under the hooves. She, Ella, seeming shy, still talking little in those days, had been bolder, thrilled to see the cowboy holding on, daring the horse to unseat him. She thought then that she might like to be a *cowgirl*. The American word makes her laugh out loud, and she stops walking to let the silliness pass, lest she slip. There was not, in the end, so very much wrong with her.

The path leading down the hill from the blue and yellow house is slick with new-fallen snow, too fresh to have been tamped down with the passage of many neighbors. Ella remembers with pleasure the years when there were hardly any neighbors. Now, though, the hillside has sprouted low, wide houses with back gardens. She does not know who lives in these houses. Presumably families with children. She sees the outdoor toys, the small bicycles, and in the summer months sometimes children kick around a football in the early evenings after the suppers have been cleared away. She has never introduced herself, though she suspects Johannes has. It may be that he has even kicked the ball with some of the neighbor children. It would be like him.

She makes herself walk carefully, placing each boot as though she were tracing a design with her feet, a pattern of foot and foot and cane and pole, writing a message in the snow like Morse Code—dash, dash, dot, dot. To whom would she send her message, this calling out from the high hill? She is uncomfortable thinking about it, and again she stops herself. It is all the fault of that letter, that stupid request to sit and be gawked at. She needs to get away from that letter and the pinched feeling that comes into her chest.

She thinks about the snow and patterns. If the snow were thicker, she could stomp an upside-down city of negative space—down through the snow to the ground instead of up upon it. This foot the town hall. This one the train station. If there were more snow, at least, and if one could stand on one's head to see what one has made.

On the pavement next to the road, she can hold her cane and pole in one hand and warm the other in her pocket. There is a bit of a grade downwards, but the going is not so slippery as before. Still, she thinks, she has not had much experience with building of any kind. Most of her life has been a kind of erasing—a smudging away of the old rules, a cleaning up and getting down to principles. And storing. Saving. And that moment worries her just now. She had saved *him*, had she not, when she hid those things she is now about to give away? But might there have been a better future for them than in the hands of those grasping business-types, those speech-makers and sitters upon daises, those city fathers just waiting for her to die? Surely better for herself not to have to sit on a dais and listen to a passel of speeches that will not come even remotely close to the truth, speeches about *then, did, was.* As soon as she has raised these questions in her mind, she feels much better. She is often a teapot, she knows, and it does her good to spout and sputter, release the steam that swells inside and pushes against her brain. And why shouldn't she just keep the paintings? Especially when it took so much to secret them out of Munich and keep them hidden and safe. But, of course, there is an answer to that question, too.

The sky is mottled white and gray, and she fears that she may be

caught in another fall of snow. But just now there is no wind, so perhaps she is all right for a bit. She considers returning to the house but
then remembers the small cafe just below the church. If she gets a
chill, she can take shelter there, and perhaps she can eat something.
At night she sometimes dreams of being hungry and sitting down to
something delicious, a lovely pike in cream sauce, a pungent cucumber salad, some crisp potatoes, a baked onion. But when she wakes,
she often finds that she cannot imagine eating such food, and she
prepares a slice of plain, toasted bread that she does not always finish. Her drink of choice is water and lemon.

The street goes up a small hill, now, and Ella walks more slowly.
To the right, stone steps lead to a narrow path that winds past the
house of the priest. When she reaches the churchyard, she unlatches
the gate and turns to the left to walk around the old stone structure,
imposing and cold on the outside. Johannes has said that inside, the
church is magnificently ornate, the organ pipes hand-carved from
a sleek, golden wood, the sanctuary peopled with gilded saints, the
monstrances and chalices hand-wrought by Renaissance artisans
earning acceptance into the silver guilds. Someday she might look
inside, if she feels like it. So far, she has not. She turns around the
back corner and goes directly to her final resting place.

No one is there today, and Ella is grateful for that. She imagines
that she and Johannes will be glad not to be seen for long stretches.
If she had her way, she would rest for eternity in no one's company
but her own, with Johannes to turn over to from time to time. She
imagines herself a heap of silt rolling to one side, shifting the weight
of the dirt in the coffin. She sometimes thinks that the coffin will
surely split and crack and parts of her will sift into the earth, itself.
That, too, suits her.

The spot is lovely today, all black and white and grey, polished, the
sheen of the land and the sky solid and eternal, like being in a jewel
box of pearls. She likes a black and white day, like photographs be-

fore they invented color. Her eyes feel stronger in this light, keener. The grave markers stand out against the snow like a theme and variations, the rectangular shapes repeated smaller, larger, their angles softened by time, or not. She sees nubbles on the grave markers of her neighbors, little pits of stone blackened and rough, and above them she looks out over the hill to the wide expanse of valley lidded just now with a fat, dark cloud.

She sets down her cane and pole on the path between the graves that lean up the hill behind her and those that point down the hill to the valley. She will lie there, just below the path, like being in the last row of seats in the front section of a theater. The view will be good. She slides her shoulders out from the straps of her backpack and sets it down. Someone has swept the snow off the path already. She doubts it would be the priest who sold her the spot, but she cannot be sure. He did not seem like a man to sweep a path. She unbuckles the flap of her pack and removes her camera. Now she must take off her gloves, or she will not be able to adjust the lens. But the camera knows her touch, and the dial turns effortlessly for her. She has a very fine camera, a Leica IIIf Red Dial ST, not that she knows what that name indicates. She has memorized its designation to stop the conversation when nosy people ask her what camera she uses. They rarely have another question after that. They leave her alone then.

She takes a dozen pictures, moving the lens ever so slightly this way and then that, adjusting the settings so that the depth of field sometimes pulls in the mountain opposite and sometimes casts the mountain as a shadow on the gravesite. It occurs to her that she must ask Johannes if he cares which side will be his. Likely he will want the right side. But she must remember to bring it up. They will need to make that clear. She moves from one side of the site to another. She likes to see it from several angles. She will not be able to look around when she is buried here, she understands, and she finds it important to pack her head with images for later.

Now that she has what she has come for, she looks around at those who are already her neighbors on the hill. Some are whole families, grandparents and parents and even babies. Many are couples, like her and Johannes, although perhaps not quite like them. Very few are single people lying alone, at least. She can understand that. As much as she intends to rest alone, she will be glad to think that Johannes is nearby, doing his own resting. But there are not so very many neighbors at all, to be sure. She will have lots of room to stretch out, lots of time to consider.

The black cloud that put a stop to the endless sky is gaining bulk and mass, and Ella feels chilled. A brisk wind is rising from the valley, and Ella lifts up the little fur collar on her coat and pulls her wool hat lower around her ears. She ought to go, but she hates to leave the spot. She feels she can't drink in the day sufficiently to ward off forgetfulness. The photographs will help, though, help her know the place in this very weather, on this grey and white day. Her photographs will stop time, and when she looks at them later, she will know where she was and where she will be.

She repacks her rucksack and hoists it over her shoulder. She picks up her cane and the pole with the claw and holds them together in one hand while she puts on first one glove, then the other. To get to the village, she will have to turn around, and she places her feet carefully, making V-shaped wedges of them until her whole body is pointed back down the path toward the church and the gate. She walks past the house of the priest and past the garage where she once saw five chickens pecking at the dust on the floor. Once she is on the walkway to the village, she begins to hope she will be hungry enough to stop in the cafe. She is feeling very cold, indeed. She wants to get warm and sit down.

Ella has been in this cafe several times, though always with Johannes. The owner is a fat, bald man with a white apron. His daughter has a large burn on her face, and her skin is puckered. Today, Ella is too cold not to go inside. She has not fallen, but her legs do not feel trustworthy, in spite of the cane and the claw. So she opens the heavy oak door, and when she is inside the little reception area, she rests the pole with the claw in the corner, but she takes her cane with her into the large room with the tables. The room is dark and very old, paneled with heavy woods, the windows studded with red and blue and green glass in a diamond pattern outlined in black so that only a little light from outdoors brightens the interior. At first she stands just at the entrance, and she cannot see very well. She seems to be alone in this room. Her legs are beginning to weaken, and her spirit fails her utterly. She must sit down, but she cannot move forward. And then she feels herself sinking, curling forward like a heap of snow dissolving. She does not fall forward or backward, just down, her hips and back bending slowly beneath her. When she is just about to touch the floor, a woman grabs her under her arm.

"Frau Münter," the woman says. "Are you all right? Come, let me help you."

Ella cannot answer, but she can stand up again with the woman's hand under her arm, and she can be led to a booth with a tall back and high sides. She can sit down, and when the fat man in the white apron asks her a question, she can say yes, she would like a cup of tea. And when it comes, hot and strong in a brown pot, someone puts milk and sugar into her cup, although Ella would have drunk the tea black, as she does at home. And then, in a minute or so, when the tea has cooled and she has drunk nearly half, she can look up and see where she is. The girl with the burn is beside her, and the fat man is filling her cup. She is not in the graveyard; she is in the cafe of some people who know her name and who do not say she lives in the "Hurenhaus."

‡

Finding a dress is not so difficult, after all. It is actually a suit—a deep grey-blue skirt and jacket that calls forth the blue of her grey eyes, and the blouse that the shop girl recommends is blue of a lighter shade. Emmy would have liked it, though she could not have worn such a skirt, herself. Even as a girl she was plumper. Olga, too, was plump. And later plumper. Fortunately Friedel does not take after her mother in that way. In other ways, perhaps, cautious ways, careful ways. We did not buy our clothes from a shop in those days, Ella recalls. We went to the dressmaker and we chose a fabric. We did not always like the way we looked when the dressmaker was finished. But then it was too late. Ella would like to show the suit to Emmy, to model it for her, to turn and demonstrate its features. To feel young again. But Emmy is gone, the only one who would remember Ella as a girl.

Johannes approves the suit, and when he goes to pay, he is pleasant with the shop girl. It is always a pleasure to buy clothes for a beautiful woman, he tells her. The shop girl smiles. Undoubtedly she thinks that Ella is his wife. Such a girl must think it charming when elderly people hold hands or kiss or pretend to find one another attractive. Ella is certain that the shop girl does not use the word "sexy" in her thoughts. It would not occur to her. Johannes does not speak about the color, Ella notices. Blue is the best color, Wassy had always said, a spiritual color and the color of truth. Even when she loved him, Ella had not understood. Truth had no color at all to her. Truth was something you understood and felt, and for a time, truth and pain were the same. That feeling lasted quite a long time.

Wassy had admired her eyes, too, in the first years, though they were not the shade he preferred. Who would know that but her? Later, of course, he had stopped saying lovely things to her. And now, well. She has not seen or spoken with him for over forty years. Ella imagines herself talking to the men on the dais. "He has been dead these last thirteen years," she imagines herself saying. He would have been old, too, when he died. Not as old as she is now, but old enough to die. Certainly that. She is glad she never saw him old. In her memory he will always be strong and slim with black, black hair. That is the picture she prefers. The last time she saw him alive, they were in Stockholm, and she insisted that they be photographed. She thought, at the time, that the photograph would show clearly that they were a married couple, married in every sense but one. She made him go with her to the photographer's studio, and he did not want to. And he did not look happy in the photograph, like a man who has missed a train. Or a man who did not want to be married. To her. And she wore an ugly coat and hat and her usual downturned mouth. When she looked at the photograph afterwards, even before he left for the last time, she saw that it had been a mistake, and she put her copy in a drawer she never opens. She does not know what he did with his copy. She certainly has never seen it again.

And why is she now resurrecting him, driving home from Munich with her new suit in the back seat? She is better at burying than un-burying. She would not say these things to Johannes. He would tell her she was torturing herself needlessly. Well. How could it be otherwise? One would hardly torture oneself needfully. Ella considers that perhaps she has said a joke to herself, but then decides that she has not.

Besides, when she sits on the dais, what will the gawkers be thinking? She will not be able to look at them. Some of them will have known her and about the Russian's House and what went on there. Rather, what they imagine went on there. Such high jinks, they will think. They will be imagining interesting sexual acts and all manner of behavior. They will not imagine working very long and late, nor will they imagine arguing over philosophy and *synthesis* and states of being and the meaning of the soul and blue as a spiritual color, which is how they really spent their time. These people would not be able to imagine such discussions at all. Or that there are many kinds

of high jinks and not all of them involve sexual acts. And that some
high jinks are better than others. When the paintings were fresh, it
was all cruelty and gossip, meanness and narrowness in the village.
That is what, at least, she supposes. She may be wrong about it, she
knows. She did not always tell herself the truth, she knows.

And now, when she sits on the dais, they will call her a heroine.
She cannot see what they can mean by that. What else could she have
done? Where is the heroism in saving your own flesh and blood from
ruin? She is still bitter when she remembers what she remembers. In
the days long past that the people on the dais will remember, he was
her own dear, dear Wassy. Now, he belongs to everyone else. And that
is fine with her.

Johannes helps her fasten the pearls he gave her the second or third
year they were together. She smoothes her hair and flattens her
stomach with her hands before she can face the mirror and adjust
her face. Even as a girl she had not been much to look at. Small.
Brownish. Plainish. But the face that looks back at her now is a horror. She can only bear the looking for a moment, she with her wattle,
crevasses in her cheeks. A heroine. Not a bit of it. Johannes cannot
have been more wrong. She would be a corpse but for the filament
holding her to those paintings she is getting ready to give away. Truth
to tell, the buzzards at the museum already have them. But tonight,
after the speeches and all that, when she goes home with Johannes,
the thread will be snapped. They will not be hers in any sense. And
will she then disappear?

She is giving away the best part of herself. She cannot blame Johannes. He had persuaded her, it is true. But she has hardly needed
convincing that their days are dwindling rapidly. "Let's make a gift of
them, Gabriele," he had said. "It's so much better to give them than

have someone just take them after we're gone." Like grave robbers, she thinks. "All right, then," she had said. "We'll give them away."

Johannes drives them to the Lenbachhaus early. Ella knows she will need time to prepare herself for the onslaught of well-wishers. But as they walk along the stone path through the courtyard and past the large, ornate fountain in its center, Ella begins to feel weak. She has not brought her cane. Her legs feel insubstantial, and her dress shoes hurt her feet. She clings to Johannes, wanting only to reach the stage and her chair and have done with it all.

In the crowded assembly hall, she sees dozens of people she has known from the art world—gallery owners and their wives, mostly. But she counts on Johannes to shield her, as he has done in the past. He stops, though, and extends his hand to a man whose face looks vaguely familiar, a man she wants to remember. The man bows to her, his hands behind his back, and then he reaches out and kisses one cheek and then the other. When he is pulling away, she recognizes him. He has grown small, and bald, and his face is red with a fringe of white whiskers. His eyes are the same, though, kind eyes, and his smile is the same. He is Herr Bauer, and she has not forgotten him. How could she? No, in her bed at night, she often recalls him and pictures herself at his side on that long, dark road, Bauer beside her driving her precious cargo toward a destination she could only hope would save them all. "Frau Münter," Bauer says, and smiles. "*Gnädige* Frau Münter," he says, and she remembers again that the Nazi detective called her that. "You look well," Bauer says. And just then, for the first time in ever so long, she feels very well and very happy.

"I am well, Herr Bauer," she says. "And I am glad to see you. Very glad."

Then Johannes turns her toward the front of the room. Several men are there, waiting. She does not recognize the mayor, but she shakes his hand after Johannes does, nodding but shy. She does not look at him directly in the face. Dr. Röthel, from the museum, she has seen several times as they negotiated the transfer of the paintings. Back in her house on Kottmüllerallee, she often thought of him as a pirate and imagined him chortling over his great good fortune in being offered what many a pirate had to take by force. But here in the museum, on the night she is to sit on the dais and listen to speeches about herself, she gives him her hand when he extends his own, but she cannot smile. She is grateful when he escorts her up the steps of the stage and lets her sit down at last.

The speeches are not long, though there are three of them, not two. The mayor talks about the growth of Munich as a magnet for artists for over a century. Ella's gift has brought the city international standing. She could correct him, Ella thinks. Munich only arrived on the art map some sixty years ago. It would have been 1896, she thinks, when Wassily arrived. Those earlier Munich picture-makers—Stuck and Lenbach, himself,—well, some could call them painters if they liked. Ella sits on the dais and looks down at the floor and listens to no more of the mayor's speech.

Then a man who is introduced as the Chairman of the Museum Board speaks about the benefit to the world of the Blue Rider, a "bold new artistic movement," as he puts it. He turns to look at Ella, gesturing with his fat hand. In the face of danger, he says, she courageously preserved the works of "masters of abstraction." Ella makes her face a mask. Who, after all, is this fat boor in his green Bavarian jacket with its silver buttons? A burgher, that man. What can he know about abstraction? About the agony of letting figures go, of searching the essence of elements and freeing them from recognizable forms. Not that she, herself, fully did it. But she had been there when Wassy broke through. This boiled wool Bavarian knows nothing.

Finally, Doctor Röthel speaks, praising Ella for her generosity in making such a significant contribution to the Lenbachhaus. She has heard him talk during their meetings, of course, and has immured herself to his hyperbole. She hears herself described as a patriot, a defender of art in the face of its detractors, and wants the Doctor to stop speaking. She wants to go home and lie down and remember.

Ella's head buzzes and rings. At the back of her head, she thinks she hears crickets chirping sharp and fast. Distracted by their high whine, she cannot follow the museum director's line of thought. He is speaking about her and about Johannes, too. She hears the words *treasure* and then *heroine* and *savior*. None of it matters. What part of her being could be excised at any greater cost to herself? It is her own heart that she is giving away. And yet she sees that in saving him, she has saved herself after all.

At last come the flowers. She nods at the dirndled woman who presents them. She fancies herself dead in her coffin, her arms holding the spray of gladioli. When Johannes takes her elbow and makes her stand, she does. It seems that he has been sitting beside her all along. Clapping comes from far away. It is the sound of a sea she can neither see nor smell but whose roar she feels through the soles of her shoes. The standing people with their smiling faces and hands batting together seem mysterious, vibrations of an instrument no one has ever played before. But she finds that she can smile and bow, and her heart grows large, and the top of her head feels light, and she begins to cry. She might really go now, she thinks, drift away in this expansion of joy. The abyss is waiting for her, and she thinks she could be sucked into it now and take with her this moment forever.

Johannes escorts her down the steps and out to the gallery rooms where *he* is hanging, the final parts of him she has saved and kept and no longer belong to her. On one wall and then another, she sees them, villages and onion domes and striped roads and flying blue horses and swirls and lines and curves and shapes with no name, the music of color and form. And she hears the music and it lifts her up. She sees his brilliant blues and rich reds, and the lights in the room scatter pieces of the colors around so that she feels she might be dancing, though she can tell she is holding onto Johannes and he is standing still, and she begins to cry again, first in her heart and then in her eyes. These are her paintings, and she has given them another life, now, and they will be alive when she is not.

She will go home with Johannes, back to the yellow house. He has stood by her and will be with her to the end, and beyond the end. He sensed better than she, at the time, that the weight of her history was crushing her. But now that the paintings are truly hers no longer, she feels light, nearly transparent, and now that she is free of them altogether, perhaps she can rise up and climb the hill above the slope and feel the cool wind lift her hair and hear the silence of the hills all about her and so enter the mountain dancing in her heart, entirely and forever.

Acknowledgements

My deepest thanks go to the friends and family whose knowledge, wisdom, and kindness supported me as I launched this craft, helping keep both it and me afloat.

Lauren Abramo, Alexander Basson, Duncan Basson, Jacob Basson, Stephen Basson, Martha Bergland, Kathleen Collisson, Brigid Globensky, Nancy Jaeger, Silke Kleuver, Roseann Lyons, Nancy Matthison, Kevin McIlvoy, Irene Morgan, Diana Muehlenkamp, Barbara Wuest, Laurel Yourke, Benjamin Zarwell

And special thanks go to my many friends at the Milwaukee Art Museum who generously encouraged me.

About the Author

Mary "Peetie" Basson serves as a Docent at the Milwaukee Art Museum that houses the largest collection of paintings by Gabriele Münter in North America. A native of Northern Kentucky, Basson now lives in Milwaukee, Wisconsin and Brooklyn, New York.

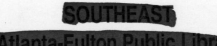
CPSIA inf
Printed in
LVOW04
45114

149605